Reflections

Jim Pinnells

Reflections

Matador
9 Priory Business Park,
Wistow Road, Kibworth Beauchamp,
Leicestershire. LE8 0RX
Tel: 0116 279 2299
Email: books@troubador.co.uk
Web: www.troubador.co.uk/matador
Twitter: @matadorbooks

ISBN 978 1789015 843

British Library Cataloguing in Publication Data.
A catalogue record for this book is available from the British Library.

Printed and bound in the UK by TJ International, Padstow, Cornwall
Typeset in 11.5pt Bembo by Troubador Publishing Ltd, Leicester, UK

Matador is an imprint of Troubador Publishing Ltd

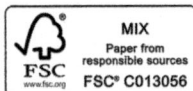

*This book is dedicated to Malcolm
who kept it alive when it might
otherwise have died.*

Day 1

'He wants you to go where?' Diana put down the battered menu and looked at him drily.

'The morgue. That's what he said.'

'Merr wants you to go to the morgue?'

'He said everyone goes to the Temple of the Dawn, but no one goes to the morgue. He thought I'd be interested.'

'And are you?'

'Not really,' Ed shrugged. 'I'll just meet him there. Say hello.' He scanned his own menu. 'What exactly is *jellyfish in chilli*?' he asked. 'Sounds slimy.'

'Just order duck,' she said. 'That's why everyone comes to Poon Sin. To eat duck.'

'If everyone eats duck, what happens to the jellyfish?'

Diana smiled at him across the table, and he saw again how beautiful she was. And how dangerous.

'When?' Dy asked, jumping back, as she always did, to what interested her.

'The morgue? This afternoon. Three o'clock.'

'Your second afternoon in Bangkok?' She shrugged, biding her time. 'Shall I order?' She liked ordering – she had the knack of it.

'Sure,' he agreed.

She beckoned the waiter and gave him the menu-numbers of half-a-dozen dishes. 'And two Cokes,' she added. 'Open them at the table.'

The waiter nodded, snatched up the menus and disappeared downstairs.

'You got through to Merr okay?' Dy asked. 'On the hotel phone?'

'Sure.'

'How was he? His usual sophomoric self?'

'You haven't seen him…in a while,' Ed answered indirectly.

'Not since the wedding.'

Not since the wedding. Unlike Diana to be so tactful.

The wedding. Four years ago. Four ugly years. Finished and done with. When she'd taken this job in Bangkok, they'd agreed – it was over. A long assignment in a far-away country – a clean break. Clean and final. Then, despite everything, her e-mail: *We need to talk things over.*

He glanced at her left hand, just to be sure. *Look, how this ring encompasseth thy finger.* It astonished him, as always – anything you ever wanted to say, Shakespeare had said already. Not that he was King Richard, and not that Diana was Lady Anne. He studied the ring. It was strangely impressive – gold engraved with a pattern of sphinxes. From the day they got married, she'd worn it for five weeks. Then it had disappeared. And now it was back.

Well, maybe they would *talk things over.* He'd arrived the afternoon before. She'd met him at the airport in a hotel limo. And yes, they'd talked. But not about *things.* Not even about her job.

The waiter climbed the stairs with two bottles of Coke and two glasses on a tray. The bottles were already opened. He put a glass in front of Diana.

'I asked you to open the bottles at the table,' she said. She didn't add: *We have a contract and I expect you to keep it,* but the lawyer's snarl was in her voice.

'No unnerstann,' the waiter replied putting a glass and a bottle in front of Ed.

'Then listen…' she began.

The waiter half-filled her glass, put the bottle on the table and walked away unsmiling. Ed found his expressionless back encouraging – you had to admire anyone who could silence Diana.

For once she was gracious in defeat and swung back easily to Merr and the mortuary. 'Where is it?' she asked. 'The morgue?'

He took a folded sheet of paper from his shirt pocket. 'Got it off Google Maps,' he said, unfolding a street map. 'Institute of Medical Jurisprudence. Seems to be in a street called *Thanon Henri Dunant.*' He looked at her enquiringly.

She shrugged.

'Merr said there's a big sign outside. In English. You can't miss it.'

'If Merr says so.'

'You want to see him?' Ed offered. 'I could ask him. Supper maybe?'

Merr and Diana had been living in the same city for six months without exchanging as much as an SMS.

'He's going up-country tomorrow,' Ed explained. 'That's what he told me. So tonight might be the last chance.'

'It's up to you,' Diana said.

The waiter brought a basket of soft, bappy rolls. Ed looked round the other tables. Everyone else in the place was Thai – or maybe Chinese. Oriental anyway. None of them had a basket of rolls. He sipped his Coke. 'So tell me about the job,' he said, trying to get closer to her fear, her anxiety, or whatever it was that had dragged him to Bangkok. 'Is it what you expected?'

'Let's not spoil lunch,' she replied.

He heard pain in her voice, and it surprised him – not the pain itself but the sudden hint of vulnerability. After Terry had been born, she'd retreated into herself, become untouchable. And during the few hours he'd been in

Bangkok, that's how she'd been — friendly but remote, lively but beyond his reach. As yet, she hadn't so much as mentioned Terry. But maybe soon, maybe that was the point of the lunch-date.

'So what's the problem at the UN?' he asked. 'Bureaucracy?'

'It's huge,' she said.

'Lazy?'

'Lazy and corrupt.'

'The UN corrupt?' he grimaced. 'Worse than Judas Iscariot? Or better?'

Dy shook her head. Her blonde hair rippled in the down-draught of the fan. It was short now, shorter than he remembered. But still pretty. Still Diana. 'You remember the brief?' she continued. 'Or probably you don't — you weren't particularly interested at the time.' There it was — the prettiness and the stab of accusation, simultaneous and deadly.

'International Protocol on the Eradication of Child Abuse?' he offered. 'Something like that?'

'Not bad,' she smiled. 'Actually it was Child *Exploitation* and Abuse.'

'Bitten off more than they can chew?' He tried to sound concerned.

She nodded.

'What's the hold-up?'

'Listen Ed — I've been here six months. The programme's been going for five years, and they still haven't decided if *abuse* and *exploitation* are the same thing.'

'*Eradication*?' he asked. 'Defined that yet?'

'No. Not even *child*.'

'That always happens when you start with definitions.' Words from the ivory tower, he realised, smug and discouraging — probably what Diana had come to expect of him. But at least he hadn't quoted Shakespeare at her.

4

Though he could have: *Define, define, well-educated infant.* Neat and apposite, but not worth risking until things had settled down.

He reached for one of the rolls. He'd missed breakfast – overslept. Dy had gone to work without waking him. Jet-lag always hit him hard for a day or two.

'I told you what our budget is, didn't I?' she asked.

'Millions.'

'Eighteen. And how much do you think is spent?'

'Most of it?'

'Right,' she shrugged. 'And on what?'

'Travel. Entertainment. Feasibility studies.' He knew from his teaching days how research budgets are frittered away – twenty percent focus, eighty percent fritter.

'Exactly,' she sniffed. 'And I think it's disgusting.'

'You mean, they should have warned you before you took the job?' At one time she'd enjoyed jokes like that. But now, he could see by her expression, she'd have been happier with *You're right Diana, it is disgusting.*

'I didn't exactly *take* the job,' she flared up. Then she backed off: 'You already know why I came here.' She shrugged and smiled. 'Go to Bangkok, or go to hell. At the time I thought it was a choice. Now I see it comes to the same thing.'

The waiter appeared again. He lit the chafing dishes on their table and opened a trestle for the tray he'd bring in few minutes.

'Ed,' she said, suddenly soft. 'Thank you for coming. It means a lot to me.' She filled her glass with Coke and sipped it. 'So how's painting?'

His painting? What could he say? He'd refused a commission for a portrait – a cat, the only love of an overexposed teeny head-banger. More hopefully – Warner Brothers was doing a film on da Vinci, and they'd asked him to fake a couple of portraits the great man forgot to paint. And his real work? Reflections? Diana had a problem with reflections. *Pseudo-philosophical bullshit*, she'd called one of his reflection pictures, driven not by spite but by a kind of puritanical outspokenness that had once seemed to him one of her attractions. Steer away from reflections. The story about Seymour Doll and her pussy would last through lunch, and the Leonardo fakes would cover coffee. But still, it was almost wifely, her sudden interest in his work. And it sounded real, as though she still cared in the same way she'd cared before… Before everything went to hell. He was puzzled.

*****

The ice-cold taxi growled its way into the sunshine from the shadow of the Skytrain tracks. It crawled past a building identified by a crest and a name-board as the Headquarters of the Royal Thai Police. Ed glanced at the Google printout. The Institute of Medical Jurisprudence would be round the corner now – the second building. Another crest, another name-board, just as Merr had told him.

'Here.' He leaned forward and pointed left. The taxi-driver turned into the guarded forecourt. A policeman peered into the taxi and then dragged aside a steel barrier. The taxi edged forward and stopped under a flimsy concrete porch. Ed glanced at the meter – thirty-five baht. He paid the driver from the wad of fifties Dy had given him and opened the door. For a second the broiling, filthy air of the city drove him back into the deep-freeze of the cab. Then the opposite door of the taxi creaked rustily open, and two women peered in. Ed scrambled out of the taxi, slammed the door closed, and made for the main entrance of the Institute. It was just before three o'clock. Merr had said he might be late. But no – Merr was there before him, waiting in the lobby.

'Dr Scarman, no less,' Merr said holding out his hand.

'Hi,' Ed said, shaking Merr's hand uncertainly. It was an unexpected formality, like drinking Bud out of a wine-glass.

'Still working out I see!' Merr exclaimed. 'Gym? Jogging?'

'Both.'

'You look great.'

'You too.' Ed tried to match Merr's locker-room cheeriness, but it wasn't easy. And Merr *didn't* look great – not at all. His waist was thicker, his hand felt pudgy, and his eyes had gone yellow and dull. Unreflective.

'It's tough, staying in shape in this climate. But I do okay,' Merr said.

'That's for sure,' Ed agreed.

'So how's Art?' Merr asked. It was a long-standing joke between them. Art Buchwald? Art Garfunkel? Art Schopenhauer? But somehow Ed couldn't keep the ball in the air. 'If this is the morgue,' he said flatly, 'it's a good place to start looking.'

'That bad?' Merr's laugh was loud and mechanical.

'Art's dead. Though you can still sell lousy pictures.' He told Merr about the commission to paint Seymour Doll's cat.

Merr made the obvious puns and then asked: 'So what's her real name, Seymour Doll?'

'Dorothy Sagmour,' Ed replied. 'Old Irish family.'

'How'd she get hold of you?'

'I did a car picture for her choreographer. And a dog picture for her dealer.'

'And you turned her down?'

'I hate her songs.'

Merr shook his head and laughed. 'No reason to hate her money.'

'And I hate cats. That a good enough reason?'

'You get to meet her?'

'Talked to her on the phone. Once.'

'Could've been worse,' Merr played along. 'Could've been twice.'

Ed tried to smile, but the old joke had lost its edge. 'So you're disappearing up-country,' he said. 'Tomorrow?'

'Up north,' Merr apologised. 'Lousy timing. Sorry about that.'

'But you'll be back?'

'Yup. Not sure when though.'

'Well if you're here this evening,' Ed offered, 'we can do dinner.'

'With Dy?' Merr's voice lost its deliberate lustre. *With Dy* were the first serious words he'd spoken.

'I think you're off her shit-list, Merr.'

'No sure why I was ever on it,' Merr objected mildly. 'She's never been on mine.'

There had been a quarrel of sorts. Merr had said something Diana didn't like, and she'd called him a stupid sod. He hadn't replied, perhaps because the word *sod* had been new to him. He'd sensed the insult, though, and a chilly friendship had turned to ice. 'So, you want to come?' Ed asked.

'Sure,' Merr said without conviction. 'Sounds great. If the Oriental's okay, I'll call and get a table. Eight o'clock? On the terrace?'

Ed nodded, and Merr made his call. Then Merr began again more cheerfully: 'You got your passport with you, like I said? You have to turn it in for an ID.'

'If we're doing dinner,' Ed said, 'maybe I should skip this afternoon. I'm real jet-lagged.'

'No,' Merr protested. 'You told me about those reflections, and immediately I thought of the morgue. It's all steel. Like you said – if you saw the reflection, would you know where you were? I thought that was real interesting.'

'I'm not sure.'

'Oh come on. It's really something. Take your mind off Dy anyway.'

Ed was tempted. Merr wasn't the brainless jock he sometimes seemed. At least he'd understood about the reflections. 'I'm not allowed in here, am I?' Ed asked.

'Allowed?' Merr repeated. 'That never stood in your way before.'

Before? Ed had never been a rebel. What the hell was Merr talking about? Somehow there was a gap between them that old jokes and half-erased memories couldn't bridge.

'So, if I stay,' Ed asked, 'who am I?'

'Doctor Scarman. That's what it says in your passport. I assume.'

'And why am I here?'

'Usually I come with our own doctor. From the embassy. But he's on leave.'

'Listen Merr. I'm not that kind of doctor. What the hell am I supposed to say?'

'Don't say anything. Just look the place over. I promise you…'

'And why are *you* here?'

'I'm looking for Felicity.'

'Aren't we all? But not in the city morgue.'

'Felicity Porntip Andrews. American citizen. Nineteen. Last heard of… You get the idea?'

'Bit gruesome, Merr.'

'Just look at the reflections.'

'And if the people here find out? I don't want you to get in trouble.'

'I won't,' Merr assured him. 'Look – if they ask who you are, say you're the embassy semiotician.'

Ed laughed. 'You don't change, do you?' he said, but it wasn't true. The distance between them was almost a coldness.

'Let's get your badge. Hirsch said 3:15. He'll be here any minute.'

*****

Hirsch was late. After Ed got his badge, the two men stood silent for a while. Ed felt unsure and uncomfortable in the cold, silent building. Then he asked: 'You often get cases like this? Felicity?'

'More often than I like.'

'So why are you looking for her? In the morgue?'

'Felicity's a NAM – *Notified as Missing.*'

'By her parents?'

'Yeah. With most NAMs, it's parents worried about their kids, specially their daughters.'

'That it? Daughters?'

'Mostly. Though you'd be amazed how many husbands go AWOL in Thailand.'

'No wives?'

'Most guys leave the old lady back home when they come to Thailand.'

Ed smiled. Merr had majored in Foreign Relations. Searching for missing daughters among the newly dead – it wasn't what Ed had expected. They fell silent.

'And there's a nastier side as well,' Merr said at length. 'Like I told you before.'

'The organs?'

'Yeah. Hirsch gets half-a-dozen corpses a week with the marketable bits removed.' Merr shrugged. 'That's why we're here.'

'T-CAN?'

'T-CAN.'

'Remind me what it stands for.'

'Transnational Crime Affairs Nucleus.'

'Nucleus?'

'Makes us sound hi-tech.'

'Ballistic even,' Ed agreed.

Merr shrugged. 'Not my idea. They wanted a name that doesn't make it too obvious what we do.'

'And what do you do, you guys? On work-days?'

'Gather information. Collect statistics. Whatever else it takes.'

'I see stuff in the papers sometimes, and I sometimes read it, knowing you're out here, trying to…'

'Trying and failing. You can't change human nature.'

'That bad?'

'We still buy slaves. We still sell kids. We still drown refugees. So why not trade livers? Livers, hearts, eyeballs? Whatever.' Merr's voice was gravelly and rebellious.

'Is that the latest from Hillary's desk?' Ed asked, flinching away from the pain in Merr's voice. 'Can I *quote* you on that, Mr Croft?'

'Never quote a man when he's telling truth – he's sure to deny it later.'

'You sound pretty pissed, Merr.'

'I guess.'

The two men fell silent again. 'I saw one story in the paper,' Ed said finally. 'Couldn't get my mind around it. Blood. Kids kept in camps – farms almost – and, like, milked for their blood? Specially kids with useful groups?'

Merr said nothing.

'Anything in that?'

'Useful?' Merr queried.

'I mean, like Terry. She's O rhesus D negative. So they tell me. The universal donor. But not much of her type about. When she needed a transfusion, they had a helluva job finding a couple of litres.'

Merr had nothing to say.

'They found some in the end, of course,' Ed rattled on. 'They told me where, but I can't remember.'

'Blood-farms? You know about that stuff?' Merr's tone had sharpened – he wasn't just stoking the conversation.

'Only what I read in the paper. It kind of struck me. Because of Terry.'

'I'm not the right guy to ask. Blood's another department. I do organs.' The sharpness was tuned out – Merr was backing off.

'So it's true? About the blood? It said *Thailand* in the paper.'

'Anything could be true in this fucking country,' Merr shrugged terminally.

'But you asked for a second tour? Didn't you say so when you wrote at Christmas?'

'Yeah, I put in for it. Two years ago. We all make mistakes.'

Silence again. Merr glanced at his watch. 'So how *is* Terry?' he asked flatly.

'About the same,' Ed replied.

Terry. Teresa. Four years old. Vocabulary of three words. Still in diapers. Still not walking. And a life expectancy of… Nobody knew. 'Thanks for asking.'

'How's Dy feel about it now?' Merr's voice was flat, as though he didn't expect, or even want, an answer.

Two security guards walked by, women in tight skirts and tailored blouses with dark blue forage caps. They carried nightsticks. Holsters and handcuffs dangled from their belts.

'Prefer my dommes with a bit of meat on them,' Merr switched track. 'So skinny these women. And so ugly.'

They watched the retreating guards. Merr was right – they were skeletal. Bloodless and threatening.

And Merr? *So why not trade livers? This fucking country?* But at least Merr had asked him about Terry. Which Dy hadn't. Merr and Dy – was there any point in trying to mend their quarrel? It they had dinner together, would it end in a fight?

Merr had met Dy for the first time not long after she'd arrived in the States. 2003. She and Ed were already shacked up. Merr had a girl-friend called Gré, and the four of them got along fine. Then Merr got a job with the State Department and started his first tour in Thailand. Gré had been left behind. He'd been away for about a year when Ed and Diana decided to get married. Dy was pregnant, not that it showed. Ed had wanted Merr to be best man, and Merr had jumped at the idea. Unfortunately Merr's boss had been sticky about leave, so the wedding had been put off month by month till Dy was eight months gone. She'd not been too pleased about the wait, but she'd made the best of it. Terry had been born, a few weeks premature, not long after the wedding. Then the quarrel. Ed had taken Merr to the clinic to see Dy and the baby. Merr had been floored, couldn't handle it, a kid with no proper brain. He'd mumbled something tactless – something about testing. The word *womb* had been in there somewhere. And Dy had ripped into him. Her anger, her raw feelings, had caught all three of them unawares. The storm hadn't lasted long, and Dy had lost herself in a fit of crying. With a quick *Sorry*, Merr had left the clinic. He'd gone back to Thailand without seeing Dy again. At Christmas he'd mailed a few lines to Ed, and Ed had replied. Otherwise silence.

The Christmas mail had unfortunate results. When Ed mentioned it to Dy, she took it as a provocation: *Wilt thou provoke me? Then have at thee, boy!* She tossed back the Jack Daniels she was drinking and threw the glass at Ed. It cut him painfully on the cheekbone. What could he do? Hit her back? He retreated to his studio and sank onto the chesterfield where his models sometimes posed – his mother's old chesterfield, with kapok poking out of rips in the leather. Dy followed him into the studio. 'Good,' she said. 'That's where you'll sleep from now on. I don't want you in my bed again – ever.'

The two guards rattled some locked doors and disappeared down the corridor.

'Better not mention Terry tonight,' Ed said. 'Unless Dy brings it up. It's still a touchy subject.'

'With her?'

'Yes,' Ed agreed. But that wasn't quite fair. 'With both of us,' he added reluctantly.

'Whatever you say,' he agreed. Then, 'Hey, there's Hirsch. Finally.'

Dr Ignatz Hirsch was sixty, Ed guessed. He was wearing a crumpled white lab coat over crumpled white clothes. His shoes were white leather, trodden down and shabby. His hair, which was also white, needed cutting. Beside him on extremely high heels trotted a Thai nurse, as mercilessly starched as an engraving of Florence Nightingale.

Hirsch shook hands with Merr and then looked enquiringly at Ed.

'Doctor Scarman,' Merr explained.

Hirsch held out a pudgy hand. 'Hirsch,' he said, with a guttural German *r*.

Ed shook the extended hand. 'Scarman,' he nodded.

Hirsch turned to Merr. 'What you know about this girl – the one you are looking for?' he asked, shambling toward the elevators.

'I sent you the RFI this morning,' Merr replied. 'You got it?'

'Sure.'

'Felicity Andrews. Generic Thai-American. You saw the photograph. Only definite ID is dental. Half-a-dozen fillings. And calluses on her left fingertips.'

'She play *Geige*? Violin?'

'Guitar. So the paperwork says. Make it easy to learn the harp, won't it? Where she's going.'

Ed flinched – Merr was a joker, not a cynic.

'You are not musical, Mr Croft?' Hirsch asked with a fine irony. His German accent gave a professorial edge to everything he said.

'No,' Merr replied. 'Strictly work and basketball.'

'And, as you once told, you are not religious.'

'No. Not that either.'

Ed felt ever more out of place. Probably he should back out now, remember an appointment or something.

They reached the elevators. The polished granite floor, dark red and black, reflected the lights of the lobby. And there was an altar with a seated Buddha surrounded by baskets of fruit, bunches of flowers, and lotus wreaths. The altar itself was garish, like the paintings in Mexican churches, but the reflection in the granite... Hirsch pressed the down-arrow.

'And you? Doctor...' He read Ed's name-tag. '... Scarman?'

'Just passing through,' Ed mumbled.

The elevator doors opened. Two women and a girl with a bandaged head were perched in the cage, forlorn. Hirsch stood patiently aside to let them out.

'You are in general practice?' Hirsch asked Ed without much interest.

'Supply,' Ed told him. 'I'm in supply.'

'But I can see you are sportsman, like Mr Croft.' He ushered the two men and the Thai nurse into the elevator. The nurse pressed *S3*, and the doors closed.

'Sure,' Ed replied.

'And what do you supply?' Hirsch pressed.

'Nothing. Supply is what we call procurement. Where I work.'

'Then what do you procure?'

'Look,' Ed replied. 'I'm not...' He caught Merr's eye and thought again. 'Blood,' he said flatly, remembering the newspaper story. 'I procure blood.'

S3 was the deepest cellar. The cage stopped with a terminal thud, and the lights cut for a second. The doors opened. The smell of formaldehyde was sickly but not strong. Extractor fans hummed. The cold was bitter, worse than the taxi, worse than a Chicago street in a cold snap.

A white-coated orderly greeted Hirsch respectfully. 'Dottor Hish,' he said.

The lighting in the big cellar room was white and intense. The walls of the room were lined with stainless-steel drawers, part satin-finish, part shiny. There was an island of stainless steel in the middle of the room and more drawers. Merr was right – the reflections were stunning.

'Obductions we perform upstairs.' Hirsch waved in the direction of the ceiling. 'It is less cold.'

Each of the drawers, Ed saw, had a grey LED label. The lettering was Thai – unintelligible.

Hirsch followed Ed's glance. 'We have place for fifty *Leichname*,' he said. 'Cadavers. A gift to Thailand from the last chairman of Sony. Unlike our obduction-room which was perhaps a gift from the last Kaiser.'

He looked at Ed enquiringly, expecting a smile, but at that second Ed saw how the only two touches of colour in the room – his red shirt and Merr's blue polo – were contorted, re-formed and reflected in the mirroring steel.

'Something wrong?' Hirsch asked.

'Sometimes Doctor Scarman suffers from double vision,' Merr explained. 'It's probably the cold. Let's start on Felicity.'

'It's nothing,' Ed added. 'I'm fine now.'

Hirsch went to the steel island and pressed a button. A keyboard and a letterbox screen unfolded from the table top. The screen blinked into life. 'What date?' Hirsch asked.

'Last word to her folks was a postcard. After that nothing.'

'Postmark?'

'August twenty,' Merr said. 'Two months ago.'

'Teeth?'

'Four fillings, back left, top and bottom. Amalgam.' Merr shrugged at Ed. 'If it was gold,' he explained in an undertone, 'it would have vanished long ago.' He grinned menacingly at the orderly, who smiled in return and said: 'Missa Clott.'

Merr's name was Croft – at first Ed didn't make the connection.

'Age?' Hirsch asked.

'Nineteen. Slight build. Black hair. Brown eyes. American mouth, but nose and eyes Thai. No distinguishing marks apart from those calluses on her fingers.'

Hirsch touched the screen half-a-dozen times.

'How many you got for me?' Merr asked.

Names and photographs flicked up on the screen 'Three,' Hirsch grunted. 'But really only one. I know who is your Felicity.'

'I better see them all,' Merr said. 'Looks better on the report.'

Hirsch said something to the orderly. Nothing in the old man's voice suggested the nasal rise and fall of Thai speech, but the orderly understood immediately and went to one of the drawers – second tier, hip-high. Hirsch read something off the computer screen, evidently a code, and the orderly touched a keypad on the drawer. A handle sprang out of the metalwork, and the orderly pulled out the drawer.

The three men crossed the floor to the open drawer. The nurse stayed at the console. Ed looked down at the body resting in a disposable cradle of silver foil. A girl, not long into puberty. Her skin was brown, but somehow it looked bleached. There were no blemishes on her body, but her right arm ended in purple and white tatters just above her elbow. The severed part of her arm rested between her ankles.

'Too young,' Merr said, 'and zero percent American.'

'I know,' Hirsch agreed.

'What happened to her?' Ed's voice was dry with the cold, the formaldehyde, and the shock of seeing the frozen, mutilated child.

'Factory accident,' Hirsch told him. 'They run the machines without guards. She caught her arm. Usually it's the hair. Sometimes the scalp is torn off the head completely. Or the cranium may be drawn in. In such case, it is mutilated or sometimes flattened, depending on the machine.'

'I don't get it,' Ed replied. 'I mean, what about her family? How can someone who works in a factory be unidentified?'

'It isn't an American factory,' Merr explained with a hint of impatience. 'It's Thai. They have barracks. No one's allowed out. The parents collect the wages each month. When they come for the wages and the girl isn't there, the factory says she's run away.'

'Why?'

'The girl's dead, so they dump the body somewhere. If they report she was killed in the factory, they have to pay compensation.' Merr's voice was edgy. *Not here, not now – I'll tell you later.*

'You are only short time in Thailand, Doctor Scarman?' Hirsch asked.

'Yes, short,' Ed replied.

'Some people become accustomed to such things,' Hirsch said. 'Some do not.' Ed heard revulsion in the old doctor's voice. Revulsion and anger. It was a surprise, but somehow it calmed him – calmed him enough to stand in silence and stare at the butchered girl.

'It's getting better though,' Merr said. 'The new factories aren't so bad.'

'Yes,' Hirsch agreed, 'the new factories are better.'

The Thai nurse was studying the computer screen now. She said some words, and the orderly moved to another drawer. Number 3454, Ed saw. The nurse read out the unlocking code.

The second corpse was also in a cradle but it was further wrapped in a sheet of silver-shiny foil. A faint mist formed on the foil as it was exposed to the warmer air of the room. The mist cleared slowly, allowing the foil to reflect the lights, the faces, the clothes, and the two splashes of colour, red and blue.

'We reported her to you since five days,' Hirsch said. He folded back the foil. The body had been obducted. A Y-shaped slash from the tips of the shoulders to the breastbone and then down to the girl's scant pubic hair had been crudely sewn back in place. One side of her chest protruded unnaturally high, as though her rib-cage had been removed and dropped back asymmetrically. From her breast-bone to her womb, her body had collapsed – it seemed to be empty inside. Her eye-sockets too were caved-in and empty.

'I saw the report,' Merr said. 'Lethal injection.'

'As always,' Hirsch confirmed. 'Professional. They are professional.'

Hirsch held out his hand to the orderly who opened a drawer in the central table and produced latex gloves in a plastic wrapping and two wooden spatulas. Hirsch put on the gloves and used the spatulas to open the girl's mouth. 'Bad teeth,' he reported. 'No dental work. You want to see?'

'No,' Merr replied. 'It's not Felicity. But they've been thorough, whoever she was.'

'Yes,' Hirsch agreed. 'The eyes are gone with the rest. First time for four, five years.'

'You'll write her up for T-CAN?'

'As always,' Hirsch replied.

'So our girl is the third one,' Merr said casually.

Ed said nothing. He was transfixed by the reflection of the corpse in the array of stainless steel around her, learning it by heart. The orderly closed the draw.

The last girl also bore the Y-shaped scar, but Hirsch had neatly restored her body – cadavers like her were always identified, and the next-of-kin always wanted the corpse. She'd killed herself, Hirsch said, with a mix of alcohol and some kind of tryptamine – probably what the dealers called *foxy*. Her last hours had been torture. She'd been dumped under the Expressway vomiting until her oesophagus had ruptured. She'd drowned in a mixture of alcohol, bile and blood. Ed heard grief in the old man's voice – as though he knew what it meant to lose a daughter.

★★★★★

The terrace of the Princess Hotel overlooked the swimming pool. Whether that was a good thing or not, Ed had trouble deciding. The Princess wasn't much of a place, but it was near the UN building, what the locals called *ESCAP*. Economic and Social Commission… Ed couldn't remember the *A* and the *P*. He caught sight of Diana and stopped.

Dy was sitting at a shady table, her back to the pool. Two men were sitting with her, a bulky Indian and an oriental. A Thai? Dy said that after a while, you could tell a Vietnamese from a Cambodian, a southern Thai from a north-eastern. Ed hoped he wouldn't be staying that long. Then he remembered – she'd asked the head of the project to have tea with them. Patel. That must be the Indian. The Thai, if he was a Thai, must be someone else from the team. Ed didn't want to meet them. His hour at the mortuary had left him harsh and uncivil. After they'd identified Felicity, Merr had become ever more edgy and defensive. Ed was puzzled. The old doctor had been quite different – unmistakably angry even though such ugliness was nothing new to him. Angry – and rightly so. Three shattered girls. All of it vile and shameful.

And Merr? What was up with him? He was out of shape, close to burn-out on his job, and he certainly wasn't in love with Thailand. Ed had gone over their conversation already half-a-dozen times. The story about the blood-farms… Somehow he'd wrong-footed Merr on that. But why would blood-farms make Merr uncomfortable but not stolen livers?

Diana glanced in his direction and caught his eye. She waved her royal English wave. He raised a hand in blunt acknowledgement. She beckoned. The two men from her project were looking in his direction too. He shrugged. He'd say hello. Not sit down. Not have tea. He began to weave his way among the tables toward Diana. She watched him the whole way, her brilliant smile like a beacon. Her fake smile. But she was still good-looking – that was undeniable. Magazine quality. Paris Hilton with a decent nose. Her thick, blonde hair, her strong, intelligent face, her elegant gestures.

He reached the table. Diana stood up. Patel stood too. Failing to take the hint, the other man kept his seat. Diana introduced Ed to the two men, and he shook hands with them. 'My husband, Ed Scarman,' she said. So easy, so natural. While the truth was: my not quite ex-husband, Ed Scarman. Ed, the father of my half-dead, brain-sick daughter. She was right, of course – he was her husband, at least from the demographic point of view. And if she could squeeze some advantage from it…

Diana sat down, indicating Ed's chair with a compelling little gesture. Patel sat down too, but Ed remained standing.

'Ms Tarn has told us very little about you,' Patel began. 'I believe you are some kind of *artist*.' His voice was wearing latex gloves, and he held up the word in tongs.

'That's mostly in my spare time,' Ed replied. 'Actually I'm in procurement.' He saw Diana's eyes widen in surprise, though otherwise her smile remained intact. *Ms Tarn*, his handsome English wife, who'd never contemplated becoming *Mrs Scarman*, not even for a second.

'Procurement, Dottor Scamman. What you procure?' Ed had guessed right – the second man really was Thai. The accent, the expression, the way he moved his hands, they were all familiar already. The orderly in the morgue had spoken in just the same way – the orderly who, according to Merr, stole gold teeth from corpses.

'Blood,' Ed replied. 'I buy blood. For hospitals.' He saw Diana's smile die completely.

'Would you like some tea, Ed?' she asked. 'I can easily order more.' She was shutting him up, willing him to say *No* and go away.

'Perhaps I will,' he said sitting down. 'I asked Merr about this evening. He said to be at the Oriental at eight. We've got plenty of time.'

★★★★★

'So what was all that about?' Dy asked as Patel and his colleague retreated from the terrace and disappeared into the lobby. Patel had excused himself quickly – a *Kanya Daan*, the giving away of the daughter. In other words, Patel had explained, a wedding. There would be many people there. Even so, he couldn't possibly be late.

Ed looked at Diana, weighing her question. He'd seen her with Patel now, her boss for the last six months. The man was the pattern of ignorant superiority, male condescension, and arrogant wealth. Ed knew without prompting what a humiliation it must be for Diana to work for such a man – every hour of every day, week in and week out. 'I didn't want to hear Mr Patel's views on art,' he said gently. 'I hope I didn't go too far.'

She shrugged.

'It was stupid what I said,' he admitted. 'But at the morgue… Something…' His voice trailed away. Dy didn't want to hear about the morgue. She had her own fish to fry.

22

'Well, you got Patel right,' she said. 'From the first minute.'

'And the other one?' he asked. 'What was his name again?'

'Chitanawa. Patel is lazy and stupid. Chitanawa is lazy and sly.' She wasn't begging for sympathy or spinning a hard-luck story, just filling in the details, hoping he'd understand. The fingers of her left hand were combing through some grains of sugar spilled across the tablecloth. The ring caught his eye again – the sphinxes. On a sudden impulse he took her hand. She froze and eyed him with suspicion. As so often, she shied away from affection, like one of Graham Greene's dreadful Englishwomen.

'Shit happens,' he said, wishing he'd kept his hands to himself. 'And this particular truck-load happens to be your boss. Until they promote him.'

'I wish,' she said. Then silence. Dy had many shades of silence. This one meant she was waiting for a prompt.

'Everything okay?' he prompted.

'I called Damian this morning.'

'In Boston?'

'Yes.'

Ed eyed the dead tea-things, waiting.

'Ed, there's a serious chance I may lose this job. And you know what they said at Lambfields: *Fuck up on this, and don't bother to come back*.'

'You think they meant it?'

'With the downturn, yes. They're cutting back. Bopple's gone. And Dowell. Damian said it's getting tough.'

'No chance of a partnership then.'

'Not unless I buy one. Quarter of a million dollars. Which I don't have. And which they wouldn't necessarily accept if I had it.'

He looked at her uncertainly. 'Dy,' he said, 'you were seconded here for two years. Judging by what you said, no one expects the Protocol any time soon. How can you fuck up?' At last they were talking, talking about *things*. And he was getting involved, ready to fight her corner. He wasn't sure he liked the sensation.

'If I got kicked out...'

'Is that likely?' The question answered itself. The remarkable thing was that Diana had lasted six months. 'No one here on your side?' he asked. 'What about that woman you told me about? The new Madame Big from Malaysia.'

'She's brilliant. She could be secretary general one day. But, Ed, I've never actually seen her. I'm stuck with the Patels and the Chitanawas of this world.'

'Come on,' he said. 'There's always someone. Some blighted pervert who'd sell his soul to get into your knickers.' He used her English word – quaint, oddly provocative.

'Oh, you mean Vadim,' she replied without blinking. 'You'll meet him tonight. He's Russian.'

'Tonight?'

'I thought it might be awkward with just us and Merr, so I mentioned it to Vadim. Provisionally anyway. And he can bring someone with him. An artist. I know her from work. I wanted...'

'...you wanted me to have someone to talk to?' No! It was too much. It was completely outside Diana's range. Or was it? It was a stupid habit he'd got into – putting her down, finding fault with everything she did. In fact, it *was* thoughtful, asking the woman from work. Why was he always so churlish?

He saw her shrug – she knew exactly what his words implied and refused to take offence. 'Merr said eight at the Oriental?' she asked.

'On the terrace.'

'Did he reserve?'

Ed nodded. 'In my name. But only for three.'

'I'll call. Get a table for five.' While she telephoned, Ed watched her, so familiar and so surprising. He listened to the

24

inflection of her voice. He saw how she turned away from him so he wouldn't catch her eye while she was talking. She'd taken off the jacket of her green silk suit and hung it on the back of her chair. Sometimes her eyes had a pretty green light in them, and the suit brought out the colour. She should've posed for Rossetti – awful stuff he'd painted, but he'd worked miracles with green.

Then she keyed in an SMS, presumably to Vadim. 'Sorted,' she said, easing her phone back into its slip-case.

He said nothing.

'But...' She hesitated. 'You were going to tell me something, a few minutes back.'

'Yes,' he agreed.

She looked away from him, nervous, listening.

'I wanted to tell you about the morgue,' he said quietly. He had to talk to her. He had to find words for his anger.

'Okay,' she said. 'But tell me about Terry first.'

Whichever way he turned, the ugliness defied words. 'I need a shower,' he said. 'I'll tell you later.'

*****

It was magic. After the disgusting little street –a *soy* Dy told him – after the pompous entry and the tumultuous lobby, they walked into the sudden serenity of the Oriental garden. The night sky, the glow of floodlights on tropical plants, the glitter of the wide river – Ed surrendered to the place immediately and without reservation. So this was Thailand too, the legendary hotel where Somerset Maugham had written his exile stories and Conrad had ordered tiffin.

Diana took his arm. Perhaps she sensed his pleasure in their new surroundings. Perhaps she wanted to establish with her friends that she really was a married woman and that this was her man. As they reached the broad terrace above the river, a Thai waiter in a dinner jacket bowed discreetly and said: 'Mr Scamman?' Ed nodded. 'Your table is this way.'

The waiter led them to a table on the edge of the river. Two people were sitting there already – mid-twenties, simply dressed but not casual. The man stood up to greet them when they were still some yards away. 'That's Vadim,' Dy whispered. 'The girl's Irina. They're both Russian.'

They shook hands. Irina didn't stand up. Ed wondered why not.

'Before I forget,' Vadim said to Diana. They sat down, the waiter holding Diana's chair for her. 'Meeting tomorrow start at nine, not ten. So you come early. Okay?'

A riverboat covered in lights swung into sight half a mile away. Shreds of New Orleans jazz carried across the shimmering, rolling water. The river sucked and splashed among invisible pilings below the terrace. Vadim chattered with Diana about the meeting next day. His fractured English was somehow civilised and comfortingly distant – nothing he said was of the least concern to Ed. As he gazed at the river, Ed felt at ease for the first time since he'd opened Diana's e-mail back in DC. His chair was large and comfortable. The table was set for five with silver, glass, and a handsome red tablecloth. Now if he had a tumbler of Jack Daniels in front of him, the world would be perfect.

A waiter had approached the table unseen. 'Would you care for an aperitif?' he asked quietly. 'A sherry perhaps for the ladies? Bourbon for the gentlemen?'

They ordered.

'Do they read minds here?' Ed asked when the waiter had gone. 'They knew my name. This guy knew what I wanted ten seconds after I knew myself.'

'This is Oriental service,' Vadim said as though he owned the place. 'Dy not warn you?'

Diana was smiling. He expected her to say something brittle and clever, something that would break the spell of the place, but instead she demurely straightened a kink in the tablecloth, and that was all. She could be nice, she could be so goddam nice when she felt like it.

There was a moment of silence, welcoming rather than awkward. Then Irina said, 'You are looking at the river, Doctor Scarman.' Her voice was soft and low...*an excellent thing in a woman*. Whose voice was *soft and low*? Juliet's?

'Yes, the river,' he agreed. 'It's amazing. Specially the reflections.'

'The Chao Phraya.'

'I saw the name on the map. What does it mean?'

'In English? Nobody really knows,' Irina explained quietly. No, *soft and low* wasn't Juliet – it was Cordelia, Lear's daughter, dead in his arms.

'Don't call him Doctor Scarman,' Diana broke in. 'Or he'll give you a lecture on semiotics.'

'Semiotic?' Irina exclaimed, suddenly more alert. 'Dy say you are photorealist.' Her emphasis fell on the last syllable, photoreal-*eest*. She sounded like a Russian spy in an old Bond movie.

'Well, if Dy said so, it must be true,' Ed laughed. 'I'm a mess really – started out in literature, taught semiotics, and finished up as a painter.'

Irina nodded. 'You like the reflections. On the river?'

'Don't you?'

'Yes, I like. But Dy tell me you are *painting* reflections. Is it also true?'

Ed was startled. They'd hardly said hello, and already this Russian woman was ready to turn him inside out. But he liked her – her ludicrous accent, her extraordinary directness.

'Look at the river,' he said abruptly. He formed his thumbs and two fingers into a square and peered through it. 'If I painted just that – the reflections – would you know it was a picture of Bangkok? Would you know there was a riverboat out there? Would you hear the music?'

'Hear the music?' Vadim asked derisively – the question irritated him.

'And maybe if I hear it?' Irina dismissed Vadim with a flick or her wrist. The idea interested her. 'What is the point? Why paint like this?'

'Because for me it's an important question,' Ed replied. 'Specially for a painter. When you see something – a cat or a car – you know what it is, or you think you know, but what are the signs you've picked up? Why are you convinced that you know what you're seeing?'

Diana was laughing. 'Ed! Have a heart. We've been here three minutes! We're still supposed to be at *How do you like Bangkok?* And *Is Loy Krathong this week or next?*' But there was sweetness in her laughter and a hint of relief – there goes God-Almighty Ed on his high horse again, nothing's changed.

'The signs?' Vadim asked. 'What signs?'

'Signs?' Ed cleared his throat. He felt stuck-up and pompous lecturing Dy's friends, but somehow he'd been sucked in, as always. 'Your brain works with signs,' he began with a grimace at Diana – *I'm sorry. Forgive me.* 'Like here. With the waiter. He reads our signs. These people would like a drink. One of the women is English – she looks as though she'll order sherry if I suggest it. Given a hint, the Yank will order bourbon and the Russian will follow suit. It's all signs. If a painter knew how to put the right signs on canvas, you'd hear the music.' Dy was laughing. 'Well maybe,' he added.

'I don't know why Dy think is funny,' Irina said with gentle familiarity. 'I think is *een*teresting. Very.'

The drinks arrived. The conversation became energetic, witty, intimate. The two women enjoyed each other's company – Irina fed Dy with subjects for her sarcasm, and Dy let Irina win all the arguments. How Vadim fitted in was less obvious.

The waiter brought the dinner menus and discreetly called Ed to the house-phone – cellphones were forbidden on the terrace. It was Merr. He was sorry he couldn't make it – maybe they'd see each other when he'd finished up-country.

'Sure,' Ed told him. 'Whatever.'

'How long you be around?' Merr asked.

'No idea. Depends how things go.'

'With Dy?'

'She'll be sorry to hear you're not coming.'

There was a silence at Merr's end of the line. Then 'Take care,' and the phone went dead.

★★★★★

Diana wanted to walk. 'At least as far as Silom Village,' she said. Ed objected – the street outside the hotel was dark and ugly, and it was nearly midnight.

'I walk on my own at night,' she replied. 'Take the subway. Or the Skytrain. This isn't Washington.'

'Judging by what I saw this afternoon…'

'Don't,' she said. 'It isn't Washington, I promise you. I can go anywhere I want at any hour of the day or night, it simply isn't dangerous.' She took his arm, and they set off down the pompous entry ramp toward the *soy*. Beyond the protective range of the Oriental porters, a gaggle of taxi-drivers ambushed them, offering them destinations Ed didn't understand and activities he understood all too clearly.

'We're walking, thank you,' Dy said, and the drivers returned to their gossip.

'It really doesn't scare you – a woman on her own, walking at night?' Ed asked and then winced. *Men always know best*. Dy had told him the streets weren't dangerous, and he'd told her, from his extensive knowledge of Thailand, that she was wrong. He was in hot water now – and rightly so.

'No,' Dy replied crisply. 'It doesn't.' She caught her breath, biting back a sarcastic reply. 'You know, Ed,' she said quietly, 'it was so nice tonight.'

And he was spoiling it. But at least she'd given him space to turn round. 'I have to buy a white suit,' he ventured, 'and a Joseph Conrad hat. Hard to believe the great man ate in that garden when he was just a gun-runner.'

The *soy* was dark. They were walking in the road keeping to the right, clear of the broken sidewalk. A *tk-tk* without lights rattled down the middle of the *soy* toward them. Ed wasn't sure which way to dodge – the left-hand traffic still puzzled him. The *tk-tk*-driver slowed down and shouted something. The only word Ed understood was *laydee*. 'We're walking, thank you,' Ed told him.

'No problem,' the driver shouted and roared on toward the Oriental.

They walked in silence until they reached a wider, busier road. 'Charoen Krung,' Diana said. 'One way goes to the Temple of the Emerald Buddha. The other to the Thieves' Market.'

'Which way are we going?'

'We go Thanon Silom,' she said, imitating a Thai accent. He laughed.

They stopped at a brightly lit shop on the corner of the *soy*. It was crammed with bronze statues – life-size lions, winged horses, dragons, golfers, dogs, baroque peasant-girls with exaggerated breasts, and the Empress Maria Theresa in endless configurations, one of them ten feet tall. Maria Theresa? Or was it Maria Theresia? Or was that someone else altogether? Behind their shop-window, the statues were bizarrely lit by neon reflections from the other side of the street. The monstrous empress had a yellow halo that read

Fingerlicking Good 4U

They moved on, heading away from the Emerald Buddha. Ed glanced back at the window, intrigued. He'd never seen such a shop – he'd go back when it was open. 'Interesting shop,' he said pleasantly.

Diana made no reply. Then suddenly: 'Nothing I say will make any difference, will it?'

Ed knew what she meant – and it had nothing to do with bronze statuary. She'd gone back to something they'd agreed six months before.

'Nothing,' he repeated, surprised at the hesitation in his own voice. 'It's over. That's what we both wanted.'

'Yes,' she repeated. 'That's what we both wanted.' She said the words without inflection, draining them of meaning.

'Dy?' he began. 'I'm baffled. Why did you ask me to come?'

They walked in silence as she pondered her answer.

'Why did you come when I asked you?' she replied at last, not, it seemed, in a spirit of repartee but because nothing was clear to her either.

'When you left there was so much anger in me,' he said. 'And it's still there. So I thought… I thought if we saw each other it might… I might…'

She said nothing.

'And I came for another reason too. I still don't understand about you and…'

'…Teresa.'

'Terry. Yes.'

She hesitated, shaping her next remark as she often did. '*Brutal, selfish and emotionally crippled,* that's what you called me.'

'Yes,' he agreed reluctantly.

'And you still think that?'

'I never thought it, Dy. It's because I never thought it…'

'…that you came here.'

'We've never talked about it properly. Not that talking does much good. I just wanted…'

'We have to cross here,' she said. 'Go up Silom Road.' They crossed the road. 'You just wanted…' she picked up the thread.

'…to make some sense of it all,' he said hesitantly. 'I don't know.'

She pondered his words and seemed to reach a decision. 'Even without…what happened to Terry…it wouldn't have worked, would it? You and me?'

She was leading with her chin as Merr would have called it, inviting him, begging him almost, to annihilate all they'd been to each other. *No, it wouldn't have worked.* The words formed, but he couldn't say them – they'd have been a lie. 'I don't know,' he repeated quietly.

'I don't know either,' she agreed, hardly moving her lips.

The Expressway on its enormous stilts sprang across the road ahead of them. To make way for the new monster, a chasm had been excavated through the old buildings on both sides of Silom Road. Beneath the black shadow of the monster, down-and-outs from the city, migrants from the north-east, addicts, the maimed, the insane – all found a home. Merr had told him about it that afternoon. It was here they'd dumped Felicity. And it was here that the police had found the unclaimed factory girl with her ripped-off arm. The traffic on Silom Road squeezed itself into narrow lanes, barricaded off from the eerie wasteland on either side. And now he must cross the divide, cross it with Diana. In the no-man's-land of dust and rubbish, a pimp approached them dragging a little girl dressed in rags. Then two whores, holding hands. They'd do anything, they said, anything for 500 baht. As he and Dy walked on, the price dropped to 300. Then to fifty. A dollar – anything for a dollar. A beggar twitched in the dirt, prostrate and inarticulate.

Then they were across the Badlands, back into the hideous normality of Silom Road.

'And when you're on your own?' Ed said. 'Is it like that? Those terrible people?'

'Some places worse than others,' she said.

'And you're okay with it?' Dangerous ground again, but Dy would know he was asking out of uncertainty, not arrogance.

'Sure. Sometimes I pretend it isn't happening, like we just did. Sometimes the girls speak English, so I ask them if they're hungry. Usually they are, so maybe we go eat.'

Ed heard in her words a purpose beyond bravado and beyond the mockery he most probably deserved.

'Sort of field research for your project?'

'No, Ed,' she replied. 'I quite like talking to them. And other girls too. Cleaner and better-looking mostly.'

'Are you…?' It was a delicate question. 'Are you…?'

'*Nostalgie de la boue*? Probably not. Though primeval slime is not without its charm.'

'Dy,' he said. 'Is that what you wanted to talk about?'

'Not really,' she said. 'But I'm…' Ahead loomed another monstrous bridge. 'Ed – I'm lost. I've been lost ever since Terry was born. You can't help me, I know you can't. And I've no right to ask…'

'Let's get a taxi,' he said – the day had been too long and his legs were tired. 'It's late.'

Day 2

Diana was gone. He glanced at the spidery red figures of the TV-clock. Gone ten already. She'd be at her meeting now with Patel and Vadim and the others. He studied the reflection of her bed in the mirror. He made a 4:3 box with his fingers and framed an interesting section. Her bed. For six months Dy had lived in a one-bed suite. Then, when she knew he was coming to Bangkok, she'd moved into a twin-room. He'd have preferred separate rooms – *I do desire we may be better strangers.* But no – all the single rooms were taken and they'd finished up like an old married couple in twin beds. So what did that make them? Intimate strangers? Estranged lovers? Strangers certainly. Though some things about Dy were still familiar, the mercurial girl he'd married had more or less vanished. And the tough, disappointed woman who'd fled to the Far East – she was gone too. So who was she – this new Diana who'd left the room hours before? Gone about her business, but still hopelessly entangled in his life.

The room was cool, though the sun was bright through the net curtains. He got up and splashed his face with water. Dy's hairbrush was on the mirror-shelf. He picked it up and looked at it – a few short blonde hairs were trapped among the bristles, only a few, but somehow unmistakably female. His own hairbrush was in his case somewhere, so he used hers. The mirror. The mirror-*trap* as Sartre had called it. His reflection – undistorted, unattractive, not worth painting. But at least his hair wasn't receding. Not like Merr's. Merr would be bald in ten years.

Ed found his swimming shorts in his half-unpacked case. Two brown bathrobes hung in the closet – two *dressing-gowns* hung in the *wardrobe* as Diana would have said with her insistence on all things English. The robes were new and thick, one large, one small. He'd eat breakfast by the pool and take a shower afterward.

The pool was quiet. A middle-aged woman was swimming inexpertly while a man shouted instructions in what sounded like German. The man was clattering away at her with a Nikon. A D2X Ed saw. He had one himself – it was the camera that put the *photo* into *photorealism*. He helped himself to muesli and slices of mango from the breakfast buffet and sat down at a shady table. A waitress in a brown uniform brought him coffee. A young girl, nervous about making mistakes. She looked weary and tyrannised. Another daughter, like the factory-girl in the morgue, slaving for her parents. My poor fool.

And my poor Fool is hang'd. That was Cordelia. Again. Cordelia, Juliet. Had Shakespeare lost a daughter? Ophelia. And… His mind flicked through the plays. Lavinia – she'd been the first. Daughter of Titus Andronicus – Shakespeare's only unreadable play. Shattered, raped Lavinia, crawling onto the stage, her hands cut off and her tongue cut out, only to be butchered by her father. But years later, when the *vpstart Crow* had retired to Stratford, the miracle of Miranda, the daughter who survived. And Perdita. The herbs. *Reverend Sirs, for you there's rosemary and rue, grace and remembrance.* The signs. He said the line to himself over and over, painfully aware that his own daughter, his poor little Terry, would bring him no grace and no remembrance. But he was no Leontes. Far from it. If he was any of Shakespeare's fathers, it was probably Titus. Titus Andronicus, the butcher.

A voice interrupted his musings: 'Doctor Scarman?' It was an Indian, plump and sleek like Patel but not so well-dressed. One of his front teeth was edged with gold, and his tie was inhibited by a gold tie-clip.

'Yes,' Ed scowled.

'I regard myself as very fortunate in having the opportunity of making your acquaintance,' the man said, displaying as he spoke the beautifully buffed fingernails of his right hand. 'In fact, *extremely* fortunate.'

'Oh?' Ed replied. 'Why?'

'Perhaps if you would allow me just two minutes of your most valuable time…'

'Forget it,' Ed replied. 'Whatever you're selling, it's exactly what I don't want.'

The man laughed. 'Allow me to present my professional card,' he said, slipping from his breast pocket a white card embossed with a gold motif. He didn't simply hand the card to Ed – he laid it on the table like an oblation.

Mrs Nikon reached the ladder at the corner of the pool and heaved herself out of the water. The D2X clattered as though the woman was Seymour Doll trying to leave a limo without showing her Caesarean scar.

Sardar Chaudhary, Ed read. *Andronicus Medical Services.*

Andronicus? 'What do you want?' Ed asked.

Andronicus? So far he'd guessed that the Indian was trying to sell him a suit, a trip up the river, or a timeshare in the Princess Hotel. Dy had warned him that he'd be harassed.

'You are a buyer. Medical procurement,' Chaudhary explained. 'May I sit down?' He sat down without further invitation.

Medical procurement! Who was this Chaudhary? Who had he been talking to? What the hell was going on? 'No. Listen,' Ed protested. 'I'm…' This was the moment to come clean – yesterday's nonsense had gone far enough. But, startled by the name on the card, Ed changed tack. 'I'm on holiday,' he said.

The German woman had dripped her way to the breakfast buffet. In a dissatisfied, colonial bark she ordered orange juice, fresh pressed.

'You find this hotel agreeable?' Chaudhary asked.

It was a subtle question and difficult to answer. If Ed told the truth, he'd create a thousand opportunities for Chaudhary to lament the condition of Thailand, to sympathise, to suggest alternatives. If he told a convincing lie, he'd show that he was a man without taste or discrimination – at least on the subject of hotels. 'Yes,' Ed lied, but without conviction.

The Indian smiled, knowing the game. 'If you would do me the honour of allowing me to leave a catalogue with you. Or perhaps I could send it to your office in…?'

'Let me take a look at the catalogue,' Ed said. It was a stupid thing to say. He should have kicked the man out and got on with the day. Done something about Dy. In the taxi last night, they'd hardly said a word. Back at the Princess, they'd not even had a nightcap. He hadn't promised to help her – not even to talk to her. His options were still open. If he moved fast enough, he could be on a plane back to DC before she got home from work. He had to decide, and a masquerade with this Indian was the last thing he needed.

Chaudhary bent down and unfastened his briefcase. It was a sturdy case, almost a Gladstone bag. He withdrew a slim catalogue, letter size, from a stack of papers and presented it to Ed.

The catalogue was expensively printed. Ed leafed through it. Medical instruments, hospital equipment, gloves, buckets. Art suppliers came to his studio all the time on similar errands with catalogues not very different. 'Price list?' Ed asked, keeping up the game by one more question before he let it drop.

'On our website,' Chaudhary replied. 'You'll find us competitive.'

'You do bigger equipment?' Deeper and deeper! How stupid! Ed tried to remember the name of the machine that had tomographed Terry's half-missing brain. 'MRI scanner for example?'

'Unfortunately not,' Chaudhary apologised. 'We offer essentially supplies, not equipment.'

'Blood supplies?' Ed asked. The cat was out of the bag. The winds were out of the sack.

'Yes, Andronicus supplies blood,' Chaudhary confirmed. 'Your special field, I believe. You will find a reference on page fifteen, but no details.'

Andronicus supplies blood. The game was over – something seriously unpleasant had just begun. 'How did you know I was here?' Ed asked, his voice lower and tighter.

'I was given your name and the name of your hotel. That was all. By our marketing manager, Mr Bhatnagar.'

'And how did *he* know?'

'I'm a sales representative, Dr Scarman, as you can see from my professional card. The ways of marketing managers are sometimes inscrutable.' He risked a knowing smile. 'As I'm sure you are aware.'

'So you don't know how he knew.'

'You are correct. You are absolutely correct.'

'And what about procurement managers? Are their ways inscrutable too?'

'That is not for me to say, Dr Scarman. But…'

'But?'

'Am I correct in believing that our company interests you, small and insignificant as it is?'

'Hard to say,' Ed remarked. Who was this eloquent Indian? What was going on?

'Naturally you can decide nothing at the breakfast table. Indeed, I must apologise for what can only be seen as an intrusion, but I wanted to be sure of leaving my professional card with you. With you personally.'

'With me personally,' Ed repeated.

'If by any chance you wished to learn more about Andronicus, you could, of course, visit our offices. The Kingdom Tower. Sathorn Road. A taxi will take you there in fifteen minutes.' He glanced at his watch. 'Thirty minutes at this time of day.'

Ed nodded. 'Thirty minutes,' he repeated.

'Shall I make an appointment for you? With Mr Bhatnagar?'

'This your number?' Ed picked up the card.

'Indeed it is. You'll see both my personal number and the number of the switchboard.'

'I have to tidy up my schedule,' Ed said. 'If I need anything, I'll call you. Maybe tomorrow.'

Chaudhary evidently saw that he'd made his point and had nothing to gain by staying. He stood up, shook hands, picked up his bag, and walked slowly to the lobby.

Mrs Nikon had removed the top of her bikini. She stood by the buffet sipping her orange juice while the D2X resumed its fearsome work. *Her breasts,* Ed remembered a remark of Saul Bellow, *looked as though they had been washed but not ironed.* The sack of winds. The thousand ships of Agamemnon trapped behind Aulis. Iphigenia murdered in exchange for a west wind. *I am slain, I perish, slaughtered by a godless father.* He blinked away the shadow-images of a lifetime – Iphigenia, Lavinia, Gilda, daughter of the godless Rigoletto, dead and tied up in a sack of her own. Reflections. The same patterns, the same situations endlessly reflected, endlessly repeated, endlessly distorted. Euripides, Shakespeare, Verdi. In the confusion of his thoughts, a decision had somehow made itself. He'd stay – at least till Dy got home from work. And maybe for a day or two more. He'd talk to her. No, he wouldn't talk to her – they'd talk to each other. She'd said she was lost, his handsome wife. Well probably he was lost too. Perhaps that was the real question – last night under the Expressway they'd been lost in the same wilderness, but was there just one wilderness? Or were their wildernesses as separate as the rings of Dante's inferno?

★★★★★

'And how many people heard you say you buy blood?' Diana's tone was female, matriarchal – a mother half-listening to tattle about a schoolyard fight.

'Hirsch, Patel and Chitanawa. Three.'

'It's nonsense, Ed,' she said. 'Forget the whole thing.'

They'd walked down from the ESCAP Building to the Old Palace by the river and taken tickets for the water-bus to Wat Arun, the Temple of the Dawn. They'd waited for the boat among the hubbub of stallkeepers and the raucous smells of cooking stands. They'd enjoyed balancing on the pontoons, tossing and heaving in the wash of passing junks. Ed had put his arm round Dy as if to protect her, though she was in no imaginable danger. Usually she disliked such gallantries, but this time she'd submitted, perhaps even enjoyed the momentary closeness. He'd told her again about Chaudhary's visit. She'd listened half-heartedly until the roaring, crowded boat arrived, and they'd set off across the Chao Phraya.

Now they sat on a wooden bench, looking across the river, with the *stupas*, the wall of the temple, and the half-spent afternoon sun behind them.

'You're right,' Ed said. 'I should forget it. But it was so odd – Chaudhary coming like that. And the name of the company.'

'Andronicus?' She shrugged. 'You wrote a paper once, *The Semiotics of Offal*. Do you remember? The Romans looking for signs in the entrails.'

'It's called *extispicy*,' he said. 'Exposing the entrails and interpreting them.' Number 3454. He couldn't get the girl out of his mind. They'd gone further than extispicy with her. Exposed her entrails, sure enough. And then sold them. Her eyeballs as well.

'Well...' Diana smiled.

'Well?' he replied, his mind lurching back to their sunlit bench.

'...you know, you're just as...' Ed guessed she wanted to say *extispicatious* but wasn't sure it would come out right. '...just as superstitious as they were. It's just a coincidence, the name of the company.'

'I know it's a coincidence. But even so,' he insisted, 'someone *did* tell Andronicus I was a buyer.'

'So what?' Diana replied. 'What's sinister about that? It was Hirsch. Probably he's a shareholder.'

'I guess I'm seeing too much in it,' Ed conceded. 'Did you ever hear of them? Andronicus? Or this whole blood racket? I mean, at the UN you must get to hear things.'

Diana hesitated and then shook her head. 'Not really,' she said. 'Just rumours. Live drug testing. Experiments on nerves. On brains. Stealing livers. Snuff films. There's rumours about everything. What else do you want to hear about?'

'None of it,' Ed replied. 'I hate every word of it.'

'So, I hear rumours, but I don't follow up on them. I hate them as much as you do.'

'And your project?'

'I already told you,' she replied. 'We don't do actual work. Just definitions.'

'So this Indian coming and asking me if I want to buy blood. You obviously think it's a case of *malum non presumitur*.'

'That was one of my father's stupid expressions.' She looked at him sourly. 'You know how I hate that Latin crap.'

Yes, she'd told him more than once. Her father's legal Latin – a hundred inkhorn terms, as inauspicious as the rough and speckled livers Ed had described in *The Semiotics of Offal*. They fell silent sitting on the bench, the dark shadow of Diana's father falling across them. He'd had a stroke, a bad one, during his daughter's last semester at Harvard, 3,000 miles from England. Dy had flown home, but she'd been too late. A second stroke had laid the old man low as she was landing at Heathrow. She'd told Ed, and she'd told herself, that she'd gone back for her father's money, a last-ditch try for an inheritance. She was his only child, but even so he'd threatened to leave his money *away from her*. In fact, her inheritance story had been a fig leaf. She'd really gone to England to make peace with the old man. Too late. As it turned out, he'd written to her not long before his second stroke. A vile letter. Her uncle, the executor had given it to her after the funeral. Her name in black ink on the envelope had disturbed her, and she hadn't opened it. She'd brought it, still sealed, back to Boston, back to Ed. True to form, the letter had been a masterpiece of gall – a spiteful letter, self-righteous and vindictive. He'd left her £3,212. She knew the figure already from the will. This meagre sum, the letter informed her, was what her dead mother's jewellery had fetched at auction. Diana, the old man carped, had defied him in everything. He'd wanted her to become a solicitor and take over his practice. But after King's she'd gone to America, had studied in America, would qualify for the bar in America – entirely against his wishes. One by one, this unlovable nobody rolled out the grievances he'd hoarded during a quarter of a century against his clever, pretty daughter. *Better thou had'st not been born than not t'have pleased me better.*

Diana often said she'd been at war with her father from the day she was born, from the day he'd decided, over her mother's objections, to call her Diana. 1981. The year Diana

Spencer had become engaged to Prince Charles and married him. What flux of pre-senile chauvinism had persuaded her father to name her after the new bride? It was not even Diana Ruth or Diana Jane so she'd have an escape route, but plain Diana! At school, at St Cunegunda's, she'd truncated her name to Dy. What was Dy short for, people sometimes asked her. *Diamond*, she told them, *as in a girl's best friend*. That got her a few speculative looks and a few giggles. Not that she cared either way. On the other hand...

'Ed. Promise me you'll forget it, this blood thing.' Diana's anxious voice broke his train of thought.

'Probably you're right,' he agreed. He looked over his shoulder at the temple. 'Why do they glitter like that?' he asked. 'Those steeple things?'

'Come on,' she said. 'They're called *stupas*. I'll show you.' She stood up quickly.

She was neat, he saw, clean in her movements, and old-fashioned in her plain dress and straw hat. She'd come from work, otherwise she'd be wearing jeans and a baseball-cap like everyone else. He preferred the dress. Not that he had the right to any kind of preference. At one time though... Don't go down that route, he corrected himself. It's over.

She led him briskly to the gatehouse of the temple. Unusually for Dy, she held out her hand to take his, but he kept himself out of range. 'We have to buy lotus flowers, and joss sticks, and a square of gold-leaf,' she explained. 'But it's okay if we just pay for them.'

They were in the temple precinct. The steeple-like forms of the *stupas* were solid, or so it seemed. The huge central *stupa* towered into the sky like... Like a naked arm? Like the chimney of a monstrous crematorium? Like a giant phallus? No. Like nothing he'd seen before. And the four smaller *stupas* firmly planted around it? They formed a system of signs, but he had no access to it. None at all. He liked the place.

'Can you see now why they glitter?' Diana asked, excited. He was a child, and she was taking him on a treat.

'No,' he said. 'But those steps? Can you go up them?'

All the *stupas* had steps, senseless, dizzying staircases that narrowed as they rose. At the top, the steps were just an inch or two wide.

'I won't in sandals,' she said decorously.

Then he understood the glitter. 'That's not china, is it?' he asked. 'Broken plates? And cups? Reflecting the sun?'

She laughed.

'The whole thing?' he exclaimed. 'From top to bottom? Broken pots?'

She laughed again.

'That's so cheap. And yet it looks...' He grabbed her hand and dragged her along the gravel path, eager to look more closely.

The sun fell rapidly as they explored the place. It was almost dusk when they reached the river again and sat down on one of the benches.

'Dy,' he said reluctantly. There would never be a better time. 'What is it? Why did you ask me to come?'

'You?' she said. 'Well, I hardly know anybody else. For the last six years of my life, there hasn't *been* anybody else.'

Strictly speaking it wasn't true. But... *I have been faithful to thee, Ed Scarman, in my fashion.*

'I asked you...' she began, uneasily. 'Ed – I'm in trouble.'

'Must be serious trouble,' he replied easily, 'if you're being so goddam nice. And for two whole days.'

She laughed. 'I thought it was going to be an effort,' she said. 'But it isn't.'

'So?' He'd noticed it too – it wasn't an effort. And somehow that decided him – if he could help her, he'd do it. Short of getting back together, he'd do it.

'You know...before I met you..., at Kings..., at school even...'

'Yes,' he prompted, unsure what was coming next.

'You know… You know how I was.'

'I know what you told me.' As teenage horrors went, Diana had been distinctly high-end. Not that it bothered him. Some of it was funny even. She'd done some hair-raising things – but more as a rebel than as a dropout. She'd played with fire, and she'd gotten away with it. Or so he'd always thought.

She said nothing more, and he turned to look at her. Tears were streaming down her cheek – tears without sobs. Heartache. An agony of mind. What was it? AIDS?

'Are you…sick?' he asked quietly, trying to stay calm in the face of her grief.

'In a way,' she whispered. She looked at him. In her tear-filled eyes was a soft affection he hadn't seen for a long while.

'Something to do with how you were…before I met you? Is that what you're saying?'

'Maybe how I *was* is how I *am*,' she said.

'You raised a little hell,' he said. 'Kicked some ass. Dropped out and dropped back.'

'I told you about it,' she said. 'I didn't hide anything.'

'Why should you? You weren't the only one. That's how it was back then…' His voice tailed off – he should shut up and listen. She didn't need his platitudes. Or maybe she did.

'If I drank,' she said, 'I'd be a binge drinker, wouldn't I?'

She wanted him to reply – and with more than a plain *yes*. 'No one's perfect, Dy,' he risked. 'And you *do* drink. At the Oriental, you downed a sherry, a bottle of Chardonnay, and three brandies.'

She tried to smile, sniffing away her tears. 'You know what I mean. A binge addict.'

Addict? Where was she going now? 'It's easy to confuse a predilection with an addiction,' he said hesitantly. Jesus!

As pompous remarks went, that hit the jackpot. If he was trying to piss Dy off, that was the way to go.

'Oh for fuck's sake,' he heard her say, though without much venom.

They sat in silence, giving each other a chance.

'You remember once,' she began at last, 'a long while ago, I wanted you to sum me up in one word. And you couldn't. You needed two words, or so you said.'

Ed remembered. They'd been walking home, unsteady after a party in Boston. He remembered the words too. 'Yes,' he said. 'One of the words was *beautiful*, as I recall.'

'And the other was *fearless*.'

'Yes,' he agreed.

'Well I'm not fearless anymore. I'm shit-scared if you want to know the truth.'

He said nothing. Now she was started, she'd find her own words.

'Scared, Ed. Scared my father never loved me. Scared you're going to pack up and go home. Scared I can't love my own kid. Scared she doesn't even know who I am. Scared the people at work see me as some kind of stuck-up piece of horse-manure. Scared I'm no good at my job. Scared of everything really.'

He looked at her, sharing her hopelessness. Then suddenly her mood shifted. 'And *scared* is the wrong word,' she burst out, 'because most of it's true.'

He would have denied it if he could. But half of it *was* true, and the other half – he didn't know. He simply didn't know.

'Oh for fuck's sake,' she repeated viciously, stood up and stalked away.

A river-bus bounced toward the battered landing stage of the temple. Ed watched the reflection shifting violently on the clear plastic awning – the bizarre temple behind them, the heavy sky, the river.

Diana turned back, walking slowly toward him, her white sandals crunching the gravel. Her lips were tight closed. After her few painful words, she had no more to say.

'*Give sorrow words. The grief that does not speak whispers the o'er-fraught heart, and bids it break,*' he said to the river, but quietly so that Dy wouldn't hear him. At one time she'd enjoyed his Shakespeare, it had made her laugh, and he'd memorised dozens of useful lines to amuse her. And, of course, a couple of plays he knew line-for-line from directing them, though only at the Agassiz. Now, sadly, her laughter had dried up though the quotations still flowed through his mind.

She sat down again. 'I've got a stone in my hoof,' she said, reaching down to take off her sandal.

'Your trotter, would be more accurate.' It was a well-worn joke, a cheerful insult from their happier days.

She smiled. 'Ed,' she said quickly grave again. 'It's not going to work – talking.'

'I know,' he agreed.

'Would you...?'

'Would I what?'

'Go somewhere with me? I'd like to see it through your eyes.' She hesitated, shying away from too much explanation. Then: 'It isn't the problem, but it might be a way of looking at it.'

'I only see reflections,' he replied. 'Will there be any?'

'Mirrors. Dance poles,' she said. 'Best see for yourself. Tonight?'

He shrugged. 'If you want.'

'I'll ask Vadim and Irina. That might help.'

★★★★★

Back at the Princess Hotel, a note was waiting for Ed.

47

Esteemed Dr Scarman,

Please forgive this suggestion if you find it intrusive, but our Mr Bhatnagar is leaving tomorrow evening for a short trip. If it were convenient with you, he would be honoured to see you in our office in the Kingdom Tower tomorrow morning. May I take the liberty of suggesting eleven o'clock?

Yours most respectfully
Sardar Chaudhary

He didn't show the note to Diana. She was right – he should forget the whole thing.

★★★★★

There were reflections, many and curious, but even so Ed hated the place. It was exactly what the word *Bangkok* had conjured up when he'd read Diana's e-mail – thunderous music, flashing lights, drunk Australians and girls dancing, each with a number dangling from her bikini.

The rowdy tout-girls who'd grabbed them from the street a few moments before were subdued now. Their trawl-net was full – four well-heeled, sober customers heaved into the bar in one go. Now if they could stop their victims slipping away...

Three rows of benches upholstered in fagged velvet were banked round a narrow stage. A dozen girls were dancing listlessly. The touts knew their job – the question for their captives should not be *whether* to sit but *where*. And whatever happened, keep the newcomers facing the seats, not the stage. Ignore the lifeless go-go.

'We go top row,' Vadim said to his tout-girl. He went first, quick and familiar, then the two women. One of the girls moved in after them, cutting off their retreat. Ed stayed below, still unconvinced. Two girls stayed with him. One of them grabbed his arm.

'No problem, mister,' she said.

'That's a comfort anyhow,' Ed said with a laugh. *'Where words are scarce they're seldom spent in vain.'*

The girl laughed back, not understanding. She was dressed in a cheap bikini top and a blue-and-white skirt that just covered her panties. It was her uniform, just as a soldier might wear a forage cap and camouflage fatigues. She wasn't pretty. Just a skinny kid working as a bar tout. He smiled at her. It was a lousy job. The girl smiled back, wearily but with an unexpected warmth. With understanding even. *It's work*, she seemed to say. *Everyone has to live. It's not so bad.*

He glanced up at Dy and the others. They were sitting down. Casual. Jeans and t-shirts. The music was too loud. It hurt his ears. What was that song anyway? *I'm just a juv'nile scumbag, baby.* Cornus. A golden oldie. From the time before he'd met Diana anyway. Vadim was beckoning. *Oh no, scumbag. Oh no, scumbag.* It's what we give our kids instead of poetry. Ed shrugged and climbed the steps.

In a gaggle, the tout-girls ran back to the street, Soy Cowboy, Vadim had called it. As Ed sat down, the music changed. Seymour. *Get your clothes off baby.* Subtle choice! Well, Seymour practised what she preached – you could say that much for her.

He sat down between Dy and Irina. He saw the reptilian manager, a middle-aged woman with a sharp jaw, signal two of her waitresses to *Get busy*. The girls approached. They were dressed like the touts, only in red. They were better-looking – pretty even – and a year or two older than the blue girls outside. Diana wanted to drink beer, so Vadim ordered four Singhas.

For the first time, Ed tuned out the noise and watched the stage. The benches in front of them were empty – the view was perfect. Twelve girls were dancing at fourteen poles. They were dressed in bikinis of various styles, but nothing exotic. Not much different from the beach. Dangling from each bikini was a number – it helped if you took a shine to one of the girls, Ed guessed. Most of the girls had long black hair, though two or three had lightened their mops to a murky shade of blonde. But the girls were striking, all of them, slender, and elegant if unenthusiastic dancers. That wasn't how bargirls looked back home, at least not in the far-off days when he'd visited such places. A young girl at the back, Ed saw, furthest from the door, was watching the front girls, imitating their steps in a stiff, childish way. An artless beginner in one of those *professions that go the primrose way to the everlasting bonfire.*

'How old?' he asked Diana. He spoke directly into her ear, raising his voice above the music. Irina wanted to hear the question too, so he repeated it for her.

'In these places, eighteen,' Diana replied.

'They don't look it.'

'It's controlled,' Dy told him. 'In bars like this.'

Ed shrugged. The point of the visit escaped him.

The beers arrived – bottles in polystyrene holders. A few seconds later, the third wave of girls broke over them – half-a-dozen kids dressed like the girls on the stage, ready to sit with them, chat with them, have a few laughs for the price of a drink. They infiltrated the row below, blocking off the stage. Ed glanced at Dy, still unsure what she had in mind.

A slim, pretty girl was smiling at him. Perhaps she really was eighteen, but it seemed unlikely. Her smile was warm and open, not shameless but unashamed. Like the tout outside, she was doing her job, and it would go better if Ed liked her. 'What your name?' she asked, seeing that she'd caught his eye.

'Ed,' he replied. 'What's yours?'

'My name Miao. Like cat.' She laughed.

Diana moved a foot or two up the bench, making room for Miao to come and sit between them.

'You want a drink?' Diana asked the girl as she sat down. The girl nodded. One of the waitresses caught the gesture and hurried off.

Ed saw Vadim signal one of the new arrivals *Next to me*. He saw Vadim's hand rest on the red velvet, waiting for the girl to sit on his splayed out fingers. Ed flinched. If Vadim was a sample, Dy was making some unlovely friends. The other girls drifted away. The red-skirt waitress arrived with two small glasses and put them in front of the girls. She put the check in a little pot in front of Vadim.

Miao put one hand on Ed's knee and the other more tentatively on Dy's. Dy put her hand over Miao's, and the girl relaxed. For a few minutes Miao joked with them, her shrill voice stabbing through the music. 'Where you from? How long you stay Bangkok? You like Thailann?' Probably she couldn't hear their answers and wouldn't have understood them if she had. But that wasn't important. As long as she kept them on their seats, she was doing her job.

Then a buzzer sounded. Seymour was cut off in the middle of the word *clothes*, and the girls on the stage abruptly stopped dancing. They clustered at the top of the little staircase that led down from the stage. Dy let go of Miao's hand, and the girl stood up. Vadim's girl stood up too. 'Dance now,' Miao said wearily.

When the stage was clear, two red-skirts climbed the staircase with tea-towels and carefully wiped the dance-poles. The music changed to a brisk German march, though scarcely louder now than the chatter of the bargirls.

Diana moved toward him down the bench. She sat further away from him than Miao, and he missed the warmth – the air-con was painfully cold.

Vadim looked significantly at his watch. 'Eleven,' he said and then something that sounded like 'Bye-bye bikini.'

Irina sighed. 'So, Doctor Scarman. Dy tell us you want to see the famous Bangkok night-life. To me, I think you are bored.' She shrugged. 'Very.'

'Not bored exactly,' he said. 'Just out of place.'

'After eleven, is more interesting – if you like to look at naked children.'

Vadim said something to Irina in Russian and grinned – some obscenity, Ed guessed.

'Shut up, Vadim,' Irina replied in English, unimpressed.

'I didn't quite catch that,' Ed said, grinning in turn at Vadim.

'Not important to know,' Irina broke in. 'Vadim talk like dirty schoolboy. Always.'

Ed shrugged. Vadim had been put in his box. From the *always* Ed guessed that Vadim had taken Irina to bars like this before, though they left her cold. But what attracted Diana to the place? *Dy told us you wanted to see one of these places.* Evidently Dy had blamed the trip on him. Of course, in a way she was right. If he'd been able to talk to her, they could have gone somewhere pleasant. Or to take the idea a step further – if he'd been able to talk to her, they wouldn't be in Bangkok at all.

The music began to build, an unstoppable fascist march. The next cluster of dancers had gathered at the bottom of the staircase, Miao among them. They were all naked now except for over-the-knee latex boots, some black, some white, some red. Their number-tags hung now from their boots. The march rose to a deafening volume as the girls climbed the stairs and took up positions at the poles. The march stopped, lights flashed mercilessly, and a devastating beat shook the bar. *When you're freezin' in the street and you still can feel the beat, Poundin' your F-off jeans.* Yma. The girls began their amateur writhings. Well, Ed mused, you needn't be a ballerina to push your pussy to that stuff.

The Chinese manager wasn't happy. She stormed along the gangway, looking up at the dancers. She was screeching orders so loud Ed could hear them over the music. The girls livened up, generating a shade more friction with their poles but only a distant imitation of arousal. Perhaps it was mildly erotic, but mostly it was sad. Some of the girls were beautiful. Miao for example. A Waterhouse nymph with her youth and charm crushed out of her night by night. How long did she have left? A year maybe? Six months?

'Well?' Irina asked him, speaking close to his ear. 'Are you inspire? Or you are waiting for more?'

Ed had no ready reply. 'Naked children,' he repeated her words at last. 'What else is there to say?'

Irina pulled away from him, folding her arms across her breast. She eyed him closely. Then she leaned forward again. 'So come here is not your idea?'

'Yes it is,' he grunted loyally. Then: 'Not really.'

'The nasty part starts around twelve,' Irina said, close to his ear again. 'We can go before. No problem.'

There was a sudden eruption at the doorway. A gang of men in their twenties staggered into the bar, spilling the blue-skirts along with them. Australians Ed guessed from the way one of them shouted *Oh fucking hell!* The dancing picked up instantly. Some of the girls abandoned their poles, flaunting their nakedness at the newcomers. Miao, Ed saw, was not playing that game. She glanced in his direction or maybe in Dy's. He caught himself nodding to her – skip the Aussies, come back to us.

Diana put her hand on his knee. 'Do the girls get it right? D'you like that?' she whispered, coming closer to him. Then she took her hand away and swigged her beer.

'Not much,' he replied, but she didn't hear him. He said the words again, louder.

'There's something to be said,' she pitched her voice into his ear, 'for places where it's hard to talk.'

'So what's the procedure? Just drink and gawp?' he shouted back.

'I don't think I'm gawping?' she replied. 'And you certainly aren't.' She held up four fingers at a passing redskirt. The girl nodded: four more beers.

By the time the Australians were sitting down and suckling on their Singhas, the girls had danced through *Help Yourself*, *In my Bed*, *I'm a Slave*, and a couple of others Ed didn't know. The buzzer sounded again half way through *On a Night like This*. Ed saw Miao glance at him again from the stage. He nodded – she should come back.

Five minutes after she'd left the stage, Miao came to them dressed again in her bikini. She was leading another girl by the hand. 'This my frenn,' she explained. 'She name Phu. Mean *crab*. You buy drink?'

This time Ed and Diana sat together, with Miao and Phu on either side. Vadim's girl fought her way back to him, beating aside the opposition. Vadim enjoyed the little scuffle for his favours. More naked girls humped dance-poles until the buzzer went again at midnight. Then, as Irina had predicted, the less innocent part of the evening began. Two girls writhed in a plastic pool in half-hearted intercourse. Insertions and extractions took place to the accompaniment of exotic laser beams. Ed found he wasn't paying much attention. Phu spoke better English than her *frenn*. The girls were funny. Diana began to tell them about when she'd danced go-go in London. Reduced to language the girls could understand and shouted into the huddle of heads, Diana's experiences lost their rebellious edge, even their faded eroticism. It began to amuse him, the little sisterhood of strippers. Then, leaning across Miao's bare legs, he tried to explain to Irina the reflections on the dancing poles, how shatteringly rich they were in half-identifiable shapes and colours, but it was too noisy, and he gave up with a laugh. Diana was deep in conversation with Phu. The girl was holding Dy's hand, her slender brown fingers clutched, it seemed, round Diana's supple wrist. In the uncertain, changing light, their varnished nails shaded from brown to blue and then to sudden vermillion. Whatever the colour really was, they'd both chosen the same shade, the girl and the woman. Ten years – maybe there were ten years between the two of them. But beside the little prostitute, Diana looked older than her twenty-eight summers, older and even less of a survivor.

And then the buzzer. The acts were over. The music cut back. The fascist march began again, low and threatening. Miao and Phu stood up reluctantly. They had to get naked again and work on their poles. They finished at five – unless someone paid their bar fine and took them back to a hotel somewhere. '400 baht for the bar,' Diana explained. 'And the hotel adds 500 to your bill – double occupancy – something like that.'

'And the girl?' he asked.

'Up to you. Another 500 probably.'

All told, twenty-five bucks. Ed glanced at the girls. 'Shouldn't we tip our two?' he prompted.

'I already did,' Diana told him. 'But so the manager didn't see – she takes half the tips.'

Ed remembered what Diana had said at the Temple of the Dawn. She wanted to know how he saw the place. He glanced around, hoping he wouldn't have to see it again.

Dy stood up to go. He stood beside her. The red-skirts were cleaning the poles again. Miao and Phu were standing arm in arm stark naked waiting to climb up onto the stage. No boots, no numbers. Phu caught his eye, and he raised his hand to wave her goodbye. She waved back as though they were old friends casually parting.

'How much did you give them?' Ed asked.

'500,' Dy shrugged. 'Between them.'

'Good,' he said, wincing as the march jerked up a hundred decibels. 'Such beautiful kids.'

They had to walk the length of Soy Cowboy to reach the taxi stand. The street was still lively. Outside each bar, tout-girls dressed in every variation of the same outfit stood ready to harass passers-by. Unthreatening. Cheerful. In Washington the girls would be bagging groceries, Ed thought, though not at this hour of the morning.

Diana took his arm. She seemed to have absorbed the atmosphere of the street – unthreatening, cheerful. They found a taxi, ice-cold as usual, and squeezed into it. Vadim sat in front and told the driver to turn off the air-con. Ed sat in the back between the two women. They each put a hand on one of his knees and began to exchange obscenities in exaggerated Thai accents. Clever women. Funny women. No longer afraid of flying as the Jong woman had described their mothers – just afraid of crash landings.

Then Irina said: 'If you're not busy, Ed, come to my place tomorrow. You can tell me about the reflections, but properly.'

'Sure,' he said.

'I can meet you at Princess?' Irina offered. 'We can take taxi?'

'What time?'

'About one?'

'Sure,' he repeated.

Diana made a claw of one hand and mouthed a long *miaaoww*.

'As you see, Dy has no objections,' Ed remarked, 'and anyway, she won't find out because she'll be at work till four.'

'Till six,' Vadim broke in. 'Tomorrow is monthly meeting.'

'Oh fuck Patel, and fuck his meetings,' Diana pouted.

'Well, he go to KL Thursday evening,' Vadim said. 'You not see him for a while. Good news?'

'Next beggar I see gets ten baht,' Dy replied.

'And another thing,' Vadim told her. 'He call me this evening. Patel. About seven. He said: How much I know about Ed?'

'What did you tell him?' Diana asked, suddenly alert despite the evening of beer drinking.

'Nothing. What do I know? Ed paint music? Ed like Jack Daniels?'

'What did he want?' Diana persisted.

'Something about Ed's work. I tell him I have no idea – he best call Ms Tarn. Ask her.'

'What did he say to that?'

'He say, no problem.'

★★★★★

Ed sat on his bed. Diana was brushing her hair. She was in her pajamas already – *pyjamas* as she called them, stretching the *y*. She'd always worn her hair short, but now it was even shorter. Hardly worth brushing. Pretty though and provocative. Her back was to him, but her face was reflected in the mirror, a little too pink from the ugly mirror-light. She caught his eye, but she didn't smile.

'So you ever paid any bar fines?' he asked, sure that the answer would be *no*.

'No,' she replied, still brushing.

'So what's in it for you? Places like that?'

She shrugged. She didn't know, but she wanted him to talk it through.

'You and that girl Phu. You seemed to get on okay.'

She stopped brushing. 'What does that mean?'

'Nothing,' he replied. 'You held hands a lot, that's all.'

'She held my hand. That's what she's paid for.'

'That's true.'

'And you hated the place,' she prompted.

'Pretty much. Disco dancing. And all those fucking Australians.'

'Well, I agree about the Australians,' she said. 'But the dancing.'

'You like the dancing?'

'It gives you a different feeling, having naked girls around.' She put down her hairbrush and glanced at his reflection in the mirror.

'Does it?' he asked.

'Totally unlike real life. Maybe not *your* real life, Ed. But life at the UN.'

'I guess,' he agreed.

She laughed: 'Why should I excuse myself anyway? You knew how I was when you married me.' The old excuse. In a way it was like the jokes he shared with Merr, except that it was funnier.

'I had to laugh,' he said. 'You telling those girls about your misspent youth.'

'They thought it was brilliant. They wanted me to go on stage with them.'

'You could have,' Ed said factually. 'You're still in shape.'

She weighed the compliment carefully and then nodded agreement. 'And what would you have done if I had?'

'Walked out probably,' he replied. 'Taken the next plane home.'

'Exactly,' she agreed. 'But why? Would you have been shocked? Disgusted? Ashamed? What?'

'None of those, Dy,' he replied. 'I'd have been irrelevant. Completely irrelevant to your life.'

'And now you're not?'

It was a false step. She didn't mean it. He didn't reply.

'It just slipped out,' she said. 'Sorry. As long as you're in this room – in this city even…'

He nodded. 'So why did Patel want to know where I work?'

'That's a change of subject,' she protested. 'I liked the old subject better.'

'As you wish,' he said, bending forward to take off his Nikes.

'One thing I'm scared of, Ed…,' she began tentatively.

They were getting there at last, edging toward why she'd dragged him half way round the world. And maybe when they'd talked about it, they could talk about Terry.

He sat up, one shoe on and one shoe off, looking at her. Dy liked to be looked at – she knew her strong suit.

She turned her head away, almost shyly. 'What I'm scared of,' she repeated, 'is losing it.'

'Losing it?'

'You saw Vadim? How he was?'

'Unfortunately yes.'

'That's how guys are. Out here. Everywhere, more or less.'

'Surely not.'

'Yes, the kind of guys I meet. The kind of guys who are interested in me.'

'Maybe.'

'No, Ed, not maybe. I'm telling you. That's how they are, and when I see it, I can't stand it.'

'But Vadim's a friend of yours, isn't he?'

'Colleague.'

'So – what do you mean by *losing it*?'

'I took you there tonight… You hated it, but you were chatting with Phu. You didn't hate *her*. Vadim you found repellent. But Phu you liked.

'How could anyone take against her, poor kid?'

'Well, sometimes I wonder…'

'What?'

'About bar fines.'

'Really? With a bargirl?' Paying? A girl? Unless Diana had changed trains, it seemed unlikely.

'Not now, Ed. Not here. Not with kids. I don't think so anyway. But… What do I have in my life? Where the fuck am I going?' She picked up her hairbrush again and stared at the bristles.

Dy had gone to school in England. St Cunegunda's. Boarding. Girls only. She'd told him stuff… Dy and her little clique of rebels searching for barriers to trample. And when they'd trampled the landscape flat, they'd searched around for higher, thornier barriers simply to prolong the fun of trampling. They'd livened up vacations with protest marches, and term-time with selfies bashed off to porn blogs. Later it was sit-ins and an occasional riot. For the web, they'd perpetrated videos – self-conscious solo epics and lesbian lampoons of love. In the summer between St Cunegunda's and Cambridge, she and a girl called Harriet had signed up with a theatrical agency as go-go dancers *available for private parties only*. Altogether, a risky trampling package, though it hadn't proved fatal. One time in Harvard Dy had showed him a dozen JPEGs and some movie clips. Then, in a sacrament of repudiation, she'd reformatted her hard-drive. It wasn't long before the old Dy faded into a distant legend. Far more important, the here-and-now Dy, who was she? Was post-repudiation Dy likely to pay a bar fine and all the rest of it? It seemed unlikely. On the other hand, Dy wasn't entirely tamed. She'd given the girls 500 baht so the manager couldn't see. It was a protest – not much compared with the protests against Larry Summers back in 2005, but even so it was an ember of the old fire. Diana leading the bargirls of Soy Cowboy in the fight to end tyranny. Tyrants? Arabs owned most of the bars, or so Irina had told him. Arabs, some of them rich and all of them tyrannous.

Dy waited for his thoughts to catch up with her. 'I've met a few people here,' she said seriously. 'UN types. Embassy. Mostly men – but women too. A few bar fines at first. A binge or two. Harmless enough. But what's to stop it becoming a way of life?'

'For you?' he asked.

'So much drunken wreckage about. And all of it despicable, God knows. But chatting with girls like Phu, suddenly it seems possible. Why not pay up? Why not drop out once and for all?'

He saw her point – what *was* there to stop her? She knew what she was talking about. In her years of trampling, she'd had some lucky escapes. And now she was knocking thirty. No one's luck lasts for ever.

Diana started to brush her hair again. He watched her, aware for the first time of a subtle change, a shadow line. He asked himself again – what *was* there to stop her? In truth, not much. She'd never paid a bar fine. Not yet. That wasn't much to hang on to. The *not yet* would frighten her, his fearless, defiant Diana. It would frighten anyone. Was that what she'd wanted him to see in Soy Cowboy – her choices? Guys like Vadim? Or girls like Phu? Or maybe he was off track – and not for the first time.

'You see what I'm saying?' she asked, not looking at him.

He nodded, still unsure.

'I hit rock-bottom a couple of times,' she said. 'My last Christmas at Kings. In Harvard after my father died.'

'Yes,' he agreed.

'But I always left something behind. Getting a first. You, Ed. There was always something I wanted badly enough to bring me back.'

'Me?'

'Of course, you. How long was I gone? That time in Harvard?'

'Six days, four hours and eleven minutes,' he improvised. 'Not that I was counting.'

'You see!'

He wasn't sure what he was supposed to see, but he let it go.

'So when I lose this job, what's left to go back to? Nothing.'

He nodded.

'You understand?'

'I guess. But what does it all add up to? The future is a black hole, and it scares you. Join the club.'

It was her turn to think. She sat pressing the bristles of her brush into her fingertips. 'I'd be happier about the future,' she said at last, 'if I was happier about the past.'

'But that was all years ago.'

'No. Not that. I mean…' She turned away from the mirror, her voice suddenly bleak, bleak as a mountaintop.

She meant Terry. Terry was why she wanted him there. And Terry was why he'd come. His courage faltered and collapsed. Not now. He wasn't ready. He had to escape.

'But I don't see… I don't see how I can help you, Dy,' he said. He took off his other Nike and threw the pair of them into a corner of the room with a thud.

'You *have* helped me,' she replied with cold finality.

'So help me in return. Why did Patel ask about my work?'

Day 3

Wednesday 28th October 2009

'I thought we'd settled this last night. It's none of your business. Stay out of it.' She was dressing, more concerned with the sit of her skirt than with his imaginary problems.

'If Patel is asking questions about me, it *is* my business.' Ed had got up before Dy, the jet-lag already slaked off. He'd spent an hour googling on Dy's laptop *blood supply chain management, blood groups, Haemonetics Corp*, and other leads. He'd taken a swim.

When Dy was ready, they went out to the cool of the breakfast terrace. He walked behind her, preoccupied, but not too preoccupied to admire the assertive modesty of her walk. He couldn't believe that only the Vadims of this world were *interested in her*.

'So?' he said, ironically holding a chair for his pretty lady to sit down.

'Patel may have many things in mind,' she said. 'I tell him you're a painter. Then you tell him some tarradiddle about buying blood. He can't cope with contradictions.' She shrugged. 'Like you said – he starts with definitions.'

Ed sat down, the right-angle of the table between them. 'What else did you tell him?'

'Nothing. Nobody at the UN knows anything about you. Or about Terry.'

'What's Terry got to do with it?'

Dy fell silent, weighing her words. 'In a way, Ed,' she said quietly, 'we've been talking about Terry ever since you got here.'

He fell silent in turn. Perhaps she was right. Perhaps they had nothing else to talk about, nothing that didn't go back to climbing Denali – the big one.

Denali. They'd booked it, trained for it, talked about it incessantly for almost a year – all through Dy's bar exams and his last semester of teaching. Mount McKinley – 6,000 metres. Then to Dy's fury, she'd missed her period – if they still went on the climb, she'd be ten weeks pregnant. Abortion? Culling a life so they could take a holiday? Impossible. They'd talked to Siggi, Ed's doctor friend. There was a risk, a small one, from the altitude – but Dy was fighting fit. If she felt bad, there were helicopters on McKinley – medevac wasn't a problem. They'd talked about postponing the climb or giving it up altogether, but not often and not seriously. They'd planned it for so long, and the challenge was so desired, even more of a challenge now that three of them would climb the mountain instead of two. Then Denali itself – the thin air, the ever more strenuous climb, the battering winds. Somehow Dy had struggled through, but Terry hadn't. Just at the time when Terry's foetus-brain should have grown faster than it would ever grow again, it had begun to suffocate. In Dy's womb. And back in Washington, no one had guessed. Everything seemed normal. Then, not long after the climb, Dy had suggested they get married. And he'd agreed. Because he loved her. And because she loved him.

After the excitement of Terry's birth, they quickly understood what they'd done – to their daughter. Their marriage fell apart. A few bitter quarrels. Then silence. Ed hadn't blamed her. He'd blamed himself. Absolutely. He'd known the risk – he should have cancelled the trip. His unforgivable failure drew him to the damaged child. From the first Terry had needed love, so he'd loved her, held her, cared for her. Loving the helpless little scrap of life had helped him hide the guilt and the ugliness of what he'd done. He'd hidden behind his work too, and behind Lucía, the Mexican girl who looked after Terry most of the time. Somehow he'd coped. And Dy? She'd climbed the Big One and found at the summit nothing but shame and self-disgust. Every glimpse of Terry was a new wound. Ed had seen her pain and felt its intensity, yet her coldness had shocked him. That had been what they'd quarrelled about – her unbearable coldness. Their suffering had driven them apart. Dy had withdrawn from the baby, and he hadn't. It was an absolute difference.

In the wreckage of their lives, she'd finished her exams and joined Lambfields. He'd painted. Good paintings, most of them. Easy to sell anyway. Myron had taken everything he did. Took it still. The perfect gallerist.

The breakfast terrace was almost empty. They ordered coffee and a basket of croissants. 'I took her to see Ohrenstein,' Ed began.

Dy looked at him intently – was this the news that had hung over her for three days?

'She's probably epileptic, as well as the rest.'

'So if she has a fit…?'

Ed nodded. 'Could be the end. Very easily.' For a second he steeled himself – he'd trusted Dy with the ugly new fact. Now he trusted her to spare him the obvious, the *welcome-release* crap everyone spouted at him. Ed's mother – Terry's grandmother for Christsake – had buried him under an avalanche of it. But Dy said nothing – she retreated deep into her most closely guarded self. She poured coffee for both of them and took a croissant. Ed took one too, and for a while they breakfasted in silence, though somehow the silence was more intimate than their words had been.

At length he said: 'If you're right, I'm not changing the subject, just seeing it from a different angle. I'm going to call Merr.'

'Call Merr? What about?'

'About Patel. Maybe Merr will tell me what the hell's going on.'

'Going on? What do you mean *going on*?'

'This blood racket. I can't get it out of my mind.'

'Selling blood is a perfectly respectable business. Distasteful to you perhaps, but perfectly respectable.'

'Dy, I've actually been approached on this terrace by a guy *selling* blood. And there's at least a possibility Patel put him on to me. Isn't there?'

'No,' Diana replied. 'You don't know Patel. He wouldn't touch anything like that. Wouldn't soil the fingertips of his white gloves.'

'I just can't bear to think about it,' Ed objected. 'Kids locked up so bastards like Patel can sell their blood.'

Dy's cold anger struck out: 'What's got into you, Ed? In some obscure way, this really is about Terry, isn't it? So what's the plan? Start a crusade against the blood mafia, the organ mafia, the drug mafia, the sex mafia in a country you don't know, in a language you don't understand, without a single friend in your corner? It won't help anybody – not you, not Terry, not the poor kids. Don't be so fucking crazy.' The frigid tone, the sarcastic curl of her mouth – Dy at her ugliest.

'Can I have your phone?' he said.

She unzipped the phone from a compartment in her shoulder-bag and gave it to him. 'Hold down the 8,' she said icily. 'I put in Merr's number yesterday.'

The number rang. Merr answered. Ed asked him if he knew anything about Patel.

'Why?' Merr asked.

'He thinks I buy blood.'

'Why?' Merr repeated.

'I met him on Monday. I didn't like him much. After that stuff we pulled at the morgue, I told him I was a blood-buyer. Totally stupid. But yesterday a guy came around trying to sell me blood. So there must be a connection.' Silence. Ed held the phone away from his ear so Diana could hear Merr's answer when it came.

'I shouldn't tell you this, Ed, but we did a background on Patel. As far as we know, and as far as your question's concerned, he's clean.'

'Good,' Ed told him. 'That saves me a lot of bother.'

'You're still in country though!' Merr's voice began to pick up its locker-room edge. Deliberately it seemed. 'Something keeping you? Found yourself a Thai girl?'

'Merr. Dy's listening.'

'Well, maybe she can give you a few tips. I guess she knows the ropes.' Then: 'Say, I'm not going to be up here as long as I thought. If you're still in Bangkok Friday, how about a rain check on that dinner?'

'Sure,' Ed told him. 'Call me soon as you're back.'

'Great. Take care.'

Ed pressed disconnect and gave the phone back to Diana. 'Looks like he's done a background on you too.'

'You think so?' she said, suddenly less remote.

'*I guess she knows the ropes.* That's plain enough.'

'Merr always talks like that.'

'Dy – how indiscreet have you been? I mean, do you go to those places on your own?'

'No.'

'Who do you go with?'

She hesitated. 'A woman from work, Adina. I went once with her when I first got here. And with Vadim on the way home from work – a couple of times. A while back.' She began to tear the remains of her croissant into shreds, crisp little flakes of mangled pastry.

She'd gone with Vadim? That was new. Vadim and *Irina* – they went places together, or so Irina had told him. But Dy? Whenever Dy took what she called *an evening off*, it had always been with a girl-friend. It was safer that way, easier. At Kings, it had been her old school chum, Harriet. In Dy's first year at Harvard, it had been Mirah. From Oman or some such place. *Mirah, Mirah on the wall, who is the fairest of them all.* Poor girl – she'd modelled clothes for a couple of magazines. Then she'd got her face slashed by one of her cousins who decided modelling was unIslamic. But Vadim? A little shit who liked bargirls sitting on his fingers.

'If Patel's checking up on you,' Ed pursued, 'how would it look, going to a place like last night? I mean, in DC it wouldn't look good at all.'

'In Bangkok it's okay for men. Bit less for women.'

'So Patel might use it to get rid of you?'

'He can get rid of me easily enough. *Inadequate cultural adaptation* is what they call it. *Insufficient respect for persons of a different cultural background.* Especially if their name is Patel.' She made the gesture of slitting her throat.

'Have you been getting up people's noses, Dy? You can be a real bitch when you like.'

'On the whole not,' she said without taking offence. 'I learned that lesson at Lambfields.'

'What then?'

'Patel's a bureaucrat. Worse, he's a UN bureaucrat – an *apparatchik*. If things go wrong, he finds a Jonah to throw to the sharks.'

'And this child abuse project is going badly.'

'Exactly. So…he'll fill up my file with crap and then dump it on me. All of it. Going to a bar on the way home from work isn't worth a footnote. But maybe I've done worse things than that. A woman's place is under a man – and I'm not. That's why he's ferreting around, asking questions. And he's interested in you too, or so Vadim says. It didn't help much, you know, that nonsense about buying blood.'

Ed nodded. 'I see what you're saying about Patel. But it sounds like Merr's been on your tail too. I just don't get it. I mean, he's known you for years – he was fucking best man at the wedding. I think he's being devious.'

'Merr checked me out. So what? Let's say he did it thoroughly. Let's say he knows I've gone to a couple of bars. That's all he can possibly know. There isn't anything else. And if he'd asked me, I'd have told him anyway.'

'That's not what worries me. If he's being devious about you, how do we know he isn't being double-devious about Patel? He says Patel is clean, but…'

Diana fell back in her chair. 'How do *we* know?' She stood up. 'Count me out, Ed. You've gone paranoid on Patel. He's a blue-chip arsehole. But that doesn't mean he steals blood and trades it in the marketplace. Get back on the planet.'

Ed struggled for words but found none.

'Ed.' She looked down at him, incredulous. 'You think my boss, Patel, and your buddy, Merr Croft, are in some sort of conspiracy? Is that what you're telling me?'

'I'm telling you nothing. I'm simply pointing out that we don't know… I don't know…'

She stood up. 'I've got to be at work. I'm late already. With poor cultural adaptation *and* bad time-keeping, they can sell your corpse to the crocodile farm. Article 112.'

And she was gone.

Blood, blood, blood. Were they quarrelling about blood? Or just quarrelling? A *crusade* she'd called it. Most of what he knew about the crusades he'd picked up from *The Talisman*. If you went on a crusade, at least according to Scott, all the sins you'd ever committed were forgiven, every last one. *Plenary absolution* the church called it. All your old sins washed away – plus the sins you *might* commit in the future. Something like that. Maybe *crusade* was the right word. After Denali, that was maybe what he needed – plenary absolution. And Dy too.

Ed reached out for the shiny vacuum flask on the table, glancing at the reflections. A face, a brown face, hideously distorted, was staring at him. Patel? He turned abruptly, confronting the bogeyman. It wasn't Patel – it was Chaudhary, just out of earshot, waiting for a chance to intrude.

'Well?' Ed said.

'Such a charming lady.' Chaudhary nodded at the door through which Diana had just disappeared. 'So exquisite in every particular.'

'Yeah,' Ed agreed. 'I met her in a bar last night. She may look okay, but a couple of hours and you find out she's a total bitch.'

'I have so little understanding in such matters,' Chaudhary replied delicately. 'There is nothing...'

'So what do you want?' Ed broke in.

Chaudhary smiled as though he'd been paid an exorbitant compliment. 'I know this is an extreme liberty, but should you be planning to visit our office, we find that ten would be more appropriate than eleven. At least for us. I can take you in my car, if you wish.'

'Sit down Mr Chaudhary,' Ed invited him, swallowing his anger. 'Would you like some coffee?'

Chaudhary poured his slick body into the chair Diana had just vacated. 'Most kind,' he said.

Ed beckoned the waitress and ordered a clean coffee-cup. 'I wanted to ask you something, Mr Chaudhary.'

Chaudhary smiled and bowed slightly.

'Is there a big Indian community in Bangkok?' Ed ventured.

'Yes,' Chaudhary replied. 'It is considerably sizeable.'

'Considerably sizeable,' Ed repeated. 'Do you happen to know anybody here by the name of Patel?' He watched Chaudhary's face closely for any sign of surprise. It was a clumsy trap, he realised immediately.

'Several people,' Chaudhary began helpfully. 'Patel is a very common name in India. Also in Pakistan. Of course

I cannot speak with any certain knowledge for the Indian community in Indonesia or in Malaysia, but I see no reason not to believe…'

Chaudhary was a master – unbeatable. 'Just that somebody offered to make me a suit,' Ed broke in. 'He said his family was the best-known tailor in Bangkok. Is it?' The night before Ed had seen the name *Patel* on a tailor's shop near Soy Cowboy – even so, he was swimming in unnecessarily murky water.

'Patel in Sukhumvit, you mean in all probability. Perhaps he was exaggerating… A little.' Chaudhary began a circumstantial account of the history of Indian tailoring in Bangkok. Too circumstantial, Ed thought. The cup arrived, and Ed filled it with coffee. Chaudhary's chatter flowed seamlessly to traditional handicrafts in Chennai. Serious overkill.

Ed glanced at his watch – 9:15. He took his decision. 'We could leave in ten minutes if you like. I just need to pop upstairs.'

'Take your time, Doctor Scarman,' the Indian said. 'Take your time.'

★★★★

Scar, Ed said silently to his reflection in the mirror as he cleaned his teeth, you know this is totally fucking stupid, don't you? Let's say Patel really is connected with Chaudhary, Andronicus and the rest of it – what are you going to do? Report it to Merr? Report it to the UN? Report it to Hirsch at the morgue? All three? And what difference would it make? You don't even know there *is* a blood racket.

He found himself repeating the words *totally fucking stupid* as the escalator bore him upward among the fish and fountains of the Kingdom Tower. It was a vast place, built to impress and crushingly successful. Huge volumes of unused, air-conditioned space, marble, altars, inscribed stone tablets, bronze effigies, all the signs told the same story – the Kingdom Tower was not an office block, it was the Wat Arun of Thai commerce.

'There are fifty-eight floors and fifty-two lifts in this building,' Chaudhary informed him. 'Or elevators, as you might call them. In all, a third of a million square metres. But we occupy only a small part of floor twenty-nine.'

The elevator was programmed to skip the first twenty-eight floors. The doors rolled open in silence. A hint of disinfectant hung in the air of the modest lobby. There were three offices and a public toilet on the twenty-ninth floor. Two of the offices were empty. *Andronicus* – the name in gold letters guarded by two bronze dragons stood outside a double swing door. The doors and most of the walls were made of thick, greenish glass. The empty offices had white lining paper Scotch-taped inside the glass. The unpapered glass walls of the Andronicus office hid nothing.

Chaudhary grabbed one of the heavy, vertical door-handles and hurried Ed through the glass door. They passed a Dilbertian landscape of cubicle-dwellings, heading for a corner office screened off completely by walls of plastic rosewood. Chaudhary tapped on the office door, opened it, and ushered Ed ahead of him. An Indian was sitting behind the desk. He was shorter, darker and skinnier than Patel or Chaudhary. A different tribe? A different race? The pits of Bhatnagar's eyes were almost black, and his pomaded hair was slicked back. The name on his desk plate was *J.N.K. BHATNAGAR*. Inscribed below the name was the word *Bloodproducts*.

'Doctor Scarman,' he said, standing up with ill grace. He shook Ed's hand without looking him in the eye and sat down again. 'Mr Chaudhary…' He said the name as though it gave him ear-ache. 'Mr Chaudhary said you wanted to see me.'

'Not exactly, no,' Ed replied.

Bhatnagar said something, and Chaudhary replied in a language Ed didn't understand – Bhatnagar challenging and Chaudhary apologising, Ed guessed.

'You are a buyer, I understand,' said Bhatnagar. 'May I have your business card?' He held out his hand, curt and aggressive.

'Maybe I should explain,' Ed began. 'I'm actually a gynaecologist. But owing to a mistake, I can't get professional indemnity insurance anymore.'

'A mistake *you* made?'

'A mistake I made. Unfortunately yes.'

Bhatnagar shrugged his shoulders – what did this have to do with him?

'And so,' Ed continued the story he'd been putting together all morning, 'I've found another field altogether. Administration. When I get back to the States I *shall* be a buyer. But a total novice.'

'Which hospital?'

'Not a hospital. A company.'

'Haemonetics?'

'Much smaller,' Ed replied, 'and niftier. We like to think we're Haemonetics' competition.'

'But you're not going to tell me the name?'

'My contract hasn't started yet. I can't speak for the company. It was Mr Chaudhary's idea that I come here. Well, I thought, why not? I might learn something useful.'

'Something useful,' Bhatnagar repeated sarcastically. He added some words in the language he'd used earlier.

Chaudhary replied, conciliatory, almost obsequious.

'Maybe,' Ed broke in. 'Maybe I should mention that my department – when it is mine – has an interesting budget.'

Bhatnagar looked at him intently for the first time since he'd entered the room.

'I'm not at liberty to tell you how much. Obviously. But there are two figures in front of the million. And diversifying our suppliers is – will be – a priority.' *Diversifying our suppliers* – a distant memory of *MGMT 5005* in his last year as an undergrad.

Chaudhary cleared his throat, suddenly relaxed and self-satisfied – it seemed he'd won the skirmish with Bhatnagar, *scotched the snake*, though perhaps *not killed it*.

Ed had come to the end of the story he'd prepared. It had played okay – he'd said nothing the Indians could google and use to disembowel him. But even if he slipped up? Impersonating a failed gynaecologist wasn't a capital offence.

Chaudhary and Bhatnagar began to wrangle again, but this time Bhatnagar seemed less aggressive. He looked at his watch. 'I have to leave for the airport shortly,' he said to Ed. 'And I still have many things to do. You understand?'

'Of course,' Ed replied.

'Go with Mr Chaudhary. He will show you round the office.' Bhatnagar stood up to shake hands. 'I'm sure we shall see each other again,' he said. His eyes met Ed's. Ed was ready for curiosity, distrust, hostility maybe, but all he saw was emptiness, a soulless, inexpressive void. He shuddered.

*****

As they walked round the office, peering into cubicle after cubicle, Chaudhary explained the workflow of offers, orders, order confirmations and dispatch notes. Ed flattered him with questions.

'So you are learning the supply-chain business,' Chaudhary returned the flattery. 'Compared with the intricacies of your former profession, supply management has few secrets. Common sense and a handful of simple procedures.'

'If it were really so simple, every firm would be rich,' Ed improvised. 'I'm sure there's much more to it, Mr Chaudhary.'

Ed realised that Chaudhary was not trying to steer him – he saw columns of figures on computer screens and addresses on letterheads. Nothing hinted that Andronicus was anything but a well-run business – not that Ed knew for sure what a well-run business looked like. Yet Chaudhary and Bhatnagar had been quarrelling – apparently about him. Bhatnagar evidently distrusted him. Why? If everything was above-board, why was a potential customer treated with suspicion? But perhaps it was always so – he had no way of knowing.

'I like the glass walls,' Ed ventured, eyeing the double and triple reflections bouncing around inside the erratically shaped building. 'It gives the place an air of transparency.'

'A company with nothing to hide is not afraid of transparency,' Chaudhary remarked sententiously. 'And in any case we have our Archive.' He indicated another fake rosewood office like Bhatnagar's with the word *Archive* in bold letters on the door.

Andronicus' office was not big enough for Ed's tour to last more than a few minutes. It was time to try another move. 'You have a plant?' Ed said. 'Here in Bangkok? So I was told.' That morning he'd seen on Andronicus' website the word *Production* and a street-address in Bangkok.

'Yes, a plant,' Chaudhary agreed.

'That's where you make your instruments I guess.'

'We have five factories in Thailand. Four are outside Bangkok. The minimum wage in the city is excessive.' Chaudhary began to explain the economics of production in low-cost countries.

'Interesting,' Ed said. 'You're an excellent teacher. I'm learning a great deal from you.'

'I can hardly believe you are such a novice as you claim.' The war of politeness was escalating.

'Compared with someone of your experience…' Ed raised the stake.

Chaudhary came to a decision. 'There is not much to see in our office,' he said. 'Would a short tour of our factory be of interest to you?'

Ed regretted that his schedule was too tight to allow him that pleasure. Chaudhary said it was a pity and pleaded for a short visit that afternoon. At tea-time? Ed conceded – perhaps he could reshuffle his engagements.

'Shall I pick you up at five?'

'Sure,' Ed agreed. 'I think I can fix that.'

★★★★★

'Don't look at my stuff too close,' Irina said.

'Why not?'

'This morning I was on your website.'

'How did you know where to look?'

'Dy told me. *Lovis.Scarman.com*. Strange choice.'

'Lovis Corinth was my great-grandfather.'

'He was impressionist, I think.' Again the spy-girl impression-*eest, I theenk.*

'German though. Have you seen his early stuff?'

Irina shook her head.

'He worked with Bouguereau.

Irina shrugged – she'd never heard of Bouguereau.

'So, how did you like the website?' Ed asked. 'What did you think of Evil the Weevil?' Whenever Ed wanted to bring himself down to earth, he invoked the Weevil. Mascot of some redneck basketball team. 8,000 bucks the Weevil had brought him. Finished like a Bouguereau nude. And the most worthless piece of...

'It make me sick and jealous,' Irina said with an honest shrug.

Ed looked round the studio. One room. Cheaply furnished. Uncomfortable – but colourful enough. A mix of posters in Thai and English decorated the walls, blow-ups of fashion sketches and bold drawings of Thai girls, short-haired, long-haired, in stiff, unlikely poses. 'All yours?' he asked, trying to sound enthusiastic.

She shrugged – as close to denial as she could come without saying *No*.

'What are you working on now?'

'Something very difficult,' she said, glancing at her workbench. Scattered on the bench were dozens of cut-outs, all the same shape – six squares arranged like a crucifix. Most of the crucifixes bore a female figure arranged so that each square was decorative but, as he guessed, enigmatic.

'Packaging?' he guessed. 'A cube?' He went to the workbench, interested.

'Perfume,' she replied.

He looked at the failed sketches – awkward poses distorted to fit the unpromising outline. Only one human shape belonged on the cross – the expiring carpenter of Nazareth.

'How would *you* do it?' Irina asked. He'd had a Russian model once, Raissa Petrovna. Of all his models, she was the only one Diana had disliked. Now Ed saw in Irina's dark eyes the same subdued, inviting flame he'd seen in Raissa's. It piqued him, and he picked up a stick of black pastel. For a moment he studied one of the empty, six-box cutouts. Irina was holding her breath in expectation.

'Pauline Bonaparte,' he said. 'Canova. You know the thing. Leave off her drapery. Take away the silly pillow from under her arm. Turn her thirty degrees.' He began to draw, unambiguous, confident lines. He was showing off – unambiguously, confidently. Luckily the sketch wasn't bad for a first try. The tight hair knotted on the back of Pauline's head – it was almost okay.

'Fix it, and we'll see how she looks as a box,' Ed said.

Irina sprayed the sketch with fixer. She waited a few seconds, then folded the shape into a cube, holding the edges with Scotch-tape. Ed watched her nimble, work-worn hands – too worn for a girl her age. He'd thought the same thing the night before when she'd been drinking beer.

She held up the box, admiring it from every angle. 'So tell me about reflections,' she said quietly.

Ed paused to collect his thoughts, as he'd done with the drawing. Irina was intelligent. He'd pay her the compliment of talking to her intelligently. 'You have any photographs?' he asked. 'Not photoshopped?' He glanced round the walls. 'Like that one.' He pointed to a picture thumb-tacked to the wall – half-a-dozen grinning children in Thai costume. 'An untouched image like that isn't arbitrary in any way. It derives from the laws of physics.'

'*It derives from the laws of physics*,' she repeated with a smile. 'This is from your lecture, yes?'

'Yes,' he admitted. 'Sorry.'

'No, don't be sorry,' she said. 'It is interesting. Listening to someone like you. If I try for a year, I can't make anything as good as…' She gestured at the little cube on the bench.

'Dy hates it when I lecture her.'

'I know. She told me.'

'What else did she tell you?'

'She said you are the smartest man she never met.' Irina eyed him archly, wondering what he'd say.

'Diana said that?'

'I think she mean it too,' Irina replied. She was laughing. Her teeth were not even and not particularly white. Amalgam fillings. Like Felicity. The memory stopped him dead.

Irina sensed his sudden arrest and waited, saying nothing.

'But a painting?' he picked up the thread. 'Take a Cézanne. A landscape. Every square inch, taken out of context, is a mystery. You need rules to understand the picture – the simplest of which is how far away to stand so you can see it.'

'I never heard this rule before.'

'You've seen pictures by Ocampo? Mexican?'

She shook her head.

'Most of his stuff is a bit overdone. But one series I really like – if you get close, all you see is birds and branches. From a bit further away, elegant faces. The rule of distance.'

'Can we google him?'

On Irina's ancient laptop, Ocampo's pictures were unimpressive, but she saw the point immediately.

'So there is rule about distance,' she agreed, 'and maybe thousand rules more. But why you must *understand* a picture? Why is not enough to *see* a picture?'

'The fancy word is *recuperate*,' he replied. 'You recuperate a picture. You see it intelligently, not like a scanner sees it, not as a billion pixels.' He was standing with his arms folded, not looking at Irina. Looking at nothing, thinking. He was enjoying himself, talking to someone who didn't mind the professorial edge in his voice, someone who asked the right questions. People bought his stuff, paid good money for it, but the only questions they asked were: *How long did it take you to paint that?* And *Do you ever paint nudes?* That was one great advantage of photorealism – nobody asked what the picture was *of*. At least, they hadn't asked till he'd started on reflections.

Irina was studying intently the side of the box that showed Pauline Bonaparte's feet. 'You draw her with a broken foot,' she said. 'For a reason?'

'It's a sign,' he replied, looking again at the broken line, 'and it has a meaning. For me anyway.'

She thought for a second. 'In art so many perfect women,' she said, 'and in real life no perfect women? Not one. So you broke her foot?'

'It frightens me,' he nodded. 'Girls like Pauline. Like Miao and Phu.' And Dy, he added silently. And Dy.

'But reflections?' she said. 'Like you told us with music on the river. Is it possible?'

'The second day I was here, I went somewhere. I won't tell you where. Give me a sheet of paper.'

'For pastel?' she asked.

'Sure.'

She found a new block on her paper-shelf and tore off the plastic wrapping.

'Nice paper,' he said.

'Bought it in Singapore,' she replied. 'They don't sell it here.'

He began to draw. Grey. Black. More grey. Steely textures formed on the paper. Then an enigmatic shape in red and another in blue. Then unaccountable shapes in dingy colours, suggestive, ugly, frightening.

'It makes me feel sick,' she said. 'Stop.'

'Smell,' he replied. 'What does it smell of?'

'Cold,' she said. 'It smells like the last level of hell.'

'It is,' he said quietly. 'That's where I was.'

He waited for the obvious question, but with a sensitivity to his mood that also reminded him of Raissa Petrovna, she simply said: 'You allow I fix it?'

'Sure,' he replied. He turned away and went to a clumsy sofa-bed at the other end of the room. He sat down. He heard the hiss of the aerosol as Irina sprayed the sketch. Already he could see the picture he'd paint back in Washington, as heart-rending as a Hardy novel, his own *Tess of the d'Urbervilles*.

He heard Irina's footsteps. She was barefoot. He glanced at her. Jeans. T. She walked like a farm-girl, as though her next chore was to muck out the hen-roost. Dark-haired. Almost black. Sallow. She wasn't pretty – but he liked her. Raissa Petrovna hadn't been pretty either, though Diana had resented her. Hated her even. That had been years before, back in their *good time*. Ed had been fond of Raissa. He'd had sex with her, of course, but Diana never resented that, expected it even. With her invincible fear of emotion, it was the fondness she couldn't stand. Then Raissa got her film contract. After that they'd e-mailed sometimes. But not for a long time now.

Irina sat beside him on the bed. 'Who teach you to draw like this?' she asked.

'I never went to art school, but I don't think anyone can teach you to draw,' he replied. 'All anyone can do is help you *see*. A lot of people did that for me. Starting with my mom.'

'So I can't see, and this is why my drawing is lousy? Is your opinion?'

'What's your second name?' he asked.

'Sergeyevna,' she replied, puzzled for a second.

'Well, Irina Sergeyevna, I think when you look at your models, you see position and not movement. It makes the drawings a bit static.' He waved his hand at a wooden sketch of a Thai girl holding a baby and forcing a smile. Always the professor, always *de haut en bas*. Sometimes he hated himself.

'Well, of course, my models are posing, not moving,' she laughed. 'Maybe this is enough reason.'

'Maybe,' he agreed.

'But I know what you are saying.' She made a rueful face, and they both laughed, provoked and already curious about each other. At least she hadn't clammed up when he told her what he thought of her drawing. It might have been a safe moment for a kiss, but Ed didn't kiss her.

'Can I ask you something?' he said.

He watched a dozen clever, bitter, flirtatious replies flicker behind her eyes. Then she said simply: 'Yes, of course.' The sudden drop in tone, the plangent softness of her Russian voice, brought them closer than any kiss might have done.

'I had a strange meeting this morning,' he said. He began to talk. They sat down. They went into the kitchen so she could make tea. They sat down again, drinking. And still he talked. The story in the American magazine about the blood-farms – children with useful blood-groups locked up and robbed of their blood. He told her about Merr. About the morgue. The blood. Chaudhary. Bhatnagar. And Irina listened – Irina Sergeyevna as he'd begun to call her, like a younger sister in a Chekhov play. Of course, he realised, she had little choice but to listen as long as he chose to pour out his problems to her. But she wasn't just listening. She took his part, she shared his suspicions and, it seemed, his *anger*. He wondered why. What was it in her life that made her angry when he told her the blood-farm story?

'This man, Chaudhary – he pick you up at five? At the Princess?' she asked.

It was four-fifteen already. He'd better get moving if he wanted to make the meeting. 'You think I should go?' he asked.

'No,' she said.

'No,' he repeated.

'I think *we* go. You and me.'

'You come with me? What for?' She was serious – he didn't understand it.

'Not go together. I follow you.'

'Follow me?'

'On motor-bike.'

'You watch too many spy movies,' he replied.

'All Russians are spies. Check it in Wikipedia.'

'I don't get it,' he said.

'Listen,' she told him. 'What you're doing – it is very dangerous. If I was doing something so crazy like to go with this Chaudhary, I want a friend to…wait, see me go in, see me come out – okay?'

A friend? She was the friend who'd go with him? He'd only met her two days ago. In fact, though, her thinking was one jump ahead of his. A back-up would be vital if anything went wrong. Not that it was dangerous – not for him and not for her either. Or was it? But what was her *real* reason for coming? Maybe she was bored and wanted a bit of excitement. But no. It was her character – so abrupt, so impulsive. He remembered their dinner at the Oriental – she'd been demanding explanations almost before they'd sat down.

'Well, if you're sure,' he agreed, trying to sound enthusiastic. There was something shocking in her generosity – he found it difficult to respond. 'But do you have a motor-bike?' he asked.

'Bike on every street corner. Fast. Not very safe.'

'That's what Dy told me. If ever I was late, take a bike. But…'

'But nothing. You go. I follow. Is already decide.'

★★★★★

'That was very impressive,' Ed said, sitting down. A windowless office, brightly lit. A circle of plastic armchairs round a low glass table.

Chaudhary said a few words in Thai to the small, skinny man with an unpronounceable name who ran the plant. 'I asked him if tea could be arranged – but only, of course, if you would like some,' Chaudhary explained. 'Or Coca-Cola?'

'Coke would be great,' Ed agreed.

The Thai clapped his hands. Despite his meagre size and shabby Mao suit, everyone treated him with a respect that shaded into uneasiness. As they'd walked round the plant, all his workers had greeted him with the same gesture – palms pressed together and fingertips raised to the forehead. Each time, he'd replied in the same way. In the labs, it had been white-clad, androgynous figures in white helmets. In the packaging bays, tough men in bright yellow shirts and pants trimmed with green tape. No name, no badge, no logo. But all respectful.

The door opened. A woman from the front office. The Thai said something, and the woman disappeared, silently closing the door behind her.

'What in particular did you find impressive, Doctor Scarman?' Chaudhary asked modestly.

'From the outside, this building looks like nothing at all. Windows painted over. Bars everywhere.'

'This area was formerly warehouses. Belonging to the tobacco monopoly.'

'Yes. You told me.'

Chaudhary smiled – for his excellent friend he would repeat the same information from now until midnight. With pleasure.

'But inside,' Ed continued. 'Modern equipment. Beautiful tiling everywhere. And so clean, so hygienic.'

'Perhaps hygiene should go without saying.'

'Please don't mistake my meaning,' Ed back-tracked. 'It doesn't surprise me. Just the contrast with the outside.'

'Ah,' Chaudhary said, not deceived. 'But at least you have a clearer idea now of how blood products are processed and packaged? I must say, I have learned some interesting particulars myself. It is a considerable while since I visited these premises.'

'A considerable while.'

'Yes, Doctor Scarman. Quite considerable.'

Ed smiled, wondering if anyone ever wrong-footed Chaudhary. 'Well I must say,' Ed began again, 'I'm immensely grateful for your time and for Mr...' Ed struggled for the name of the Thai manager, but it was hopeless. 'The only thing you didn't explain is where the blood actually comes from.'

Chaudhary said something in Thai to the plant manager. The manager replied – a stream of nasal sounds that Ed couldn't break down into words.

'He says,' Chaudhary began, 'there are donation centres all over Thailand. Volunteers give blood, much as they do in your country. It is chilled and sent here overnight. You saw the containers. They usually arrive here in the morning. Though from a scientific point of view it is unnecessary, we like to complete all processing within forty-eight hours.'

'Impressive,' Ed repeated the word.

The woman came in with three Cokes and three glasses on an aluminium tray. She put the tray on the low table. Ed saw a bowl of tiny fried octopus and another of what looked like algae-covered hydroponic gravel.

'So,' Ed said, watching Chaudhary pour him a Coke. 'How much of all this huge space is yours?' And what he didn't say: especially that area with the padlocked steel doors and the smell of ammonia and formaldehyde behind them?

Another Thai sentence from Chaudhary. Another reply from the manager.

'None of it is ours. We only rent.'

'One warehouse?'

'One warehouse is more than enough for our needs,' Chaudhary replied.

Ed nodded. Slowly he drank half the glass of Coke.

As Ed drank, Chaudhary glanced at his watch and came to a decision. 'Shall I call you a taxi?' he asked. 'I myself must go to another part of town altogether.'

'Please,' Ed replied.

Chaudhary took his cellphone from his breast pocket, asked the Thai for a number, and keyed it in. A brief pause and some words in Thai. 'Perhaps we should leave already,' Chaudhary suggested. 'The taxi will be here in a few seconds.'

'No problem,' Ed replied.

A guard in a brown uniform unlocked the warehouse door and saluted them through. Outside it was dark already. 7:15. The guard locked and bolted the door behind them.

The cluster of warehouses was surrounded by a desolate truck-park – pebbly concrete, vigorous weeds and saplings of what looked like sumac trees growing in every crack. An expressway straddled the plot on Pharaonic concrete columns. Fluorescent strips lit up the outside walls of the warehouse. A few were dead. Some were flickering. The street and the perimeter fence were perhaps fifty yards away, alive with headlights and the bright butane lamps of evening stallholders setting up or already selling.

Ed looked back at the buildings. Four warehouses, he'd been told. He could make out three, the shapes picked out by the illuminated walls. In the Andronicus warehouse, lights burned behind some of the painted-out windows. One window must have been open – it was edged on three sides by a narrow slit of light. He pictured the ground-plan of the workshops he'd seen. The light came from a part they hadn't showed him.

He walked with Chaudhary across the empty truck-park toward the gatehouse. A red-and-white barrier was down and padlocked in position. A rusty gate for pedestrians hung open and useless. Feeble floodlights created deep shadows but hardly lit up the road. Chaudhary's car was parked outside.

They were in Chatuchak. With tireless goodwill, Chaudhary explained how the old weekend market in Chatuchak had become an all-week affair. How the Skytrain had brought new life to the whole area. How the city planned to redevelop the old tobacco warehouses and the railroad station at Bang Sue, though the plans had been put on ice during the crisis and not yet revived. Probably similar cut-backs had occurred in the United States?

'I will give instructions to your taxi-driver, and then I will leave myself,' Chaudhary concluded as they reached the gatehouse. Ed saw that the padlock and chain on the barrier were new. From the roof of the empty guard-hut, a CCTV camera pointed downward at the barrier. Ed scanned the forecourt and glanced up and down the busy street, smoggy with exhaust fumes. Where was Irina? Would she see him when he got into his taxi?

In the forecourt, a meter-taxi was parked at the kerb behind Chaudhary's car. Chaudhary checked with the driver – yes, the driver knew the Princess Hotel.

There was no sign of Irina. 'Mr Chaudhary,' Ed began. 'I may not see you again before I go, so perhaps I can clarify a couple of points. It won't take a moment.'

Chaudhary looked at his watch and pressed a button to illuminate the dial.

'If you're in a hurry, of course…' Ed apologised.

'Perhaps tomorrow morning,' Chaudhary offered.

A motor-bike swung off the street and into the car park – a bike and two dark, skinny figures with black balloon heads. The engine cut and then the headlights. A female voice said *Spasiba* unnecessarily loud.

'Perhaps I'll call you, Mr Chaudhary,' Ed said, getting into the back seat of the taxi. 'Tomorrow.'

★★★★★

Every hundred yards or so Ed glanced back. It was a while before he picked up the motor-bike following his taxi, the balloon heads merged into one. He told the driver to pull into the kerb. The bike stopped behind them. Irina climbed off and unlatched her helmet. She paid off her driver and joined Ed.

'Is okay?' she asked as the taxi swung resolutely back into the traffic.

He told her about the lit-up window. He told her about the locked doors and the smell.

'Formaldehyde and ammonia? Might be gesso.' It was still there – her spontaneous interest in his problem. And not just interest – it was her problem too.

'Yes, I thought of gesso too. But why?'

87

'There was smell of paint?' she asked. 'Acrylic?'

Her cellphone played a phrase from *Rigoletto*. He'd seen the opera at the WNO. With Diana, when they'd got back from Mount McKinley. *Bella figlia dell'amore* – not long before Rigoletto finds his dead daughter in her sack. Irina glanced at the display. 'Dy again,' she said. 'You want to talk to her?'

'What did you tell her last time?'

'I didn't answer.'

'Don't answer now,' Ed told her.

'She'll worry.'

'She's not the type,' Ed replied.

The music stopped.

'Yes,' Ed picked up the conversation. 'There was a smell of acrylic, but I assumed it was the walls. Freshly painted – some of them anyway. Why?'

'Well, you seen those huge posters, specially outside movie houses?'

'I saw a couple on the way from the airport. Monsters. Hideous.'

'Well, they still hand-paint them.'

'They're painting posters? In a medical warehouse?'

'Don't think so western,' she said.

'And if they *are* painting posters?' he asked.

'Children paint,' Irina said. 'A poster is just – how you say? – painting by numbers.'

'So following through on my obsession – they have a warehouse, they have kids. Why shouldn't the kids in the warehouse stay busy painting posters? Anything's possible.'

'Tell me how the place is like inside,' she said, mulling over the idea. He liked her. She trusted his instinct, his impulse – however thin the evidence. But why? Because he could draw and she couldn't? Because he'd helped her with Pauline Bonaparte? It wasn't enough.

The taxi came to a halt. They were near the centre of town – the permanent traffic jam. He described the warehouse to her. The gatehouse. The empty, half-lit truck-park. The locked door of the warehouse with its guard. The painted windows and the windowless inside-rooms.

'You really think they keep kids in there?' she said.

'Not impossible.'

'No. Anything's possible,' she agreed, echoing his words. *Anything could be true in this fucking country.* He heard the same tone of resignation in her voice that he'd heard in Merr's, that he'd heard in his own voice seconds before. And he bridled. *Life's uncertain voyage.* This time he wasn't going to settle for uncertainty! He'd had enough of it. And now – at least with these kids, at least with this warehouse – he wanted to know for sure. He wanted to *know.*

'If I go back,' he said with sudden urgency. 'Take another look at the warehouse. Would you say I was nuts?'

'Nuts is like crazy?' she asked.

'More or less.'

She shrugged. 'Tell me who isn't crazy?'

She was on his side. She understood. 'Listen,' he said. 'Can you get Diana on your phone for me?'

A few seconds later, Dy's voice was with them in the taxi. 'Oh Ed, it's you. Where are you?'

'Irina is taking me to a place where they paint movie posters. We're stuck in the traffic right now. Not sure when I'll be back.'

Silence. One of Dy's silences.

'Dy? Everything okay?'

Silence. Then: 'Patel told me I was doing a good job. At the meeting.'

'Is that good or bad?'

'Fucking disaster probably,' she said and cut the connection.

Irina told the driver to go back to Chatuchak. To the market.

'How come you speak such good Thai?' Ed asked.

'Enough for taxi and for shopping. That's all. I am three years here.'

They were near an intersection. With lights flashing and horn blasting, the otherwise docile driver forced his taxi across the traffic and into the turning lane.

'Dy said your husband went back to Moscow.'

'Not Moscow. Kiev. He is Ukrainian.' Her tone was dry.

'You stayed on. You must like the place.'

'Nobody likes Bangkok,' she replied.

'Then why stay?'

'I don't want to talk about it.' Her voice flashed anger, straightforward and immediate. Remembering Raissa, Ed took her aggression as a sign of friendship.

The taxi made a heroic sweep into the oncoming traffic and headed back toward Chatuchak. He felt Irina's hand rest lightly on his knee as it had done after their trip to Soy Cowboy. He rested his hand on hers and pressed it for a second – her outburst hadn't upset him. Reassured, her hand slipped away.

The taxi turned into a broad yard. He read the words *Chatuchak Weekend Market* on a big, unlit signboard above a locked gate.

Ed paid the driver, and they got out of the taxi. The hot, sticky air was heavy with the exhaust fumes of two expressways.

'Why get out here?' he asked.

She pointed to a big map next to the gate – the market, the park, the railroad stations. 'I remembered this map,' she said. 'Sometimes I come this market. At weekend. Mostly they sell reject. Very cheap.' She held out her hand to him, and he took it automatically.

They went to the map. It was behind glass that reflected uninvitingly the street lamps and the lights of passing cars. Two dark figures, hand in hand, formed a sinister silhouette against the reflections. The map was labelled in Thai and in

English. Despite the awkward light, he found the Tobacco Monopoly warehouses, four of them, standing in a huge compound. Rail tracks penetrated the compound from the north. He found the gatehouse and the car park where he'd left Chaudhary not twenty minutes before.

'This warehouse,' Irina pointed. 'I saw you go in.'

'The window was about here.' He pointed in turn, remembering the façade of the building, the lights in the yard, and the busy street outside the fence.

What was the plan? Why had they come back? What came next?

'This compound have fence along street,' Irina said. 'No gap. Gate have TV camera.'

'I saw it,' he agreed.

'Maybe there is back way,' she said, pointing at the map. 'Railway enter the compound. Somewhere.'

'I'm not sure I want to go back into the compound,' he said. 'It doesn't make sense, what we're doing.'

'Then we can look again from street,' she suggested. 'From front fence.'

It was almost half a mile to the warehouses. The street-lighting was patchy. Most of the passers-by were exhausted women carrying bundles. Some of them dragged dirty children by the hand. Ed felt out of place. He was tall, Irina too. They were foreigners in the wrong place – awkward and conspicuous.

They found the chain-link fence that fronted the yard. It was rusty and topped with three rows of barbed wire. Along the fence, especially near the gatehouse, food stalls were busy. Painted stools and greasy folding tables blocked the sidewalk. On the opposite side of the street, shops sold plants and garden ornaments, their fluorescent lights greenish and sickly.

If there were TV cameras along the fence, Irina said, the other side of the street would be safer. They crossed the street. It was closing time. Barefoot girls were hosing down plants, Thai gnomes, and concrete altars. The sidewalk of broken red tiles glittered with shattered, unreadable reflections. Bats flitted in the ugly light.

For a while they picked their way along the sidewalk and stopped when they were opposite the Andronicus warehouse. The yard, the fence, and four lanes of crawling, belching traffic lay between them and the building. Two floors. The lower floor had no windows. The brightly lit window above was still a slit open. They watched slow silhouettes darken the painted-over glass, as unreadable as the reflections on the sidewalk.

'Strange shadows,' Irina said.

'It could be painters,' Ed said. 'It could be children painting. It could even be imprisoned children painting. Or it could be the ghosts of murdered tobacco monopolists.'

'We can cross road again,' she said encouragingly. 'Eat something from a stand. See better from there.'

They dodged through the traffic and went to the last food-stand, as far as possible from the gatehouse. A fat woman in a yellow dress was boiling a bucket of corncobs over a gas-ring. The steam from the bucket swirled yellow-grey in the light of her simple lamp. Irina asked for two cobs. The woman gestured them to sit down on her stools. She pushed sharp sticks into two corncobs and presented the cobs with a rough flourish.

The stools were inches from the chain-link fence. The wire was ancient. Waste paper, dirt and weeds anchored it to the ground. In places the rusty mesh sagged open, and the crown of barbed wire had come adrift.

'Ask her what she knows about the place,' Ed said.

Irina thought for a second, then said some words in Thai. The woman replied.

'Something about tobacco monopoly,' Irina translated.

The woman continued her explanation, turning cobs in the boiling water with wooden tongs.

'Now tobacco is finish,' Irina told him. 'It is factory.'

'Ask her if children work there.'

Irina asked. The woman answered, pulling cobs from the boiling water and arranging them on a rack over the bucket.

'Yes,' Irina translated. 'Children. Many. Lock in so cannot run away. I think she say so.'

'Ask her again.'

'My Thai is not so good.' Even so, Irina asked again.

'Yes. Lock in. Like in old factories. This is all she know.'

'How does she know it's children?'

Irina asked the question in Thai.

'So people say. She is not sure.'

'Those shadows?' They stared across the empty truck-park at the warehouse windows. 'Any ideas?'

'Shadows are same like your reflections, yes?' she said.

'Not really. No depth. No colour.'

'I see space behind the shadows. How big?' Irina wondered.

'Huge, it seems to me. A hall. Like you get in a warehouse.'

'For poster, you need big floor.'

'You and your posters,' he smiled. 'What else do you feel?'

'People,' she said. 'Definitely I feel people.'

'Working?'

'Mmm.' She wasn't sure. 'Not playing basketball,' she said. 'Not dancing. Not sitting still. I guess working.'

'One peep inside would be enough,' he suggested. 'Just one peep.'

'Peep is like look?'

'Yes.'

'Up to you,' she shrugged, testing the corncob against her lips in case it was still too hot.

He scanned the empty truck-park. 'I don't see any guards or any TV cameras. Do they use dogs in Thailand?' he asked.

'Fence have too many holes. Dogs can escape. And get eaten.'

'Maybe we can try the railroad. Like you said.' He looked at her. She was gnawing her corncob, spurting hot water onto her clothes.

'You're hungry,' he said.

'Eat,' she replied.

★★★★★

Most of the strip lights were dead. Round the few lamps that were still working, bats dived through huge swarms of insects. In the street he'd seen a few bats – here there were hundreds. Ahead of him the expressway towered on its stilts. Its unhealthy light glowed orange against the black sky. He could hear the beating of bat-wings above the *whoosh* of the traffic overhead.

He stopped. Ahead, maybe 200 yards away, on the other side of the expressway, was a hall where Thai children might or might not be painting a movie poster. On the worst possible interpretation of the little he'd seen, what was he up to? What was he doing in this abandoned, bat-infested ruin? Looking for a way to strike back? For a chance to play hero? For some kind of remission? That's what Diana had said: *In some obscure way, this is all about Terry.* He didn't know. He couldn't think it through.

He'd left Irina at the gap where the railroad ran into the warehouse-yard. There'd been no guard. Irina would wait till he came back. If he wasn't back within half an hour, she call Diana – make some waves.

Irina? She was on his side, unequivocally on his side. In a way, that was comforting. But at the same time it was alarming. Why? Who was she, this hopeless Russian artist who couldn't draw a straight line if you gave her a ruler? What was in it for her, chasing shadows on a warehouse window?

A bat flew close to his head. Sensing the warm-blooded beat of its wings, he flinched. But there was no danger. Not from the bats, not from the derelict, unguarded buildings. All he had to do was follow the railroad, check the back of the Andronicus warehouse, and try again to understand the shadows. Then he'd go back to Irina. And that would be the end of it.

Between the overgrown railroad track and the warehouse lay a concrete strip wide enough for two trucks to pass. Ahead, black shapes blocked the railroad. He hurried toward the shapes, his Nikes squelching on the ribby concrete. He tried to walk without making a noise, but he couldn't. As he squelched under the expressway, the black shapes resolved themselves into old railroad wagons, some with tattered canvas tops, some open to the sky. Andronicus was still fifty yards away. He could see a lighted window. It seemed to be symmetrically opposite the window they'd studied from the corncob stand. On the night air, he caught the faint smell of paint. Acrylic.

He reached the window. Like the window on the other side of the building, it was a few inches open. From below, all he could see through the slit were steel roof-beams and corrugated panels. Dull galvanised panels. The light inside was intense and white. Good enough to paint by. The mysterious shadows were less active on this side, but he could hear a radio playing snake-basket music, and the occasional *clank* of a bucket handle. The line of railroad wagons was unbroken. They were uncoupled, cannibalised, abandoned. If he climbed on top of one, opposite the window-slit perhaps...

The bright strip of window-light fell across one of the wagons. A cattle wagon. It had closed doors, at least on his side. He checked one end of the wagon for the usual iron ladder. Then the other. Nothing. Two wagons further on was a chemical transporter. Its ladder was still intact. He grasped the ladder with both hands and shook it. It seemed solid. He climbed up, his hands flinching away from the rusty, crumbling iron. From the top of the ladder, his view was no better. A catwalk ran along the top of the giant drum. Fearfully he crawled along it. He was still too low to see anything. He stood up, giddy and trembling. Still nothing new. He crouched again, waiting for the vertigo to pass.

Then an outcry. From the warehouse. Children's voices in a tumult of protest. A shrill cry – a woman's screech rising above the din. The children fell into an uneasy muttering. The woman's voice, joined by others – two or three it seemed – screamed orders. The shadows on the painted window became suddenly eloquent. A definite line of heads. Then an ugly *thwack*. A belt against a human body? A scream of pain. A child's pain – or so it seemed. More screams. Shouted orders. What sounded like a rain of blows. A man's voice now, bellowing. Silence.

If only he could see. Shadows and sounds were not enough. He scuttled back along the catwalk and down the ladder. As his toes touched the wooden rail tie, the warehouse went dark inside and out – long seconds of silence and darkness. Then, with the *ping-ping* of their starters, the strip lights outside flickered back to life. The warehouse windows stayed black. He crouched for a second, suddenly afraid. Coming toward him, between him and Irina, two men were silhouetted against the orange glow of the expressway. Guards? Ed's white shirt, his white pants and white shoes were painfully luminous. He scuttled under the chemical wagon, hiding in the angle of an axle and a black wheel. The track smelled of lubricating grease and of some kind of corrosive poison that had leaked from the wagon.

The men stopped for a cigarette, leaning against the wall of the warehouse. They were wearing coveralls and baseball-caps, and they carried t-batons. Definitely guards.

Ed waited. They hadn't seen him. He was safe. A light flicked on again inside the warehouse – a single bulb, nothing more. The window slit closed slowly, and then the light was switched off again.

As soon as the guards moved on, Ed scrambled from under the wagon, but now on the dark side. Too dark to see. He smashed his shin against some kind of metal bar. Silently cursing, he slipped between two trucks, back to the concrete and the half-light. He began to run, jogging at first, then speeding up as he neared the expressway.

He followed the railroad track, unsure now of his bearings. Switch lines branched off in unexpected directions. He came to the gap in the perimeter fence. Where was Irina? He peered around. Was it the same place? Had he left her here? Or somewhere else? Perhaps she was hiding.

'Irina!' he called, trying to whisper. It was ridiculous. 'Irina,' he called again, much louder. The *wah-wah* of the expressway was the only answer.

Against the fence, he saw a white glint – a discarded plastic bag it could be, or a scrap of newspaper. No. It was something more. He moved closer. A face with white hands covering it. Dark clothes. A stretched out body. Irina.

He felt for her pulse, for the throb of the carotid artery against her windpipe. When Terry stopped moving, that was how he touched her neck, assuring himself that she was still his child. The artery was pumping. Irina was alive. Was she injured? Had she passed out? Perhaps she'd been hit by a passing car? If her backbone was damaged… If she was bleeding inside…

He could see nothing. Irina's shoulder-bag must be nearby. He fingered among the rank vegetation and the garbage till found her bag. Her cellphone was an old-fashioned Razr. If he opened it, there'd be light enough to see.

By the light of the phone, Ed saw blood on Irina's face.

Her hair and her neck were bloody. Irina had called Dy from the taxi, so her phone must have Dy's number in it. He found the number and called Dy.

'You calling to tell me about the posters?' Dy asked caustically.

'No,' Ed told her. 'There's been an accident. Irina's hurt.'

'You want me to call an ambulance?'

'No I want you to come here. With a taxi.'

A silence. Then, 'Where are you?'

'Listen Dy. You've heard of the Chatuchak Weekend Market.'

'I've been there. With Irina as it happens.'

'Go to the map. At the gate.'

'The map?'

'You'll find it. Call me when you're standing in front of it, and I'll tell you how to get where we are.'

Irina came round while Ed was calling. Two guards, she told him painfully. They'd knocked her down and kicked her.

'And be quick,' Ed said into the phone, but Dy had already hit red.

Day 4

'Coffee.' It was an order, not an invitation.

'How is she, Dy?' They'd taken turns through the night, watching Irina. He stretched himself awake now, aching from three hours of broken sleep on the floor of Irina's studio. A mug of instant coffee steamed beside the cushion he'd used as a pillow.

'She's still quiet.' Dy was sitting beside him cross-legged on the floor, sipping her own coffee. 'I have to get back to the Princess and change for work.'

'What time is it?'

'Six. The doctor's coming again at ten.'

'You're sure we can't get her into a hospital?' He sat up and reached for his coffee.

'Her work permit ran out ages ago – so she said last night. A hospital would report her to the police. They'd have to.'

'And she doesn't have health insurance.'

'Most people don't,' Dy said. 'Did Lavinia?'

'Who?'

'You were talking in your sleep, muddling up Irina and Terry and someone called Lavinia.'

'Lavinia, daughter of Andronicus,' he said.

'Listen. I've got to run. Call me after the doctor's been.'

'Sure.'

'And maybe tell me what the hell was going on last night. Your story – I think *unimpressive* is the right word.' She finished her coffee and stood up.

He looked up at her. Nothing wrong with Diana's bullshit detector – never had been. Nothing wrong with her Good Samaritan act either. She'd gone to Chatuchak. Got Irina home. Called a doctor and taken over when the doctor left. Yes, that's how she was sometimes – a rock when you needed her. And all without nasty questions – at least till two minutes ago.

'See you,' Diana said abruptly. She went to the door, grabbing her handbag from Irina's workbench. 'And don't forget to keep the ice-pack going,' she said over her shoulder. 'I just took one off.'

He drank his coffee and went through his *unimpressive* story again. He'd gone with Irina to look for a warehouse where they painted movie posters. Irina had thought they were near, so they'd got rid of the taxi and walked. Then Irina had lost her way. He'd left her for a moment to take a leak. Nothing improbable so far. While he was gone, Irina had been hit by a passing car. That was where the problems began. Irina's bruises and the lump on her head looked like anything but a car accident. The doctor had been discreetly dubious, but he hadn't made an issue of it – he wasn't paid to ask difficult questions. And Dy? Thank God she hadn't snapped into her lawyer's cat-stalking-bird mode, but she'd known Ed was lying. And it wouldn't be easy – telling her the truth. After all, she'd told him to forget the blood thing, and he'd more or less agreed. Still, after the way she'd come through for him – and for Irina – maybe he owed her a little honesty. *Though honesty be no puritan, yet it will do no hurt.*

He glanced at the sofa-bed. Irina was lying on her side with her back toward him. Part of her skull was shaved. A bugling, ugly dressing was held in place by criss-cross white tapes. The end of one tape had come away from the skin. Probably from the wet towel and the ice-cubes. He'd better stick it down again. He stood up, still in his street clothes from the night before. His hip hurt from the hard floor, and he staggered a few steps rubbing the painful bone. Irina's studio was unusually comfortless – nowhere to sit, a noisy air-con that kept the temperature at a steady seventy, a tile floor with only a battered kilim to cover its nakedness. He wondered where she'd lived with her husband. Somewhere consular – not a dump like this.

Irina stirred.

'Irina,' he said quietly. 'It's okay. I'm here. Don't roll onto your back.' He hurried to her and held down her shoulder to stop her moving. 'Are you awake?' he whispered. He'd never been much of a nurse, but looking after Terry had taught him to foresee pain and to head it off.

She said something in Russian. Her voice was half way between a growl and a moan. Then: 'Those bastards. Is it bad? My head?'

★★★★★

Ed signed a passing taxi, but it didn't stop.

The doctor had visited Irina at ten and told her she needed some x-rays. He couldn't do tomographs, but old-fashioned stuff he could do in his office. X-rays should be enough. Her appointment had been at twelve. Ed had gone with her. The doctor had been thorough. No ribs were broken, though she had deep bruises from a couple of nasty kicks. Her head would be okay – her parietal bone was unusually thick – eight millimetres in some places. Irina hadn't been surprised. As a kid she'd been hit all the time, mostly round the head. Maybe that had something to do with it. Thick skull or not, the doctor had suggested, she'd need watching for another thirty-six hours.

Ed hailed another taxi. Then another. Hopeless. The uncompromising sun beat down directly on their heads. Irina had covered the ugly dressing with a head-scarf – Bolshevik red, like a peasant scarf in an old Soviet poster. A few yards from where they were standing, a palm tree cast a patch of shade. Ed steered Irina toward it, out of the sun, and tried again for a taxi. After three more failures, a filthy brown car pulled into the kerb. Ed opened the door for Irina. The car was dirtier inside than out. He held his hand above her head so she wouldn't hit the doorframe.

Irina moved awkwardly across the seat to let him follow. Her bruised ribs stabbed her as she moved.

He waited till she'd recovered, then sat beside her and slammed the door. The driver tutted – tourists slamming his door.

The taxi was hot inside, hotter than the street. Ed told the driver to turn on the air-con.

'Bust, mister,' the driver explained. 'Where you go?'

Irina had written her address in Thai and in English on a slip of paper so Ed could show it to taxi-drivers if need be. The paper was in his billfold. He took it out and showed the address to the driver. 'And start the meter,' Ed told him. 'Now.'

As the taxi picked up speed, Irina's cellphone rang *Bella figlia dell'amore*. It was Dy. Irina passed the phone to Ed.

'Listen,' Dy said urgently. 'Patel's sending me to KL.'

'Sending you where?'

'Kuala Lumpur.'

'Where's that?'

'In Malaysia.'

'Why?'

'He was supposed to go himself, but he can't be bothered. He says something's come up. He has to stay here.'

'Can he make you go? Are you going?'

'It's only till Monday evening, Ed. Or maybe Tuesday.'

'Tuesday? I'm not sure I want to hang around till then.'

'It's Loy Krathong on Monday. They say it's pretty. They float candles on the river.'

'I'm not in the mood for candles,' he said.

Silence. Then: 'You finished at the Doc's? Sounds like you're in traffic.'

'Yes. But we're making time for once.'

'How's Irina?'

'Okay. No nasty splinters. She'll be alright by Sunday. Want to talk to her?'

'Not right now.'

'When will you leave? For Malaysia?'

'Five. I've got to get back to the Princess and get packed. More or less now.'

'Will I see you?' he asked.

Silence. 'Before I go to KL? Or before you go home?' A lawyer's question – with hooks. The fraying cord that bound them could snap in the next few seconds. Was that what he wanted? And Dy? What did she want?

'Before both, maybe,' he replied cautiously. He glanced at his watch – it was nearly two. Then, almost despite himself he said, 'If I was at the Princess at four-thirty…?'

'I'd like that,' Diana said, with a little catch in her voice. 'Really.'

'Four-thirty then.' He hit disconnect and passed the phone back to Irina.

'Ed?' Irina asked him. 'Are you going away?'

'Going away? Not till you're okay. The doc said Sunday. But if it takes longer…'

Irina nodded and winced.

'What did you think? I'd leave you like this?'

'I think you *might*. I don't know what Dy…'

The traffic was slowing down. The driver dodged in front of a black Mercedes and gained a few yards. They were following a hotel limo, grey and polished. It stopped, and they stopped behind it.

'Ed, can I ask you – another question?'

'Sure.'

'Are you walking away? From those kids? The blood? All of it?'

'Do I have a choice? Look what happened to you, and you were only hanging around by the railroad. What would they have done to me?'

'Tell me what you saw. And what you heard. It's not clear to me. Not at all.'

He'd described it all to her twice already. Patiently he told her again, but this time she was alert, asking questions, getting the details clear in her mind.

'Isn't that enough?' she asked when he'd finished.

'Enough for what?'

'To tell someone. In that warehouse blood is process. There's kids in there. Locked in. Guards hit people over the head, so is something to hide.'

'Tell who, for example?' His voice had a sarcastic edge – he'd broken into an ugly sweat in the heat of the taxi. It was time to forget Andronicus and the rest of it and get back to Washington. Talk to Diana before she flew to Malaysia. Get Irina on her feet, hopefully by Sunday, and then go. If there was a blood racket, it was no concern of his.

'Dy works at the UN,' Irina suggested.

'The UN. That's a joke if ever there was one. A team of six people. Working on child abuse. And two of them – your friend Vadim and my wife – go to watch kids take their clothes off in Soy Cowboy. And God knows what else. And the others I met – Patel and that Thai guy… I told you about them already. Forget it, Irina.'

'Your friend at America Embassy then.'

'Merr?'

'I don't know… He is your friend? Or?'

'Maybe he'd know what to do. But the other day when I mentioned blood, he just clammed up.'

'So you not trust him?'

'I trust him, but…'

'You trust him, but also you not trust him.'

'More or less. And anyway…'

The grey limo in front of them began to move. The taxi-driver slammed the old car into gear, and they ground forward.

'Anyway, what?' Irina prompted.

'I've got a sick kid at home.'

'Terry?'

'Yes. I talked to her nurse. Ever since I left, she keeps crying and saying *Daddy*. That's one of her three words.'

'What are the others?'

'Sounds she repeats. One means *bottle*. But she can't say real words. Only *Daddy*.'

Irina was puzzled. 'And you not get angry with her? For being stupid?'

'She isn't stupid.' He told Irina about Denali. She listened, her bloodless face tight and urgent.

'And Dy came here?'

'Yes.'

'And you look after Terry? In your studio?'

'Mostly. She has a nurse. A Mexican girl. Illegal.'

'What's her name? The nurse?'

'Lucía.'

'Lucía,' Irina repeated, somehow testing the word for its integrity. 'You trust her. If you leave your little girl with her…'

'Yes I trust her. She's the only person in Terry's life beside me. Terry's fond of her.'

'And does she get angry? With Terry?'

'No. She loves her. Same as I do.'

Irina shrugged. 'Not easy to understand,' she said. 'A father… My father…' She couldn't explain, and Ed couldn't help her out.

The traffic slammed to a halt again.

'Proof.' Irina picked up the old thread. 'If your friend Merr have proof? Something bad? In that warehouse? This can help?'

'Proof? You mean evidence? Something concrete?'

'I mean photographs.'

'Taken where? And who by?'

'I have friends,' she said. 'You stay in Bangkok a few days. Till Loy Krathong.'

★★★★★

Dy was flying economy. The evening flight would land her in Kuala Lumpur around eleven – ten o'clock Bangkok time. Ed sat with her and her packed suitcase drinking bourbon on the Princess' terrace. Her laptop was on the table in a bag of its own. The limo was booked for five-fifteen. They had another ten minutes. Patel had spent most of the afternoon briefing her – something he'd never done before. It had made her queasy – after a briefing like that, he'd find some way to slaughter her when she got back. And what was she to do in Kuala Lumpur anyway? Break a five-year log-jam in two days – that was Patel's idea. 'Like being the Minister of fucking Agriculture in fucking Somalia,' Diana mused. She was being set up, and she knew it.

'Can you call me?' he asked. 'When you get there?'

'You'll worry about me, Ed?'

'I'm worried about Patel,' he said. 'I don't know why he's sending you.'

'A stiletto in the ribs in the slums of KL? If he wants to get rid of me, poor cultural adaptation is a lot deadlier. I told you that already. And I'm not going to the slums anyway.'

'I guess not,' Ed agreed, and they sipped their bourbon.

'Ed?'

'Hmm?'

'If I get kicked out… When I get kicked out…'

He nodded.

'…I'm going to need money.'

'Yes, you said – to buy a partnership.'

'Any idea where I'd get it?'

'The banks?' He shrugged.

'They don't lend to out-of-work lawyers. Since the melt-down, they only lend to the Fed.'

'I don't know then,' Ed said quietly. 'If I had any spare, I'd lend it you. But…'

'You're a penniless artist. With Terry hanging round your neck.'

'Terry's not a burden, Dy,' he said, suddenly ashamed for her.

Dy fell silent. She glanced at her watch. 'Why do you think I'm like that? About Terry?'

He looked at her uncertainly. 'That's a hell of a question.'

'And we've got four and a half minutes to come up with the answer.'

It erupted without warning from some locked chamber in his memory – her joy, her curiosity, the sublime peace that came over her in the weeks before Terry was born. The vitality of their love, so oddly, so unexpectedly heightened by marriage. He remembered with a pang of longing the bright, clever, sensual world they'd created for each other. And now, on the other side of the rattan table, sat this harsh, unloving wreck of his beautiful Diana, the only woman he'd ever loved. Beyond his reach, headed for a distant and evil shore. Unless…

From nowhere the bell-hop appeared beside their table. 'Limousine, Miss Ta'an. Waiting now.'

'Early for once,' Dy said. 'I'll call you from KL. On Irina's mobile.'

'I'll get one of my own,' he said, 'if I stay in Bangkok.'

She looked at him emptily, her face a mask.

'One phone more or less,' he said. 'It won't break the bank.' How could words fall so far short of intention? He'd gone to the hotel to be with her. Why? Because of what she'd said – *I'd like that. Really.* And because he knew what the words had cost her. He'd gone because she'd stood by him in the night and because she'd stood by Irina. If only he could find the right reply, even now…

'Sure,' she said, standing up abruptly. The bell-hop pulled out the handle of her case. 'Take care,' she said, looking away. He watched her as she followed her case out to the waiting limousine. Maybe, by some miracle, she'd be successful in Kuala Lumpur. Though maybe that wouldn't help with Patel. Success might damn her worse than failure. His Diana.

He sat down. She'd hardly touched her bourbon, he saw. Kuala Lumpur? In a few hours Dy would be there. KL they called it. He formed no image of the place. Nothing. She was taking over Patel's mission. Why? What was keeping Patel in Bangkok? So many imponderables, not the least of which was a meeting that Irina was setting up, a meeting he didn't want, with two guys who sounded like the scrapings of the scrapings. He'd have to say no. No, no, no.

★★★★★

Irina was asleep. Just before ten, her phone vibrated on her workbench. She'd turned off the Rigoletto so it wouldn't wake her. Ed picked up the phone and pressed green. He thought it might be Diana, but it was Merr. He was at the airport – Suvarnabhumi. The late hop from Chiang Mai had just got in. Merr had the day off tomorrow – if Ed wanted to do some of the sights, it might be a good time. Impossible, Ed explained – he was keeping an eye on a friend who'd been hurt in a car accident. In her studio.

Merr sympathised. 'That Russian art girl? Friend of Diana's?'

'As it happens.'

'Sounds like her residence ran out. Or she'd be in the hospital.'

'Want to come round in the morning?' Ed said. 'We can chat. Catch up a bit. No reflections. No corpses. No Diana. She's gone to KL.'

'I called her a minute or two back,' Merr said. 'She gave me your number.'

'Irina's number,' Ed corrected him. Odd. Ed glanced at the wall-clock. Ten to ten. Diana should still be in the air, somewhere short of KL. How could Merr have called her? Maybe the flight was early, and she'd landed already. She was flying Malaysian – maybe they had planes where you could use your cellphone. Maybe. Maybe.

'She went to KL instead of her boss,' Ed explained.

'Patel?'

'Him. Precisely.'

'What's this girl's address? Irina, you said her name was.'

Irina Sergeyevna Porzova. Almost Chekhov, but not quite. He fished out Irina's address from the paper in his billfold and read it to Merr.

'Tomorrow, eleven?' Merr asked. 'Will you be decent by then?'

'I'm taking her to the doc's at nine-thirty to get her dressing changed. Stop laughing. It's not what you think.'

'Dy's away, so ten seconds later you shack up with a beautiful Russian spy. Most guys go to Pat Pong, but you always had more class, Ed. The entire class one semester – if I remember right.'

'Merr! Shut up will you.' He laughed. It hadn't been an amusing day. Merr's humour was almost welcome.

'No Scar. You won't talk your way out of this one. No way.'

'Listen,' Ed said. 'That business about the blood. I may be onto something. Can we talk about that? Tomorrow?'

'Good idea, even. There was something I wanted to say last time you brought it up. Something's not quite straight. We can chew it over tomorrow.'

'Eleven?'

'Eleven.' Merr cut the connection.

Ed looked at the wall-clock. And what about Terry? It would be ten in the morning at home in Washington. He keyed in his home number. The phone rang for a few moments. He pictured Lucía putting Terry in her playpen. Then picking up. It took longer than he'd expected, but at last the girl answered. Yes, everything was fine. Yes, Terry missed him. She was still crying a lot. No, Terry hadn't been up to any mischief. Yes, they were going to the store soon, in about half an hour. No, no urgent messages. Usually Lucía was more talkative. He guessed her boyfriend was there.

Lucía. Lucy, the lost bride of Lamermoor. One more scalp for the collection.

Ed didn't know much about Irina's friends, but he already disliked the hours they kept. They'd be round at eleven, Irina had said. Or maybe later. Midnight. Whenever. They weren't really her friends, Irina had told him – just guys she knew. A while back they'd been friends of her husband. She talked about her husband freely now. Andrey. He'd worked at the Ukrainian Embassy – Commercial Section. Commercial in name, but in fact devoted to pilfering drawings of Japanese electronics and German car-parts. The Commercial Section, that was who these two guys still worked for. Ed hadn't been sure where the Ukraine fitted into the great scheme of things, so she'd filled him in – Russia, the Soviet Union, the Ukraine. The old Soviet Embassy had turned itself into the Russian Embassy years ago, at about the time the Ukraine became independent. For more than ten years there hadn't been a Ukrainian Embassy in Thailand. When it opened again in

110

2002, there'd been a lot of local hires – Ukrainians left over from the old KGB days, security men who'd hung on in Thailand mostly working as heavies in tourist bars. In fact they'd worked for anyone who wanted a dirty job done and no questions asked. Irina had arrived with Andrey in 2006. Andrey's hobby had been weight-lifting – still was as far as she knew. He was good. He'd just missed being on the Olympic team in Athens. There was a gym in Bangkok where all the Ukrainians went – some from the embassy, some not. The gym was where Andrey made most of his friends. She'd gone there sometimes to watch him or to work out herself. That was where she'd met Stepka and Vanka, the two who were coming at eleven. Or maybe twelve. If Ed wanted photographs, that was something they did, Stepka and his buddy.

The phone rattled again on the workbench. Diana? No. It was Vadim, asking after Irina. Ed told him she was okay. Vadim was pleased but not inquisitive. Ed asked Vadim for his take on Kuala Lumpur. Why had Dy gone there? Was it a dirty trick? A mission impossible? Vadim didn't know and didn't sound particularly interested. So Ed tried something else, unsure where it might lead. 'That bar we were in the other night...'

'Rawhide?' Suddenly Vadim's tone was more alive. 'You like it?'

'It was okay,' Ed replied. 'But...'

'But?' The question was eager – Vadim wanted to know the answer.

'But somehow...' Ed took the plunge. 'Somehow I thought those places were more raunchy.'

'Yes. Rawhide is not good place,' Vadim agreed. 'I tell Diana: We go good place. Show Ed really Bangkok. But she say – no, we go Rawhide.'

'So you and Dy? You go to the good places?'

Silence. Then: 'Dy not tell you? Where she go with me?'

'No. She didn't.' Why was he playing Vadim along? What was the point? He ventured one last shot: 'But it sounds interesting.'

'Really? You think maybe we go one time?'

'Maybe.'

Slowly a sluice-gate opened in Vadim's imagination. He couldn't stop talking. The places he and Dy had gone together! As he told it, Dy was the ice-cold English lady, *debosh'd and bold*. Omnivorous as a guillotine, remorseless as a barracuda. Ed listened shaking his head and adding an occasional *Yeah*, or *You don't say*. He didn't believe a word of it. Dy said that nothing had happened – not yet anyway. That meant nothing had happened. Nothing. But Vadim's brutal perfidy took him by surprise – the little rat. Still – it was good to know who you could trust, and Vadim had erased himself terminally from the list.

Irina stirred on her bed. Ed cut Vadim off with a quick 'Gotta take care of Irina. Bye.' He went to her. She'd have to wake up soon. Stepka and his buddy were due in less than an hour. How could Irina get mixed up with a guy like Vadim? How could Dy? Except that Dy wasn't mixed up with him. They'd gone to a few bars together. Dy had a wonderfully obscene way with words. Probably she'd amused herself firing him up with bizarre ideas. Her idea of a joke. But not…

Irina was awake. 'Who was on the phone?' she asked. 'What time is it?'

'Not long after ten. Vadim called. Wanted to know how you are.'

'Did he? Usually he want something different. What you tell him?'

'I told him you were at death's door, and if he wanted to see you alive, he'd better hurry.'

'What did he say?'

'He'll call again tomorrow.'

'Ed!' she laughed painfully. 'But you're right. This is how he is.'

'So, why…?' He backed off. 'Sorry. None of my business.'

'Why? Me and Vadim?' she shrugged. 'Dy asked me. He was making trouble. For her. With her. She wanted me to…'

'…take Vadim off her hands?'

'Something like that.'

Ed said nothing.

'Many men are same like Vadim,' Irina explained. 'For me is no big problem. But for Diana – she has no… Do you say *experience*?'

'Dy has no experience?'

'She has fun. Take off her clothes for *fotokamera*. Dance go-go. But now she is lawyer. A filthy man like Vadim – she cannot.'

'Let's talk about Vadim. He was saying some strange things on the phone just now. About Dy. Quite unpleasant things.'

'Yes, he has very dirty mind.'

'Did he say things like that to you? About Dy?'

'Sometimes. But I don't believe.'

'And to other people? At the UN?'

'Is possible.'

It made sense. If Vadim had been undermining Dy in the office… Probably he hadn't risked the Messalina routine, but there were a dozen other ways. Repeating words Dy had let slip. *Fuck Patel and fuck his meetings.* A few gems like that and Dy would be dead meat. Dy's tongue had a way of getting her into trouble.

'Oh,' Ed grimaced. 'Poor Dy.'

'Dy is, for me, like friend,' Irina said slowly. 'She is good. I like her.'

'So how did you meet her?' Ed asked, suddenly wanting to see Dy from Irina's perspective – someone who liked Dy but who found her inexperienced.

'At the UN. Her department had a conference. They want me to do poster.'

'Did you?' He glanced round the studio.

'No. Patel said there was no budget.'

'After you'd agreed the price with Dy?'

'Something like that,' Irina repeated. 'But one or two small jobs – she have help me already. And perhaps a big job is coming.' She closed her eyes suddenly and covered her face with her hands.

'You okay?'

'I must go to bathroom. I feel…'

Gently Ed swung Irina's feet off the bed and onto the floor. He helped her stand up, holding her till she got her balance. She was awkward with him, unused to being fussed. He led her to the bathroom.

'I'm okay,' she said. 'I'd like a bath. Hot and deep. But I only have a stupid shower.'

'There's a tub at the Princess,' he replied.

'They wouldn't let me in,' she said. 'Thai whores only. No *falang*.'

'Shout if you need anything.' He left her and sat again at her workbench with his back to the open bathroom door.

★★★★★

That afternoon, after he'd got back from the Princess, Ed had told her *no*. He didn't want to meet the Ukrainian heavies. And there was nothing he needed to know about Andronicus he didn't know already. He wanted out.

'You afraid?' she'd asked him, not as a challenge but simply because she'd wanted to know.

'Afraid? Yes,' he'd agreed. 'Those guys aren't playing softball. Look at your head. Look at what they did to you. It isn't my fight, it isn't yours. Let's drop it while we're still alive.'

'It *was* your fight, Ed. You wanted to go to warehouse with Chaudhary. And later you wanted to go back again with me.'

'Maybe I did. But not anymore.'

'Why you want to go yesterday but not today?'

'I don't know.'

'Ed, can I say something?'

He'd gestured *yes, go ahead*.

'You told me about Terry. You told me you look after her. You find a Mexican girl to help you – illegal girl. You have Terry in your studio, not lock away in hospital…'

'You're making a connection? Between Terry and those kids?'

'Yes. I am wrong?'

'That's what Dy thinks too.'

'And you?'

He'd shrugged. In a way everything was linked to everything else. The real question was not *if* things were connected but *how*. 'So let me ask you something, then,' he'd said. 'When I told you about Andronicus, you were on my side. Immediately. Absolutely on my side. Why was that?'

'It disgust me – about those kids.'

Such an easy answer, though it didn't quite tie up. 'But in the Rawhide – watching children taking their clothes off in front of a gang of drunken swine, that *didn't* disgust you.'

'Why you say that?'

'I was watching you. You were ice-cold. It didn't touch you.'

'Is that what you think?' she'd asked. '*You* hate the place, but you not believe *I* hate it. This is because you are more sensitive? Or more moral? Or what?'

A long silence. Then, 'You know, Ed, I google *semiotics*. It mean studying signs. Yes?'

'Yes.'

'You were teaching this. Well, I think you are good artist, but perhaps you are not so good teacher.'

'You mean I read the signs wrong.'

'You know why I went to Rawhide? Because Diana ask me. And to meet you again – because you are unusual man. But the place? I am happy if someone burn it down.'

He'd said nothing, remembering how she'd been in the club, her stony face, her curt gestures. Had it been an act? Had she been faking indifference to keep on the right side of Diana. After all *perhaps a big job is coming up.*

'You study signs,' Irina had pressed on. 'You understand about signs, so you think you understand meaning of everything. But you do not. At least, you did not understand me in Rawhide.'

Her words had been *a very palpable hit.* Of course, he could have said, signs must be interpreted within a system of signs – where access to the system is denied, correct interpretation is impossible. It would have been a line of defence. But why bother with defence when you're not being attacked. Irina had been setting the record straight – nothing more.

'What can I say?' he'd muttered. 'I'm sorry.'

She'd closed her eyes, shutting out the argument.

He'd given her a moment or two of respite. Then, very gently, 'But can you answer my question? Why were you on my side from the first? And you've set up this meeting? What for? Why does it matter to you?'

And then she'd explained. The guards at the warehouse had hit her. It wasn't the first time in her life she'd been hit. She'd seen stars many times. Too many times. And she'd been laid out too – woken up where she'd fallen minutes later, hours later. Or woken up somewhere else altogether. Most of it had been years ago. In Russia, in her village in Siberia. She'd been the youngest and the smallest, and so she'd been hit all the time. It wasn't unusual. Most families were like that. Her grandmother had been the worst. That's

116

why she couldn't understand about Terry. In her village, kids like Terry didn't last long. It was a bad place. She'd never go back. Never to Siberia. Not anywhere in Russia.

★★★★★

Ed sat now at the workbench, mulling through what she'd told him. In front of him was a block of drawing paper, pens, brushes, pencils – everything to hand. So far it had been a day without reflections, but he had no urge to draw. He stared at the white paper, trying to imagine the life of an intelligent kid in a Siberian village, the youngest, slapped, kicked, sworn at every day by more or less everyone around her. Her father had hit her when he was drunk – the rest of the family whenever they felt nasty. He'd read about that kind of thing in Gorky. *My Childhood*, surely the ugliest book ever written and the most frightening. He'd vaguely thought the revolution had ended it all. Apparently he'd thought wrong. But at least she'd escaped. Run away to Moscow. Survived somehow through art school. Somehow. He pictured again how she'd been in Soy Cowboy. Angry. That's what she'd told him, and, after all she'd said, he believed her. But on the surface she *had* been unblinkingly cold. It had been an act, but what had she lived through that made her act so convincing? Part of the answer might be how she was with Vadim – she'd taken Vadim off Dy's hands, or so she said. Men like Vadim were *no big problem* for her, though poor, inexperienced Diana might have difficulties.

And somehow she'd won Ed over – he'd changed his plan. He'd talk to her friends when they came. Talk – that was all. But, as he saw now, even talk a lousy idea. He regretted it already. Still – she hadn't wheedled him, she hadn't bullied him, she hadn't even tried to persuade him. It had come from him, a tribute somehow to her awful life and the way she'd survived it.

★★★★★

Irina took her time in the bathroom. He heard her shower. He heard the little sounds of bottles and jars opening and closing. He heard her take clothes from the closet by the bed, but he didn't turn round. Just before eleven she came back into the studio looking bright and fresh. Only her head-scarf, a Hermes fake, looked odd indoors. With her friends coming, though, at least it covered up the bump.

They'd been gossiping quietly for half an hour when the doorbell rang. Stepka was alone. Vanka had lost a bout at the gym – he was in bad shape. But he'd be okay by the morning. Probably.

Stepka was not the villain Ed had expected. He looked at least fifty. He was clean-shaven and respectably dressed – the manager of a supermarket rather than a KGB dropout. He greeted Irina in what sounded like Russian, looking ruefully at her head-scarf. He said *Hi* to Ed as though they were old acquaintances, and shook hands. Ed sensed behind the blunt, sinewy fingers, a strong arm and a limitless reserve of brute force. Irina certainly knew some strange people.

They sat down, Stepka on the bed, Irina on her work-chair, and Ed on a folding chair he'd found in the kitchen. Irina offered Stepka something to drink.

'No thank you,' he said. 'Nothing to drink. Just tea.'

Ed stood up. 'I'll fix the tea,' he said. Better just listen, let Irina do the talking. 'But talk in English so I know what's going on.' He went to the tiny kitchen, little more than a broom closet.

'So your head?' he heard Stepka ask. 'How?'

'Got hit,' Irina said.

'Who?'

'Security.'

'Take it off.'

118

Take the scarf off, Ed guessed. He heard the bed creak as Stepka stood up.

A quick indrawing of breath from Irina. Then Stepka: 'He didn't hit you square. Too far left. Must slip off your head. Hurt your ear.'

'My ear. Yes.'

'And your shoulder.'

'Yes.'

'Must be short guy, shorter as you. Why? Why they never reach up? Time and time I tell them: Reach up, hit square. But never they listen. Lazy bastards, I guess.'

'Lucky for me,' Irina said.

'Lucky for you, yes. Fracture head is not so fun.' The bed creaked again as Stepka sat down.

Ed decided to wait in the kitchen while the kettle boiled. He put out Irina's three mugs and three tea-bags from a red package – Twinings British Breakfast Tea.

'So,' Stepka continued. 'This security. You want him hurt? Or finish?'

'No,' Irina said. 'Not hurt, not finish.' She said a sentence more in Russian, ending with *Styopka*.

'What then?' The rough KGB voice sounded puzzled.

'You still do photographs?' Irina asked. 'Like that Jap factory one time. Engine parts. I remember you tell Andrey about it.'

'How is Andrey?'

'I don't know. We never write.'

'You make divorce. This you tell me, in August – Independence Day.'

'Andrey wants divorce. I don't have enough money.'

'You work artist? Little money, I think.'

'The scarf? Can I put it on again?' Irina asked submissively.

'Yes. Okay.'

Silence. Irina must be tying her scarf. The kettle boiled. Ed poured water onto the tea-bags.

'So, what photograph?'

'You ever hear of kids lock up – like a sort of blood-bank? Blood taken and sold?'

'Blood-bank? Sure,' Stepka said. 'You mix in it?'

'Not directly.'

Ed stirred the mugs, watching the brown tea seep into the swirling water. Stepka knew about the racket – took it for granted. If it was common knowledge, why…?

'What then?'

'If we told you the place, could you get in? Take pictures?'

'That where you got hit?' Stepka asked.

'Yes.'

'Trying to take picture?'

'No.'

'Picture is expensive.'

'How much?'

'We have to check the place out. How many guard? How many door? How many CC?'

'CC?'

'Television. Close-circuit.'

'*Roughly* how much? For the pictures?'

'You said *we*? If *we* tell you… Who is *we*?'

Another silence.

'Guy in kitchen?' Stepka asked. 'Plenty-money American? Or same like you – artist American?'

'Artist,' Irina told him.

Stepka burst suddenly into voluble Russian – or it might have been Ukrainian.

Ed took in the tea. As they drank it, Stepka lost his volubility. The word *artist* had obviously dampened his interest. When his mug was empty he stood up. He had to go. It wasn't easy for him, all the talk in English. Vanka spoke English much better. Vanka maybe can call Irina and her artist Yankee in the morning. He left without shaking hands.

Day 5

'A background on Dy? Yes, we did one. I thought I told you?'

'Told me? Indirectly I guess.'

'Since when did the great semiotician need everything spelled out?'

'Guys?' Irina broke in. 'The waiter. He want order.' Tentatively she adjusted the knot of her head-scarf behind her neck – the red peasant scarf again. She winced slightly but then smiled, a pale, strong smile.

Merr had invited them for lunch – a sprawling, shady place, a brick terrace with whitewashed walls, clinging somehow to the fringe of River City. The mid-day sun crackled on the broken surface of the Chao Phraya. Concrete steps led down from one part of the terrace into the river. Two boys in khaki shorts were splashing in the water. Further out in the main stream, clumps of green weed drifted down toward the Gulf, lilies with enormous leaves and roots that had never known earth. Rice barges, long-tail boats and raucous river-busses battered their way through the golden, glinting water.

They ordered lunch – *khao phat kai*, chicken and cashews, Chinese cabbage, spring rolls, omelette.

They talked about the floating weed, wondering where it started, wondering if fish and crabs lived among the roots, wondering how long river life would survive in the ocean.

Ed searched out the shiniest spoon on the table and held it up to reflect the sun and the water and the weed. It was a dim, distorted picture. Meaningless. He showed it to Irina. She took the spoon and turned it, trying to form an image.

'Why?' Ed asked abruptly, watching Irina's hands. 'Why did you check up on Dy?'

'Maybe this isn't a good time,' Merr replied.

Irina put down the spoon immediately and stood up: 'Back in a minute,' she said. 'I must wash my hands.' She left the terrace without glancing back.

'Nice girl,' Merr remarked appreciatively. 'Crocodile hide. Right through.'

'So Dy? Why?' Ed pursued.

'It was routine. We did a background on her whole department. Patel, Chinkiwana I think his name was, some Russian guy, Dy, couple of others.'

'Why?'

'It's confidential, Ed.'

'So why?' Ed persisted.

Merr didn't answer immediately. Then: 'There was an informer. Told us about a racket – selling blood.'

'So you knew about the blood? Already?'

'Did I deny it? And this woman told us something else. Because the racket involved children, and because the UN has agencies that deal with kids, she'd reported it to them – now listen carefully – to them *first*, before she ever came to us.'

'To Patel?'

'To his department.'

'Who exactly?'

'She didn't give us a name.'

'Why not?'

'Ed… When you're a whistle-blower, you're an insider. You make a phone call. Usually just one, because you're scared, specially in a country like this. And when you're talking to a whistle-blower, you don't say: *Who am I talking to? Please hold the line while I make a note. How is that spelled please?*'

'Okay. I get the point.'

'So, like I said, she'd already called the UN – that's what she told us. Then, apparently they did nothing about it, so she called us. One call. From a prepaid cellphone.'

'Why *you*? How'd she know about you?'

'She called the embassy. Switchboard put her through to T-CAN.'

'And after you'd spoken to her, you checked backgrounds – at the UN?'

'Exactly. It's possible someone at the UN had suppressed the information. Sat on it. For whatever reason.'

'What sort of reason?'

'Blackmail probably.'

'Blackmail? How'd that work?'

'The woman – it was a Thai woman, she didn't speak much English – she gave us the name of a firm.'

'Had she given the name to the UN?'

'We did ask her that. She said yes.'

Ed hesitated. Then: 'Was the name *Andronicus*?'

Merr made no reply. He stood up and walked to the whitewashed wall that bounded the river. Ed eyed his back with distrust – if Merr already knew about Andronicus…

Merr turned slowly back to face him. 'Who told *you* about Andronicus?' he asked flatly. 'Diana?'

'Absolutely not,' Ed countered. 'I mentioned Andronicus to *her*. She'd never heard of it. Unlike *you*.'

Merr thought for a second. 'Me?' he questioned. 'Ed, you don't think *I'm* mixed up with…' He moved back to the table and sat down. '…with Andronicus?'

'You clammed up at the morgue when I talked about blood. And you're not coming clean now. Not completely.'

Merr drummed his fingers on the table doubtfully. 'Listen,' he said at last. 'We did a background on Dy to see if she was spending more than her income. The same check we ran on her whole department.'

'And was she?'

'No. They were all clean. Except maybe the Russian guy. What's his name again?'

'Vadim.'

'Yeah, him. But listen. In the morgue, when you suddenly brought up the blood thing, it did occur to me – if Dy was in some way involved, she might have asked you to sound me out. To see if I'd got anything on her. I mean, she knows roughly what we do at T-CAN.'

'So you thought not only Dy was involved, but me as well?'

'It seemed possible,' Merr replied with a shrug. 'But if you say Dy never heard of Andronicus – then that's the end of it.'

It took Ed a moment to think it through. From Merr's perspective, it added up, given what the woman, the informer, had said about calling the UN. 'And what about Andronicus?' Ed asked. 'Did you run a background on them?'

Irina appeared again on the terrace. A Thai dressed in a white suit stood beside her, an old man – the manager probably, or maybe the owner. Irina glanced a question at Merr – was it okay for her to join them?

Merr nodded. 'Does *she* know about Andronicus?' he asked quickly. Ed watched Irina thank the old man and saw him reply with a *wai*, the graceful, two-handed gesture Ed had seen in the warehouse.

Irina crossed the terrace and sat down. With the eyes of three men on her, her walk shed some of its farmyard angularity.

'How you feeling?' Merr asked with an edge of concern in his voice. Ed was surprised. Usually Merr took other people's aches and pains with heroic apathy. Maybe he really did think crocodile-hide Irina was a nice girl. Ed wasn't sure he liked the idea. Merr and Irina? None of his business, but…

'Feeling?' Irina said. 'Nearly back to normal – thanks to Ed.' There it was again, just for a second – the inviting warmth in Irina's eyes that Ed found so appealing. Nothing brazen, no hint of demand masquerading as invitation. And no trace of the reptilian hide Merr had observed. Rather the opposite. *If we ever became lovers, there's nothing I'd hide from you, and nothing I wouldn't do for you* – that was the message. If. In the unlikely event that…

'This is a big place,' Irina said. 'Private dining-rooms. Apartments. Rent by the hour – so he told me.' She raised her chin slightly in the direction of the old man.

'That's with River City being so near,' Merr explained. He grimaced. 'Not what you're thinking, Ed.'

'River City?' Ed asked.

'The antique market – so-called. In fact they're not allowed to sell antiques, certainly not to foreigners. So the dealers bring their punters here to do business. Upstairs. Rent by the hour.'

'That part of T-CAN too?' Ed asked.

'Yes, but a different department,' Merr laughed. 'Everything's a different department.'

Irina looked quizzically at Merr. 'You know Bangkok very good,' she said.

'I could return the compliment,' Merr replied.

Ed watched them, startled. A cat-and-bird game had just started, though who was the cat and who was the bird he wasn't sure.

'T-CAN have a file on me?' Irina asked casually. 'Or only on my husband?'

'Both,' Merr told her. 'Yours is pretty short.'

'That's good to know,' Irina said, flat, neutral. Ed heard the words – there was a file on Irina, but how long it really was, or how long Irina believed it to be, he had no idea.

'Nothing on Andrey for two years,' Merr volunteered.

'But everything about me.'

'Not really.'

'What is missing, for example?'

'For example, I'd like to know who gave you that bump on the head.'

'A guard.'

'Where?'

'Chatuchak.'

'The old tobacco monopoly?'

'Yes.'

'Andronicus?'

'Yes.'

Merr nodded. He understood – Ed and Irina had been on the prowl together. 'Dangerous game,' he said.

Irina shrugged. Merr fell silent, watching.

'First and last time,' Ed assured him. 'But something's definitely going on. That's why we thought – maybe we should talk to you.'

'What makes you think I'd listen?'

'You're listening already,' Ed replied.

'But not unconditionally.'

'So tell us – what are the conditions?'

'That you've got something resembling proof.'

'Merr, if you put two and two together, it's obvious.'

'You asked me just now if we'd ever done a background on Andronicus,' Merr replied. 'They're clean. Far as we know.'

'I don't agree,' Irina said. 'They're not clean. Absolutely not.'

'You know that for a fact?'

'More or less,' Irina replied flatly.

'More or less,' Merr repeated.

'You say you want proof. I think there is proof. But...' Irina hesitated.

'But?'

'If there are photographs…?' she pressed.

'Photographs?' Merr asked. His tone hardly changed, but suddenly the game had new interest for him. 'I tell you – we get tip-offs, we get rumours, we get corpses, but we never find out who's behind this stuff. You know – evidence the Thais can't walk away from. Whatever I show them, they always say the same: *Yes, but, but, but, but…* I get every kind of proof that a crime's been committed – Ed saw some of it with me – but hard evidence on who did it? Evidence the Thais would act on? I've never had it in my hand. Not once in five long years.'

'So,' Irina said. 'What kind of pictures you want?'

'What kind have you got?'

'First theory,' Irina said. 'What you are looking for?'

'Well, nothing blatant. Obvious stuff is always fake.'

'What then?' Irina pursued. 'In theory.'

Merr stood up and went to the railing again. He stood with his back toward them, brooding. A dangerous man, Ed saw. A lonely man. A man who databased the names of people he invited to lunch. Ed glanced at Irina. She shrugged. An eloquent gesture. Of course T-CAN has a file on me, the gesture said. My husband was in Ukrainian security. Your friend Merr doesn't trust me an inch. He'd be a fool if he did. Then she smiled. Not a social smile like Dy's, but a smile rich with meaning: *But* you *can trust me. They nearly cracked my skull open, Ed. You won't let them get away with it, will you?* Or maybe it wasn't that at all. Maybe it was more like: *This Andronicus business is important to me, Ed. Your friend is really interested. I can go ahead with just him, but I'd be much happier if you were on board too.*

Merr turned back slowly to face them. 'Either you're setting me up, or you're not,' he said, 'and I guess you're not. But it's flat against regulations, ordering stuff from the KGB without a say-so from Washington.' He shook his head. 'Okay, listen.' He went back to the table and sat down. 'The best pictures simply show things that don't belong. You know – big square crates on the deck of a rice boat.'

'Merr,' Ed said. 'Slight course correction if I may. This crap about the KGB. Or whatever they call it now…'

'SVR,' Merr cut in. '*Sluzhba Vneshney Razvedki*. No. You're strictly ACP.' ACP was a Merr-joke, a neat distraction.

'ACP?' Ed repeated, playing dummy.

'Artists Chasing… Something to do with Seymour Doll.'

'Pussy,' Irina said coldly. 'Ed told me already. Please, we talk about photographs.'

Merr nodded. 'Well,' he said. 'We'd be looking for things that don't belong. If they process blood, Andronicus will have separators, testing equipment – that sort of thing. That would be legit.'

'Yes,' Ed agreed. 'Chaudhary showed me that.'

'But if they're taking blood directly, they'd need donor-level stuff that isn't legit – not for processing.'

'Such as?' Ed asked.

'There's a firm called LabTop. In India. They specialise.' A small black shoulder-bag hung on the corner of Merr's chair. He put the bag on the table, unlatched it, and took out a tablet. 'We can google it,' he said.

After the tablet had booted, Ed watched Merr's chubby fingers call up the keyboard and then key in *LabTop*. If Merr had a name like LabTop at his fingertips, he knew a hell of a lot more about blood than he'd given away so far.

LabTop, according to its website, made everything from collection monitors to needle destroyers. 'Donor stuff would be hard to explain in a plant where there aren't any donors,' Merr said. 'Especially in quantity.' His voice took on a naive edge: 'You got anything like that? Among your pictures?'

'We'll see,' Irina said. 'Anything else?'

'You got any records? Or pictures of records?'

'What records?'

'Dates, donor names, blood groups – though records like that might be part of the business. Better, something that goes beyond donation – records of daily iron supplement. Something like that.'

'How would we know?' Irina asked. 'Records are all in Thai.'

Merr nodded. 'Just give me what you've got,' he said. 'I'll sort out the language.'

'You told me blood was another department,' Ed objected.

'That was Tuesday. This is Friday. Listen – I'm assuming these pictures exist. I'm also assuming that the source is Irina's buddies from the... From the good old days.' He glanced at her – she gave no sign that she'd heard his words, let alone understood them. Ed saw appreciation flash for a second in Merr's eyes, lively and unmistakable.

'That's one possibility,' Merr continued. 'The other is that the pictures don't yet exist, but that you're going to commission them. Probably from the same source. If that *is* the idea, then please, both of you, don't even think about it. It's too fucking dangerous.'

Silent-footed, the waiter stood suddenly beside their table carrying a wide aluminium tray. It was time to eat.

*****

It was an unpleasantly informative afternoon. Merr, it turned out, had studied the files on blood-farming, and – as a down-payment on the pictures – he told them what he knew.

Blood-farms were documented in Indonesia, but, despite rumours, not in Thailand. Children were bought or kidnapped. Kids, especially girls, were easier to guard, easier to control, and girls were an age-old way to supplement your workers' wages. At first the farmer took blood every six weeks, then more and more often. The more blood you take from a body, the more blood it makes, provided there's enough iron. After a while, the body can be tricked into making far more blood than it needs – a kind of general *hyperaemia*. In nature, there was no such thing, but the condition had been induced by Nazi doctors experimenting in the 1940s. It was like stimulating cows to produce unnatural quantities of milk. And there was a similar down-side – an unmilked super-cow goes through agonies before it dies. With blood it was the same. As soon as overproduction set in, blood had to be taken regularly. If not, blood vessels would rupture, especially in the nose and ears and, with girls, in the uterus. In a few cases *hematidrosis* might occur – sweating blood. Children sweating blood.

★★★★★

Merr's taxi dropped them off at Irina's apartment. Ed stood with her for a moment on the broken concrete sidewalk, unsure of their next step. Two dogs, stifled by the heat, lay panting outside the hairdresser's shop that occupied part of the ground floor. Irina's cellphone jangled *Bella figlia...* Almost certainly Stepka – he'd called three times already that morning, talking prices, discussing terms. She hit the green button expectantly and said 'Hello.'

But it wasn't Stepka, it was Vadim from the UN. Where the hell was Diana? Irina passed the phone to Ed.

'Where's Diana?' Vadim asked.

'In Kuala Lumpur,' Ed replied.

'Has she called you?'

In fact Dy hadn't called as she'd promised, but she often changed her mind about things like that. 'No,' Ed replied.

'Well, she didn't turn up for her meeting this morning.'

'What time was that?'

'Ten-thirty. Nine-thirty our time.'

'Was she on the plane?' Ed asked, remembering Merr's call to Diana the evening before. 'The plane last night?'

'Listen, Ed. If you know something... Where is she?'

'I don't have the faintest idea. Check the airline. See if she was on the flight. Check her hotel. And get back to me.'

'Patel's mad as fuck.'

'Time to get mad when he knows what's happened. Wouldn't you say?'

'You think she have accident?'

'Listen Vadim. Call the airline. And the hotel. Now.'

'Sure,' Vadim said.

Ed hit disconnect. Irina had been listening intently. 'We better call Malaysian,' she said. 'Perhaps Dy miss her flight.'

In Irina's studio, she googled Malaysian Airlines and found the telephone number. Twenty minutes later, they knew for certain – Diana hadn't been on her flight, nor on any of the morning flights to KL.

They called Vadim at the UN to tell him, but the line was permanently busy. They called Merr. Diana was missing, they told him – how could they find out if she'd had an accident?

For a long time Merr said nothing. Then: 'Is she involved with this Andronicus business? Tell me straight.'

'No,' Ed replied. 'Absolutely not. I mentioned it to her once or twice, and she was dead against it. Totally.'

'But she knows Irina was hit.'

'I told her it was a car accident.'

Merr said he'd ask around and call them back. In a few minutes he was on the line again – nothing. No *falang* in any of the emergency wards, no unidentified bodies in Doctor Hirsch's cellar. If she'd started out for KL in the hotel limo, Ed should check with the Princess – maybe she'd never made it to the airport.

★★★★★

Ed took a taxi to the Princess. Irina went with him. She should be resting, he told her – Dy wasn't her concern. But Irina insisted, and Ed was grateful.

The driver who'd taken Diana to the airport was certain – he'd dropped her at Suvarnabhumi, at the international terminal, not long before six. He showed them his logbook. It was a scrappy book, untidily kept in Thai, but the details of Diana's trip were logged beyond question.

As they were leaving the Princess, Stepka called. He was at the studio. It would soon be dark. He'd had some bad news. Where the hell was Irina? She was on the way, she told him. She'd be there soon – depending on the traffic.

They found a taxi, but after a hundred yards, the traffic ground to a halt – not even an inch forward in five minutes. Ed called Merr again. Should they register Dy as missing? With the consulate? Brits? Americans? With the police?

'She's not a Brit anymore?'

'No. American as Lizzie Borden.'

A long silence while Merr pondered. 'Where do you think Dy is?' he asked. 'Best guess?'

'Well, she might have…'

'Might have what?'

'Well, once or twice – in the past – she…' It wasn't easy to explain Dy's habits.

'…she went on a binge?' Merr prompted. 'You told me about it before. Years ago. You think that's what's happened?'

'No. But it's possible.'

'What's the UN doing?'

'First the line was busy,' Ed told him. 'Now it rings, but no one picks up. I can't get through…'

'Nobody ever got through to the UN, Ed. They're impenetrable.'

'So? Consulate or police?'

'I'll make some calls,' Merr said. 'Find out if the UN's registered her as AWOL.'

'Right.'

'And I've got friends in Bangkok Vice. If I ask nicely, they'll nose around the places Dy hangs out. There aren't that many in her file…' He paused, letting the word *file* sink in. 'There's a couple of lesbian knocking-shops. Not on her list. Think she might try that?'

'No,' Ed said firmly. 'I don't think so.' His throat felt suddenly parched and tight. 'No,' he repeated.

'Okay. If she's not turned up by tomorrow and the UN's done nothing, you can register officially. With our consulate. It'll take a while, specially on a Saturday. Then we have to start looking for her. Okay?'

'Okay.' *We have to start looking for her.* For Merr it was that simple – Diana was missing so Diana had to be looked for. Another Felicity Andrews, more or less. Ed pictured Felicity in her wrapping of silver foil. Was Dy in that same *undiscover'd country*? Already? No. The idea was unbearable. Merr was right – they had to start looking. Tomorrow. Tomorrow at the latest.

The six o'clock traffic jam was at its height. They were stuck, with no apparent hope of reprieve. Ed gave the phone back to Irina. 'This deal with Stepka?' he asked. 'What do we say to him?'

'You want to work with Stepka?'

'I don't know. I can't get my mind round Diana. People don't just disappear.'

'Maybe Dy disappear is connected with Andronicus?' Irina suggested. 'This is Merr's first idea. When you tell him.'

'There can't be a connection. Andronicus doesn't know about her.'

'Chaudhary saw you and Dy at the hotel.'

'But Chaudhary had no idea she's my wife.'

'He saw you together.'

'I told him I'd picked her up in a bar.'

'Maybe he asked. At reception.'

'Why should he? And even if he did, I'm Scarman, she's Tarn.'

'But hotel knows you are married.'

'Yes, they know we're married.'

Irina sighed – she had no more arguments, but she didn't concede the point. 'So what about Stepka?' she asked. 'He says there is bad news.'

'Maybe he's trying to put the price up.'

'If you prefer, we can stop. Tell Stepka – forget the whole deal.'

'What do you think?' Ed asked uncertainly.

'Ed, it's your money. I cannot decide.'

'So, what has he suggested so far? Tonight a reconnaissance. Then the full-scale thing tomorrow or whenever.'

'Yes.'

'500 bucks for the reconnaissance. And 3,000 for the pictures.' Ed shook his head. It wasn't so much the money. In fact $4,000 was already at the Princess, in the big safe, in an envelope with his name on it. His credit card was good for 10. Visa had asked him to call, of course – 4,000 was a big sum in a foreign city – but in the end they'd let it through. He didn't want to chuck the cash away, not that 4,000 was the end of the world. The problem was everything else piling up – Dy gone, Terry back in Washington crying for him, Irina injured – too many problems and none of them under control.

'Not 3,000,' Irina said on the defensive. 'He want three-five for pictures and 500 for reconnaissance. He is not doing it for less. I told you this already.'

Yes, she'd told him already – Stepka was insisting on three-five for the pictures. And she'd told Stepka she didn't want her ten percent, so he could drop from three-five to three-one-fifty. And Stepka had refused. Refused! He was robbing her of $350 that belonged to her – absolutely to her. She'd been nervous when she'd explained it all to Ed – she hoped he didn't think… Ed had laughed and said it was the same with his pictures – he painted, somebody paid, and Myron in between took his percentage. Except in Myron's case it was twenty-five. 'But I'm not Myron,' she'd insisted. And for the first time he'd kissed her – to calm her down and comfort her. But instead it had baffled her, his incomprehensible kiss.

'So what will we say?' she repeated. 'To Stepka?'

'Whatever happens, you'd like to see those bastards behind bars? Right?'

'If it is my money, I say okay. Let Stepka get the pictures. Then Merr can use them. But…'

'Forget the *but*,' he decided. 'Let's do it.'

'Yes,' Irina said. The single word, as so often with Irina, had many shades of meaning. Mostly what he heard was: *I was afraid you'd changed your mind, but you haven't. And I think it's marvellous.* He didn't much like pedestals. The last person who'd stood him on one had been a girl called Velusha. *Semiotics 100.* Smart kid, nice-looking. She'd do anything for an A on his course, she'd told him. And he'd told her that an A was just a component in a system of signs – the A meant nothing in itself. She hadn't understood – just raised his pedestal six inches and repeated her proposal. In the end, he'd given her an A, though he'd never found out what she'd meant by the word *anything* – just a quick BJ probably. That had been the going price of an A, or so he'd heard. Not Velusha's fault.

And now his pedestal was 4000 bucks high. 4000 bucks in hundreds, and still in the hotel safe. 'Let's talk to Stepka one more time,' Ed said. 'Maybe we can beat him down a bit.'

★★★★★

Stepka was waiting gloomily in a wicker chair in the street outside the hairdresser's shop. Vanka wasn't with him. After his beating at the gym, Vanka would be out of action for a while. That was the bad news.

They walked up the four flights of stairs to Irina's studio saying nothing. Stepka was angry – the surly *scuff-scuff* of his feet on the concrete steps was not encouraging.

'I not can work without helper. Without Vanka,' he complained as Irina closed the studio door behind them.

They sat down. 'No Vanka, no job,' Stepka repeated obstinately.

'How long is he out?' Irina asked.

'Month. Six weeks.'

Ed found himself staring at Stepka's hands, a blatant mismatch with his store-manager's suit. His fingers were stubby and seemed to be all the same length. His nails were ribbed and thick, like tortoise-shell. Ugly scars criss-crossed his skin, as though he'd spent his life punching holes in steel lockers.

Now that Stepka was backsliding, Ed began to push forward. 'But it's only reconnaissance tonight,' he argued. 'Just counting doors and windows. You can do that on your own, can't you?'

'No,' Stepka insisted. 'First you must tell exactly what you want. Then me and Vanka must reconnaissance outside. Also perhaps inside. Later we get pictures. Only later.'

'But I don't understand – if you get inside tonight, why not take the pictures right away?'

'Who understand photograph business? Me or you?'

'You, but…'

'So I talk, you listen.'

'I am listening. And you say you can't do it.'

136

'Without helper, not possible. And Vanka is broken nose. Very bad injure.'

There was a silence. Stepka folded his arms – a nice little job was slipping away.

Irina stood up and went to the bathroom, her outdoor sandals clattering on the tiles. The men sat hopelessly, saying nothing.

When Irina came back, she'd had an idea. 'Listen Stepka,' she said. 'What about Ed? He knows the place. What if he was your helper?'

'What are you talking about, Irina?' Ed sat up abruptly. 'Isn't it enough, what they did to you the other night? More than enough?'

'But Ed, you know what to look for. If you are there, Stepka doesn't need the reconnaissance. One trip is enough.'

'No,' Ed said. 'I'll pay. That's as far as I go.'

Sensing a reprieve, Stepka perked up. 'To be truth,' he explained, 'job not is difficult if…' He gestured toward Ed. 'Stand up,' he ordered.

Reluctantly Ed stood up, submitting himself to the will of the stronger animal. Stepka stood too and took Ed's arm between his iron thumb and forefinger, feeling Ed's bicep. Then with his clenched fist he pressed Ed lightly in the stomach. 'Artist American not bad fitness,' he said, sitting down again.

'Glad you approve,' Ed retorted. 'But so what?' He sat down again.

'Like I said, job is not difficult. Two men – me professional, you fitness American – can do it easy.'

'The warehouse isn't Fort Knox, Ed,' Irina added flatly. 'When I got hit, I didn't know what hit me. We didn't know about the guards. But now we know. We're ready.'

'You got hit because Andronicus is a bunch of evil bastards.'

Irina shrugged agreement.

'So give me one good reason why I should risk my neck,' Ed pressed. Somehow she'd cornered him, put him on the defensive.

'No, Ed,' she said quietly. 'I don't give you good reason or bad reason. I'm not try persuade you.'

'But you want me to go. Or so it seems.'

'I am not important. You must decide. If you not want to go, then don't go.'

'It's not that I don't want to go,' he said, dangerously manoeuvred into shifting his ground. 'But right now, with Dy missing...' Why drag Dy in? Why hide behind Dy? 'To me, as it stands,' he said, 'finding Dy is more important than taking a bunch of photographs.' A false dilemma – if he couldn't do better than that...

'Who is Die?' Stepka asked. 'Some person is dead?'

'My wife,' Ed told him. 'She's on a UN mission. To Kuala Lumpur. But she never got on the plane.'

'She is in Bangkok?'

'Probably.'

'Find wife is easy work. More difficult work is *lose* wife.'

Finding wife? Losing wife? Stepka seemed to be on home ground again. 'You mean you can find her?' Ed asked.

'I find everyone in Bangkok. Everyone.'

Ed glanced at Irina. She nodded.

'You have picture?' Stepka asked. 'Of wife?'

'Yes. At the hotel.'

'So listen,' Stepka said. 'Listen careful. We make new package – warehouse pictures *and* wife – everything 3,000.' The false dilemma had been resolved. Could it be that Stepka, the annihilator, was outsmarting Doctor Ed?

'But with condition,' Stepka added, his case almost won.

'Condition?'

'Condition is you come with. We make just one trip, no problem.'

Maybe it was a good deal. Maybe a well-connected KGB man was worth the UN, all the consulates in Bangkok, and T-CAN rolled into one. 'What about it, Irina?' Ed asked quietly. 'You think he'll find Dy?'

'I am sure he'll try,' she said. 'But – no one can promise.'

It was a fair answer.

'I find. If wife in Bangkok, I find,' Stepka protested. He glanced at Irina then back at Ed. 'You are sure?' he asked.

'Sure about what?'

'Sure you *want* to find wife? Is not so normal.'

Ed still hesitated. Merr had warned him off Andronicus altogether. Maybe he should call Merr again. It'd mean confessing that the promised pictures didn't exist, but Merr had guessed that already. He called Merr's number three times. It was busy. Somehow that decided him. 'Who's driving?' he asked.

'Guy from embassy,' Stepka told him. 'Security, same like me.'

'That's the Ukrainian embassy?' Ed queried.

'Good driver,' Stepka countered. 'Not important, Ukraine Embassy, France Embassy, China Embassy.'

'3,000?'

Stepka nodded.

'1,000 up front,' Ed offered. 'Another 1000 when I get the photographs, and the rest when you find my wife.'

'Very tough, mister.'

'Take it or leave it.'

Stepka glanced at Irina. She nodded – *take it or leave it.*

'Okay, take,' Stepka said, and he shook hands with Ed.

'And Irina Sergeyevna?' Ed asked. 'Is she coming?'

'She wait in car. No problem.'

Day 6

Saturday 31st October 2009

Face and hands dark brown, hair black, clothes black with a greeny swirl pattern – not camouflage but similar. Black, silent sneakers. Stepka's baggy jacket hid rope, a jemmy, a CCTV-alert – everything they needed. All Ed had was the camera. It was in a dull black pouch fastened to his belt, an HDR-XR, not new but functional. Stepka had decided on video for the pictures because the camera had infra-red. In a guarded warehouse with big windows, flashlights inside would be dangerous. With the camera and with Stepka's night-glasses, they could find their way in the dark, no problem.

Exactly as before, the bats flitted, and the expressway towered over the warehouses. The line of abandoned wagons hadn't moved. Nothing had changed. Stepka moved cautiously, silent as a weasel. They kept the wagons to their left, between them and the concrete road. Often Stepka paused, learning landmarks for the way back. They reached the chemical wagon, Ed's hiding place two nights before. They crouched, invisible beside it. The big windows were dark now, and the compound was quiet. Ed whispered again to Stepka what he knew about the inside of the building. Stepka looked at his watch – it was two-thirty, and Chatuchak was sleeping. They waited, silent, alert. Two men carrying nightsticks and flashlights sauntered toward

140

them, silhouetted against the orange glow of the expressway. Guards. They tested doors and played their yellow flashlights over windows. Twice the feeble beams of light swung along the line of wagons, hesitating, prying.

'Why guard have this useless light?' Stepka muttered angrily. 'Very old-fashion. Stupid.'

The guards passed the transporter, picking out the big windows of the warehouse with their flashlights. Then they stopped at a door with *E7* painted above it in white. One of the guards opened the door with a key. He went into the building for a few seconds, then emerged again and locked the door behind him.

'He sign log,' Stepka whispered. 'Wait.'

The men set off on their next circuit.

'How do we get in?' Ed asked when the guards had disappeared round the corner of the building. 'Pick the lock?'

'We wait. See how much minutes their round. Each round they must sign, so they must regular.'

'And where do we get in?' Ed repeated.

'You not see. They not see. Big window. Not tight closed.' He fished his night-binoculars out of their pocket, switched them on, and passed them to Ed. 'Middle window.'

Ed took the binoculars and focussed them on the window. A greenish image, not much magnification, but Stepka was right – the window was a crack open. 'Good,' he said, 'and we get up there like you showed me at Irina's.'

'Yes. We hook rope over... *podokonnik* – I forget name.'

'The windowsill. With your telescope thing.'

'Yes.'

'Clever idea.'

'But,' Stepka ignored the compliment, 'I have question.'

'What?'

'You saw guards? On Wed-*nes*-day?'

'Yes.'

'They make same? With flashlights? Test doors?'

'No. Not that I remember.'

'Why is this? Thai guard is lousy guard – not careful. But tonight is careful.'

'You think they know? That we're coming?'

'Not possible. Who tell them? You? Me? Irina Sergeyevna? What other person know?'

'No,' Ed replied flatly. 'No one else knows.' Though Merr knew of course – or at least he'd probably guessed. But whether he'd guessed or not, Merr could be trusted. Ed liked Irina – Merr was on their side. Unless they'd both read the entrails wrong.

It took the guards twenty minutes to circle the building. As Stepka had foreseen, they checked in at E7 and then disappeared again round the corner. As soon as they were gone, Stepka sprang into action. Making no more noise than a night-moth, he flitted across the concrete road. By the time Ed caught up, Stepka had extended his telescope stick with a simple grappling hook and a thin rope attached to one end. A second later the hook was over the windowsill, and Stepka had collapsed the stick back into his jacket. The rope was too thin to climb with bare hands. Back in Irina's apartment, Stepka had showed Ed how to use climbing gloves that gripped the rope in metal clamps. They'd climb hand-over-hand – Stepka first.

Ed watched Stepka's burly figure float evenly upward. With one arm hooked over the windowsill, Stepka pushed at the big window. Would it open? Usually high-up windows opened from the ground through a system of levers – perhaps the window would block. With a violent effort, Stepka thrust the window half-open. Then, with an awkward heave and a fling of his leg, he was astride the windowsill, taking off the gloves. He dropped the gloves for Ed to pick up. Then he took out the binoculars, checking the way ahead.

Stepka had told him not to brace his feet against the wall – sneakers always left marks. The climb was a straight pull, hand-over-hand up the rope. If he needed a rest, the gloves would take the strain. It was twenty feet to the windowsill. Ed made it without stopping, and Stepka helped him on to the sill.

There it was again, the smell of gesso and acrylic, though much stronger now. Ed looked down, straining to make out a movie poster covering the floor, but it was too dark.

Stepka adjusted the hook, gathered up the rope, and let it fall inside the warehouse. He took the left glove from Ed. 'Go down one-hand,' he said. 'First you hold tight with glove. Then you make open your hand. But only little. Very little. Slide down. You go first.'

Ed clambered awkwardly off the windowsill. Twenty feet down. He gripped the rope as Stepka had told him. When he and Dy had trained for Denali, they'd learned how to repel, but this was far more dangerous. If he fell... If he fell, Stepka would be out of the building and back in the car faster than a hungry cockroach. Cautiously Ed released his grip. The rope slipped through his grasp. Too fast. He tightened his fingers in the glove. The rope jerked but held him. He released again, just a fraction, and lowered himself clumsily to the floor. He looked up. Stepka's black silhouette slipped off the windowsill, closed the window to its original crack, and coasted down the rope.

With quick, neat movements, Stepka recovered the hook from the windowsill with his telescope-stick. Then, mountaineer style, he took his time re-coiling the rope and securing it inside his jacket. He put the climbing gloves back in their special pocket. The man was competent and systematic. That should have made Ed feel safe, but it didn't – now they were in the building, Stepka was his only way out, and competent, systematic Stepka would leave him in the lurch without notice and without hesitation. Was there still time to go back? *I am stepped in so far that returning were as tedious as go o'er.* Stepped in? Yes, he'd stepped in it up to his neck.

'You okay?' Stepka asked in a gravelly whisper. 'You did good on rope.'

'Can I take pictures?' Ed whispered back. 'In here?'

'Check first,' Stepka replied. He took the CCTV-alert out of its tight pocket and turned it on. 'I check infra-red already.' He scanned the dark, hidden space with the detector. 'Nothing,' he said. 'No TV. If is TV, LED go red.'

'Good,' Ed said. 'Microphone?'

'If no TV, probable no microphone. Microphone too old-fashion. Even in Thailand.'

The dim orange light from the big windows at either end of the hall showed the size of the place but not much more. 'Did you see a poster?' Ed said. Irina had explained the poster theory to Stepka the night before.

'*Plakat*? Look yourself,' Stepka grunted. 'Use camera.'

Ed had practised with the camera in Irina's apartment. It was pre-set to *Night Shot*. He unzipped the pouch. All he had to do was open the viewfinder.

The picture came up immediately, dim and greenish. The invisible infra-red beam hardly reached the far wall of the warehouse, but in the viewfinder, as Irina had predicted, loomed a movie poster perhaps forty feet by twenty. Ed went to the edge of the canvas. Stepka followed close behind. The big lettering, still unfinished, was in Thai. He found the title in English, small but clear – *The New Daughter. Kevin Costner.* He'd never heard of it. Maybe it wasn't released yet. He took a few seconds of film. Then he filmed the painting gear – buckets, paint canisters, mops, brushes. It was new to him, the cat-like thrill of seeing in the dark. Faulkner. In an essay somewhere – a woman was seeing in the dark. Who? Anna, he remembered. The beautiful Anna Karenina – as she lay in bed listening for the first time to her beloved Vronsky snoring. Listening and seeing in the dark. Without thinking, Ed pointed the beam upward, scanning the window.

Stepka's quick hand jerked the camera down. 'Not on window,' he growled. 'Is glass. Is...' he hesitated. '*Refraktsia.*'

'You mean it might show red outside?' Ed interpreted.

'If you know, why act stupid?'

Because I was thinking about Anna Karenina, Ed confessed to himself. If he couldn't stay better focussed than that...

'And turn off camera. Not so good battery.'

Ed folded back the viewfinder and slipped the camera into its pouch. The world went black. Even the orange shapes of the windows were blurred. He screwed up his eyes, trying to see clearly again, but the unhealthy blur remained.

While Ed had been filming the poster, Stepka had mapped out the hall. He pushed his binoculars into Ed's hand. 'Use this,' Stepka said. 'This battery is twenty hour. Check out the doors. This side.' He put his hand on Ed's shoulder and turned him to face one of the walls.

The image was tele, not wide, but the picture was sharp. Quickly Ed picked up a double-door. The handles were chained together and padlocked.

'You see the chain,' Stepka said. 'And the lock – *patt*lock you say.'

'Yes.'

'And when you with Mr India, you also see two door. Also steel. Also with *patt*lock. You tell me.'

'Yes.'

'And this smell?'

'Yes. I must have seen exactly these doors – from the other side.'

'Yes,' Stepka agreed. 'Lock this side. Lock other side. Why?'

'It means the doors aren't used. They can't be opened.'

'Correct. You are not experience. But you are not stupid.'

Ed scanned the other walls. 'There's a roll-up door,' he said. 'A big one.'

'Here was tobacco store. That is where trucks bring in tobacco.'

'You know? Or you think?' Ed challenged him.

'Think. Know. For me is same.'

'And where do you think the children are?' Ed asked still studying the walls.

'You tell me.'

'How should I know?' Ed objected.

'When you here, Wed-*nes*-day night, children leave hall? You see from outside?'

'Yes.'

'Which door you think?'

It was a smart question. Without hesitation Ed turned to face the big window. There was a steel door in the wall to the right.

'We check the door,' Stepka said. 'Me with glass. You with camera. Turn it on.'

The door was steel with heavy hinges and old-fashioned barrel bolts top and bottom.

'Bolts. This side,' Stepka said. 'See? Closed.'

'Yes.'

'Turn off camera.'

Ed folded the viewfinder closed. The screen cut out. Darkness again – the blinding, menacing darkness.

'So,' Stepka resumed. 'What it means? This bolts?'

'It means the door's bolted from this side. Probably the children go out this way when they've finished painting. Then it's bolted behind them.'

'Who bolt this door?'

'Someone who stays on this side.'

'Where is he now?'

'He must have left the hall by a different door.' Ed heard a quaver in his voice. He was scared. Stepka must have heard it too. They should get out now! Now!

'You afraid?' Stepka asked. 'Of dark? Many people afraid of dark. Me not.'

'No,' Ed told him. 'Not of the dark.'

'Door now,' Stepka said, heading toward the blackly invisible doorway. 'Come.'

They reached the door. Stepka fumbled for a second in his jacket. Ed heard fingers cracking – he guessed Stepka was pulling on gloves. Then a slow, rusty grind and a clunk – Stepka sliding back the top bolt. Then the bolt below.

'Good,' Stepka said quietly, trying the door-handle. 'No lock – only bolt.'

Somewhere in the distance a door slammed shut. Stepka glanced at the luminous dial of his watch and then showed it to Ed. Twenty minutes had gone. The guards were checking in again.

Stepka eased down the door-handle and cracked open the door. He took the CCTV-alert from its pocket, switched it on, and held it through the open crack. Nothing. But there were sounds now and the yellow gleam of a nightlight ahead. Stepka pushed the door open.

'Quick,' he said. Ed followed him through the door, and Stepka closed it behind them, quietly letting the latch engage. By the yellow nightlight, Ed saw that they were in a windowless corridor. To the left was the outer wall of the building, to the right a plywood partition with three doors. The wood was new and unpainted. The doors were plywood too. The sounds were more distinct now – a faucet running, an electric motor, or perhaps several, and a quiet moaning that seemed to come from one of the rooms in the corridor.

Three plywood doors. The first was only a few steps down the corridor. It was half-open. Stepka pulled a flat

LED flashlight from his jacket. He panned it round the room, a weak bluish light. Steel bookshelves with files lined the walls. Perhaps 500 files with the backs labelled in Thai. Half of the shelves were empty.

'Can you read Thai?' Ed whispered.

'Not necessary. Only old dates.' Stepka held the blue beam steady for a second and then panned it to another set of shelves. Stepka was right – the file-backs were from the eighties and nineties. Ed glimpsed 1998. Nothing later.

'Where is desk?' Stepka asked. 'No one work in this room.' He glanced round the walls without pointing his torch at them. 'And no windows.'

'Can we check a couple of files?' Ed suggested. 'If we're looking for records, we might find something.' Stepka grunted approval. Ed pulled a file at random. The back was dated 1997. It contained letters, invoices, bank deposit slips. Everything was dated 1997. Some of the papers were in English. Ed tried to spot the word *Andronicus*, but the company names were all acronyms. He pulled another file – old catalogues for building supplies. They went back into the corridor and tried the second plywood door. It wasn't locked. Stepka pushed it open. A store-room, Ed saw by the glow of the nightlight. Old paint cans, coils of electric cable, buckets of worn-out tools, and discarded canvas posters, some bundled up with rope, some not.

The final room was locked – a SmartScan lock, Stepka told him. American. The lock recognised fingerprints. Fifty-two fingerprints. Impossible to get around. All you could do was break the door open with a *lom*. The moaning sound they'd heard before seemed to come from inside the room. The moan grew suddenly louder, then ended with a shudder.

'Someone in there?' Ed asked quietly.

'Possible. Also possible is old *refrizherator*. With compressor.'

'That's not what it sounded like to me.'

'You want I break down door? Huh? But we know this room very secure. Essepp…'

'Except what?'

Stepka pressed his fist against the plywood wall. It buckled slightly. 'Five only.'

'Five what?' Ed prompted. 'Five ply?'

'*Pyat sloy*. Half centimetre. Good lock, stupid wall. I make hole in ten second. But not now.'

'Okay,' Ed agreed. 'Let's move.'

Ahead of them now was the door that led out of the corridor. Again it was bolted, though with a single bolt, waist-high. As before Stepka slid back the bolt, cracked the door open, and directed the CC-detector into the space beyond. Nothing.

Behind the door was a big room, lit again by dim yellow nightlights. Four of them. There were no windows. Two long tables took up most of the room – bare wood. Down the centre of each table, twenty glasses – maybe more – were lined up, aluminium water jugs, bottles of sauce, toothpicks. Benches were pushed against the table legs. It was a canteen for forty, maybe fifty people. The place smelt, though not strongly, of burnt cooking oil and bitter spices. Along one wall of the canteen were gas burners on dirty tables. Blackened woks, ladles and slices hung on the wall. The far end of the room was partitioned off with plywood and glass. Mostly glass. The space behind was unlit, but it seemed to be tiled. Ed hurried past the tables to the partition and peered through the glass. Stepka stayed by the door. There it was – what Merr had told them to look for – equipment for taking blood but in the wrong place, in a canteen. Ed pressed his nose to the glass, remembering the website images he'd studied that evening, trying to identify what he could see. It was going to be easier than he thought. He took out the camera. Would the infra-red work through the glass? He began to film. A quick pan first. Then hopping from item to item. Ten seconds. Twenty seconds.

He heard Stepka's soft footstep behind him. 'This is exactly what we want,' Ed said, aware suddenly of a reflection forming behind the glass. A distorted face. Unfamiliar. Whoever it was, it wasn't Stepka.

★★★★★

Ed had no weapon. He imagined a gun pointed at the small of his back, ready to smash his spine. He imagined a nightstick raised to batter his head. What now? He flung himself down and to the side, still clutching the camera. He twisted to see his attacker. It was a Thai girl, perhaps fifteen, empty-handed and dressed in a cotton nightshirt. She said some words he couldn't understand and let out a little cry.

Then a sound Ed somehow recognised though he'd never heard it before – the single *phut* of a silenced pistol. The girl's chest burst forward and open. Blood splattered the glass, drenched the plywood. The girl's nightshirt went black with blood. She staggered forward and collapsed against the partition.

'Finish the pictures quick,' Stepka's voice growled. 'We not come back this place.'

'Why'd you do that?' Ed yelled, scrambling to his feet. 'It's just a kid.'

'Shut up,' Stepka hissed. 'Or whole place wake up.'

'What do we do about her?' Ed demanded.

'Nothing. She dead,' Stepka replied, slipping the gun back into a holster under his arm. 'You take pictures? Yes or no?'

Ed went to the wreck of the girl's body and instinctively knelt beside it. Worse than a wreck. Nothing human left of her. He looked back at Stepka. The door stood half-open, but Stepka was gone.

There was nothing Ed could do for the girl. He stood up. He heard movement, Thai voices. He ran to the door, slipped into the corridor and swung the door closed behind him. He slammed the single bolt home. More voices. Shouts, muffled by the steel. A woman's scream. He ran down the corridor to the other door – if he caught up with Stepka, he could still escape. He reached the door and jerked down the handle. The door didn't budge. Stepka had bolted it – from the other side. He was trapped in the corridor. In a few seconds, the hubbub in the canteen would alert the guards. Or the alarm system would go off.

A steel door behind him, a steel door ahead of him. In one direction the canteen, in the other the film poster and the guards. All he could do was hide. He scuttled to the store-room and opened the plywood door. By the glow of the corridor light, he saw the old canvases just as he remembered them, folded, unfolded, and dumped in untidy heaps. Paint cans were stacked against the wall, brush cleaner, oil. The noise in the canteen grew louder. He heard more screams and then the blast of a whistle. The noise cut back. He left the door a crack open – just enough light for him to dive at a heaped-up canvas, find an edge, and burrow himself into a hiding place. A stack of paint cans toppled over. He froze, dreading the clatter, but the cans settled with a dull *thud-thud-thud* – they were full. He pulled the canvas to cover him completely. Then, curled up, he lay for a moment, his heart pounding and his body shaking as though he were naked and freezing. He was still holding the camera, though the viewfinder had somehow closed itself.

The dark was suffocating. He had to breathe, he had to see. Nervously he twisted his way back to the edge of the canvas and made a peephole. He heard a steel door crash open, shouts, and a stampede of boots. The corridor flashed into harsh, bright light. Men flickered past the door-slit. The steel door into the canteen, the one he'd just bolted, was flung open. The building boomed as the door smashed against the wall. The noise from the canteen stopped abruptly. He heard a shouted question and a storm of replies. A bellowed order. The whistle again. A sudden silence. What was going on?

For long minutes he heard nothing more, and his panic began to subside. They weren't looking for him – not yet anyway. But they must have found the girl. What did they think had happened? More to the point, what *had* happened? The last few minutes were a blur. He tried to work through them. The girl? She must have gone to the canteen, maybe for water. Stepka had heard her coming. Perhaps he'd hidden behind the door. Perhaps he'd just stood still. The girl must have seen someone standing at the glass – at the partition. Apparently she had no idea anything was wrong – she hadn't run, she hadn't said anything till he'd thrown himself on the floor. And then Stepka had shot her. Once. From behind. Some kind of filthy KGB bullet it must have been – it had torn the girl to pieces. With just a single *phut*. The *phut* and the instant disintegration of the girl's body filled him with loathing. Another life ripped apart. Another Iphigenia. No doubt her body would show up in Hirsch's morgue in a day or two, unidentified, unclaimed, meaningless.

Stepka had butchered her. Perhaps he'd thought she had a gun, a gun aimed at Ed's back. But no. Stepka didn't make mistakes like that – he read the signs too clearly. He'd decided that a single *phut* was safer than letting the girl scream the place down. But one sign Stepka had missed. Completely. He knew Ed was an amateur, but he hadn't allowed for the way Ed would react. The shot had been all but silent, but Ed's shout had roused the whole building.

Then the bastard had disappeared. Locked the door so Ed was trapped in the corridor. Well, Ed had known it would happen. Had Stepka got away? Or was he hiding somewhere in the big hall? No, he was up the rope and out of the hall already. That was why he'd bolted the door – there was time for *one* to escape, but not for two. What a treacherous animal, corrupt as Odysseus.

For a long while the corridor was busy. Thai voices, some male, some female, argued and explained. Ed sensed bafflement – more questions than answers, though the sing-song, nasal language confused him. Perhaps the girl's body was being taken away – or perhaps not. After a few minutes, Ed heard new voices – one seemed to be a Thai speaking in English. The other sounded Indian, not that he could make out what they were saying. Chaudhary? Bhatnagar? Patel even? Or someone else altogether?

Finally the footsteps drained away into the big hall, the bright light went out, the door slammed shut, and the bolts were shot. What time was it? How long had he been hiding? He risked opening the camera. *Menu. Time and date.* СУББОТА 31 ОКТЯБРЬ 2009. 05:09. Fucking Russians. He shut up the camera again and put it in its pouch – the battery was still at 80%.

★★★★★

A piercing, heady smell – acetone – was getting stronger. One of the cans he'd knocked over must be leaking. He crawled out from under the canvas. Still on his hands and knees, he fumbled for the cans, standing them upright. One of them was wet. A screwtop. Half a gallon. The can felt heavy. He shook it. It was half-full. The smell took him back to the Princess Hotel, back to Diana changing the colour of her nail varnish. Acetone – he never used the stuff himself, not even to clean brushes. He stood the can upright and dried his wet fingers on his shirt. As his fingers dried, he felt the skin freeze and tighten, the devil's touch on his warm hand.

His best hope now was Irina. She knew where he was, and she knew Merr's number. Right now she'd be sitting in the car with Stepka's driver, waiting. Would she call Merr? That depended on what Stepka said when he got back to the car. He'd have some story ready – the son-of-a-bitch.

Ed saw two options now – stay where he was with no water, no food, and acetone to breathe till Irina called Merr and Merr sent out a search party. Assuming, of course, the guards didn't find him first. Or? Think up a Plan B. For a breathless moment no Plan B suggested itself. He was trapped.

Then the floorplan of the corridor outside began to take shape in his mind. Three plywood doors and two steel doors. The steel door into the big warehouse was closed and locked. But what about the canteen door? Open or closed? Had they left a guard in the corridor? No way of knowing without taking a look. He stood up, his head unsteady from the fumes. He peeped through the door-crack. Nothing. He listened into the silence – no sound of breathing. He widened the crack. No guard – the corridor was empty. The canteen door was closed.

He retreated again into the store-room. A single bulb hung from a wire in the middle of the room. He closed the plywood door behind him and flicked on the light-switch. The bulb glowed, a feeble fifteen watts but enough to show him the chaotic room in detail. Years before he'd shared a studio with two old men. Over the decades they'd accumulated a mountain of art-rubbish, much like the room he was facing now. Then the fire brigade had run a safety inspection, and that had been the end of the studio. An idea began to take shape.

The moaning sound he'd heard earlier picked up again, very faint. It was coming from the next room, through the panelling. Stepka had guessed a refrigerator – but that wasn't what Ed could hear. The dividing wall was mostly lined with crude wooden shelves and racks. Between two racks Ed saw a patch of plywood, the bare wall. He put his ear to the plywood and listened. The sound was definitely a moan. One of the children? Locked up as a punishment? Not his problem. And he had to hurry – his new idea wasn't so simple.

Acetone. That was the clue. Six screw-top cans on a shelf. He tested them. All full. One litre each – enough to kill a hundred huffers. And enough to burn down a dozen warehouses.

If the acetone was his explosive, what was his ignition? A light bulb. He glanced at the bulb hanging from the ceiling. There were other bulbs, one in the office next door, and a couple in the corridor. If he took a bulb and broke the glass without breaking the filament, it would flash when the power went on. There was plenty of left-over cable about. He could wire the bulb easily. If there was acetone about, there'd be an explosion. A fire-bomb.

He'd stay in the store-room. The bomb would be in the office next door. He could make a hole in the plywood and wire the light-bulb through the wall. At some stage the guards would come back, unlock the steel door, and enter the corridor. How could he lure them into the office? Leave the door half-open and the light on. The door should be open, but not too wide. He wanted the guards to push their way in. That was the booby trap. On a couple of laths, he'd balance a can – an *open* can – of acetone above the office door. It would crash to the floor when the guards barged in. Then, the instant he powered up his bulb, *flashing fire will follow.*

Explosion, fire, chaos. In the confusion, he'd get to the main hall. And then? He'd find a way. For now the problem was to set up the whole thing. He had wire, he had buckets of old tools, it shouldn't take long.

He worked quickly, his mind flickering, as it always did, through a dozen memories and half-invented pictures. He saw a fireball spewing into the corridor, a burning stunt-man *arrayed in flames, like to the prince of fiends.* And suddenly Ingrid Bergman, her gaze fixed on heaven, burning at the stake. Dy often told him he had a grasshopper mind. Probably she was right, though if everything was a reflection of everything else, he couldn't see the problem. Diana with her cold lawyer's logic got things wrong far more often than he did. Or maybe not? And what the fuck had happened to her anyway? Where was she? Stepka, the bastard, was supposed to find her. *If wife in Bangkok, I find.* Well, Stepka wasn't going to find her. Wasn't even going to look for her as things stood now. So with Diana, Irina, Stepka and all the rest, what had he actually put together? Nothing. *This is nothing, Fool.* The blast of a horn? Yes, far away on the road. Then voices. *The isle is full of sometime voices.*

Distantly he heard the *crunch* of marching feet. Nearer. The can was already in position over the door, but the ignition still needed ten minutes work. He barely had time to cut the lights and scamper back to his hiding place under the canvas.

Far off, muffled, he heard the feet stop at the steel door. The bolts were scraped open, the door creaked, and the main light flashed on in the corridor. He heard a low-spoken word of command, not crisp or military.

The footsteps, not marching now, headed toward the canteen. Six, maybe eight people. They passed his door and stopped. He heard the SmartScan lock open with a *beep* and a mechanical *clack* – presumably it had recognised a fingerprint. He heard words spoken in Thai – another casual order and what must have been a *Yes sir.*

Through the plywood partition he heard voices and muffled sounds. A shrieking cry – definitely a girl. Then what sounded like a slap. More muffled sounds. Footsteps again. It seemed the guards were dragging the girl out of the room. She was struggling. From the sound of her cries, he guessed she was gagged. The footsteps drained away into the hall. The main light in the corridor was cut. But the big steel door? Had it slammed shut? No – no slam. Just the retreating thud of boots, crisp and clear, hardly muffled at all. He scrambled out from under his canvas and peeped into the corridor. Empty. The light was on. And yes – the steel door stood open.

Now!

★★★★★

The darkness of the big hall was shot through with a grey hint of dawn. Where could he hide? He slipped across the dark concrete floor toward the poster and crouched beside a bucket with half-a-dozen mops standing in it. The guards were nearing the far end of the hall, dragging the girl with them. She'd gone limp, like a protester at a rally. Back in 2005, he'd seen Dy dragged away like that. *End sexism at Harvard*. The only time he'd seen her in Joan-of-Arc mode, though she knew how to fight. After all, at St Cunegunda's she'd been centre-forward of the hockey team.

At the other end of the hall, the girl was struggling again. Poor kid – he could guess what was in store for her. And maybe not for the first time. If she'd been locked up, they must have been at her for a while. *How long wilt thou forget me, O Lord?* How fucking vile it all was. *End sexism in Bangkok.* When was *that* going to happen?

The hall was getting lighter by the second – the equatorial dawn that he'd never seen was exploding over the city. In the far corner of the concrete hall, the girl was led out and away – God help her. Then one of the guards went back to the steel door, to lock it Ed guessed, crouching, silent and motionless, beside the mops.

How long wilt thou forget me, O Lord? For ever? How long wilt thou hide thy face from me? How long shall I take counsel in my soul, having sorrow in my heart daily? How long shall mine enemy be exalted over me? Consider and hear me, O Lord my God: lighten mine eyes, lest I sleep the sleep of death. He'd learned the words in high school. For a competition. *Elocution* Ms Massinger had called it. Three pieces – the psalm, the *noiseless, patient spider* thing, and a page of Faulkner. But, of course, he owed old Massinger a lot more than that. Shakespeare, Tennyson, Langston Hughes – she knew screeds of poetry by heart, though she never just rattled things off. It always seemed to him that she extracted each word from her own deep, invisible and perhaps painful experience. She was batty, of course, and the kids gave her a hard time. For Ed though, her class was often the only part of the day that made sense, though he'd never told her. Now he said the ancient psalm as a kind of threnody for the gang-raped girl and her sisters. And old Massinger? She'd died of a heart attack half way through twelfth grade, unmourned, unappreciated, *sans*, as the old man said, *everything*.

The guard locked the steel door and ran back to join the others. The hall was nearly light.

*****

'So what the fuck happened?' Merr was sitting at Irina's workbench. She was still at the street-door paying off Ed's taxi-driver.

Ed went to the bed and sat down with a crash. 'I guess Irina told you most of it,' he said.

'That you went with this guy Stepka to get the pictures. And never came back.'

'She was waiting in the car.'

'I know.'

'So what did Stepka tell her? When he got back?'

'Nothing. He never got back either.'

'He didn't? What do you mean?'

'He never get back.' Irina's voice from the doorway.

'You stayed in the car?' Ed asked disbelieving. 'How long?'

'Till dawn. Like we agreed. Nobody came. Not him. Not you. So the driver bring me back here.'

Ed said nothing.

'And I called Merr,' Irina added. She glanced at Merr with a mix of gratitude and curiosity.

'Stepka left Andronicus about three,' Ed objected. He sketched the story right down to the green button by the roll-up door. Eighteen inches had been enough. He'd squeezed under and hit the red button on the other side. He'd walked out of the building, across the switchyard, and found his way to Bang Sue Station. There he'd picked up a taxi, the taxi Irina had just paid off.

Irina was seething. The shit! The murderous *таракан*! She hit Stepka's cellphone number, then glanced at Merr, her finger poised on connect. But Merr shook his head. Stepka was a KGB man, a dinosaur. That was how he'd been trained – shoot first, ask questions afterward, and above all make a clean get-away. But now they had to move carefully. If Stepka knew Ed was free, then Stepka's safety was compromised – at least if you saw it from his point of view. Who knew what he might do? Let him stew – for twenty-four hours at least. Irina calmed down and hit red.

Merr was more interested in what Ed had seen – the canteen, the guards, the locked up workers, children probably but still not for sure. And the equipment. They looked at Ed's film frame by frame. The Kevin Costner poster, the big hall, and then the shots through the glass. They were enough to identify the equipment, Merr guessed, once they'd been enhanced. And the girl? As he'd dived for the floor, Ed's camera had picked up the image of the girl exactly as he'd seen her – skinny, terrified, screaming. The rest of the film was blurs, streaks, confusion, walls, tables, the girl, all in the hazy green light of an infra-red camera. The machine had run till the viewfinder snapped shut. The last shot seemed to be Stepka. The soundtrack was surprisingly clear: *Nothing. She dead.*

Was the film enough? Was it what Merr needed? Merr wasn't sure. The pictures were probably okay. He'd have to wait for Washington to run an enhancement. But...

'But?' Ed repeated.

'Couple of things,' Merr said. 'First – with you and Stepka blundering round like that, they may well move the kids out. Get rid of the evidence quick as they can.'

As he spoke, Merr hit a key on his cellphone. He gave a curt order: the warehouse had to be watched. Back and front. Starting *now*.

'Maybe it'll happen,' Merr said, ending the call. 'But I doubt we have the people.'

'What is it mean, *get rid of the evidence*?' Irina asked with a frown.

'I'd say they've got three choices,' Merr told her. 'Leave the kids where they are, move them, or remove them – permanently.'

'You mean...' Ed began.

'Unless of course you've already finished them off.'

'Me? How?'

'Let's go back to that bit again – the bit where you're in the store-room. Making a booby-trap,' Merr said, taking his tablet out of its shoulder-bag. He booted it and googled *acetone*.

'*Acetone begins to vaporise at minus 18° centigrade,*' he read. 'Listen, Ed. That go-down has a sheet-iron roof – I checked it out on Google Maps. A few hours from now, the temperature in there's going to hit forty. More maybe. And you left half a gallon of acetone sitting over a door with the cap off. And five more on the floor for good measure. And all that stuff in the next room. Oil. Canvas. Paint. The whole building's a booby-trap. Any kind of spark – switching on a light, opening a cellphone even…'

'My God,' Ed said. 'The kids…'

'Yes, the kids,' Merr pursued. 'If they're still there…'

Ed shook his head, too disgusted to speak.

'Ed.' Merr's tone softened. 'The kids are bad enough, but actually there's more.'

'Worse?'

'Depends how you look at it,' Merr said. 'Look, let's say the kids die in the fire and the story comes out – which it may. Think about it. Good old Merr knew what was going on, so T-CAN itself, the State Department in Washington, isn't clean.'

'Your job?'

'My job, yes. But there's Irina to think of as well. And Dy at the UN. As fuck-ups go, this is Iran-Contra and the Bay of Pigs rolled into one. Potentially.' Merr exchanged a look with Irina – *You see what he's landed us in?*

'Merr, what can I say?'

'No need to say a word. If you've burned that place down, and if the Thais pick up on it, which, not being totally stupid, they might…' Merr threw up his hands in despair. 'They still execute murderers here, you know. Lethal injection.'

'Merr… I didn't mean… I had no intention…'

'So let's say you're lucky. No fire-bomb. What do you think'll happen when my report hits DC? If I follow T-CAN procedures, your name will be in it. And in DC they just love people like you. You might even end up with a red file.'

'A red file?'

'It means you're on everyone's shit-list for the rest of your life, Ed. Once it starts, it never stops.' Merr was deadly serious. 'They'll bug your phone for evermore. They'll read your e-mail. They could take Terry and put her in care.'

'My God…' Ed's voice was a dry croak in his throat.

'I warned you, Ed. *Don't even think about it.* That's what I told you. *It's too dangerous.* And Irina should know better too, the stable she comes from.'

Ed shook his head in denial, cornered, at his wits' end.

'Saturday morning,' Merr said abruptly. He looked at his watch. 'Seven. You two go to that Internet café downstairs. Get some breakfast. Maybe good old Merr's got an idea.'

★★★★★

Ed sat with Irina in the almost empty café next to the hairdresser's shop. At one of the computers, a skinny boy in headphones was trapped in a world of bloody dungeons and predatory monsters. Perhaps he'd been there all night – there was no way to tell. The overdriven headphones spat out every snarl and screech as he *zapped* his enemies.

A weary girl brought them coffee and American donuts with pink icing.

'You think he can fix something?' Ed asked.

'He must. If there is fire and a lot of dead kids, he's in trouble too,' Irina said. 'I remember with Andrey, my *stable* Merr call it. That is first rule: whatever happen, keep your nose clean.' She shrugged. 'Merr is clever man. I didn't see the problems – not with calling Stepka, and not with acetone. Not till he explain.'

'So what'll happen? At the warehouse? If we're lucky?'

'Nothing. Nobody will go there. Nothing will happen. Somehow your fire-bomb vanish from the earth. And life continue exactly as before.'

'You think so?'

'This is the Thai way,' she said with resignation.

'Gloss over everything?'

'Ed, they had riots here in the summer. The yellows. The reds. A mob close the airport. Tanks at every street corner. Busses got burned.'

'I saw it on TV. But it never came to anything, did it?'

'Exactly. It all disappeared. That's the Thai way. Pretend you don't see. Nothing is happen. And nothing will happen – not till next time.'

'But it's not just in Thailand is it? It's everywhere.'

'Perhaps yes,' she shrugged. 'Maybe that's how it is.'

He nodded.

She stretched out her rough hand to him across the table. 'I made mistake,' she said. 'About Stepka. You don't...'

He took her hand. '...blame you?'

She nodded.

'No. It was my choice. You stayed out of it – pretty much,' he reassured her. 'It just astounds me – my total stupidity. Thinking I could...'

'Well,' she said, gripping his fingers tightly, 'I also think you could. And Merr has his pictures.'

'*Probably okay*, that's what he called them.'

'The pictures are perfect. Or Merr isn't sending them to Washington.'

'You think so?' Ed was exhausted. All he could think about was the kids in the warehouse. And the girl the soldiers had dragged away. The screaming of the headphones blurred into the roaring of a truck in the street outside. For a second he closed his eyes.

'Sorted.' It was Merr's voice. He pulled a chair up to their table and sat down, eying their uneaten donuts and linked hands.

'My God,' Ed said. 'What did you do?'

'Fire department. I know a guy there. Routine inspection.'

'And when they find the cans?' Ed asked.

'What cans? Why should they find cans?'

'And your report?'

'A few matters subject to further enquiry. Should cover it.'

Ed glanced at Irina. He saw her familiar shrug – it would go, as she'd said, the Thai way.

'So,' Ed began again with a vicious glance at the zapping boy. 'On what might, or might not, be an altogether different subject…'

'Dy?' Irina asked.

'Dy,' Merr repeated quietly. 'Ed, this girl you say was in the next room, the one the guards took away…'

'That wasn't Dy?' Ed was suddenly wide awake. 'It wasn't Dy. Definitely not.

'How do you know? You never saw her clearly.'

'It wasn't her voice.'

'She was gagged.'

'It wasn't Dy. But you think it was?'

'No, I don't. It was just a question.'

'Did you find out any more? About where she is? Anything more about yesterday?' Yesterday seemed a year ago.

Two kids came into the café, twelve, maybe thirteen. Fat girls with bad complexions. They went straight to one of the computers. They cackled something in ugly, loud voices to the waitress. She went to the control desk and hit half-a-dozen keys. Merr ate one the donuts and ordered coffee. The fat girls opened a website, read messages aloud to each other, and shrieked with nasal laughter, covering their open mouths with their hands.

'The UN reported her missing,' Merr picked up. 'To the police and the consulate. About ten last night.'

'You know who made the report? Was it Vadim? The Russian?'

'I saw the report, at least the one to the consulate. Yes, it was Vadim.'

Ed let go of Irina's hand and took a sip of his coffee. 'What did he say? Do you know?'

'She failed to show up in KL. At first nobody worried much because *Ms Tarn is given to erratic behaviour…*'

'Vadim wrote that? The bastard!'

'He had to explain why the UN took twelve hours to report,' Merr replied.

'Damn fools.' It was a ritual curse, without much venom.

'Listen, Ed. If you want some advice, I'd say get packed and go home. Now.'

'And leave you to find Diana?'

'No. It's not my job. The consulate does that.'

'You just examine the bodies after they're picked up.'

'Something like that.'

'It may seem odd, after all you know about me and Dy, but...'

'...you'd rather stick around till you know she's okay.'

'More or less.'

'That's not odd – that's exactly how you've always been. Hang in there! Never give up! *To your own self be true.* That kind of thing'

'*Thine own self*,' Ed corrected him.

'So, let's cut the crap. Listen...'

Irina stood up. 'I'm going up to my apartment,' she said. 'Get some rest.'

'No, stay,' Merr said. 'You know this town better than any of us.'

Irina sat down again, with a weary smile.

Merr paused. 'I still have a feeling,' he said, 'that Dy disappearing is connected with Andronicus.'

'Through Patel?' Ed asked.

'I don't know,' Merr shrugged. 'It's just a feeling, okay?'

'Okay.'

'I've called around. There's no trace of her. The UN report means she's officially missing, so the consulate takes over. Not that they're likely to get off their asses and do anything.'

'So you're off the job?' Ed heard the edge of accusation in his own voice.

'T-CAN's off the job, yes. But me? Obviously not. What's got into you, Ed?'

'Sorry,' Ed said. 'Lack of sleep. Not thinking straight.' Why was he accusing Merr? Without Merr he'd be on death row. *Your own. Thine own.* What the hell did it matter? What was so superior about knowing Shakespeare back to front? He felt Irina's hand shyly cover his, a warning, a sign of solidarity.

'If you stay in Bangkok,' Merr picked up, 'you could generate a bit of pressure, call the UN, call the consulate, follow up on leads. It might help.'

'Help find Dy?'

'Dy and... There's probably more behind this, Ed. A lot more.'

'Okay, assume I'm staying.' He felt Irina's hand tighten over his. She was pleased. 'So what happens next?'

'Let's start at the Princess. Go there and talk to the driver again, the one who took Dy to the airport. Get him to take you to the exact place he dropped her off. Then scout around. You'll need a photo of Dy. Ask everyone – officials, shop-people, whatever – ask them if they recognise the picture. Try all the shops, specially perfume.'

'Perfume?'

'I left a bunch of orchids for Diana in your room. Last night. Just an excuse to nose around a bit. Dy has enough perfume to make a fair size Molotov cocktail herself.'

★★★★★

The lump on Irina's head has almost disappeared, though she still wore a scarf. She drove with Ed to the Princess through the morning rush-hour. The driver who'd taken Dy to the airport would be on duty at four. Till then, nobody knew where he was.

They ate a second breakfast on the terrace, enjoying the cool and the quiet. No screeching girls, no zapping boys, and no pink donuts. Half-asleep, Ed took Irina to his room – his room and Diana's. The clerk at the desk said nothing when he showed his hotel-pass and asked for the room-key. Ed knew that the night shift looked out for prostitutes – the extra room-rent was a handy source of income for the check-in clerks, or so Diana had told him. The day shift seemed more relaxed.

Ed unlocked the door and waved Irina ahead of him. It was cool – the maid had left the air-con running. Irina was wearing jeans and a plain white shirt. Her dark hair was pulled into a rough ponytail that spilled from under her scarf. There was nothing eye-catching about her, none of that instant appeal that radiated from Diana. She was simple, not remarkable in any way. Yet...

She turned back to smile at him, exhausted as he saw. He held out his arms to her, without intention but also without hesitation. She'd been worried about him, anxious and frightened to the end of her strength. And she was pleased that he was staying. She came to him, putting her arms round his waist, resting her head on his shoulder.

'I thought they kill you,' she said. 'I thought you aren't come back.' Her voice throbbed with emotion. 'Thank God you're safe.'

He held her, frankly and tenderly, as if she were some long-cherished part of his life. He kissed her forehead and felt her tremble.

'Lie down,' he said. 'You need to sleep. You were up the whole night, and you're still not over the concussion.'

He sensed her agreement in the softening grasp round his waist. He led her to the bed and sat her down. He took off her sneakers and her socks and lifted her feet onto the bed. For a second she trembled, then her whole body relaxed. She closed her eyes.

He stayed for a moment on his knees beside the bed, too weary to stand. He looked at Irina, struggling to understand who she was and what she was beginning to mean to him.

He went to the shower. In Irina's apartment, he'd already cleaned off most of the hair-black and the make-up Stepka had rubbed into his skin. Now he showered and soaped himself clean. He pulled on a bathrobe and went back to the bedroom. Irina's clothes were in a heap by the bed. Her slight body was outlined under the sheet. She was fast asleep.

He lay on his own bed, trying to figure out how he knew the gagged girl in the warehouse wasn't Diana. What were the signs? Six hours later the door-buzzer roused him. The ugly rasping emerged from a crackle of fire and faggots round the tormented, ecstatic face of Ingrid Bergman. Irina stirred but didn't wake. The limo-driver had arrived early. If Ed wanted to talk to him…

★★★★★

Ed arranged with the driver to take them to the airport at five-fifteen – that way they'd coincide exactly with Dy's trip two days before.

Ed was thirsty, and his head ached. He sat on the terrace and ordered tea. He had Tylenol in his medical kit, but he was too weary to fetch it. And he had no phone to call Merr. He'd better get himself a phone. He closed his eyes tight for a moment, trying to squeeze back the headache.

He felt two hands rest on his forehead – tentative, affectionate. Irina. 'Stay there,' he said. 'For ever.'

She laughed and sat down. She was dressed exactly as before. She even had her bag over her shoulder.

'If you wanted…' he began. She could maybe find some clean things of Dy's to wear. But he didn't finish the sentence – she was fine as she was.

'I ought to call…' he began again.

'Merr?' She took her phone out of her bag and gave it to him.

The hotel manager brought Ed's tea smiling diplomatically. 'Madame?' he asked.

'*Cha ron*,' she said. 'Same.'

'Will madame be staying?' the manager asked. 'In the hotel?'

'No,' she replied quickly and firmly.

'You can if you like,' Ed broke in, finding Merr's number and pressing connect.

'No,' Irina repeated to the manager. 'Get the tea, please.'

'Thank you, madame,' the manager said and left them.

'If I stay in a hotel, I must register. And my permit's expired,' Irina explained. 'You know this already.'

Merr picked up.

'Any progress with the warehouse?' Ed asked him.

'It's sorted,' Merr replied.

'What is?'

'Whatever it is you're talking about.'

'They found it?'

'Found what? Nobody found anything, Ed. I could have asked, I suppose, but I didn't. And even if I had asked, I wouldn't have believed the answer.'

'The Thai way?'

'How else?'

'You keep your job, and I don't get a red file.'

'Mission accomplished,' Merr assured him. 'You out looking for Dy?'

'We're going to the airport at five. Like you said.'

'She with you?'

'Irina? Yes, she's here.' He smiled at Irina. 'You want to talk to her?'

'I want to ask her out to dinner. Think she'd come?'

Ed held out the phone to Irina. 'Merr. Wants to ask you out to dinner.'

'Me?' she said. 'Tell him no.'

'You tell him.'

Irina took the phone. 'Hi. Hi Merr,' she said. She was making her voice brighter, Ed heard, hiding her weariness.

Ed began to pour his tea, politely looking away from Irina as she talked to Merr.

'Tonight?' he heard her say.

Merr's voice was a distant buzzing.

'I'm very tired. Tonight...no.'

What did that mean? Tonight *no*, but another night *maybe*. Keep trying, Merr.

More buzzing.

'No really,' Irina said. 'So many things for catch up in the studio. I'm days late with all this...problems.'

That was better.

'I'll give you back to Ed.' She passed him the phone.

'Sounds like *no* means *no*,' Merr said to him ruefully. 'Still, you'll be back in DC soon. Making room for your betters.'

'Listen, Merr...' Ed repeated.

'Give us a call if you dig up anything at the airport,' Merr said and disconnected.

Ed gave the phone back to Irina, and she put it in her bag. 'He likes you,' Ed said as casually as he could. It was ridiculous. He was behaving like a tenth-grader.

Irina shrugged and smiled. 'You guys,' she said.

★★★★★

For a while the road followed the elevated track of the new Skytrain through rice fields and new housing projects. The trains weren't running yet, the limo-driver told them over his shoulder. Ed asked if the trains would hurt the limo business. The driver thought no – busses would suffer. And taxis. But not limos.

The Thai way, Ed thought. Maybe it wasn't such a bad way either. *Sufficient unto the day is the evil thereof.* It was one of his mother's favourite sayings, though what she thought it meant, he'd never understood. He tried to remember where the words came from. And there he was – back in DC, in church with his mother. St Mark's. Romanesque brick. Skinny columns. Stained glass – Gustave Doré no less. And put together by Tiffany. The window was a jewel, something to boast about to visitors. Not that many visitors came to St Mark's back then – in the eighties. He remembered sitting beside his mother on an uncomfortable plastic chair, loathing the smell of the incense. *Take no thought for your life, what you shall eat, or what you shall drink; nor yet for your body, what you shall put on.* Something about the lilies of the valley. That was where it came from, *Sufficient unto the day...* The chair, the incense, and his mother's Sunday hat, a hat about which, in defiance of the scripture, she'd taken considerable thought and decided it was just right for church. Red, with a brown feather. She hadn't worn it to the wedding though. For the wedding she'd bought a new hat. White, with lots of feathers. He pictured it, the only hat among the little circle of heads on the chancel steps. And then, together with the hat, the ancient, alienating smell of St Mark's. Five of them had stood there – bride and groom, the groom's mother, Merr, and an English friend of Dy's from way back when – a girl called Lizzie. Tin Lizzie, Merr had christened her. No, not five. Six. Terry had been there – the unknown, unborn, half-life they'd created.

He looked at Irina. 'Do you ever go to church?' he asked.

Her tired eyes smiled. 'No,' she said. 'I never been in a church. Not any of my family. I think not.'

It was a luxury – they didn't have to talk. Nothing obliged them to discuss the role of the Orthodox Church under President Putin, Prime Minister Putin, or whatever the man was called now. Likewise they could ignore the invisible line that separated Episcopalians from Roman Catholics under Mr Obama. They understood each other without wallowing in talk.

The limo reached the giant arrows that directed traffic within the airport. The driver already knew where they wanted to go. 'Essackly where I drop Miss Ta'an?' he confirmed.

'Yes,' Ed said. 'Exactly the same place.'

They had Diana's flight number and a photograph. The picture was a Polaroid taken in a bar a few months back. Dy had poked it into the mirror of her dressing table. In fact it was half a picture. The other half had once been Vadim, but Dy had *snipped him off* – as she put it. Though it was only a bar-hopper's snapshot, the picture showed Dy in all her disturbing beauty, with the faery light in her eyes that beamed up after a few drinks.

The driver manoeuvred the car through a police barrier and along the kerb outside International Departures. 'Here,' he said. 'Essackly here.' He stopped the car.

'You sure?' Ed asked.

The driver craned round and gave Ed a smile of seraphic innocence, though seraphs probably had better teeth than the driver's brown stumps. The smile confirmed what Ed already suspected – the seraph neither remembered nor cared where he'd dropped Miss Ta'an. 'No problem,' Ed smiled and gave the man a 100-baht tip.

'You're learning fast,' Irina said with a fleeting grin. The Land of Smiles – Ed had heard the phrase often enough, but suddenly there it was. Three smiling people, four if you counted the Polaroid of Diana.

Ed was certain they'd find nothing – there were agencies that specialised in searches like this. Professionals. But Merr had been adamant. In a place like Thailand, with an agency, even a respectable one like Spyonthai, you were never sure where your information might end up. And if there really was a link to Andronicus, then the quieter the better.

Level 4 Departures. The flight to KL was a codeshare. They went straight to the check-in counter, jumping the lines. The flight manager was unhelpful – if the passenger had not checked in, then nobody would remember her. That meant there was no point in finding out who'd been on duty on Thursday evening. In any case, security did not allow an airline to release information about its staff schedules.

Ed asked if Diana had perhaps checked in but not boarded the flight. Apparently that would have brought the entire aviation of South-East Asia to a standstill, so it couldn't have happened.

At the tail-end of the lines was a small, thin man who directed lost passengers to their check-in. He didn't speak English, and he didn't recognise the picture of Dy.

Opposite the check-in were shops, stylish and glittering. Perhaps Dy had bought a newspaper or a book. The assistants in the bookshop looked with interest at the picture but none of them remembered Dy. Next to the bookshop was a huge display of cosmetics and perfume. Merr had told them to concentrate on perfume. Most of the assistants were young, perfectly dressed, perfectly made-up Thai women. Some were young men, just as well-dressed as the women and made-up with just as much attention to detail.

'Let's try the boys first,' Ed said. They started with the Te Amo stand. 'Were you here at this time on Thursday?' they asked a bored young man.

'Yes.'

'Do you remember seeing this woman?'

The young man looked at the picture thoughtfully. 'She is very beautiful,' he said. 'A beautiful *falang*. Perhaps…' He called a name, a loud nasal cry, wild and unexpected.

A young man at the Givenchy display turned his head.

'Perhaps my frenn remember?' the Te Amo boy said.

Yes. The Givenchy boy remembered Dy clearly. She'd joked with him. Told him his eyeshadow was too red – blue would go better with his black hair. The boy smoothed his pomaded, already sleek hair with an affectionate hand. Without hesitation Ed nicknamed the boy *Giv*.

'You're sure it was her?'

'Yes.'

'Did she buy anything?'

'Yes.' Giv looked petulant for a second.

'What did she buy?' Ed asked kindly. He liked the boys – so unutterably un-American. Strange though, Ed thought. Why did he find it unnerving, talking to boys who wore mascara?

'I hope she will buy many thing, but a man come.'

'A man?'

'Yes. A man.'

'He talked to her?'

'For five minute. Perhap more.'

'What happened?'

'She buy only lipstick. Come I show you.'

They all went with Giv. He led them to a display of lipstick and without hesitation picked out *Number 15 Rouge Interdit Gold Brown*. 'I tell her it is completely wrong for her. Completely wrong.'

'But she bought it anyway,' Ed sympathised. 'Can I see the colour?'

Giv took out a sample from under the counter. He uncapped the stick, and took Ed's hand delicately in one of his. He drew a little heart of the back of Ed's hand in a shade of streaky gold that might better have been called Combat Zone Gothic.

'You see!' Giv said triumphantly. 'Completely wrong.'

'Did she take it with her, the lipstick?'

'She buy two. One duty-free. One cash.'

'If something's duty-free, you send it to the gate?'

'Yes,' chipped in the Te Amo boy. Inevitably Ed had nicknamed him *Take*.

'Do you have a sales record? A sales slip? Anything of that sort?'

'It is forbidden to show such a thing,' Giv said severely. 'Not possible.'

'This lady in the picture,' Irina broke in modestly. 'I'm her... She's my...partner. And I'm afraid something is happen to her. Something bad.'

Irina's confession seemed to put things in a new light. Giv sucked in air through his teeth. 'I will ask,' he said gently. 'Please you wait here.'

Ed and Irina waited. Take waited with them. Nobody spoke. A few minutes later Giv returned. 'I see daily sales return,' he said. '18:22. Two Number 15. Thirty-seven dollar pay in Thai baht. Duty-free go to gate – I can't remember gate. Anyway, flight to Kuala Lumpur. No boarding card number. Only ticket number. Name was Ms D Ta'an.'

'This is so helpful,' Irina said. 'Specially with the name. It really is her.' She put the back of her hand to her eye as though to wipe away a tear.

'So what happened?' Ed picked up. 'After she paid for the lipstick?'

'She went off. With the man.'

'Did you hear any of their conversation? Even one word might help.'

'No. I try but not possible.'

'Did she still have her case with her?'

'Yes. Louis Vuitton. Real.' He sighed. Ed guessed a case like that would cost the boy three months wages.

'What did the man look like?' Ed asked.

'Indian.'

That was interesting. 'Well-dressed?' Ed pursued.

175

'Business. Ugly tie.'

'Short? Tall? Fat? Thin?'

'Tall. Fat. And exceedingly ugly.'

'Well, we can't all be beautiful,' Ed remarked.

'No,' Giv and Take chimed together.

Two of the girl-assistants sidled over to where they were talking – they'd sensed something unusual and wanted to be part of it. Ed showed them the picture, but they had no recollection of Diana, none at all.

'Which direction did they go?' Ed asked.

Giv pointed toward one of the huge arched walkways.

'Where does it go?'

'The car park,' Giv said, 'and other places.'

'Taxis?'

'The other way.'

No one worked in the car park except the attendant who sat by the barrier in case anyone had trouble with the mechanism. He hadn't seen Diana. In fact, with the heat and the fumes in the car park, Ed doubted he'd seen anyone for years.

They took a taxi back to town, picking over the new information. Diana had blazed a trail – she'd bought the two hideous lipsticks, kept one and sent the other to the gate. Odd. Deliberately odd, it seemed. Did Dy already know she wasn't going to check in? Probably yes. Had she gone to the airport to meet this tall, fat, ugly Indian? Had she planned to abort the trip? It seemed unlikely. Yet she'd gone off with him – apparently without much argument. Probably she'd gone with him to the car park. And driven off with him. But why? And where?

'The number? Is it mean something?' Irina wondered. 'Fifteen?'

'Number 15 Rouge Interdit Gold Brown.'

Ed racked his brain for connections. Fifteen? Clothes size? Shoe size? 1915? 2015? The 15th of November was in two weeks' time. Nothing useful suggested itself. 'No,' he said. 'I think the message is the colour. *Red forbidden, gold-brown.*'

'Gold-brown might be the Indian,' Irina suggested.

'Chaudhary?' Ed speculated. 'One of his teeth was outlined in gold. And he wore a gold tie-clip too.'

'Too complicated?' Irina said.

'I think it's just the ugliness. Something she wouldn't buy because she'd never wear it.'

They called Merr. He asked if they'd like a nightcap at the Oriental. He had something to tell them.

★★★★★

Merr had suggested the Bamboo Bar. The jazz was okay, he said. Sometimes. And there were quiet corners where you could talk.

The taxi from the airport took them back to Irina's apartment so she could smarten herself to Oriental standards.

While she was showering, Ed sat at her work-table trying to capture in pastel the bizarre reflections and re-reflections he'd seen in the domes and vaults of the new airport. What he wanted was that Irina should glance at the abstraction of lines and colours and say: *Ah. The airport.*

She was ready. Beige sandals, a print dress – short, attractive, understated. She'd made herself up more carefully than before and tied a chiffon scarf in her hair – it hid what was left of the bump and made her look young and cheeky. She glanced at his drawing, then looked at it more attentively. 'The airport,' she said.

Merr was waiting for them in the Bamboo Bar, though they didn't see him at first. Unlike the Oriental garden, it was not a place of enchantment, Ed quickly decided. Merr had found a table as far away from the music as possible, hidden among the bamboo decor. Merr stood up and glanced approvingly at Irina.

'You're over your crack on the head,' he said. 'You look great.'

'And how about me?' Ed asked.

'You look like a piece of shit,' Merr replied. 'Much better than usual.'

They sat down.

'So what'll it be?' Merr invited them.

The singer finished her number, an almost tuneless deconstruction of *Stormy Weather*. Intellectual, modern – or perhaps it had been intellectual and modern back in the seventies. There was polite applause, and she left the bar. The band followed her. All black. All old. As anachronistic as sternwheelers on the Mississippi.

While they waited for their drinks, Merr circled round the question of Irina's work. What kind of work did she do? Who did she work for? Was there a living in it?

Irina answered ever more cagily. Finally she said: 'You want to know if I am legal? Is it?'

'Not really,' Merr replied quietly. 'You're not. I know that already.'

'It's in my file?' Irina flushed a little and looked away – she'd prefer to talk about something else.

And what *was* Merr after? Ed wondered. Testing the thickness of Irina's crocodile hide, it seemed.

'No,' Merr said. 'Not in your file. But it's no secret at Immigration.'

'Immigration,' Irina repeated. 'You are asking Immigration? About me?'

Ed watched Irina's coolness shade into anger. Anger and fear. Her mouth shut into a hard line. It startled him, and it seemed to startle Merr.

'Unless you get into trouble, they'll leave you alone,' Merr said. 'You know that.'

'I'm jealous,' Ed broke in, with an uneasy smile. 'Did you ask Immigration about me too?'

'Listen, Ed. You're in pretty deep considering you only arrived last Sunday.'

'Me? Deep?'

'Don't act dumb. Yes, I asked Immigration if they had anything on you. Yes, I pulled your file from the States – yesterday when I got back from River City. What do you expect? At the morgue you pull some half-assed crap about buying blood. You ask me if I've got anything on Diana's boss. You come up with a weird and wonderful story about Andronicus, a Siberian artist and a KGB hit-man. How do I know what you and Diana might be cooking up? We're old friends, okay, but I still have a job to do.'

The drinks arrived. Bourbon and ice.

'I have a file?'

'Of course you do. You're teaching at Harvard. You drop that for art. In Washington DC. You sell pictures no one understands. You're a natural subversive. You don't have to be a dumb asshole as well.'

'Anything *in* my file?' Ed asked sheepishly.

'Unpaid speeding ticket in Canada.'

There was a long silence. 'Anything on a girl called Lucía?' Ed asked at last. Lucía was illegal – the doorbell could ring any night, and she could be taken away. How would he cope with that? How would Terry?

'Terry's nurse?' Merr asked.

Ed nodded. It seemed they knew all about Lucía.

Merr paused. He was in the driving seat, and he knew it. 'Is there some reason you don't get citizenship for her?'

'I tried,' Ed replied. 'It's not so easy.' He glanced at Irina, but she was deep in her own thoughts.

'Listen, Ed,' Merr told him. 'This isn't why I asked you here – to talk about nursemaids.'

'No.'

'I had doubts about you, so I checked,' Merr pursued. 'But *you* had *your* doubts about *me*. Fair's fair. Listen – I'll ask Irina a question.' He turned to Irina. 'Has Ed ever asked you, *Can I trust Merr?* Has he?'

'Yes,' Irina replied coldly.

'And what did you say?'

'I told him: I know nothing about Americans. Russians see friendship different.' She was spoiling for a fight.

'Like Stepka?' Merr asked. It was a cheap shot. Ed winced – whatever game Merr was playing, he'd just taken it too far.

'Don't get me wrong, Irina,' Merr said, back-tracking. 'All I'm saying is, Ed would have checked me out – if he'd had the chance.'

Irina waved the argument away – it didn't interest her. 'I ask *you* something now,' she said, her anger icily under control. 'You know where I was before I enter Thailand?'

'No.' Merr shook his head, caught suddenly on the wrong foot.

'Well, I'll tell you. North Korea.'

'North Korea,' Merr repeated under his breath. 'North fucking Korea.' He was shocked, as deadly serious now as Irina herself.

'There was a birthday parade for the Dear Leader,' Irina explained. 'Andrey had to attend. We were coming here, and we made a stopover in Pyong-Yang. Husband and wife – together. Ukrainian diplomatic. It was in his file, surely?'

'It was, but I didn't make the connection,' Merr whispered. 'I…'

'What's the point?' Ed broke in. 'I don't get it.'

'Your friend, Mr Croft,' Irina explained, 'has ask about me at Immigration.'

'But if they knew about you already…'

'Perhaps they open my file again if T-CAN ask questions.'

'You mean, you might be deported. That's terrible, but…'

'Poor Ed,' she said. 'About the real world you understand nothing. Only about reflections.'

'Why is it so serious?' Ed asked, hearing something odd in her voice.

'It isn't necessarily serious,' Merr broke in. 'But it *could* be. If Irina is deported and she arrived here from Singapore, they'd send her back to Singapore. But she came from North Korea, so they'd send her to North Korea.'

'Is that...?' Ed began.

'Bad as it gets,' Merr said. Then seeing the blank look on Ed's face: 'You didn't follow the story? Euna and Laura? Two months ago?'

Ed shook his head.

'Two American journalists working in North Korea. They got twelve years hard labour for visa offences. Twelve years hard in Korean penal colony. Americans. Women. Bill Clinton went and had a personal chat with the Dear Leader about it. Got them released.'

'Okay, I remember vaguely,' Ed said. 'But these girls, Laura and the other one, they're the arch-enemy, Americans. Irina's *Russian*. Surely...'

'It doesn't help. Right now, Ed, there's the talks.'

'What talks?'

'Six-power talks. On North Korea. Putin lining up with Obama.'

'Twelve years, you said. Hard labour. For a visa problem?'

'And that's exactly what Irina would have – a visa problem,' Merr explained.

'And maybe it just got worse,' Irina said. 'Guess who went out the door?'

'Who?' Ed asked.

'I saw him,' Merr said. 'Vassili from the Russian Embassy. We kind of follow each other around.'

'Not good that he saw us together,' Irina said.

Merr made a shrewd face. 'It might put up your value,' he said slowly.

Ed looked from one to the other, out of his depth. 'I don't understand,' he said. 'Again.'

'When governments want to do each other a favour, say for example the Thais wanted to do the Dear Leader a favour, they'd give him a victim – someone he could put on trial as a traitor or a spy. Irina isn't worth much in a game like that, she's just a Russian nobody. But a Russian nobody who hangs out with the State Department – that's much better.'

'But if that guy was a Russian, how will the *Thais* find out…?'

'Who knows who talks to whom, who has access to what files in whose filing cabinets?'

'So Irina's in trouble,' Ed said flatly.

'She might be,' Merr replied. 'And I haven't helped – not at all.'

'Jesus, Merr…' Ed began. When it came to fuck-ups, he and Merr were about even.

'It's…,' Merr began tentatively. 'It's one of those problems that can be…stitched.' He looked at Irina, and she looked at him. It was a long look – the word *stitched* had been the trigger. After a moment, Ed saw that they'd reached an understanding, though he had no idea of the details.

'So why did you ask us here?' Ed asked suddenly, starting a fresh hare. 'Something on Dy?'

'Yes,' Merr agreed. 'Something on Dy.' He looked at Irina. Her anger was gone. She sipped her bourbon, inscrutably cold as she'd been in the Rawhide.

Merr turned back to Ed. 'You told me that she'd left the airport with a guy, maybe Chaudhary, you think.'

'Yes. Chaudhary. Should I call him? I've got his number.'

'Difficult.'

'Why?'

'He's dead.'

'Dead?'

'Knifed and robbed in an alleyway around six this morning. About the time you left the warehouse. Preliminary identification this afternoon just before you called me from the airport. Confirmed not long after.'

'Chaudhary isn't the alleyway type,' Ed said.

There was a hint of applause. The band was coming back. Piano, drums, bass. The pianist sat down and played a few chords. 'Thank you, thank you,' he said into his microphone, 'and now will you please put your hands together for the unforgettable…Miss Gloria Plum.'

'I already forgot her,' Merr said. 'The Dear Leader of progressive jazz. Let's drink up and get out of here.'

★★★★★

'It'll take a few days,' Merr said. They were walking down the dark *soy* toward Charoen Krung, the *soy* where Ed had walked with Diana five days before. The cluster of taxi-drivers was the same, they made the same offers, received the same refusal, and the same reflected halo mocked the head of Maria Theresa. But though the signs were the same, the situation had changed completely.

'What will you do exactly?' Ed asked him.

'Depends what Irina wants.'

Irina said nothing.

'A passport would be easiest,' Merr offered.

'US? With a Thai visa and an exit stamp from San Francisco?' Irina asked. 'Would they?'

'You gave us information. You're in danger. It's fairly routine.'

'How long?'

'Few days. A week maybe.'

'Or,' she said, 'can you fix so I fly out with no questions at the airport?'

'Shouldn't be a problem,' Merr agreed. 'Out where?'

183

'Singapore,' she said. 'Cheapest.'

'My budget,' Merr replied. 'Go where you like. States? Russia? Up to you.'

'Singapore,' she repeated. 'I know someone there. Maybe I come back here when this is blow over.'

'No problem.'

They reached the corner of Thanon Silom. 'Let's take a last drink,' Merr suggested. 'The roof of the State Tower has a good view. If you're in the mood for views.'

'I'd rather go back to the Princess,' Ed replied. 'And Irina's pretty weary too.'

'No,' Merr said. 'Your hotel. That's another thing we need to talk about.'

*****

Merr was right – from the roof garden of the State Tower, Bangkok spread itself shamelessly in front of them, a spectacular view of a hideous city. They sat down quickly, avoiding the enormous white sofas where yuppies sprawled in fashionable discomfort. There was plenty to talk about.

First Ed wanted to know about the kids? Were they gone? Or were they still in the warehouse? Merr wasn't sure. T-CAN had dragged its feet disastrously. On Saturday morning the office had been empty – everyone was off to Pattaya or someplace else with their cellphones switched off, though according to regs phones stayed on 24/7. It had been late afternoon before a team big enough to stake out Chatuchak had been in place. If Andronicus was on its toes, the warehouse would have been empty hours before. Had the kids been there during the fire check? Ed wanted to know. The firemen had seen only the building manager, or so they said. But then, the way they told it, they'd seen amazingly little, not even the booby-trap.

And Chaudhary? He'd been killed, but why? Not by some alley-thief for the sake of his gold tie-clip, though that was how it had been set up. Andronicus and Bhatnagar had no reason to love Chaudhary. From their point of view, he'd invited a blood-buyer, a buyer without even a business card, to visit the warehouse in Chatuchak. The next night there'd been a break-in, a girl had been shot, and Andronicus' operation in Bangkok had been compromised – perhaps fatally. Chaudhary must have been number one on Andronicus' hit-list. But who was number two? Almost certainly Ed.

And Irina? Was she on the hit-list too? It was possible. Ed had left the warehouse by taxi – the TV at the gatehouse, if it was working, must have picked up two figures on a motor-bike, one of them a girl, following him. Not long after that, the night patrol had caught a girl snooping in the switchyard and smashed her head in. If the guards had searched her bag, they'd know exactly who she was... Two *ifs* – but it was a plain possibility.

So, Merr concluded, Andronicus knew that Ed was staying at the Princess, and they might also know Irina's address. Given that, wouldn't it be best if Ed checked out of the hotel, and if Irina quit her apartment? As soon as possible? Ed saw the point, but where was safe, especially for Irina? Merr already had a place in mind. A hotel called Schomberg's – just up the street from the State Tower, no whores allowed and strictly anonymous. He sometimes booked people in there – dubious types, mostly without papers, like Irina. The night manager padded the bill and didn't ask questions. They could stay there till Merr sorted things out...

Day 7

Ed was sitting at the table he'd shared with Chaudhary. He stared emptily at Chaudhary's chair – it had been Dy's chair too. Not a lucky chair apparently. It was made of cast aluminium pieces, bolted together and painted dark green. It had sphinxes at the end of the armrests, the casting swamped in paint. His own chair was the same.

He was waiting for Irina. They'd taken separate taxis from Schomberg's that morning. She had to buy some things in Bang Khun Phrom, and he had to check out of the Princess. The check-out had gone quickly, and he'd retrieved his cash. $3,000 – Stepka had been given his up-front money. Ed felt the button-down pocket of his shirt – the fat envelope was safe. His bag was in the lobby, the name-tag removed. Ms Tarn would be back in a few days, he'd told reception – they should hold the room for her.

'Ah, Mizta'an,' the manager had said. 'Some visitor come for her yesterday evening.'

'Visitors?'

'United Nations. American Embassy. Police.'

'Police?'

'I tell them Mizta'an in Kuala Lumpur. Leave on Thursday.'

'Correct. What did they want to know?'

'If hotel receive message from her.'

'And did you?' he'd asked. 'Get a message?'

The manager had shaken his head with one of those smiles that Ed could now interpret – even if there had been 200 messages, the manager would say *No*. 'No,' he'd said. 'But there is message for you.' He'd given Ed a note from Vadim, handwritten on hotel paper. It lay on the table in front of him now, beside his Singha beer.

Saturday, 22:35. Hi Ed. Seem you are not here. I know tomorrow is Sunday, but we must talk. Can you be at Princess around 1? Lunch maybe. Is important. Vadim.

Ed glanced at his watch. 11:20. Irina should arrive soon. They'd planned to go back to Schomberg's together and lie low for the rest of the Sunday. On Monday Ed would raise a little hell at the UN – demand that they find Dy or else. Or else *what*, he wasn't quite sure. Merr would tell him what to say.

And now Vadim. What did the little rat want? *Is important.* Important enough to bring Vadim to the Princess late Saturday night. Too important to talk about on the phone apparently. *I know tomorrow is Sunday.* Sunday? However sacred Sunday might be at the UN, if Ed ought to know something, what was wrong with telling him on Sunday? The note made him uncomfortable – he didn't trust it.

He showed the note to Irina as soon as she arrived. She was dressed in jeans and a new grey t-shirt with *Property of Holloway Jail* printed on it in black. Her neck was wound in a muslin scarf embroidered with flowers.

'Huh,' she said after she'd read the two lines. 'So there is one place in Bangkok you cannot be at one o'clock.'

'The Princess? You think Vadim might arrive with an escort? Indian cavalry?'

She shrugged. 'In Russia we call it параной́я.'

'Paranoia. You think a dose might be useful? Right now?'

'Паранойя says: Never be there when they come for you.'

He looked at her quizzically.

'Don't forget Ed – I married a security man. His name wasn't Andrey. It was Паранойя.'

'Okay. Point taken. Let's get back to Schomberg's.'

'But perhaps it *is* important,' Irina said. 'What Vadim wants to tell you. Maybe it's something about Dy.'

'We'll never know,' Ed replied. 'We won't be here.' He checked the time. 11:45. 'You want a drink? We've got half an hour. And it's nice and cool here.'

A waiter, seeing Ed glance in his direction, approached their table.

'We must leave,' Irina said. And then a little louder than necessary: 'Your plane is at 4. Mine is at 6:30.'

They stood up. 'Leave a note for Vadim,' she whispered in the lobby. 'Say you meet him at Poor Man's at 1:30.'

Ed took the point – if they changed the venue and Vadim was up to anything dirty, for a few moments they'd have the initiative. Shrewd – she was uncomfortably shrewd, he was beginning to realise. She'd learned a lot from her *security man* husband.

★★★★★

Poor Man's was a scruffy, steaming street restaurant in the long *soy* between the Princess and the ESCAP building. Among the Europeans at the UN, it was said that you could eat at Poor Man's for fifty cents and never get the runs. Irina had lunched there once with Vadim when he'd been short of cash.

They approached the place cautiously. Their retreat was already covered – next to the huge boxing arena on the corner opposite ESCAP, a taxi was waiting for them, the meter running. Poor Man's, like most restaurants in the neighbourhood, had set up half its tables in the street. The others were inside, though the front of the building was simply an iron shutter – no windows, no walls. At one of the street tables, a Thai in dirty running shorts and a red sweat-shirt was eating with his face a few inches from his food, his chopsticks working like a windmill. Inside, sequestered in a world of their own, a Thai couple sat behind empty Coke bottles. In the cooking area, a draggle-haired woman was standing and staring into the street. A dim, speckled mirror hanging behind her woks and gas-rings reflected the tables and the street. Clever, Ed thought – while she's cooking, she can use the mirror to watch the customers. Apart from the cook and her three guests, Poor Man's was empty. No sign of Vadim.

'No one here,' Irina said. 'Sunday. No one working at the UN.'

'No different from the rest of the week then,' Ed quipped.

'You go inside,' Irina told him with a little frown – it wasn't the time for jokes. 'Sit with your back to the street and watch for Vadim. Use the mirror. I'll sit out here. I'll talk to him first. See what he says. See if anyone is with him.'

'If you sit outside, he'll recognise you and disappear.'

'No, he isn't,' she replied. She loosened her scarf – Indian muslin, long. She rearranged it to disguise the shape of her face without reducing her to purdah. Ed saw that the two O's on her t-shirt had been printed to circle her breasts.

HOLO$_Y^W$.

'Just order a Coke,' she told him, 'and wear this.' She gave him a baseball-cap she'd bought from a peddler outside the Princess. 'Wear it backward. Changes your shape. From behind.'

It was 1:20 already.

Ed put on the cap, sat down, and ordered a Coke. The

ponderous cook opened the bottle at the table and offered him a drinking straw. He waved it away – Dy had told him straws were recycled, usually in a bucket of water behind the counter. In the mirror he watched Irina sit down. The cook went out to her. Irina said something: *Wait for frenn*, it sounded like. Instead of going back to her kitchen, the cook picked up a witch's broom with tines like porcupine quills and began scratching at the sidewalk. It made a mirror-image – the broom, the cook's cheap flip-flops, and the broken concrete sidewalk – foxed, distorted, mysterious. For a while there were no passers-by, only a dirt-blasting *tk-tk*.

He saw Irina change position, her shoulders sagging, her head falling forward – she'd seen something, and she was hiding – hiding in the open street.

Vadim. A blurred image in the mirror, but definitely Vadim. He stopped on the other side of the street, studying Poor Man's. Ed waited. Irina had said she'd speak to him – but only if the street looked okay. She didn't move – something was wrong.

Vadim didn't recognise her. He crossed the street, stopping at the barrier of tables. He cleared his throat loudly. 'Doctor Scarman?' he called. 'Is that you?'

Ed kept still. In the mirror he saw Vadim glance at his watch, mutter something, and walk away toward the Princess.

A moment later, Irina stood up and headed off toward the boxing arena and the waiting taxi. She was escaping – but still she moved deliberately, masking her face with her scarf. Ed waited. Poor Man's had no back entrance. He could go out into the street and face whatever had frightened Irina, or he could sit in the restaurant and read the reflections in the mirror. Better sit.

Vadim again. Striding back now in the same direction as Irina. With him was a man – impossible to see who it was in the ruined mirror. An Indian? Ed craned round to face the street, but he was too slow. All he glimpsed was Vadim's back and the back of a man in dark clothes, stocky, with jet black hair. An Indian almost for sure. It was time to move. Ed stood up. The Thai woman moved instantly between him and the street.

'Fitty baht.' She held out her hand. 'Fitty.'

Ed fumbled in his pocket. Useless coins. He pulled his billfold out of his back pocket. Two tens. The rest was five-hundreds he'd got from the teller-machine that morning. He gave the woman a five-hundred. Still she barred his way, standing between two tables, fumbling now in her own pocket for the 450 change.

'For fuck's sake!' Ed cursed, trying to push past her. She was immovable. He dodged round the table trying now to push past the Thai couple. Their Coke bottles toppled to the concrete floor. One smashed, one rolled away. The girl began to jabber something in Thai. The cook headed him off again, waving money at him. Ed snatched the notes, stuffed them into his pocket, and pushed his way to the street.

Ahead of him, heading for the arena, he saw Vadim. Alone. Where was the Indian? The street wasn't crowded. No sign of Irina, no clue as to why she'd taken fright. Vadim glanced back over his shoulder. He saw Ed and stopped immediately. Ed had no choice but to catch up with him.

'So there you are!' Vadim said. 'I look for you. Everywhere.'

'I think I got the restaurant wrong,' Ed said. 'I saw you going down the street. Caught you up at last.'

'Poor Man's,' Vadim said.

'Yes.'

'How you know Poor Man's?' Vadim asked with a laugh. 'You broke?'

'Dy mentioned it,' Ed replied. 'She walks this way to work.' He glanced around. There were Indians now, several.

One was walking toward them. Another stared at them from the shade of a tree where he stood working his mouth with a toothpick.

'Not Irina?' Vadim asked

'Why Irina?' Ed replied.

Vadim smiled and shook his head slyly. 'No reason,' he said.

Ed shrugged.

'So you move out of Princess?'

'Terrible place,' Ed told him.

'Where are you now?'

'Which way you walking?' Ed asked evasively.

'I'm going to the office,' Vadim replied. 'Some stuff to do.'

They started walking.

'So what did you want to tell me? Is it about Dy? What the hell's going on, Vadim?'

'Yes, about Dy,' Vadim agreed with a show of reluctance. 'She's make contact. I know where she is.'

'Where?'

'She doesn't want for you to know. She give me message for you. Only message.'

'Which is?'

'Go now. Go home. You have no reason to stay.'

'You know where she is?'

'Yes.'

'And you won't tell me.'

'No. She say not to tell.'

'Let's see what Mr Patel thinks about that in the morning.'

'Mr Patel not here. He go to Kuala Lumpur. Pick up Dy's assignment.'

'When did he go?'

'This morning.'

'Do the police know Diana's been found?'

'That's why I was going to the office. To tell them. One reason.'

'So you saw Dy last night?'

'And again this morning. She wants you go home.'

They were near the boxing arena now. Irina would be in the taxi, waiting. Vadim was lying – Dy wanted Ed to find her. She'd left a sign – the golden lipstick. That was one lie Vadim had told. But did he really know where Dy was? Was that another lie? If he knew, he was in with the Indians – or whoever had taken Diana. If he didn't, he was playing a game of his own – but Ed had no idea what it might be.

'What do you think, Vadim? You think I ought to go?'

'Not my business,' Vadim said with a shrug.

'You're on Dy's side though? You wouldn't let anything bad happen to her? Would you?'

'Nothing bad will happen. Nothing very bad. Why bad thing happen? But her job. Her job. She messed up. The UN isn't easy, but she was doing okay. Then you come and... I don't know. After you come she mess up totally.'

'So again – what did she tell you? Exactly?'

'She wants you to go. And not to see her again, Ed. That's what she said. She will stay at UN till Patel kicks her out – which is few months, maybe less. Then she make new start. Here maybe, maybe in States. She don't know. She is... She is confuse.'

Ed spotted the taxi, waiting where they'd left it. He'd learned the number – 9938. Was Irina already in it, waiting? He couldn't see. 'So that's what Dy wants?' he said, trying to keep his disbelief out of his voice. 'I'd a feeling something like this was brewing.'

Vadim put his hand on Ed's shoulder. Ed shivered – the unclean touch of an unclean animal.

'I'm sorry,' Vadim said. 'You want to help her, so the best is you go home. She is not go back to work till you are gone.'

'Why not?'

'That's all she tell me. I don't know why.'

'And Patel? What will Patel do? When she goes back?'

'Patel wants… We have saying in Russian – he wants feed her to the crows. If she disappear, she make it easy for him. If she come back – tomorrow, day after – she make it not so easy.'

'Well, you know how the place works. It's good she's got you,' Ed said, stopping suddenly. 'And you're right. I've no reason to stay. I was stupid to come in the first place. I better check the flights home. Do it right away.'

'I think is good idea,' Vadim nodded and held out his hand. Ed took it, and they shook hands. Ed turned away, queasy with anger. He began to walk briskly back toward the Princess, away from Vadim, away from the taxi, away from Irina.

He kept walking till he reached the Princess. The sun was vicious. He turned his baseball-cap round the right way so the peak protected his eyes. In the tiny yard outside the hotel, two *tk-tk*s were waiting, both drivers asleep. He chose the first, clambering onto the bench, trying not to touch the sticky plastic covering with his hands. Under the shade of the plastic roof, it was even hotter than in the street. The driver woke up, cleared the filth from his throat, and spat onto the hot concrete.

'Thai Boxing. Fifty baht,' Ed offered, finding a fifty in the bundle of filthy paper the cook had given him.

The driver asked something in Thai. Incomprehensible. Ed pointed down the street, back toward the UN. The two-stroke motor spluttered then roared, the gears crashed, and the *tk-tk* clattered at full speed into the street. In two minutes they were at the arena. Number 9938 was gone.

*****

The *tk-tk*-driver had never heard of Schomberg's Hotel. It was on Silom Road, Ed told him: *Thanon Silom.* He tried to say it with a Thai accent, as Dy had said it on their way home from the Oriental. The driver threw up his hands and began to talk very quickly. Ed watched his face, trying to catch even a single word. The old man's skin was covered in eczema, his few remaining teeth were brown, and his eyes were yellow and bloodshot. Ed looked away. The *tk-tk* had pulled up outside the window of a tailor's shop. In the glass Ed saw himself, the *tk-tk* and the driver, trapped amid a mob of silk-clad dummies. He looked back at the face of the broken, exhausted driver, still angry and protesting. Nothing in Ed's life had prepared him for an argument with such a piece of wreckage. Just as nothing had prepared him for the disintegrating body of the girl Stepka had shot in the warehouse. Nor for the frozen remains of Number 3454 in the morgue. *This is no place; this place is but a butchery. Abhor it, fear it, do not enter it.*

Another *tk-tk* puttered into place beside them and cut its engine. Ed's driver turned in his seat and, without breaking the flow of his invective, directed it now at the newcomer.

'Thanon Silom,' the new driver explained to Ed. 'Not possible. Too far. Too far *tk-tk*.'

'200 baht,' Ed said. 'You go Silom Village. It's Sunday. Not much traffic.'

'Petchaburi one-way,' the new driver said.

Ed didn't get the point. 'Two-fifty then,' he ventured.

The new driver said something in Thai, perhaps an explanation of Ed's offer. Then he slammed his *tk-tk* into gear and drove off in a cloud of black smoke.

The negotiation was evidently a step further forward. Ed held out three 100-baht bills. The old man didn't take the money but grudgingly, with a shake of his head, started the *tk-tk* and roared off toward the Democracy Monument and the river.

The roads weren't busy. As the *tk-tk* buzzed along, the breeze was cool and somehow soothing. Ed sat back, thinking. What had Irina seen? Why hadn't she waited? What was Vadim playing at? Where was Diana? Above all, where was Diana?

He went over Vadim's story. Dy, so he said, had sent him to Ed with a message. Out of character – if Dy was free and wanted to say something to him, she'd say it herself. And in any case, Dy could have called – she had Irina's number. Dy didn't want to see him, or so Vadim said? That didn't tie up her lipstick message. Dy wanted him to leave Thailand immediately? That didn't make sense either. The Combat Zone lipstick again. Vadim was lying – there was no message from Dy. So why? What was he up to?

They passed an elephant. Small, female, led on a heavy chain by two men with iron prods. A barefoot boy trailed after them. The elephant's skin was discoloured, patchy and pinky-grey. The animal was padding painfully forward on the hot tarmac. Hungry and thirsty, Ed guessed. But the elephant's life was as remote from his world as everything else in this drab, dirty street.

Put it another way, whose nose would be out of joint if Ed *stayed*? Vadim's? Maybe Ed was crowding him out with Irina? Irina, it seemed, had no problem coping with Vadim's dirty little foibles, but in that she certainly wasn't alone. In general Vadim was happy enough with bargirls sitting on his fingers. More likely, Vadim was scared that Ed would ask questions at the UN, questions that might expose some racket or other? Maybe Vadim was mixed up in the Andronicus business? Or maybe Patel had told him to get rid of Ms Tarn's impossible hubby now, at once, immediately? Had Patel really gone to Kuala Lumpur? If he hadn't, then Vadim had told a stupid lie that would be exposed next day. If Vadim was in some way tied up with Bhatnagar and the Indians… Wheels within wheels. Speculations within speculations.

A familiar corner flashed by in a city where he'd found few landmarks – the bronze-shop near the Oriental. Maria Theresa. He'd be at Schomberg's in a minute or two.

*****

'Room 505.' He held out his hand for his key. Both keys to 505, he saw, were on the hook. They were old-fashioned keys attached to a bronze plaque the size of a Hershey bar. Merr had given them the choice – one room or two? They'd decided on one. Merr had agreed – there was safety in numbers.

'Fie-oh-fie,' the counter clerk repeated.

'No messages?'

The clerk shook her head: 'No message,' she said with an easy smile. 'Nothing for fie-oh-fie.'

Fie oh fie upon her. There's language in her eye, her cheek, her lip; nay, her foot speaks. Cressida. *Her foot speaks* – the epigraph of his thesis. *Fie oh fie.* It seemed a long time ago. And Pauline Bonaparte's foot – broken. That had spoken. At least to Irina. She'd understood. She had a remarkable way of seeing what he wanted her to see.

He took the elevator to the fifth floor. Where was Irina? She should have been back before him. The corridor was long. As he walked, he held the key and swung the Hershey bar on its ring. It made a little click each time it switched direction. He reached 505. With the key almost in the lock, he paused. He sensed that someone was already in the room, waiting for him. Who? Merr? Stepka? Bhatnagar? Dy? Not Dy surely. He pressed the doorbell. He heard a *ding-dong* inside the room.

'Service,' he said, mimicking a Thai accent. He listened at the door. Silence. Quickly he turned the key in the lock and pushed the door open. The room was empty. He went in without shutting the door behind him. The room was cold and dark – they'd left the air-con running. A footstep behind him. He spun round. If he had to fight… But it was Irina.

'I waited in the lobby,' she said. 'Till you came.' She was still veiled in the Indian shawl. 'I got my key and followed you up.'

'Scared there might be someone in the room?' he asked, turning on the light.

'Not really,' she said.

'Merr chose the place. Should be safe.'

'Yes,' she agreed closing the door. It was a complicated *yes*. She was leaving something unsaid. He stood, looking at her, trying to understand. Then he took her hand and pressed it quickly. She was right – if Merr had put them into that room, then Merr would get a transcript of every word they said. Why hadn't they thought of that before?

'So where do you think Vadim got to?' he asked pitching his voice a shade too loud, trying to show her that he was talking for the microphone. They hadn't said much in the room that morning, but they'd talked about Vadim. About meeting up with him. Whoever was listening in Merr's office would know where they'd been. Would Irina understand?

'Unusual for Vadim,' she said, understanding exactly. 'Usually if he make date, he keep it.'

'We ought to do something about lunch,' Ed suggested.

She shrugged. 'We can have something sent up?' She shook her head minutely as she spoke.

'Breakfast was horrible,' he protested. 'There's a Burger King up the street.'

'Try that. Why not?' she said. Then: 'Just going in here for moment.' She slipped into the bathroom and closed the door.

So where were the bugs, if that was the right word? The microphone? The camera? The infra-red? One?

Several? He went to the window and opened the heavy, puce curtains a foot or two. From the light-shaft outside, a feeble yellow glow filtered into the room. He stared at the window opposite. No point in searching the room – they couldn't debug the place. Better play innocent for as long as they could.

He heard the toilet flush. Irina came back into the room. She was feeling carefully in each pocket of her jeans, searching. 'I had a ring,' she said. 'I put it in a pocket somewhere. Now I can't find it.'

She had no ring, she wore no jewellery. What was she talking about? Searching. Searching her clothes.

'Let's go,' she said. They left the room and double-locked the door.

In a dead corner of the long corridor she stopped suddenly and turned to him, holding up her face to be kissed. He held her, surprised, and felt her arms around him. Angular, cold – not the arms of a lover. 'Check your clothes for bugs,' she whispered in his ear. 'In the toilet downstairs.'

As soon as they were outside the hotel and safely in the street, he felt her hand slip respectably into the crook of his arm. 'What did you see? Outside Poor Man's?' he asked.

They were walking away from the Burger King, down the shady side of the street toward the cluster of tourist shops that called themselves Silom Village.

'Stepka,' she said. 'With Vadim.'

'Stepka? My God! Did he see you?'

'He saw me, but he didn't recognise me.'

'And I didn't recognise Stepka,' he admitted. 'Was he the guy with the black hair? I thought that was an Indian.'

'Change your outline, change your identity,' she replied. 'This is semiotic – like what you teach.'

'Didn't teach it to the KGB,' he said, with a half-smile. Signs. All those years of theory, and Irina understood the signs better than he did. 'So Vadim?' he said. 'And Stepka? Together?'

'It makes sense,' she said. 'Stepka is in big trouble, leaving you like that in Chatuchak. He knows Dy is your wife. He knows where she works. He knows she's disappeared. And he knows you want her back. So he talks to Vadim.'

'I don't want her *back*. I want her *found*,' Ed replied.

Irina shrugged, not quite believing.

'So how did Stepka know Vadim in the first place?' Ed pursued.

'Bangkok's a small town.'

'Not counting Thais.'

She shrugged again. 'Maybe they know each other already. Or…'

'Or?'

'Perhaps Stepka look up Dy's department on UN website, and he find a Russian name.'

'Vadim…?'

'Rozhdestvensky.'

'Definitely Russian,' he agreed. 'But so what? What's Stepka after?'

'Stepka's in deep shit. He left you to die. It's important to him – are you safely dead…?'

'…or dangerously alive?'

'Exactly,' she agreed. 'So he talks to Vadim. Vadim says you are alive, but he is not sure. He goes to the Princess. You are not there. He leaves a note: *meet me tomorrow – it is important.*'

'And my note, changing the meeting place, for Vadim and Stepka it's a sign that I'm actually alive.'

'They don't know your handwriting. The note isn't enough. Stepka wants to be absolutely sure. Then he can figure what come next. Action Point Number One: Delete Ed.'

She seemed very sure of Stepka's mind. Was she…? Did she…? 'Did Stepka call *you*, Irina?' he asked abruptly. 'Did he ask you if I'd got back from the warehouse?'

'No.' Her quick anger flared against him. 'What is this question, Ed? If Stepka call…'

'You'd have told me,' he agreed. 'Of course you would.'

She pulled away from him and stopped, resting her back against a shop-window. Another tailor's. She was framed between two white polystyrene models wearing velvet tuxedos, one blue, one green. Ed stopped too, suddenly unsure.

'You are complicated man, Ed.' Her voice was serious. She was studying his face, her eyes penetrating, flickering.

He held out a hand to her and smiled. 'I'm a very confused man,' he said quietly.

She took his hand. 'If you say,' she replied, and they walked on in silence. They reached Silom Village. 'There's a place you can eat here,' she said. 'With a gong orchestra. Makes a terrible noise, but no one can hear us.'

'Hear us? Are we being followed?'

'Yes,' she said. 'By a Thai.'

'I thought we'd agreed not to count Thais,' he said.

She began to laugh. 'You,' she said. 'No one is like you. Not in the all world.' Laughter came hard to her, he saw, real laughter. Some women were prettier when they laughed. But Irina wasn't. Her filled teeth showed, and the wrinkles round her eyes were harsh and engrained. But yet…

Still hand in hand, they passed the expensive shops of Silom Village – jewellers, fine leather, Persian rugs. Shopkeepers offered them improbable discounts but without much enthusiasm – perhaps it was obvious that the tourist girl and her serious friend were not on a shopping spree.

They found the restaurant and sat down at a table half-hidden in rubber plants and philodendrons. The gong orchestra was playing sedately, though the unfamiliar sounds vibrated threateningly in Ed's ears.

'You like the gongs?' Irina asked. 'Not the sound of course. Nobody likes that. But maybe the reflections?'

'And Vadim?' Ed replied. 'What's he up to? Why does he want me to go home?'

Irina shrugged – she didn't know.

'Is he trying to get me out of the way so Stepka can't cut my throat? Seems improbable.'

'No, definitely not that. But Vadim is…Russian.'

'Meaning?'

'Maybe there are clean Russians in Bangkok, Ed. But I never meet them.'

'So what's his particular line?'

'He never told me,' she said ironically. 'Maybe no line. Maybe he is brave young diplomat fight his way to top of the UN. Clean as Snegurochka's brother.'

'As who?' He saw her smile – he'd fallen into her little trap, willingly enough.

'Snegurochka is Snow Maiden. Daughter of Spring and Frost.'

'She sounds cold.' He played along – truth was the child of many fathers.

'Snegurochka? She liked a shepherd boy and wanted to love him, but she had no heart.'

'Cold and heartless. What happened to her?'

'Her mother was sorry and made a heart for her. Then…'

'I can guess,' Ed broke in. 'Love made her warm, and she melted away.'

She nodded. 'Do you think it's true?' she asked. 'The story?'

'If stories weren't true,' he said, 'we wouldn't tell them.'

'And lies?' she objected. 'Lies are stories too.'

'Lies reflect the truth,' he replied. 'But they're like all reflections, you need both parts. You couldn't tell a lie unless you knew the truth. Or enough of the truth to create a dissonance...' He gave up – what the hell was he talking about?

'The truth about Vadim,' she back-tracked, 'is – sometimes he have money, a lot of money. And sometimes he have nothing. He have a line – for sure. And now Dy is disappear. This is problem for Vadim. There will be question. Many question.'

'Yes there will,' Ed agreed.

'And now you. You also are problem for Vadim. Maybe you go to UN and ask nasty question about Dy. Maybe Stepka find you, and...' She made the gesture of cutting her throat. 'For Vadim, if you are dead, that mean more and more question. Or – and for Vadim this is best – you disappear back to America.'

The gong orchestra ended its number. The musicians, all men, lay down their felt-covered drumsticks, and a waitress in Thai costume brought them tea in small china cups.

'There,' Ed said suddenly. 'That girl bending with the tea. The reflection. In that big gong. Perfect.'

She looked at the reflection. 'So many Snow Maidens,' she mused.

He nodded. The girl moved away, and the reflection lost its moment. He looked round the half-empty restaurant – tourists mostly with peeling noses and sweaty clothes. 'Is that the Thai guy who's following us?' he asked. 'Over there by that hideous carving?'

She followed his look. 'Yes,' she said.

'Working for Merr?'

'Who he work for?' she replied. 'Is something you never know. Not about anyone.'

★★★★★

Back in Schomberg's, Ed called Merr.

'You having us followed, old friend?' he asked.

'Shit,' Merr replied. 'You spotted him? How can I work with guys that even Ed Scarman can't miss?'

'No,' Ed told him. 'Irina spotted him.'

'Okay. That's different.'

'She knows her way around?' Ed asked.

'If you say so.'

'And the room?'

'Ed. You're getting paranoid.'

'That a yes or a no?'

'It's a yes.'

'Sound? Or pictures as well?'

'Guess.'

Ed sighed. 'You could have told me.'

'I did tell you. You weren't listening.'

'I never listen. It's the only way to keep your prejudices intact.'

'Poor old Ed. In the morning you'll wake up and find it was all a bad dream,' Merr said. 'And in the meantime, don't get any funny ideas. Just do what I tell you, and lie low.'

There was a silence.

'Anything on Diana?' Ed asked at last. 'From Hirsch's department maybe?'

'Five unidentified corpses last night. All Thai.'

'Chaudhary? Anything on him?'

'He was married. To a Thai woman. Seven children. And all he had to leave them was his gold tooth. And half a million in the bank.'

'Dollars?'

'Baht. All legit. Thousand baht a week for ten years.'

'What did Andronicus say? About him?'

'We called a guy – Bhatnagar. You mentioned him a couple of times – the one who was having a feud with Chaudhary.'

'What about him?'

'We got him on his cellphone. He said he was in Mumbai.'

'And where was he?'

'Sydney. According to IT.'

'What's he doing in Sydney?'

'The Aussies are moving him on. Permanently.'

'Moved on. Permanently.' Ed repeated for Irina's benefit. He glanced at her and smiled. She was lying on her bed, a wet hand-towel over her eyes, listening to Ed's end of the conversation.

'And he won't be coming back for Chaudhary's funeral?' Ed asked.

'Seriously doubt it.'

Another silence but not quite perfect. Ed sensed that Merr was not alone.

'And Irina?' Ed asked.

'We're moving her on too.'

Ed shivered. There was something cold in Merr's voice. What did it mean: *We're moving her on too*? Something new? Some murderous new fact they'd found out about her?

'When?'

'Tuesday. To Singapore,' Merr replied. 'Tell her.'

'They're flying you out on Tuesday,' Ed told Irina. 'To Singapore.'

'Good,' she said.

'And tomorrow?' Ed pursued. 'What's the plan?'

'Hang on a second, Ed.' Then distant and muffled: 'Pick up on the other line Joe. It's Ed.'

A pause. A click. Then: 'Okay Ed, about tomorrow. Tomorrow you go to the UN. You know where it is.'

'Sure. I walked there with Dy. One time.'

'Take your passport. Ask at security to see a Japanese guy. Got a pencil?'

There was a pencil and a notepad on the bedside table.

'Go ahead.'

'Ken-ichi Matsu-ura,' Merr spelled the name. 'He's deputy Big Cheese. You're seeing him at two. Don't be late.'

'Not Patel?'

'Patel's in KL.'

'You know that? For a fact?'

'Last sighted in KL to be exact. And this Jap guy you're talking to – he hates Patel even more that you do. Soul brothers.'

'Mr Matsu-ura.'

'Exactly. Courtesy of the consular section.'

'Good.'

'Raise hell, Ed.'

'Will do.'

'Anything else?' Merr asked.

'You got anything on that Ukrainian? Stepka? You said leave him to stew for a day or two.'

He saw Irina sit up quickly. The towel fell off her face. She caught it and threw it into a corner, listening.

'The guy you didn't quite meet at the Thai Boxing this afternoon?'

'You know about that?'

'Sure. Yes. We already moved him on. Around five o'clock. Also permanently.'

'No need to worry about him then.'

'That it?' Merr asked.

'Sure.'

The phone went dead. Ed hit the red button and silently put the phone on the desk beside the unfamiliar Japanese name.

So Stepka had reached that *country from whose bourn no traveller returns*. Ed looked at his watch. Two hours ago. And Irina? Irina was scheduled to go the same way on Tuesday. Merr couldn't have made it plainer. He'd tipped Ed off that someone else was in the room, someone called Joe. Ed remembered the name – Merr's boss. Then came the news that Irina was also being *moved on*. That was T-CAN's plan then – to remove Irina from the scene with the minimum of fuss.

'What did he say?' Irina asked. 'About Stepka?'

'They moved him on. He won't be coming back.'

She thought for a second then nodded, translating the Merr-speak. 'Stepka got what he ask for,' she said. 'So Merr is your friend. Really.'

'Yes.'

'Really,' she repeated. 'No reflections. Really.'

She was sitting on her bed, looking up at him. The fringe of hair on her forehead was wet from the towel. There wasn't anything pretty about her at that moment. Nothing at all. But somehow it didn't matter. All he wanted was that she should be safe. Out of Bangkok, safe.

Merr had confirmed – Schomberg's Hotel was wired for sound and pictures. *I did tell you. You weren't listening.* Obviously Merr wouldn't watch the room himself – he had plenty of people to do that for him. Well, let them listen, let them watch. And Merr's deadly warning – take care of Irina, or *she* won't be coming back either.

Ed had to talk to Irina. To get her safe out of Bangkok, they'd have to come up with a hell of a plan. She had Monday to escape – that was Merr's gift. Talk to her? But how? If they left the room again, they'd obviously be ducking the mikes and the cameras.

'Irina,' he said. 'I feel like a shower.'

'Take one then.'

'No,' he said, putting a wink into his voice. 'I mean a *real* shower.'

She looked at him in surprise, not refusing but not enthusiastic either. He held her look and made a tiny nod. She got the point – they had to talk.

'I hate clothes anyway,' she said, a shade too loud. 'It is happy hour. At last.'

In the next half hour, whoever was updating the files in Merr's section would have been sure – this couple might be plotting something or they might not, but they certainly knew how to overload a microphone. Lithe and soapy under the full blast of the shower, he and Irina screeched and played. But they took it in turns – while one was raucous, the other breathed secrets.

Yes, there was a way out, Irina told him in fragmentary whispers. Through Burma. You went to the Three Pagodas Pass. By taxi. There were Karen villages on the Thai side of the border. The highways out of Thailand had customs posts and emigration checks. No way through. Not even for ready money. But there were tracks through the jungle. Many. Mostly they were mined, but the Karen knew which ones were open. Once you were in Burma, it was easy to buy a visa. No one was ever sent back to Thailand. Then Yangon and a flight on to…wherever. Most of the flights out of Burma went through Bangkok. But there were others. She'd find something. All she needed was money and a clean get-away from Thailand.

Money? He still had 3,000 of the 4,000 he'd taken out of the bank. Money was no problem. But transport? Communication? Losing their tail in the morning? They had problems enough.

They threw a plan together. It was the best they could do. Finally Ed turned off the shower and the thundering accompaniment of the sink, the bathtub and the television. Irina clung to him for a moment or two, panting, pretending to recover. She faked it perfectly. Flauntingly naked. Disturbingly sexless. Cold as the Snow Maiden before her heart transplant. Two heavy brown bathrobes hung behind the bathroom door. Ed unhooked one and offered it to Irina. She didn't take it. Instead she pulled one of the bath-towels from its rail and began to dry herself, still on camera, still calculating her effects, but now without the whispers.

He put the robe back on its hook. Suddenly he heard her laugh. He'd been faking too, though not as expertly as Irina. And now he wasn't pretending anymore.

'Whatever is that, Doctor Scarman?' she asked.

He turned back to face her. 'That's how it goes with me,' he said with a helpless shrug.

She dropped her towel and held out her arms to him. 'Very unfortunate,' she said. 'Perhaps we do something about it?'

★★★★★

He'd been gentle with her under the modest sheet, careful not to hurt her head or put his weight on her painful ribs. Now she was resting, lying back with her head on his arm.

At some time in her past, Irina must have worked as prostitute – hungry, submissive, frigid but pretending always a devouring eagerness. The women who posed for him, that was how most of them lived their denuded, Potemkin lives. The *demi-mondaines,* as the great world used to call them. Half-worlders. He got their phone numbers off the web – dozens of sites listed *artist's models*. Not so many round DC, but enough. He called, and the women came to his studio. Alone. A quick conversation about cash, a glance round the studio to see who was on the menu today. Was it just one, or a whole gang? And that was it. They were ready. Mostly he photographed them, trying to glean reflections from unlikely surfaces. Photography they more or less understood. But he sketched them too, painted them sometimes, and somehow that shocked them. Hours on end in the same pose. No fingering, no *frisson,* nothing to fake. What kind of pervert paid a girl good money to sit still all day? It was a real question. For them anyway. And the strange little baby in the studio, gurgling, staring, disappearing sometimes with the nursemaid for an airing or a meal. Terry aroused a hint of curiosity but no compassion. *Yours?* one of the girls asked now and then. *Yes, mine.* And that was it.

The depressing sameness of the girls had been thrown into relief only once – by Raissa Petrovna. Raissa had been different. For one thing, she'd steered away from hardcore. She never immolated her body for the porn factories or the weekend shutter addicts. She was exactly as labelled – an *artist's model.* The only one. She liked being painted. She understood reflections. Of course she'd been too good to last. Now she was a bit-actress in soaps and mini-series. Unless she'd dropped out. Or made a breakthrough. He didn't know. They hardly mailed each other, and he seldom watched TV. *The telly* as Dy called it.

When the day's work was over, after Terry had been bathed and told her bedtime story, the models occasionally stayed for a chat and a few drinks. At the slightest hint they were ready to work a little overtime – doing what they thought they'd be doing anyway. It didn't happen often. On the whole they were better at whoring than they were at modelling. Warm-bodied, cold-hearted, submissive. Still, as his mother so charitably said when he gave up Harvard and switched to painting, *Do what you're best at, and you'll be happy.*

And Irina Sergeyevna, lying now beside him, breathing so peacefully? She'd been part of a half-world too. Where? When? For how long? Not that it mattered, but he was curious.

Irina. Her half-world had been Russian. He tried to piece together what she'd told him with what he'd heard from Raissa and with what he'd picked up over the years. Irina had been seventen when she'd gone to Moscow. The old Soviet Union had been two years dead. Gorbachev and Yeltsin were fighting things out. Prices were decontrolled, rents unpayable. Nobody had work. Irina – a runaway kid – no family, nowhere to live, and signed up for art classes at one of the institutes. But she'd survived. Escaped. Found a husband. Of sorts. Moved to Thailand. She'd kicked out the weight-lifter and kept her head above water with her drawing. She was smart, not just streetwise. Generally she understood what he said before he'd finished saying it. More – she understood things he didn't say because he didn't know how to say them. He'd known her only a few days, but at that moment she was closer to him than anyone had ever been – anyone except Diana.

Irina stirred, her eyes still closed, a sudden frown shadowing her face. The mikes were on, the cameras were running, recording the half-darkness and the silence. The white sheet still covered them, shielding their nakedness from the chill of the air-con and from the prying lens. Her pioneer-red scarf, unknotted, lay beside her head on the pillow. The bed was narrow. But no. Like Cressida of Troy, *Her bed is India; there she lies, a pearl.* He stretched out an arm and flicked on the bedside light.

A pearl? In a way, yes. As he watched, he saw a tear bead up in the corner of her eye and trickle across her cheek. *Full fathom five thy lover lies. Those are pearls that were her eyes.* Then more tears. Silent, without sobbing, without grief. Tears. They perplexed him as much as they perplexed Tennyson – *Tears from the depth of some divine despair... I know not what they mean.*

'Why are you crying?' he asked softly.

'I'm sorry,' she said at last, talking to the ceiling.

'What for?'

'For...' She hesitated. 'For you. For everything.'

'No reason,' he said flatly. The mikes were on. He found the TV-surfer on the bedside table and flicked through the channels. He found a channel playing Dave Brubeck. Radio. Sound only. He turned off the light again and turned up the music. He snuggled beside her, so they could whisper with at least the illusion of being unheard.

'You don't mind?' she asked hesitantly. 'I think you saw... I think you understand...'

'It's not important. Any of it.' The words sounded cold. 'Really,' he added, not sure what his words might imply to her, or what he wanted them to imply.

'*It's not important. Any of it,*' she repeated. He caught her mimicry.

'I don't mean it isn't important. Of course it's important. What I mean is...'

She said nothing.

'Listen,' he whispered. 'I saw. Of course I saw. A perfect show. But it's hard for me to imagine... I've no real idea...'

'No,' she agreed.

'But now?' he struggled on. 'Irina, you're someone so unusual.' The wrong word. 'So *rare*. I hardly know you, but...' But what? 'Whatever happened in the past, nothing can be changed. And why should it? You... You...' It was a struggle. It would be so easy, and so unfair, to imply more than he meant.

'That is what you think? Really?'

What did she mean? What did she think he meant?

She held him suddenly closer, kissing his mouth. There was something girlish about her now, tentative. She was a million miles from the fearless little whore who'd been thrashing and squealing under the shower.

'I think you know,' she said. 'My... With me...' She too was struggling to find words. He didn't interrupt. 'Dy and me,' she said at last. 'We're completely different – in our past. I think so anyway.'

'Yes,' he agreed, unsure why Dy was suddenly between them in the bed. 'That's why I was surprised you two were friends, you're so different.' It helped – it steered them away from more dangerous ground.

Irina thought about it for a moment. Then: 'Dy looks for adventures. Always something new. Something different.'

'Yes, that's how she's always been.'

'When she was kid?'

'When she was eighteen she worked at a place called Fetters. In London.'

'What work?'

'Waitressing. Nude.'

'Let me guess,' Irina said derisively. 'Eight in the evening till two in the morning. No dates with customers. No fucking with chuckers-out. Just a feel from the barman when she wanted a drink.'

'Not exactly. He didn't like girls. They took her drinks out of her wages. At the end of the week.'

Irina began to laugh. 'That's your world,' she said. 'Wages! Did she pay income tax.'

'Of course. She worked there nearly four months. The whole summer.'

'And what she do with her *wages*?'

'Saved up for a motor-bike.'

'Ed.' She began to laugh again – deep, almost painful laughter.

'It's true!' he protested.

'That's why it's funny. Or maybe not funny.' Her laughter subsided. 'Did she like it? Taking her clothes off? Or you don't know?'

'Far as I know, she was having fun. Like you said, an adventure.'

'Did she buy the motor-bike?'

'Yes. A Harley. Second-hand.'

'How much it cost?'

'I don't know.'

'Because you are American,' she said. 'If you are Russian, you know.'

'Maybe,' he agreed.

She fell into silent thought – but not about motor-bikes he guessed. At last she whispered: 'One day I tell you how it was with me.'

'Only if it helps,' he whispered back.

'It help. Some things I never told.'

'From the time before you went to Moscow?'

'Yes. How you know?'

'You told me they hit you. Your step-brothers.'

'Yes, them. And because they hit me, you think…? You think they…?'

'I thought it was possible.'

'It's true. But I tell no one. Never. Not Andrey. Not any one.' She became suddenly alert, wondering, Ed guessed, where else his thoughts might have carried him. 'But not my father,' she said. 'He just hit me. When he was drunk. Hard. Very hard. He was lousy father. But also he was okay.'

Ed said nothing. Her life had been excruciatingly far from the world of his doting mother in DC. And far from the places where Dy had looked for her adventures, naked, clothed and all stations in between.

'My father, he found me with Ilyushka,' Irina whispered. 'Ilyushka made me… They both made me… You know?'

'I think so.'

'And with their friends. They got money. From their friends. They hit me if I say no. Or if I do it wrong.' She stopped, remembering.

He said nothing.

'So my father. I was with Ilyushka and this friend of Ilyushka. Both. He kick out the friend and half-murder Ilyushka. Ambulance came and take Ilyushka to hospital. Then I run away.'

'To Moscow.'

'To Moscow,' she repeated. 'Where I have no father. And no one kick out anyone. Ever.'

He kissed her forehead. He kissed her eyes. And then her lips.

'Ed,' she whispered. 'Tonight…' The word was so quiet he could hardly hear it, yet somehow, after the harsh words she'd found for her childhood, it sounded like a blessing.

She'd told him things she'd never told anyone else. Her life had been beyond anything he could fully imagine. But he'd held her and loved her, and somehow he'd treasured her. And she'd treasured him. Not admired him, not envied him, not submitted to him – all those things he half-understood. But to be valued, to be treasured. Perhaps, for now, the way she'd said *Tonight* was as close as he could get to the truth about his own emptiness and his own longings.

For a moment her life had entered his. Nothing like that had happened to him before – except with Dy. But that was finished. Long for her as he might, his Diana had died. Four years ago. In childbirth.

Day 8

Monday 2nd November 2009

Ed got up at six and began to wash his dirty underclothes. Hanging over the wash-basin, he slipped the envelope with the $3,000 into Irina's wash-kit. After she'd showered, she'd hide the money inside her shirt. Then they'd eat breakfast. That was the plan.

Irina took nothing down to breakfast but a small shoulder-bag and the clothes she stood up in, jeans and a checked shirt. As they ate, they talked about Irina's flight on Tuesday to Singapore and about what Ed should say at his meeting with Matsuura. They agreed that Merr would call that afternoon to find out what had happened at the UN – and that when he did, they could ask him how long Irina would stay in Singapore and exactly where. It was a bloodless conversation with not a word out of place, no matter who was listening. When they'd finished eating, they lingered for ten minutes over coffee and *The Nation*. There should be no urgency, no hurry, nothing to suggest that they were working to a plan. Then Irina beckoned to the waiter.

He came to their table with a quick smile and stood slightly stooped so that Irina wouldn't have to raise her voice – the gentle, outdated courtesy that Ed now realised was also a part of the Thai way. Beauty and ugliness, he saw, rubbed shoulders in Thailand. Of course, that was true everywhere. The difference in Thailand was that the ugliness and the beauty came in such unexpected and unmanageable shapes.

'Is there a bookshop?' Irina asked the waiter. 'With guidebooks? Singapore, for example.'

'Soy Ni'teen,' the waiter replied. 'Other side road.' He pointed out of the breakfast-room window and down the street.

'Thank you,' Irina said. Then: 'You want to come, Ed?'

'No,' he grunted. 'I'll finish the paper. After that I need to check flights home – think I'd better go out to the airport.'

'There is many little agencies around,' she suggested helpfully. 'You can try one of them?'

'I said, I think I'll go out to the airport. Something wrong with your hearing this morning.' He put a rough edge on his voice. Last night they'd been lovers, now he needed some space – that was the message for the secret listener.

'Pfff,' she said. 'Please yourself.'

'I shall.'

She got up. 'See you when you get back then,' she said over her shoulder.

'Sure.' He didn't watch her go, scanning the newspaper instead. The words blurred. She was gone. Would the plan work? Would he ever see her again?

He gave her fifteen minutes lead, as they'd agreed. Then he went up to their room, cleaned his teeth and turned off the air-con. He opened the room-safe – 3454. *Choose any four-figure number.* The number had made him shiver when he'd first keyed it in – it made him shiver again now. He took his billfold and his open air-ticket out of the safe and locked it again. Not much left in there beside Irina's clunky laptop and some papers she'd brought from her apartment. He looked at the bed where they'd spent the night in a room full of microphones and dead poets. He decided to leave her a note:

I'll be back from the airport by 12. UN meeting at 2. Let's
do lunch.
PS If you're not doing anything tonight, maybe…

He left the note on the desk in front of the TV. Then he
remembered the little packet of colours he always kept
handy in the zip-front of his case. Pastels. He found them
and drew a childish heart in red on the note. Don't overdo
it, Scar, he said to himself. Merr isn't stupid. That business
about the guidebook was already over the top. *Obvious stuff
is always fake* – that was Merr's rule. Ed left the pastels beside
the note.

Then, in a few seconds he was out of the room, down
the backstairs and into the lobby. He went straight to the
concierge: 'Limo to the airport,' he ordered. 'Now.'

A moment later he was riding in the back seat of the
big grey BMW, swinging out into the traffic of Silom Road.
The road was divided by a railing that ran along a narrow
central island. At the first break in the island, he told the
driver to make a U-turn, go toward Pat Pong.

'Load not go airport, missah,' the driver replied. 'Not
possible.'

'Please turn. Now.' Nothing must go wrong. One slip-
up and everything was lost. Irina, they'd agreed, would
wait for the limo on the corner of Silom Road where the
Skytrain swung off toward Chong Nonsi and the Kingdom
Tower.

The car manoeuvred through the traffic and made the
U-turn. Ed peered out of the back window. The tinted glass
made it hard to see. No one else made the turn. No other
car anyway. With motor-bikes it was impossible to tell.

'Where you go?' the driver asked.

'Pick up frenn,' Ed told him. 'Chong Nonsi. You know?'

Ed caught the driver's eyes in the mirror scrutinizing
him. 'Chong Nonsi?' the man repeated shaking his head.

Ed was flustered. Chong Nonsi was the name of the station between Silom Road and the Kingdom Tower. Or maybe he'd remembered it wrong. Surely not! They were nearing the turning. Where was Irina?

He saw her. Or someone like her. Not in her shirt and jeans but in a print dress, a sunhat, and big sunglasses. She was near the corner. He'd pick her up at the crossing. 'Slow down,' Ed told the driver.

They drew level with the woman Ed had thought was Irina. For a second he wasn't sure. But then he saw something in her profile, in the curve of her shoulders... It was her. 'This woman,' Ed said. 'Stop.'

Irina was at the door. Then she was beside him, slamming the door closed behind her.

'Sorry about the dress,' she said casually. 'No time to choose properly. You like my hat?' She pulled the brim down to hide her forehead. Ed saw the point – the driver had already craned round, trying to see who she was. He was peeping in his mirror now, chafing with curiosity.

'Now airport,' Ed told the driver. 'You go Arrivals.'

He felt Irina take his hand. He felt the pressure of her fingers and returned it. Then he felt her urging him away. He took the point – if she moved away too, the middle seat would be free, and they'd be out of the view of the driving mirror.

The car made another U-turn, back down Silom Road, past Schomberg's, past Silom Village. The great ramp swept them up onto the Expressway. The driver stopped at the barrier and paid the toll. Ed felt Irina looking at him and turned to smile at her. With a gesture of helplessness, she collapsed toward him, resting her head in his lap. Her hat fell onto the thick grey carpet.

'He'll think you're...' Ed whispered.

'He can't see nothing,' she whispered back. 'And that's what girls do in taxis. Very natural.'

He covered her head with his hand, avoiding the still painful bruise. He caressed her hair with his fingertips, surprised at its softness. At the airport, they'd go their separate ways. She'd find an old taxi for the first part of her journey to the Three Pagodas Pass – no meter and no radio. Where her journey would end, where and whether they'd see each other again, Ed had no way of knowing. She had his address in Washington, though she'd never get a visa – not if Merr's buddies had a grudge against her. It might be better for her if she never even applied – no point telling them where she was in this wide world.

'You think this limo is bugged?' she asked quietly.

'Hope not.' If he was wrong, their plan was blown already. He imagined the control-room at T-CAN. A script began to run in his overcharged mind. Cast? Merr and three kids – one black, one dust-head in a bandanna, and a blonde angel with ugly glasses.

We got him chief. And the bitch is with him. That was the dust-head. Ed glanced out of the window for a landmark. *They're at kilometre seven. Heading for the airport.*

Ed glanced at the sat-nav. *ETA oh-nine-twenty-three.* The girl this time – tough kid, role-model for aspiring kick-box champions, but so pretty without her glasses.

Chief, you want a SWAT team? Ready at the airport? That was the black guy thinking ahead. Fair enough – after all, he was the brains of the outfit.

Then Merr's word of command: *Turn that thing off. It's no business of ours where they're going.*

But Merr wasn't going to say that. Or anything like it. He had his own life to take care of. With luck, of course, no one knew where they were, no one knew where they were going, and no one was listening to their idle conversation, not even the limo-driver.

They reached the airport at 9:23. Ed told the driver to pick him up in an hour at exactly the same place.

As soon as they'd left the limo, they split up. They'd each go to a different shop and buy a cellphone. And a prepaid card. Irina had left her old phone at Schomberg's. Ed would need it – Merr had the number and so did Diana. Once they'd bought the new phones, they'd have to meet up again for a few seconds to exchange the numbers. Meet at Givenchy, they'd decided. After that Irina would be on her own.

Buying the phone, buying the SIM card, topping up the card with cash, it all went quicker than Ed had expected. They didn't ask to see his passport, so probably they wouldn't want to see Irina's – with its lapsed visa, not that shops cared about visas. On a slip of paper he noted his new number for Irina. Then he wandered slowly back to the perfume store, keeping an eye open for her. He hovered at a newsstand near the perfume outlet. A girl was working now on the Te Amo stand. But Giv was still there at Givenchy. He was arranging a display, stepping back every minute or so to examine the effect, his head cocked flirtatiously to the side, though he had no one to flirt with. Where was Irina?

He saw her at last, a few yards from Givenchy. Giv had seen her too. And remembered her. Ed saw Giv greet her with an elegant *wai*. But there was more. Giv wanted to talk to her. And Irina wanted to listen. He saw Giv take a piece of paper from his pocket. It looked like a paper towel. Irina was reading so there must be writing on it. She took the towel. Then she asked Giv a question, apparently a serious one. Giv examined her professionally from several angles and then chose something for her from his shelves. They discussed it at length. Giv led her to the checkout, and she paid. For certain the paper had something to do with Dy. Ed moved in.

Irina spotted him, walked a few steps toward him, then turned abruptly away. He was to follow her. She went through an Irish bar and into an arcade of slot machines and one-arm bandits. The arcade was L-shaped. She went to the far end and stopped. There was CCTV, but the camera seemed to point at the entrance-way. As good a place to talk as any.

He gave her the slip of paper with his telephone number. She had a slip for him too.

'What did Giv want?' he asked.

'Very strange,' she said. 'The supervisor of cleaners give him a note she find in one of the toilets. Written in gold lipstick.' She opened her handbag and took out Giv's sheet of paper. She unfolded it and passed it to Ed. On one side he read:

Please give this to the handsome boy at Givenchy. Very important.

On the other side:

Mr Givenchy, Please give this to Ed Scarman or Irina Porzova.
Ed. It isn't P. Or M. I have gone with Ch. But I'm scared. Very. Pls pls pls stay till you know I'm okay.

'I'll sort it,' Ed said to Irina. 'You go now.' It was impossible to part without kissing her. 'Good luck.' For a moment she clung to him, with an intensity beyond tears.

'Get to Vancouver,' he said. 'Call me from there.'

'Vancouver?' she repeated.

'Or anywhere. Just tell me where you are, and I'll get there, Irina. I promise.'

*****

So Dy *had* met up with Chaudhary at the airport. Perhaps by design, perhaps not. After a few minutes talk, she'd decided to go with Chaudhary and ditch her assignment in Kuala

Lumpur. But how had Chaudhary persuaded her? With a threat or a promise? *I have gone with Ch.* It could only be Chaudhary. But how did she know his name? Had she seen him at the hotel? Or maybe he'd introduced himself. With his *professional card*, no doubt. *It isn't P.* She'd tried to ease his mind about Patel. *Or M.* Or Merr. Then she'd panicked. The golden writing became smeary, rushed – the lipstick tore into the soft paper. She was going off with Chaudhary, but she was scared stiff. That had been Thursday evening. Chaudhary had been killed on Saturday morning. Had he handed her over? To Andronicus? Or to some other gang? Was that why he'd been killed? Because of Diana?

The limo was speeding back along the Expressway. The driver wanted to chat. 'Nice lady,' he said. 'She Thai? Or *falang*?' With her dark hair and skinny figure, Irina might have looked Thai. Specially with the hat and the sunglasses.

'Thai,' Ed told him.

'What her name?'

'Miao. Like cat,' Ed said.

'Where you meet her? Pa'Pong?'

'Soy Cowboy,' Ed grunted, hoping to end the conversation.

'She not Thai,' the driver said, with a sudden burst of laughter. 'She *falang*.'

That's what taxi-drivers do, Ed thought. Exactly the same as waiters. They read the signs. You can't trick them. A taxi-driver's life depends on who's sitting in the back of his cab – of course he reads the signs. Better than you can, Ed Scarman, he told himself. And this business of taking Irina to the airport, who do you think you're deceiving? If Merr wants her to get away, she'll get away. If not… That was her only chance, that Merr wanted her to get away. And after? If she got to Vancouver or wherever? He'd go to her. And then he didn't know. It wasn't that he didn't care. He simply didn't know.

He was back in Schomberg's at eleven-thirty. Another hour and he'd have to set off for the UN. In the Business Center, he rented a terminal for an hour and googled Kenichi Matsuura. It was a common name apparently, but he found his man. Not a particularly interesting man, apparently. Official of the Japanese Foreign Ministry. Seconded to the UN. Doctorate in Politics at Northwestern. Dissertation on the diplomatic significance of cultural exchanges. When? 1975. 127,000 hits. The same scraps of information over and over again on countless websites. In Roman, in Cyrillic, and in what Ed thought must be Kanji. He gave up the trawl and googled *Diana Tarn*. There she was. Lambfields. And ESCAP – Economic and Social Commission for Asia and the Pacific. And, with a remarkable instinct for reflections, Wordsworth had given Loughrigg Tarn a new name – *Diana's looking glass*. He tried *Diana Scarman*. One hit. Back in the eighteenth century. Birth date but no death date. Evidently an immortal.

*****

For someone who'd taken a doctorate at Northwestern, Mr Matsuura spoke extraordinarily bad English. Not much better than the limo-driver. But he seemed to understand every word Ed said to him, which was a start.

'What I'd like you to explain is this,' Ed said slowly and – he heard it in his own voice – threateningly. 'The United Nations knew on Friday morning at eleven o'clock that my wife had disappeared. Yet you failed to take any action whatsoever until ten o'clock that evening. That's eleven hours. And I'd like to know why.'

'I can assure you Mr Scarman, that the United Nations does everything in its power to ensure the health, safety and welfare of its employees and consultants.' A complete sentence! A complete all-purpose, learned-by-heart sentence.

'That's not good enough,' Ed retorted. 'Eleven hours. A missing consultant. Eleven hours! I want to know why.' He folded his arms and tried to look grim and unmovable.

Diana had told him everyone was kicked out of the UN at sixty. Matsuura looked older – eighty perhaps. He was bony, and his cheeks had fallen in. His scant hair was a characterless grey. Apart from the name-plate on his desk, nothing in his office hinted at who Mr Matsuura was or who he might once have been. There were no photographs, no congratulatory souvenirs or trophies, no books even, except manuals in uniform UN bindings with excruciating titles such as *Exporting and the Export Contract*. Not a single sign, unless absence of signs was a sign in itself. The man was a bureaucrat – characterless as a mathematical function.

'Not possible tell you why, Mr Scamman.'

'Did your report to the American Consulate on her disappearance contain the words *given to erratic behaviour*?'

Matsuura looked at him with sudden shrewdness. 'Who tell you this?' he asked.

'I asked you a question, Mr Matsuura. Were those words in the report?'

'I not am sure. I not saw the report.'

'Who wrote the report?'

'The United Nations is not at liberty to divulge its sources or the authorship of its publications.' Another handy sentence.

Ed's temper began to rise. 'This wasn't a fucking publication. It was a report. To the consulate. A report that said my wife had been missing for eleven hours.'

'I'm sorry,' Matsuura said. 'I did not understand. Please repeat.'

Watch your language, Scar, he told himself. The old man's not a fool. What cards were left to play? Only one.

'My wife was working in Mr Patel's department. Can I assume that the report originated from Mr Patel? Either in person or through a deputy?'

Ed saw the old man's eyes light up. 'Mr Patel,' he agreed. 'What do you know about Mr Patel?' Another complete sentence. An original one this time and spoken with something like Northwestern fluency.

'Only what my wife told me.'

The Japanese raised an eyebrow, inviting more detail.

'It seems,' Ed began, 'that Mr Patel ran one of the most efficient and productive departments in ESCAP. She was very happy working with such colleagues. But you see, that makes the eleven-hour delay and the remark about her erratic behaviour all the more difficult to explain. At least to me. As a complete outsider.'

He was doing better. The old man's grey face began to sharpen. 'Was Mr Patel's name mentioned at the consulate?' he asked.

'Most certainly. And with the greatest respect.' He was about to add *with almost as much respect as your own name* but decided against it.

The old man nodded, not believing a word. But even so a smile hovered round his tired eyes. Perhaps he was already sniffing out a scheme to shaft Patel, to besmirch his good name with the almighty Americans. 'In what connection was Mr Patel mentioned at the consulate? If I may ask?'

'As my wife's immediate superior. And as a man who would be extremely concerned for her *health, safety and welfare.*'

'As we all are, Mr Scarman. Everyone in this building.'

'I am reassured to hear it.'

'I shall now call Mr Patel's department. I shall ask whoever drafted the report to bring it here. So that we may study the offending language. Together.'

Ed watched as the old man found a phone number in a

scruffy, printed directory and touched five keys. There was a long pause – nobody was picking up.

Patel. *It isn't P.* That's what Diana had written in her golden note. *It isn't P.* Was that really what she thought? Did she know it for sure? Or was it Dy's way of saying, *I don't want you making waves at the UN?*

A voice buzzed in the telephone. 'I want to speak to Mr Patel,' the old man said. 'He's in Kuala Lumpur? Until when…? Then give me his deputy… To whom exactly am I speaking…? Listen then Mr Rozhdestvensky. Someone sent a report on Friday to the American Consulate. About a missing consultant… Please bring it to my office now. In person.'

Ed sensed strings being knotted into position, snares to enmesh a victim. It was a fancy display of UN diplomacy. *The offending language.* The old fox knew *his* way around. So many worlds – so many ways.

'I've already met Mr Rozh…' Ed began.

'Rozhdestvensky. A man of the same name was director of the Bolshoi Theatre ten years ago when I was in Moscow.'

'A diplomat must see a great deal of the world,' Ed offered.

They talked, filling the time with courtesies until Vadim arrived. Ed began to warm to the old man – he was tough and gentle. With luck, Ed hoped, he'd forgive that *fucking publication.*

Vadim was ushered into the room by Matsuura's secretary. She didn't knock. Vadim had a file in his hand. He passed it to the old man nervously. After a few seconds, he glanced up to see who was sitting on the other side of the desk. His eyes met Ed's eyes. Vadim winced with surprise, the blood drained from his face, and he staggered back half a step. Vadim, it seemed, was auditioning the role of Macbeth while Ed was trying out for the Ghost of Banquo. *Never shake thy gory locks at me.*

Ed stood up, wishing he had gory locks to shake at Vadim. 'My dear friend,' he said, holding out his hand. 'We meet again.'

Vadim took his hand. 'Ed,' he said weakly. 'Good to see you. I thought you were…' *The times have been, that, when the brains were out, the man would die, and there an end.*

While Macbeth and the ghost of Banquo exchanged pleasantries, Matsuura had opened the file, found the report, and glanced quickly through it.

'I have a question,' the old man said. 'This wording – *given to erratic behaviour* – who authorised it?'

'The report is over Mr Patel's signature, sir.'

'I am aware of that. But did Mr Patel sign this paper before the text was prepared? Or afterward?'

'I can't remember, sir.'

'Who drafted the text?'

'I did.'

'You did. Well, I can easily verify the matter of authorisation with Mr Patel. But I find it hard to believe that a man of Mr Patel's exemplary understanding of UN procedures would have authorised a statement like this about one of our consultants. For presentation to the American Consulate. It hardly gives a positive impression of UN personnel, does it Mr Rozhdestvensky?'

'No sir.'

An *apparatchik* using the weapons of an *apparatchik*, Matsuura began to make notes in Japanese on a notepad. It took him almost five minutes, and the notes covered two pages. Ed watched the blood slowly drain from Vadim's face. The little shit was caught. Well and truly.

'And my second question.' The old man looked up from his writing. 'Eleven hours? Can you explain why it took so long to inform the consulate and…' He glanced back into the file. '…to inform the police, of the consultant's disappearance?

'We were checking up, sir. In Kuala Lumpur.'

'We?'

'The department.'

'In addition to yourself, who? Mr Patel?'

'No one, sir. Only me.'

'Eleven hours. You were checking up for eleven hours. That is what you are telling me.'

'Yes sir.'

'And what exactly were you checking?'

'Airline. Hotel. That sort of thing.'

'For eleven hours.'

The old man had nearly finished. 'If you say so, then of course I believe you,' he remarked and turned again to his notepad.

'May I ask something?' Ed broke in.

Matsuura waved agreement, still writing.

'Can I go to my wife's department? See her desk? As her husband, I might notice something the staff would miss.'

'It's irregular,' Matsuura agreed. 'However, my secretary will arrange a pass for you. And Mr Rozhdestvensky can show you the way.'

'Good,' Ed said.

'Mr Rozhdestvensky. Please will you wait outside. I have something to say to Dr Scarman.'

'Shall I take the file?' Vadim asked.

'I shall send you a copy. The original stays with me,' the old man answered.

Vadim was trembling. He turned and left the room. 'Thank you, sir,' he said.

When he was gone and the door was closed, Matsuura sat in silence, thinking. 'Under the UN Rules,' he said at last, 'Mr Patel can be required to take full responsibility for every act of his subordinates,' he said. 'This will be treated as a matter of the gravest concern.'

Ed nodded. 'Can I explain something to you?' he asked. 'It may take a minute or two.'

'Of course.'

As concisely as he could, Ed explained the unknown woman and the telephone call she'd made to Patel's department. He explained that the woman had received no help, and that she'd reported the matter further to the American Embassy.

'How do you know this?' Matsuura asked.

'Like you, sir, I'm not at liberty to divulge my sources.'

'What do you want me to do?'

'I think someone with your *understanding of UN procedures* will know what to do far better than me.'

'Does your source know you have told me about this?'

'No sir.'

'Then I cannot act. There is absolutely nothing I can do.'

'I fully understand, sir. Your hands are tied.' The old fox. Patel was done for.

★★★★★

'I not expect you here, Ed. Yesterday we agree different.' Vadim was showing him the way to Patel's department through a warren of corridors and passages.

'What did we agree?'

'That you go back to the States. As soon as possible.'

'Well, I decided to get some sense out of the UN before I go. Try at least. I think Mr Matsuura will help me if he can.'

'But what about…?' Vadim was twitchy as a jumping jack.

'What about Stepka?'

'Yes, him.'

They stopped.

'The office is through there,' Vadim said. 'We better talk out here.'

'What about?'

'Ed, I tried to warn you… Stepka…'

'Stepka?'

'He seemed very upset when he found out you were…'

'Alive?'

'No, of course not.' Vadim's voice faded to a whisper. 'Actually, yes.'

'So that's why you warned me – *Stay clear of Stepka.*'

'Yes, I warned you.'

A flat lie – there had been no warning. And Vadim had been in the street with Stepka. Outside Poor Man's. Working *with* Stepka.

And that raised another question – did Vadim know that Stepka had been ratfood for nearly twenty-four hours? Or perhaps crabfood? 'I had a chat with Stepka last night,' Ed said quietly. 'I think I persuaded him that you…'

'Me? There is nothing to do with me.'

'Stepka seems to think you're involved. He thinks you may have been too free with his name. Around…'

'Around who?'

'I mentioned your connections with the consulate,' Ed improvised.

'Which consulate?'

'The American.'

'Ed., you're totally wrong. I have no connection. Nothing.'

'Well, you'd better talk to Stepka then. Clarify things with him.'

'Ed, for fuck's sake…'

Vadim had no idea that Stepka was dead. 'Did you ever read *Macbeth*?' Ed asked.

'No. Why should I?' Vadim was shaking, close to tears. He'd had a terrible half-hour. And worse loomed ahead.

'I thought not. You should. Now where's Diana's desk?'

It was an unnecessarily tidy desk, the desk of someone trying to stay beyond reproach – no hint of the chaos-as-usual that goes with serious work. Ed could see that much from ten yards away. The name-plate was modest, an inch high maybe. There was a photo in a frame, but he could only see the back. Who would Dy frame up on her desk? Herself in the hockey team? A graduation pic? There was one photograph he remembered. She'd had it on her desk at home for almost a month – the two of them on their wedding day. But that was impossible. Too bitter, surely. Too painful.

Vadim had gone to his own desk and sat down with his back to Ed. He was staring at the screen of his laptop, motionless. His screen-saver was flicking through an album of holiday snaps – a tropical beach with little girls, a palm tree with little girls, a temple with two little boys.

Ed didn't move, staring at Diana's desk, reluctant to go nearer. The photograph. He didn't want to see it. He didn't want to know. But he had no choice.

He stood now by her swivel-chair, staring at the image. Himself. Himself with a baby in his arms. Terry a few hours after she was born. When the world was still in order. Finally, in that second, standing beside her chair, he saw how much, and how deeply, Diana had suffered. And she'd goaded herself day after day, month after month with that appalling picture – the man she loved holding her shattered baby. Terry, her little girl, who roused no feelings in her beyond shame and contrition. *Why do you think I'm like that? About Terry?* They were almost the last words she'd said before she disappeared. Why hadn't he understood? Why had he rejected her so murderously? All that Shakespeare crap. All that poetry. And he couldn't hear his own wife screaming for help. Why write about the language of signs?

Why paint reflections? Reflections God's sake! All that subtlety and sensitivity. And now this simple, badly taken, terrifying snapshot staring at him from her desk, this token of a pain nobody could bear alone. What had he done to her? What sort of man was he?

He hurried out of the office without even a nod in Vadim's direction. He found the elevator. He handed in his pass at the front desk. In the stifling, noisy avenue outside, he turned downhill toward the Royal Palace and the riverside, toward the place where he'd stood with Diana, protecting her against the rocking of the jetty. Protecting her... She hadn't resisted, and he'd been surprised. He winced with shame.

Just before the Democracy Monument, he passed a little stand – a couple of boxes under a broken umbrella. A girl of eight or nine was selling garlands of white jasmine, circles of flowers the size of a bracelet. The girl looked up at him and smiled. The week before she'd smiled up at him and Diana in just the same way. The girl had only one arm. Ed stopped. With her one frail arm and skinny fingers, she held up a rusty tin for money. The tin was empty but for a one-baht piece. There was a handful of loose change in his pocket. Ed gave her the coins, trying to stop them from clattering too loud. The girl put down the tin without looking into it and asked him a question in Thai. *Do you want any flowers?* he guessed.

'No,' he said. 'No flowers.'

The girl thanked him with a one-handed *wai*. In a way it was grotesque. But in another it was as tragic as anything in Sophocles or Shakespeare. Ed shuddered.

He walked down to the river and took the water-bus to the Oriental. The boat didn't stop at Wat Arun. Ed looked at the temple and the glittering stupa at its centre. Dy had wanted him to see the broken china, knowing it would amaze him. She'd wanted to run with him, holding his hand. But somehow he'd kept his hand away from her. His drowning wife. At last the tears came, the tears he'd been holding back since he'd seen that awful photograph. The roaring of the engine, the squawking loudspeaker announcing the stops, the brilliant sunlight on the water – everything disappeared.

'Dy, my darling,' he whispered to the river. 'Why couldn't we make it? For God's sake what happened to us?'

★★★★★

Back at the hotel, Ed took the elevator up to the fifth floor. He'd better call Lucía. He hadn't talked to her since Thursday. Too long. But when there's no chance of good news… As he put the room-key in the lock, he heard Irina's phone: *Bella figlia dell'amore*. He jerked the door open and snatched up the phone from the bedside table. 'Hello,' he said, trying to sound casual.

'Not smart, Ed.' It was Merr.

'You alone this time?' Ed asked.

'Yes,' Merr told him. 'You?'

'You're never alone at Schomberg's.'

'Now you are. It's turned off. The surveillance. But not for much longer. Is she there? With you?'

'No.'

'So you can tell me then.'

'What?'

'What you've got in your head instead of brains.'

'What are you talking about?'

'What you and Irina cooked up.'

'You warned me, Merr – she had to disappear before she got on that plane to Singapore.'

'Disappear? So you still haven't got the point? Nothing you do in this country is going to work, Ed. Nothing. Leave stuff like that to me.'

'But you warned me.'

'I warned you to stay put till I sorted something out.'

'That's not what I understood.'

'*Don't get any funny ideas*, I said. *Just lie low*. How much plainer does it get?'

'Must have got my wires crossed,' Ed said. 'Again, again, again.'

'And Irina?'

'She said she knew a way out…'

'And you two left a trail plain enough for a Girl Scout to follow.'

'So fill me in. What's happening?' Ed asked with sullen resignation. It was true – he'd misread every sign, and played the wrong card in every trick.

'I called her. On the shiny new Nokia she bought at the airport.'

'You found out about that?'

'Listen Ed, if you think you're out of your depth, it's because you are.'

'And my shiny new Xperia?'

'Nice phone. Good choice. But – and this you don't know – about half an hour ago Andronicus went international. From now on you do what I tell you, nothing more and nothing less. Or you're dead. And so is Irina.'

Ed was glancing round the room. Something had changed. What? The notepad on the desk. There was a drawing. In pastels.

'International?' Ed said.

'A-MISS. You know who they are?'

'No idea.' Ed went to the desk and picked up the drawing.

'Well, the A stands for Australian. They picked up your friend Bhatnagar. In Sydney.'

'Yes, you said he was in Sydney,' Ed replied, trying to make sense of the drawing.

'There's a woman at A–MISS,' Merr said. 'The Iron Lady. She really hated your film. Specially the exploding girl.'

The drawing could only be Irina's. She was imitating him, his way of getting the colour onto the paper. But abstract. A meaningless doodle. 'So Bhatnagar...?' Ed prompted.

'Bhatnagar is helping A–MISS with its enquiries.'

'In Sydney?'

'Yes.'

'Couldn't happen to a better person.' Ed put down the drawing, unenlightened and irritated. 'So you called Irina,' he said. 'How far did she get?'

'Fifty k toward the border.'

'You guessed about the border?'

'Three Pagodas. Yangon. It's either that or Cambodia.'

'So what did you tell her?'

'Get her ass back to Bangkok. By the time she got to the border, they'd be waiting for her. She saw the point.'

'So what *is* the point? Who'd be waiting for her?'

'The Thais.'

'But the Thais aren't looking for her?' Ed picked up the drawing again in his left hand, turning it in the dim light. What a pity Irina couldn't draw.

'They *weren't* looking for her. But they are now.'

'How come?'

'I just told you. It's gone international. We're going for Andronicus. Big time. A–MISS, the Thais and us. Some guys are flying in from DC – get here tomorrow.'

'So they hated the pictures too – in DC?'

'Ed.' There was a pause. 'I need a straight answer – where *is* Irina?'

'You're asking *me*? How should I know?'

'She's not in Schomberg's?'

'No. Definitely not.'

There was a silence.

'So – what made you turn off the cameras?' Ed asked.

'I was told – put all my resources on Andronicus.'

'And even T-CAN can't watch the whole world at once.'

'They said she was low priority.'

'And you lost track of her?'

'I thought she'd go back to Schomberg's. To be honest, I was calling her, but you picked up.'

'She's not here.'

'So listen carefully. This is what my boss just said – with someone like Irina there are *certain possibilities that can't be ruled out.* And worse, she's now on the list of people A-MISS wants to talk to, God help her. Came through a couple of minutes ago.'

'So she's priority again, and they want the surveillance back on?'

'It'll go on in five minutes. They want her found.'

'Alive? So they can talk to her?'

'Ed, these people know their business.'

'A-MISS knows its business – that's what you're telling me.'

'She'd have been better off dead in Singapore. Ed…'

'So what do you want me to do?'

'Find her. Tell her to stay out of sight. In Bangkok. Invisible. Give it a month. Then call me.'

'And Dy?' Ed asked.

There was a long silence.

'Dy?' Ed repeated.

'We think she may still be alive. The operation's proceeding on that basis.'

'The operation?'

The phone went dead. Someone must have walked in on Merr. In a few seconds surveillance was going back on. There was no way he could call Merr back. *From now on you do what you're told, nothing more or nothing less.* Well, he had his orders – find Irina and tell her to vanish. Ed was staring at Irina's drawing. What was the message? She'd aborted her trip to Burma and come back to the hotel. He turned the drawing back to its original orientation, with her hand at the bottom right corner. All he could see was a slight concavity – the middle of the drawing was further away from him than the edges.

Irina had left a drawing and not a note because, reasonably enough, she'd thought the surveillance was still on. She'd sat at the desk and doodled – in full view of the camera – something only he would understand. What was it? A slight concave surface. A spoon? Obviously, dimwit! River City. Friday morning. The sun, the water and the weed reflected in the bowl of a spoon. He checked her drawing again. Green smudges of weed at the top. muddy-blue squiggles in the middle. Yellow below, as the sun would be in a concave reflection. He knew where to find her.

Why were they looking for Irina, A-MISS and the others? Had Bhatnagar given her name to A-MISS? If he had, how in hell did he know it? Bhatnagar – currently helping some murderous bitch in Australia with her enquiries. With Irina lined up for the next round. What were the *possibilities that couldn't be ruled out*? On the other hand – Merr trusted Irina, really seriously trusted her. And liked her into the bargain. *Give it a month. Then she should call me.* A month? The brass from DC would be gone by then, and Merr would have room to manoeuvre.

Irina's phone rang again. It was Merr.

'Find her,' Merr said. 'Do it. Surveillance is back on in one minute.'

The phone went dead.

Ed picked up the drawing and crammed it into his pocket. He hurried out of the room, down the stairs and out into the street. He glanced around. Were they on his tail? Obviously yes. They wanted Irina – and Ed was going to lead them to her. *Find her,* Merr had said. But what did he mean this time? Find her so we *can* get our hands on her? Or find her so we *can't*? *Tell her to stay invisible* – that's what Merr had said when there was no one in the room. So, Ed decided, the hounds were certainly on his tail, and he had to throw them off. He wasn't good at that kind of thing, but that gave him one advantage – after his last effort with the hotel limousine, everyone believed he was unsubtle to the point of idiocy. Now, if he could smarten up his act...

He strolled up Silom Road toward Chong Nonsi. Instead of turning off for the Skytrain station, he kept on toward Pat Pong. It was nearly five o'clock. The bars would be open, he guessed, open but empty.

The stallholders were setting up along Silom Road for the night market. A few were open already – t-shirts with bawdy tag lines. *Aids can kill you, don't be silly. Get a condom on your willy*. Not bad advice, as t-shirts went. *No money, no honey* – Empsonian levels of ambiguity. He paused to examine embroidered caftans, socks, watches, scorpions and giant millipedes. At a conspicuous and isolated stall, he tried several t-shirts for size against his body. Finally he bought a bright red t-shirt with a blurred-out text that read: *Mastobation bad for eye*. Then he held up baggy satin pants, green and tight at the ankle. White, he tried against his legs, then black, and finally green again. The market-girl warned him: 'For lady. Not for you.' He bantered for a moment, asking her how she knew he was a guy. She answered with the inevitable *No problem*. 'You want?' she asked. He nodded. She put the shirt and the green pants into a pink plastic bag.

'You have wig?' he asked her, gesturing long hair down both sides of his face.

'Hair?' the girl asked.

'Lady hair,' he said.

She laughed and pointed him further down the street. 'My frenn. She have,' the girl said. He paid for the clothes and set off down the street.

239

The crowd thickened as he neared Pat Pong. Most of the stalls were ready for business. He found one that sold carnival masks and nylon wigs, blonde, black, punk red. He tried on three of them, studying his reflection in the mirror that the market-woman held up for him. Finally he chose a simple black one and stuffed it into the plastic bag with his new clothes.

Pat Pong was a few yards ahead now. Despite its reputation, it was, as Ed now discovered, nothing more than two overcrowded *soys* packed with market stalls and lined with more or less identical bars. Stairways between the bars climbed toward upper storeys. Ed guessed the action was upstairs. Alleyways led between the rotting concrete buildings into neighbouring *soys*. He began to circle the streets. Among the bars and restaurants, he soon found what he was looking for – a bar with a couple of tout-girls outside, like Soy Cowboy but not yet in full swing. The long, lazy afternoon was still not over. He peered in through the door.

'Go in, mister,' one of the tout-girls said. 'Happy hour till sick o'cock.'

There were half-a-dozen girls in the bar. They were sitting at two tables eating with chopsticks out of shared bowls – rice and something brown and steamy. He went in and chose a seat in a dark corner near the back entrance. A high catwalk with dancing poles ran down the middle of the bar, but there were no dancers, no music, and, as yet, no other customers.

Urged by the others, one of the girls put down her chopsticks and stood up. She was dressed in jeans, white sneakers, and a plain brown t-shirt. She was tall and her hair was inexpertly bleached. Tall, flat and awkward. Perfect.

'What you drink, mister?' the girl asked.

'Singha,' he said. 'You want to join me?'

She smiled. The first customer of the evening, and already she'd earned her first baht or two. She went behind the bar and returned with two drinks – a beer and a small glass of something reddish-brown. It was the same stuff the girls drank in Soy Cowboy – some kind of upper.

She put the two drinks on the table. 'I muss chane,' she said, indicating her jeans. 'Not popper cothe.'

'No, sit down,' he said. 'You're prettier as you are.'

'Can-*not*,' she replied. 'Madame not allow.'

'Madame isn't here,' he ventured.

She shrugged in childish indecision and sat down. After a few seconds, she picked up her glass and raised it to him. 'Cheer,' she said.

'Cheers.' He raised his beer bottle in its foam casing and took a long, cool swig.

She put her hand on his knee. He didn't stop her. If Madame arrived, he didn't want her to earn a scolding – her street clothes, he guessed, would be problem enough. They started to chat, the meaningless gossip of bargirls and lonely *falang*. Not that all *falang* were lonely. The Aussies hunted in packs. Ed hoped they'd stay away for a while. And with luck the music would stay turned off – he needed some quiet words with the girl.

Her name Darak, she told him. Customer call her Daisy. She was eighteen. She start work in bar two month before. First job Bangkok. Job okay. One thing she not like – sleep with customer. But if he want…

'How much does it cost? For one night?' he asked.

'Up to you?' she replied. 'Bar fine is fie hunred.'

'And 500 more for you? Is enough?'

'Up to you.' She sounded disappointed.

'1,000 better?' Twenty dollars.

Daisy smiled. 'Better,' she agreed.

'But you don't like to sleep with customer,' he teased her.

She shrugged. A little girl's shrug. He guessed she was fifteen, making the best of an unpleasant situation.

'I want you to do something for me,' he said.

Her eyes flashed petulance. First he'd agreed 1,000, and now he was making extra conditions. It wasn't fair. She'd been tricked. What was she to do?

Ed laughed. 'Not what you think,' he said. 'Nothing bad. But I give you 1,000. No problem.'

Daisy looked at him doubtfully. What filthy thing did he have in mind? She glanced at the other girls, still eating at their tables. Maybe she should get one of them to take over.

'Listen, Daisy,' he said, afraid of scaring her off. 'You are good girl. I do nothing bad, I promise.' Dy had warned him, there was one thing the girls hated. They all refused to do it – the young ones anyway.

Daisy was still eyeing him darkly.

While he was paying for his new clothes in the street, he'd put two 500 bills in his hip pocket. He took one of them out now and slipped it to her, invisible under the table. She took the bill and glanced down at it. Ed saw her eyebrows go up and watched the bill disappear into the hip pocket of her jeans. He had her attention.

'You know Chong Nonsi?' he said. 'The Skytrain station.'

'Yes,' she said.

'Can you go there?'

'Before seven o'cock I can go. No problem.'

Ed glanced at his watch – 17:45. Plenty of time. 'I want you to walk to Chong Nonsi. And I will follow you.'

'And after?'

'After nothing.'

'You said 1,000.'

'I put 500 more in this bag,' he said. 'In this bag are some very ugly clothes. You take the bag now and put on the clothes. Then you walk to Chong Nonsi in the clothes. And the wig.' He made the gesture again of smoothing long hair on both sides of his face. 'Understand.'

The girl nodded.

'I pay for drinks now,' he said. 'Please get the check.'

*****

He reached River City and the restaurant on the Chao Phraya not long after sunset. He'd checked a hundred times – no one was following him. The restaurant was busy, and most of the tables were taken. Thais and *falang*. Some of the foreign women were wearing Thai costume. Ed remembered the waiter, though the waiter didn't remember him. He asked to see the owner.

'He not here,' the waiter told him with a smile.

At that moment the owner appeared, dressed as before in a white suit. Now he was wearing a bow tie, white and carefully tied. He had an air of expectancy.

'Good evening,' Ed said, turning away from the waiter. 'I think you may have a guest staying here…'

'No have guest,' the owner said. 'No have loom. No have guest.'

'You have rooms, don't you? For rent?'

'No,' the man said. 'No loom. Not possible.' He waved downstream at the dark immensity of the Royal Orchid Hotel. 'Plenny loom nex-door.'

'I lunched here the other day,' Ed told him. 'With a lady and a man.'

'Possible,' the owner conceded.

'I thought the lady might be staying here.'

An explosion in the street startled him. Then another. Then the clatter of firecrackers.

'No have loom for lady. No have loom for man. No have loom.' The man slapped his hands together in a gesture of finality and laughed.

'Nothing against my sitting down and having a beer though?' Ed asked, sensing some elaborate game.

'You want beer?'

'Exactly.'

'Loyal Orchid have good beer. Why you not go there? Liverside Tellace.'

'Because I like it here,' Ed said. His voice was rising. Two Thai women at the nearest table looked up, disturbed.

Ed went to the last empty table and sat down. He had to control himself. If this was where Irina was hiding, the last thing she needed...

The waiter brought him a bottle of Singha and a glass on a small tray. There was a little plate of cashew nuts. 'Comlimet of owner,' the waiter said. And then, seeing Ed's puzzled expression: 'Is flee. You not pay.'

'Drink and go, you mean.'

The waiter nodded. 'Yes,' he agreed. 'Mean.'

It was a stupid lie – there were rooms. Rooms for rent. What was wrong with these people? They were polite, they were friendly, they were even honest – or so everyone said. But such liars. He sipped his beer, the anger cooling. Maybe... He thought it through again. No, it wasn't a lie. It was a message. So, when you know someone has rooms and that a woman is staying in one of them, and when that someone says *no rooms, no woman*, what does it mean? She's here. Go. Disappear. If that was the message, he'd better act on it.

He gulped down the beer, and, pretending an anger he no longer felt, he strode out of the restaurant, back down the *soy*. That was where he'd been told to go, to the Royal Orchid. The dirty *soy* ran parallel with the river. He'd walked along it with Irina and Merr, looking for a taxi. Occasional *tk-tk*s rattled toward him now, catching him in their dim headlights. Somewhere ahead another firecracker rattled and spat. He pressed close to the wall. It was mud-stained, ragged with old posters, and skirted with garbage. He remembered a bridge over a stinking *klong*. Had he

244

crossed it already? No, the stench was building in his nostrils, unspeakably foul. A girl was coming toward him. Then footsteps close behind. He was alert for a message, but none came.

The Royal Orchid lay fifty yards ahead, its bright lights inviting. Institutionally inviting – the kind of invitation he always refused. Maybe he'd take a beer. That was what the old man had suggested. Maybe the beer would lead to the message. He reached the hotel and climbed the few steps from the street to the lobby. The porter opened the door for him. 'Evenin' sir.' An English accent. An English porter, Ed saw.

The lobby was designed to make the world feel at home – nebulous, stylish for those who had no idea of style, international. Plenty of angular sofas. Waiters hovered discreetly. Music played, colourless and discreet as the whole place. *Riverside Terrace*. He saw the sign. *Liverside Tellace*, the old man had called it. No one tried to catch his eye. But perhaps a message had been left for him – he made for the concierge. It was worth a try. If there was a message, it wouldn't be for Ed Scarman. She'd have found a name for him. Who? *Lovis Corinth? Titus Andronicus? Doctor Spoon?* Lovis for sure.

The concierge was a European, burly, close to retirement, a clone of the porter at the door.

'Yes, sir. 'ow can I 'elp you?' Also English, Ed heard.

'I'm not staying in the hotel, but there may be a message for me.'

'Your name, sir, if I might enquire?'

'Corinth. Lovis Corinth.'

'That would be with a K?'

'No, with a C.'

'One second, please.' The concierge checked the electronic message board on his computer. Nothing. There was a rack of lettered pigeon-holes on the back wall of the little office. From the counter Ed could see the C and the K slots – both empty. There was a message in L. The concierge checked it, turned to Ed, and shook his head.

'Thanks anyway,' Ed said and headed off toward the Riverside Terrace. Was the Royal Orchid a dead-end? Had he misread the signs? Again?

'Sir. Sir.' A Thai voice behind him. Young, girlish.

He stopped and turned. A girl of about twelve dressed in a pageboy costume was holding up a silver platter with a note on it, a sheet of paper folded three times but unsealed. There was no name on the outside of the note. Ed took the paper and unfolded it. Inside was a business card written in English – for the restaurant he'd just left. The words *Rooms for Rent* were underlined. He turned the card over. On the back was written in inky ball-point:

Close at 1

That was all. He glanced round the crowded lobby. Whoever had delivered the note must have followed him from the restaurant. He saw no one he recognised. He studied the card again and nodded theatrically, agreeing the time, in case anyone was watching. One o'clock was still five and a half hours away. Why so late? Perhaps he should take a *tk-tk* back to Soy Cowboy. Best place to disappear, or so he'd heard, is in a crowd.

The huge revolving door began to spin, and a busload of noisy tourists crowded in. Some of the women were squeezed into slender Thai costumes. Others wore the towering gold crowns Ed had seen in shop-windows. A few of the men wore white masks, Venetian style. The whole mob was led by a Thai guide who wore a slender red and gold costume that fitted her perfectly. When they were all in the lobby, the guide held up her hand for quiet and began a high-pitched screaming match with the PA-music. To Ed it was incomprehensible, but the merrymakers seemed to understand her – maybe she was speaking German.

Ed looked at the pageboy for an explanation.

'Loy Krathong,' the girl said. Loy Krathong? That and the word *Sir* were evidently the extent of her English.

The concierge loomed behind her. Sensing his tread, the girl winced and stepped evasively to the side – Ed guessed that somehow she was apprenticed to the concierge and that her training so far had consisted of little more than *thick ears* as Dy called them.

The concierge smiled professionally and put his hand on the girl's shoulder. 'Loy Krathong, sir,' he explained. 'Festival of Light. When they float their candles on the water. Let all the bad things in your life float away on the river. Big firework display too. On barges. At eleven. Best place to see it from is 'ere.'

'Is that so?' Ed encouraged him.

'It's very full tonight, sir. Lot of Germans.' He indicated the guide and her troop. 'But I fink I could still get you a table on the Riverside Terrace. Dinner and show 4,000 baht. But you'd 'ave to let me know.' He paused. 'Now.'

4,000 baht. Eighty dollars. 'Yes, please. If you'd be so kind,' Ed smiled. 'A table for one.' He wanted to ask the concierge where the cryptic card had come from, but, for all the man's cockney English, this was Thailand, and he knew he'd get a Thai answer.

The concierge made no move, waiting.

'Ah, of course,' Ed said and took out his billfold. What kind of tip did the man expect? 100 baht or 500? Two dollars or ten? He decided on ten and gave the man a 500 bill.

'Table for one. I'll 'ave your name on it right away, Mr Corinth,' the concierge said. 'You can pay on the way in.' He squeezed the girl's shoulder hard enough to make her wince again, this time from pain.

'Thank you,' Ed said, turning away and flinching with the girl. What a bastard, tormenting his little page more or less out of habit.

Ed saw one of the Germans push up his mask onto his forehead. A crimson streak of compressed skin snaked across his cheeks and below his nose. The man's eyes were piggy and red-veined. But Ed liked the mask. With luck he could buy one from a huckster in the street outside. Then he'd hang around Liverside Tellace till one o'clock minding his own business. Perfect.

The concierge was marching the little page back to his counter, his plump fingers still gripping her shoulder. For a second Ed was back in the warehouse, watching the soldiers drag their girl away – the girl who might have been Diana, or so Merr thought.

★★★★★

Ed chose a mask in the lobby-shop – a Venetian eye-mask with a hooked nose and a high plume – and then found his table on the terrace. It was, as he should probably have guessed, not a table for one but a table for three. He was sharing it with a sun-shrivelled Australian couple in their late sixties. The Australians were simple people – no masks, no costumes. From a flimsy guidebook, the woman read aloud the history of Loy Krathong. The biggest celebration, she read, was not on the river but in the Lumpini Park – thousands of Krathong boats with their candles and lanterns were floated on the lake there. The inevitable argument erupted – why did they always miss the best of everything? He blamed her. She blamed him. It had been the same in Bali, in Manila, in Hanoi – everywhere they'd ever been.

All evening the threatening sepia sky flashed with skyrockets and whizzbangs. Then, at eleven, the river erupted into a Sodom of fire and brimstone. Barge after barge ripped the night apart with starshells and skyblazers. The river reflected the sky, and, in the shriek of burning magnesium, the sky seemed for a moment to reflect the river. It was a stunning effect. For a while Ed simply sat and blinked at the show. Then, more urgently, he realised it was a good time to move.

He bade the Australian couple a fleeting goodnight, hurried through the passageways and tunnels to the lobby, and out into the *soy*. The *soy* was badly lit and deserted apart from a *falang* vomiting his soul into the gutter and a gang of boys lighting matches and flicking them into the air. The sky was ablaze, and the air smelt of sulphur. The detonations were shattering. He had no idea how long the fireworks would last. He walked briskly, breaking a sudden sweat with the effort. He felt the plume of his mask nodding, absurd and conspicuous, but in fact all-concealing, like the *tarnhelm* in the sagas.

He crossed the stinking *klong*. Another hundred yards brought him to the Spoon.

The brick terrace was crammed with sightseers now. All Thais, it seemed. The women wore Thai costume. Families clung together gaping upward at the fireworks. Many carried boats wrapped in banana leaves and flowers, ready for launching. Through the confusion of dark heads and golden crowns, he saw the water by the terrace alight with floating candle-boats. He wormed his way through the crowd to the covered archway where he'd spoken to the owner at seven. The owner was still standing there much as before, though now his bow tie had wilted.

Ed pushed up his mask, then took it off altogether. 'You have room now?' Ed asked, pitching his voice above the exploding fireworks.

The owner recognised him. 'Loom? I have loom. No problem, loom.'

'And one lady. Guest?'

'Have loom,' replied the owner. 'But lady guest, she check out.'

'When?'

'Nye o'cock.'

'You know anything about this card?' Ed showed him the card the little page had given him.

The owner took the card and read the wording on the back several times. Then he shook his head and shrugged. The Thai answer.

'Can I see her room? The lady guest?' Ed asked.

'Not her loom now. New guest. Thai family,' the owner explained. 'Tonight Loy Krathong,' he said, smiling sweetly. 'No problem lent loom.'

'Did lady guest say where she was going?' A huge explosion muffled the words.

The owner shook his head. 'No,' he said, though he couldn't have heard the question.

'So what did you do?' Ed heard the rising anger in his voice. 'Murder her for her handbag?'

The owner smiled, though without sweetness this time. 'No unnerstann,' he said.

Day 9

'Two?' Ed repeated. 'Who are they?'

'I don't know,' Merr replied. 'That's why we need identification.' The phone connection was startlingly clear, a bad sign, Ed guessed.

'You've seen the reports?' Ed wanted to know.

'Very sketchy. Hirsch said to be there at 1:45. I assume you can make it.'

'Is either of them Dy?' Ed asked flatly. 'Tell me now.'

'Two women. Both around thirty. *Falang*. One with no head. Pulled out of the river. One with her head smashed in. Some kids found her in the switchyard at Bang Sue. Found her by the smell. She'd been dead a few days.'

'Chatuchak?'

'Nearby.'

'That's all you know?'

'Talk to you at Hirsch's place,' Merr said. 'You still got the address?'

'Sure.'

Ed disconnected. Two women were missing, Dy and Irina. Two women lay in the morgue. And it was two hours before he'd find out who they were.

*****

251

The smell was the same. When they reached *S3*, the lights flicked off and on in exactly the same way. Hirsch was in a vile mood. At the ID counter he'd barely shaken hands with Merr, and he'd ignored Ed completely. Of course, Ed had hardly hoped for a welcome, coming a second time and on such a different mission. Hirsch had been duped, and all three of them knew it.

Ed stood next to Merr, silent, while the first drawer was identified and opened.

The naked corpse had no head. The severed neck was ravaged and stringy. The autopsy cuts were marked in blue felt-tip but still unmade – the body had been in the morgue only a few hours.

'Why is it like that?' Ed asked. 'The neck?'

'River-crabs,' Hirsch explained flatly. 'She was in the water only for short time. In three hours the whole body will be attacked. You see already…' He indicated the vulnerable spots on the woman's body where the river-crabs had gathered to begin their work.

'It isn't Dy?' Merr asked.

'I don't know,' Ed said slowly. 'I haven't seen Dy… I haven't seen her… I haven't seen Dy naked since…'

'Could it be her?' Merr said. 'Or no?'

'Dy has a tattoo. Like wings. Here.' He touched the small of his back. 'It has a name. She told me once. She might have had it removed. I don't know.'

'It's called a *tramp stamp*,' Merr said flatly.

'No,' Ed contradicted. 'She called it something else.'

'Can you turn the subject over, please Dr Hirsch?' Merr asked.

Hirsch signalled to the orderly and said some words in Thai. The orderly and the nurse put on heavy rubber gloves and turned the body onto its side without taking it out of the drawer. Water, slime and blood oozed from the severed neck.

There was no tattoo.

Hirsch spoke again, still in Thai. The orderly looked for something on the workbench. Then, not finding it, he went to the elevator.

'I need a *Lupe*,' Hirsch explained. 'Magnifying glass. Even if a tattoo is removed, usually there remain some traces in the skin.'

'There were no clothes?' Merr asked.

'No. None.'

The three men fell silent beside the headless woman. Hirsch indicated the left hand, fourth finger. 'No ring mark,' he said, speaking to Merr. 'The right hand also not.'

'The right hand?' Ed asked, trying to fill the sickening silence till the orderly returned.

'In some countries, a wedding ring is on the right. In some, on the left,' Hirsch explained sourly.

The elevator doors opened, the orderly held out a large magnifying glass with a built-in light, and Hirsch took it. With the glass, Hirsch examined the skin where the tattoo might once have been. 'No, no skin is removed,' he said. 'At least not recently. After a few years it is difficult to be certain. I will check with the microscope later.'

'Could it be Dy?' Merr pressed.

No, it wasn't Dy. The headless, crab-eaten wreck was not his beautiful Diana. But it might be all that remained of her. 'I don't think so. I'm not sure,' Ed muttered. How was it possible? He'd been so close to Dy, and yet he didn't know if this shattered flesh had belonged to her or to a total stranger. Surely there should be some intuition, some vibration.

'This woman had at least one child,' Hirsch said. 'That is clear in my preliminary examination.'

'Yes,' Ed agreed. 'My wife had one child. But that doesn't mean…'

'This woman, as far as I have seen, did not nurse her child.'

'No,' Ed agreed again. 'She didn't…' He began to cry as he stood, looking down at the hideous female thing in the drawer. He felt tears run down his face. Then he began to sob. He felt Merr's arm round his shoulders, though not in comfort or sympathy. *Not here, Ed. Pull yourself together. Save it for later.* Ed forced back the tears and smothered the sobs. Merr was right.

'And you don't think it could be Irina?' Merr asked cautiously.

Irina? Too many questions. Too many horrible fucking questions. 'What time was the body found? In the river?' Ed asked quietly.

'Not long before six this morning. They found seven corpses in the river, five of them were Thai. Always after Loy Krathong they find bodies in the river.'

Irina? Murdered last night for her 3,000 dollars? Dumped in the river at five. The facts fitted, but the headless corpse had never been Irina. She'd been a submissive sister, a submissive whore, and, he guessed, a submissive wife though she'd never said so. He'd seen the scars of submission on her body.

'It isn't Irina,' Ed said. 'Definitely not.'

'We'll get Dy's medical records from the UN,' Merr said. 'See if the blood type matches.'

'Dy is O-negative,' Ed told them.

'I'll do the test,' Hirsch said. 'If they are the same, I'll work on the DNA.'

'That takes a week or two?' Merr asked.

Hirsch nodded. 'And the second subject?'

The other corpse was partly decomposed and partly devoured by rats which had eaten into her body to get at her entrails. But it couldn't be Dy, despite the short blonde hair. The corpse had lost her front teeth, top and bottom. Knocked out years ago, Hirsch had already decided. When Ed had last seen Dy, she'd still had her teeth intact.

The two drawers were pushed back into their cabinets. The locks clicked into place.

'Then not one of your missing persons is found, Mister Croft. Unless Number 0993 is this gentleman's wife.'

This gentleman's wife. Hirsch's tone was as sterile as the air of *S3*. But Ed understood the coldness, accepted it even. 'Doctor Hirsch,' he said. 'I'd like to have a few words with Mr Croft. Then, if you have time, a few words with you. Is it possible?'

Hirsch gave a sigh, it seemed of relief. 'I'll be upstairs in my office. Ask for me at the front desk. You wish to talk to Mr Croft here? In this room?'

'Is that okay?'

'The orderly will be in *S2* if you need something.' Hirsch switched off the overhead lights and stepped into the elevator with the orderly. The room was lit now by two LED spots, steely white.

'I hate this place,' Ed said.

Merr shrugged and said nothing.

'You changed your mind about Dy?' Ed said accusingly. 'Written her off as dead?'

'There were two *falang* corpses. I wanted to be sure…'

'But we aren't sure, are we, because nobody knows what Ed's wife actually looks like. Not even Ed.' He had no reason to be angry with Merr, but somehow his words were sharpened to hurt.

'Hold it, Ed. I want to find Diana. I want to get Irina out of this country in one piece. And I care about you. If you don't believe that…'

Ed nodded. 'Of course I believe you. I'm sorry. It's just those horrible crabs… And…'

Merr waited, staring without expression at a stainless-steel countertop.

'And I saw something…' Ed began. 'At the UN. Something…'

'Important?'

'To me. Maybe not to you.'

'Well?'

'Perhaps I've been on the wrong track. About Diana.'

'Dy and Terry you mean? Or Dy and Andronicus?'

'Terry.'

Merr looked up now, suddenly hostile. 'You know, the day you two got married, she was nearly nine months. I don't think I've ever seen a woman look so beautiful. Or so happy. You had everything in the world anyone could want.' It was an accusation.

'I know, Merr, I know.'

'And then the bottom dropped out of her world. Completely.'

'And out of mine.'

'Yours? How can you compare…?'

For a second Ed struggled against Merr's words, but they went painfully together with the picture on Diana's desk. What could he say?

'I used to think you were really somebody,' Merr pressed on. 'I thought it was great when you asked me to be your best man. And that day, you know something, I was seriously jealous. Of you.'

Ed still said nothing.

'And then, after what happened to Terry, Dy needed help. You could make it on your own. You *did* make it on your own. But Dy couldn't. And you didn't come through for her.'

'No,' Ed repeated slowly. 'I didn't come through for her.'

'Somehow I couldn't believe what I was seeing.'

Ed winced. It had never occurred to him that Merr of all people…

'I'd have done anything to help her.' Merr turned away, struggling for words. 'To help you both. But there was nothing I could do. You were the only one she gave a damn about.' He turned back to Ed, but Ed's face was a blank. 'Nothing I could do, and nothing anyone else could do either. Your mom could see it. Even Lizzie, that girl at the wedding. Poor Tin Lizzie…'

'Merr…' Ed hesitated. 'When we were in this horrible place last week, you were a bit different? Sort of distant? Was that because…?'

'Why else?'

They stopped talking. At last, after four years of silent pain, Merr had made his point.

There was a chair in front of the console a few paces from where Ed was standing. Ed sat down, swivelling the chair so that Merr was out of sight. It was a long while before words began to form again, slow, reluctant words. 'So what's happening with Andronicus? Did you clean out the warehouse?'

'We went in last night. Too late of course. No equipment, no files. Just business as usual.'

'No kids?' Ed swung the chair back toward Merr.

'They were long gone, Saturday morning at the latest.'

'No traces? The dormitory? The canteen?'

'Kids had been there, but they were gone. The poster was gone but not the paint. Andronicus said a painting team, mostly teenagers, came in to do a movie poster – couple of times a year. It was plausible enough.'

'So why did you wait two days?' They were talking mechanically. Merr had ripped the scab off an ugly wound, and it would take a while to skin over – if it ever did.

'DC told us to put everything on hold till the chain of command arrived. By the time they'd unplugged their vibrators and got here, Andronicus was just a patch of desert. Forty-eight wasted hours. How the hell's that supposed to work?'

'And you think they've got Dy?' Dy? This Dy wasn't the shattered, desperate young mother they'd talked about the minute before. Together they'd turned their faces away from the nightmare. And what was Dy now? An object – a parcel of flesh and a few clothes they were trying to trace.

'Chaudhary picked her up at the airport,' Merr replied. 'Chaudhary was killed. If they haven't got her, where is she? She's important to them.'

'Why?'

'She's UN. That gives her status. They can trade her.'

'Status,' Ed repeated, suddenly alert. 'Merr, that girl I saw dragged away? By the guards?'

'You said it wasn't Dy.'

'It wasn't. But someone with status, like you just said? Someone important? I mean, they wouldn't just give her to the soldiers? Would they? You see what I'm saying.'

'No, they wouldn't just give her to the soldiers,' Merr repeated woodenly.

'Good,' Ed grunted. What Merr had just said was comfort of sorts, but uncommonly cold. 'And you think they've got Diana?' Ed pressed. 'And the kids? Maybe they're all in the same place?'

'No. Forget the kids. They're dead. They were worth a fortune, but alive they'd be a hell of a risk.'

'So I blew it. Totally and completely.'

'No. We blew it. Washington blew it. Like they blow everything. Remember the CIA plots to kill Castro, 638 plots, and the old bastard is still alive.'

Another pause. Then: 'Listen, Ed. On another subject…'

'You want to know about Irina?'

'No details. Just that she's safe.'

Ed said nothing.

'That stunt you pulled in Pat Pong – with that whore. You're learning. You had us fooled. We lost track of you.'

Ed shrugged.

'You saw her?' Merr asked.

'No Merr. I didn't see her.' He told Merr the whole story, down to the Venetian mask.

Merr was surprised: 'She went to Chanpanich? The place where we had lunch by the river?'

'Yes.'

'How did you find out?' Merr was more than surprised – he was startled, as though a block of wood was suddenly talking Latin.

'Irina left a note. At Schomberg's.'

'That picture she was drawing?'

Ed nodded.

'Well, she couldn't have chosen a better place. Chanpanich, the old man, he's safe. We do business there – now and again.'

'Did Irina know that?'

'Doubt it,' Merr said.

'You think the old man connected Irina with you?'

'He saw the three of us together. Probably he thought I'd sent her.'

'He told me she'd gone. Disappeared.'

'And you believed him?' Merr said.

'But that's what he said: *Lady guest, she check out.*'

'I guess what he meant was – if you've got a message for her, bring it by. But don't expect to see her.'

'You're always twenty steps ahead of me.' Ed shook his head.

'Not your world, Ed. I'd be just as lost if I started painting reflections.' It was a kind word, and Ed warmed to it.

'And *do* I have a message for Irina?' Ed asked.

From the inside pocket of his shirt, Merr fished out an American passport, travel-worn and dog-eared. 'This is what we made for her when she was going to Singapore,' he said, handing it to Ed.

Ed flicked through the passport. The picture was unmistakably Irina though a few years younger. The name was Olga Maslova. 'Who's Olga?' he asked.

'Some Yankee tourist going home,' Merr told him. 'And give her this too.' It was a mobile telephone, clunky and old. 'There are two names in the memory. If she hits *Doris Manicure* she gets me. On a secure line. The number only works on this phone.' Merr switched on the phone and showed Ed the directory – *Doris (Manicure)*. 'She should leave the phone turned off unless she needs to call. Switched off, the battery lasts a year. If she tries to open the phone or change the battery, the SIM-card self-destructs. If she hits the other name in the memory, *Wells Fargo*, it'll do the same – self-destruct.'

'That it?'

'If she opens up her messages, there's biodata. On Olga.'

Ed took the phone. 'Does she take the phone with her? When she flies out?'

'Sure. Like I said, it's good for a year.'

Ed nodded. 'And what did that mean?' he asked. 'Something your boss said – *With Irina certain possibilities can't be ruled out?*'

Merr took a moment to answer. 'It means one bit of her life is a total blank. She went to Moscow in 1994 when she was seventeen. It took her six years to get a four-year diploma. Putting it politely, she was working her way through art school. For the last two semesters she had zero attendance but good grades. She married a nobody in 2004, a Ukrainian. From the Foreign Ministry in Kiev. She showed up with him in Bangkok in 2006. Via North Korea. So where she was between 2000 in Moscow and 2004 in Kiev – it's a blank. An absolute blank.'

'Sounds to me like you've been checking her out.'

'No way. Never.' Merr glanced round the ill-lit morgue. 'In thirty seconds I'm out of here. When you talk to Hirsch, ask him about the tunnel to the Police Hospital. It goes from *S2*. That'll lose your tail.'

'My tail?'

'He's been waiting for you outside, ever since you arrived at the front door.'

'If I turn paranoid, you'll be hearing from my lawyer,' Ed grimaced.

'Shut up and listen. Get the passport and the phone to Irina. If Chanpanich won't let you see her, give them both to him. Tell him *Doris Manicure* and *Wells Fargo*. Just those words. He'll understand. Don't fuck up. And make peace with Hirsch. He's on our side.'

★★★★★

Dr Hirsch's office was on the fourth floor. It smelt of coffee and of half-a-dozen red and white carnations poked artlessly into a vase on the desk. The windows were screened inside by Venetian blinds except for one which was shaded by the branches of a coconut palm in the sunny yard. Through the fronds of the palm Ed could see what looked like a track for horse-racing.

On the way up from S3, Ed had already decided to come clean with Hirsch. Sitting now opposite the old man, he quickly explained the blood-buyer story and apologised for it. That was all Hirsch really needed to know, but somehow Ed found himself in the middle of episode two – Chaudhary and the Princess. When that was finished, Hirsch said nothing, waiting, knowing there was more. As Ed talked on, he could see from the old man's nods that the details of the story were unknown to him, but the general outline was somehow familiar. Hirsch asked no questions, but an expression of anger tightened his face a dozen times as he listened.

When Ed had finished, the old man said: 'Why you are telling me this?'

'I don't know. Because of who you are, maybe.' Ed paused. 'A police doctor. You understand these things – and I don't.'

Hirsch was watching him, sympathetically perhaps, but still unsatisfied – his why-question was only half-answered. 'Mr Croft also understands them? Or not?'

'Yes. He does. But not in the same way as you,' Ed replied.

'And how do I understand? In your opinion?'

'Those three girls – the ones I saw the first time I was here. They made you angry. I could see. They made me angry too.'

There was a long silence. The quiet room was insulated from the rest of the building by an outer office where Hirsch's secretary, a Thai dragon with dyed black hair, kept guard.

'Would you like some coffee?' Hirsch asked.

Ed nodded. 'Please.'

Hirsch stood up and set out the cups himself. 'I have no cream and no sugar,' he said.

'No problem.'

'The reason for your visit today,' said Hirsch pouring the coffee with his back to Ed. 'You are looking for your wife? She is missing and you think she may be dead? Why, if I may ask?'

Yes, he was looking for his wife – angrily, passionately looking for his wife. Ed began to pour out his second story, his story and Dy's. Mount McKinley. Terry. To his surprise, he found himself using words he hadn't used before, telling the story for the first time as Dy might have told it. It was the photograph on her desk and the explanation he'd just had with Merr – they changed the lighting, they changed the perspective. It was a new picture.

Hirsch sipped his coffee and listened carefully. 'May I comment?' he asked when Ed reached the flight to Kuala Lumpur and Diana's disappearance.

'Please,' Ed replied.

'It is almost certain,' Hirsch said thoughtfully, '*almost* certain, that your wife received information at United

Nations from this anonymous caller. Information about Andronicus. But she did not pass on this information to her colleagues. She kept it private. Why?'

'I don't accept…'

Hirsch raised his hand, postponing Ed's protest.

'Doctor Scarman, in a country like Thailand such information, if documented, can be valuable. Very valuable. It is possible that your wife approached Andronicus…'

Ed bridled in Diana's defence. What Hirsch was suggesting was *not* possible.

'Shall I finish?' Hirsch asked quietly.

'Okay,' Ed agreed. 'But I don't go along.'

'If your wife contacted Andronicus – *if* she did – she naturally remained anonymous. She had, of course, a problem – a lack of definite information. Imagine that she wanted to put pressure on Andronicus, to blackmail Andronicus in fact, it would have been difficult because all she had was rumours. No facts. People like Andronicus, and whoever stands behind them, are not seriously frightened by rumours.'

'Understandably.'

'Let me ask you a question,' Hirsch pursued. 'Was your wife in need of money? A considerable sum of money?'

'No,' Ed said flatly. Then he remembered the partnership, the partnership Dy wanted in Lambfields. 'Or maybe. It's not impossible.'

'If she contacted Andronicus but without facts, Andronicus would have no reason – no reason at all – to talk to her. You must understand – in Thailand we have many rumours and much blackmail. Without facts Andronicus will do its best to ignore her. At least until…'

'Until?'

'Until *you* arrive in Bangkok. Now, for Andronicus, the situation is suddenly more serious. You are a mystery. You say you are blood-buyer. Bhatnagar must have heard this from Mr Patel.'

'You think Patel…?'

'I have met Mr Patel. He is Indian. Bhatnagar is Indian. They meet socially, they exchange information. That is how such people function. But they are not conspirators. At least, it is improbable.'

'Okay.'

'So Mr Chaudhary is sent to find out more. Obviously you are *not* a blood-buyer. You are fresh arrived from America. And already you have some connection with a woman known to work at the UN. It seems you share a hotel room with her. So, looked at from Andronicus' point-of-view, why are you telling Chaudhary this story about blood? To show that you have knowledge, *facts* – more than just rumour. They ask themselves – this woman you sleep with at the Princess, a UN woman, who is she? Is she the person who has already threatened them? It seems possible. You are taken to the office and then to the factory, rubbing your nose, so to speak, in the scent. They watch you carefully. You are good-informed, and you ask the right questions. Now they begin to take the blackmail more serious. What day you went to the factory?'

'Wednesday.'

'Exactly. And the next day, Chaudhary meets your wife at the airport, and she goes off with him. She goes, but she is very frightened. If she is so frightened, why does she go at all?'

'The way you're telling it, because she has the chance to talk about money.'

'Exactly. And why does she take such a terrible risk? Is she tired of life?'

'Because the money is important to her,' Ed suggested, not believing a word of Hirsch's theory.

'It is possible. Perhaps the money is her only way out. Without the money, she doesn't care anymore what happens to her?'

'More or less suicide.'

'I have seen this in Thailand. Not often, but maybe ten times in all these years. I think the English word is *recklessness*. Behind nearly every suicide lies despair, destructed self-esteem.'

'Suicide?' Perhaps it added up, what Hirsch was saying. Perhaps for months Dy had been toying with an idea – blackmail Andronicus. It was a brutally cynical idea, but… She'd stayed anonymous, made no false move. Then she'd wanted Ed to come to Bangkok. She'd seen herself cracking up – at work, with the whores, and maybe – it was not impossible – with this filthy blackmail idea. She needed help. Badly. So Ed had arrived. Not just arrived, but blundered in on her patch and trampled all over it. Ed and Merr. And none of it had helped her. Ever since Terry had been born, Dy had been desperate for help, and she'd got nothing, nothing, nothing. *Despair, destructed self-esteem.* Maybe Hirsch was right.

'Much of my work over the years, Doctor Scarman,' the old man was saying, 'has been cleaning up the wreckage left by criminals. You have seen five corpses in my mortuary. I have seen thousands. And I have heard many stories.'

'Stories like Dy's?'

'Some.'

'How did they end, her kind of stories?'

'In two ways. No, in three.'

Ed waited.

'To end a blackmail, you must destroy the blackmailer. If the blackmailer keeps the evidence private, it is necessary to cut only the blackmailer's throat. That is the first ending.'

Ed waited, silent.

'In the case of your wife, the blackmail has become more and more *public*. You arrive. A raid is carried out on the warehouse – a professional raid. One girl is killed. Next morning there is a fire inspection. The level of risk for Andronicus becomes unacceptable. By Saturday noon, earlier maybe, Andronicus has emptied the warehouse. The blood operation is destroyed. An excellent thing! And maybe much more has been destroyed at the same time. Blood is only a minor trade, Doctor Scarman. Much bigger is the trade in organs. The police will be active now for the first time since many years. You must not blame yourself for failure. You have not failed. You have achieved something important. Perhaps very important.'

'And in this second ending, what happens to Dy?'

'Probably they do not cut her throat. If your wife is their prisoner, she is valuable. They can exchange her.'

'Exchange her?'

'It is called an *amnesty*. The big names in the organ business get an amnesty from the government, and your wife goes free.'

'And the government does that? Gives them an amnesty in exchange for a hostage?'

'Sometimes yes, sometimes no. Your wife is an American citizen working for the UN. Possibly it will be done. But…' Hirsch held up his hand not wanting to create false hope. 'But even if it is done, it is more or less meaningless. You understand *life expectancy*?'

Ed nodded.

'For a hostage exchanged in an amnesty, life expectancy is very short.'

'The top guys go free and take revenge afterward? Is that what you mean?'

'You can say so. That is the second ending.'

'And the third?'

'Nobody knows. The story dies. After a while the file is closed. Closed but not shredded.'

'And it isn't a problem for you – which way it ends?'

'Doctor Scarman. I have outlined for you only a *hypothese*. If this *hypothese* is correct, your wife planned to use those children, in the exact same way as Andronicus.'

'That's why I don't accept your hypothesis,' Ed objected. 'My wife isn't that kind of person. No way.'

'You must obviously know her better than I do. I know only what you tell me. And the children? In the warehouse?'

'Mr Croft said…'

'…the children are certainly dead. Mr Croft is an American realist. Today is Tuesday. It is a disgusting fact, but the part of those children that is edible is already eaten. In the city by rats, in the river by crabs, in the jungle by ants. And in the sea by something else. I have no information – they do not bring corpses from the sea to this clinic.'

Ed's throat clenched tight. 'And it's my fault. I set up the raid. I…'

'The death of the children is certainly your responsibility,' Hirsch muttered, watching Ed closely. 'But the ending of Andronicus, that is your responsibility too, your achievement.'

For a moment Ed struggled to find his voice. 'I'm having a hard time coping with this,' he gasped at last. 'I'm sorry.'

'You are not a believer? Not a Christian?'

'No.'

Hirsch lapsed into silence. Reflective, threatening. An old man's silence. 'Your story touches my life in more than one way,' he said at last. 'I also…'

Ed looked at him, unwilling to share the burden of another man when his own weighed so heavily.

'I was married,' Hirsch said flatly. 'My wife was expecting our first child. She was Thai. She was near her time. A friend of mine had a boat. On Ko Samui. It is an island. Thirty years ago, it was very remote. He invited us to spend some time on his boat. I was doctor, new qualified. Any emergency – I was sure I could master. I believed that I had properly evaluated and properly decided. We would go to Ko Samui. As it happened, I was wrong. The baby was large – a German baby, not a Thai. There was what is called a breach presentation. My wife died. And the baby died soon after. A girl. If we had stayed in Bangkok and not gone to Ko Samui, the hospital could have saved them both.'

Despite his reluctance to listen, tears burned in Ed's eyes. He blinked them away. Finally, all he could say was: 'And you're still angry.'

'Yes. I kept my anger. Try to keep yours, Doctor Scarman.'

★★★★★

Hirsch led him through the tunnel that connected *S2* with the Police Hospital. They shook hands on parting but not warmly – too many years, too many differences lay between them.

For the moment, Ed was free – no tail could have followed him through the morgue and the police tunnel. It was almost four o'clock. Once he'd delivered Irina's passport and the telephone, he'd have nothing to do but wait.

The Police Hospital was on the same crossroads as the Erewan Hotel, battered by heat, noise, and the poisonous fumes of the traffic. There was an altar outside the hotel where Buddhist girls danced for the tourists each evening – he'd seen it on his way to Soy Cowboy a week before. On the same corner as the altar, a gang of boys sat on silent motor-bikes waiting for custom. If he took a taxi to River City, he'd be there in an hour. If he took a motor-bike, he'd be there in ten minutes. He approached the gang, trying to discover from their clothing, their hairstyles or their expressions which of them was widest awake and most concerned with staying alive. No signs. He picked a boy at the edge of the gang. 'River City,' he said, hoping the boy would understand. The boy held up five fingers. Fifty baht. The proper fare for a motor-bike, Irina had told him, was thirty, but Ed didn't argue.

The boy was cradling two crash helmets on his gas tank. He put one on his own head and offered the other to Ed. The helmet was much too small. The boy shrugged and motioned Ed to mount the saddle. Ed straddled the bike, holding the helmet uselessly in his lap. *Despair and destructed self-esteem lie behind every suicide.* That was what Hirsch had said. An angry old man – unable to forgive, because the evil he'd seen, and the evil he'd done, were unforgivable.

They reached River City in less than ten minutes – the boy was evidently in training for a traffic-cross championship. Ed stopped him at the huge department store where a million souvenirs were sold, and from which, Merr had said, the antique smugglers operated. The boy's nervous alertness drained away. He took his fifty baht, sagged back into apathy, and puttered off down the street.

The Spoon was deserted – too late for lunch, too early for dinner. Only Mr Chanpanich, the owner, sat under an umbrella at one of the riverside tables smoking a cigarette. He greeted Ed as an old friend, waving him to a seat at his table. A waiter appeared.

'Tea or Coca-Cola?' Chanpanich invited him. 'On the house.'

Ed sat down. 'Coke,' he said. 'Please.'

'You have message for lady guest?'

'You have no lady guest.'

Chanpanich looked shocked. 'Naturally we have lady guest,' he said. 'Why you think…?'

'Forget it,' Ed said. 'Where is she?'

The waiter brought a Coke bottle and a glassful of ice. He opened the Coke at the table.

'You have message for her?' Chanpanich repeated.

'I'd prefer to give it her myself.' That's what Merr had told him to say.

The old man muttered a few words to the waiter who nodded and scurried off.

'One minute,' Chanpanich told Ed. Then: 'It is very beautiful, Loy Krathong. You think? So many firework. More and more each year.' The Thai voice flowed on like the sunny, weed-choked river beside them – all trace of Sodom and Gomorrah now vanished.

The waiter was gone for what seemed like ten minutes. 'Where is he?' Ed asked at last, breaking into Chanpanich's monologue.

'Maybe lady guest make beautiful,' Chanpanich said, miming a girl putting on lipstick.

It didn't sound like Irina. If she was there, she'd have seen him straight away. Unless – unless there was someone with her. Vadim? Or…

The waiter reappeared, shaking his head.

'I am sorry,' Chanpanich said. 'I raise your hope. But now is not possible.'

For a second all the bile of Ed's week in Bangkok focused on the smug, smiling Thai in front of him. He gripped the glass of Coke, ready to smash it against the table and grind the sharp edges into the smirking, self-satisfied face. The incessant lying! The endless deceit!

'Say what you like,' Ed insisted, focusing his fury into action. 'I intend to see her.' He stood up. 'Show me where she is.'

'I have said,' Chanpanich replied, 'now is not possible.' Merr's orders were, if you can't see Irina, give the passport and the phone to Chanpanich. Ed took the phone out of his shirt pocket. 'I'm going to call the tourist police,' Ed said, his voice loud with anger, 'and tell them you kidnapped a woman.'

Chanpanich waved Ed to sit down. 'In Thailand,' he said, 'we not shout. Shout is bad manner.'

'Fuck you and fuck your manners,' Ed shouted. 'Let me see the woman. Now.'

'Sit down,' Chanpanich said.

'Can I see her?'

'Yes.'

Ed sat down. 'When?' he said.

'Your frenn, Irina Porzova, is staying here. Mr Cloff call me. He say, Irina Porzova must stay *here*. *Must* stay. This morning she want to go. I tell her no, she not go. Mr Cloff order.'

'And she said she didn't take orders from Mr Croft,' Ed snarled.

'Essackly.'

'So you…?'

'Irina Porzova not ready see you. Not ready see anyone. She sleep.'

'You haven't…?'

'Mr Cloff very clear – keep Irina Porzova safe.'

At last – the truth. They'd given Irina a shot. To keep her safe. 'And when will she wake up?' Ed asked.

'Difficult be sure. Irina Porzova is very…'

'She put up a fight, you mean.'

'Yes,' said the old man approvingly. 'Irina Porzova is very good woman. Very good fight.'

★★★★★

Ed was sitting by Irina's bed. The room was hot despite the slow ceiling fan churning the heavy air. The afternoon sun and the shimmering reflections of the river glowed through the chinks in the tall Venetian blind. Irina was lying on her back under a simple sheet. Her sleep was troubled, and her face and neck were running sweat.

It was gone six o'clock. For two hours Ed had studied the room and its simple contents. Irina's clothes – the muslin dress and the sunhat he remembered from the airport – were hanging on a nail hammered into the door. Her underclothes too. On a bamboo table beside the bed were her sunglasses. In the table drawer was the envelope with the cash, open now. Ed had counted it. $ 2,634.

On Irina's encrypted phone, Ed had called *Doris (Manicure)*. Merr had answered, as promised. He'd told Ed to call again as soon as Irina came round. Transport would be there after his call. Irina was flying from Phuket direct to Singapore next day. Qantas. The driver would have the booking code. That had been at five.

It was six-thirty before Irina stirred. Ed called Merr again. 'Wait till she understands what you're saying. Then go back to Schomberg's on your own – just you. Some things have come in. About Dy.'

*****

On the crowded rush-hour sidewalk, Ed and Merr passed Silom Village. They crossed the Expressway chasm, heading for the State Tower where Merr had taken them after they'd abandoned the jazz at the Bamboo Bar. Merr had a lot to tell.

The headless woman in the morgue had the same blood group as Diana – O-negative. Hirsch would have to run a DNA comparison. Merr had already sent someone to the Princess to retrieve Dy's hairbrush. But the check was routine – Merr was almost certain that Diana was alive.

Then Patel. He'd been back at the UN since lunchtime. Matsuura had questioned him first. Then Patel had been passed to the Royal Thai Police. Finally it had been Merr's turn. Yes, Patel did know Bhatnagar, vaguely. Yes, he had met Bhatnagar on the evening of 26th October, the Monday before. At an Indian wedding – the giving away of the daughter. Yes, he had mentioned to Bhatnagar that a blood-buyer was in town, but not that the blood-buyer was married to a lawyer on his staff. No, if Ms Tarn was hiding, he had no idea why or where. Patel was beginning to panic. Merr wanted Ed to go to the UN again – to keep up the pressure about Diana. At eleven next morning.

'So where *is* Dy?' Ed asked as they stepped into the elevator – non-stop to the Sky Bar on the sixty-third floor. 'Or where might she be?'

'I think I might know where they've taken her,' Merr said. 'Or where they'll take her pretty soon.'

'Where?'

'The warehouse. In Chatuchak.'

'The warehouse?'

'Yes. Don't get any funny ideas. Stay out of things. I've told you that before, and this time I mean it. Okay?'

They had the elevator to themselves. The doors closed silently. Smoothly, with no apparent acceleration, the marble cage began its ascent.

'Why the warehouse?' Ed asked. 'You raided the place yesterday. Andronicus has four factories outside Bangkok, according to Chaudhary.'

'I know. We searched them all. And a bunch of other places too. It's quite a network.'

'Did you search headquarters?'

'In the Kingdom Tower?'

Ed nodded.

'Police searched that. Took away fifteen computers and a million files. Then they locked the place up. No way in.'

'So what did you find, you and the police?'

'Not a lot. A-MISS is doing better.'

'Bhatnagar's been talking?'

'Hardly surprising. I met the Iron Lady once,' Merr said. 'In Darwin. Regional Co-operation Meeting.'

'Gruesome was she?'

'What's up with you, Ed? You're supposed to quote Shakespeare at me.'

'I gave that up. Yesterday. Cold turkey.'

'Yeah, she's gruesome. Make a rattlesnake talk if she put her mind to it.'

Maybe she is *more stubborn-hard than hammered iron*, Ed thought. Forget it. It wasn't a play he much liked anyway, *King John*. Certainly not worth wasting time on now.

The elevator doors opened. The Sky Bar.

'Isn't the warehouse locked up?' Ed asked.

'Table for two?' the *maitre d'* interrupted.

'Four,' Merr said. 'Ladies coming later.'

They followed the *maître d'*. The Sky Bar wasn't crowded. Their table overlooked the Chao Phraya and, just visible as a green glow on the riverbank, the garden of the Oriental.

'No,' Merr told him, sitting down. 'Not locked. Nor the factories. We're keeping an eye on them.'

'What ladies?' Ed asked. 'Coming later?'

'You get a better table if you say it's for four. Didn't they teach you nothing in grad school?'

A waiter came to the table, and they ordered Jack Daniels. While they were waiting, a silence fell suddenly between them, awkward, unresolved. Ed glared down at the city, so vast and spread so meaninglessly in front of them. The waiter brought the whiskey.

'There's something else,' Merr said tentatively without raising his glass. 'It's why I wanted to talk to you. Over a glass of whiskey. Not on the phone.'

Ed nodded, alarmed, guessing already what might lie behind Merr's tactfulness.

'The consular section – they had a call. From Lucía. She was trying to contact Dy.'

'Lucía? About Terry? Bad news?'

'Yes, bad news.'

'Tell me,' Ed said quietly. 'Just tell me.'

Merr nodded. 'She's been hospitalised – Terry has. Some kind of fit.'

'How long has she got?'

'I don't know. You'd better talk to Lucía.' Merr found the number on his phone, touched it, and gave the phone to Ed. 'I'm sorry,' he said. 'Truly.'

'Yes,' Ed replied. The number connected. The phone in DC began to ring. Someone picked up but said nothing. 'Hello,' Ed said. 'Is that you, Lucía?'

Day 10

Ed's meeting at the UN was not till eleven. Even so, he took breakfast at seven and was in the street by seven-thirty, heading for Chong Nonsi.

A company with nothing to hide is not afraid of transparency. And anyway we have our Archive. What Chaudhary had said in the Kingdom Tower coupled with what Merr had explained in the Sky Bar had suggested something to Ed – something that seemed less and less impossible as he'd tossed and turned in Schomberg's Hotel, thinking it over.

Merr had put it like this – if Andronicus wanted to trade Diana, they'd have to keep her healthy and somewhere not too remote. So, as soon as things were quieter, Andronicus might well move her back into the warehouse or one of their factories. Andronicus still had the keys, though, of course, T-CAN was keeping its eyes open. For what that was worth

And anyway, we have our Archive. Diana was as likely to be in Andronicus' head office as anywhere else. At least it was worth checking. He'd said nothing to Merr. Merr had warned him: *Don't get any funny ideas.* And, by Merr's standards, the Archive in the Kingdom Tower was a terminally funny idea.

He turned the corner where the Skytrain tracks veered off toward Chong Nonsi. Ahead, at the next crossroads, he could see the Kingdom Tower, where, just possibly, Dy might be – on the twenty-ninth floor. It was a long shot, but it wasn't impossible.

From his visit to the Tower with Chaudhary, Ed knew he had to exchange his passport for a visitor's ID and tell the girl at reception what floor he was visiting. Before breakfast he'd googled the Kingdom Tower. In fact there were several interlocking towers with separate elevator systems. He'd homed in on the Consulate of Verbena – it was in the same tower as Andronicus, though on the twentieth floor. That's where he'd say he was going. And his plan? He had no plan beyond going to the glass doors of the Andronicus office and peering in. If the police had locked the place up, there was nothing he could do anyway.

The business with the receptionist went slowly. It was a busy time – the huge building was filling up fast. He waited patiently in line, numb with the dismal news about Terry: *under sedation, no prognosis.* Lucía had said the unfamiliar words carefully and emphatically – holding back her tears. The girl had been fond of Terry. He ought to do something for her. And he would. He watched the girl at the reception desk as she filed passports, driving licences, credit cards even, into a system of drawers. When his turn came, he passively exchanged his American passport for a white card with a large hand-written number. He was going to the twentieth floor – Verbenan Consulate. He showed the card to the guard at the foot of the narrow escalator which climbed up through the fountains and the fish. No problem. On the upper landing he oriented himself, remembering the marble, the altars, the effigies. He went straight to the elevator lobby. Andronicus' name was on the registry board – *Floor 29/3.* The slow elevator that stopped on all floors including *Floor 20/Consulate of Verbena* was Elevator 2. He waited for it.

The elevator took five minutes to reach Floor 29. The change was startling. The lions and the signboard were inside the Andronicus office now – he could see them through the glass. The cubicles looked deserted. Under Ed's feet, scraps of office paper, mostly blank, were scattered, gritty and trampled. The heavy, upright door-handles were chained together – a galvanised chain, far from substantial, was wound several times through the handles and padlocked. The padlock looked flimsy too. Ed went to the doors. He took hold of the handles and moved the doors in and out a few inches – the bolts top and bottom were smashed. Only the chain held the doors closed. Scotch-taped inside one of the doors was a notice in Thai and in English: *Police Line Do Not Cross*. He peered through the glass. *A company with nothing to hide is not afraid of transparency*. He could see the *ARCHIVE* clearly. The fake rosewood door was closed. He fingered the chain critically – with a bolt-cutter, he'd be inside the office in seconds.

He'd need a taxi. Waiting in the ID line twenty minutes before, Ed had seen a line of taxis outside the huge, gleaming windows. He bent down, picked up a more or less clean sheet of paper, folded it, put it in his shirt pocket, and took the fast elevator down.

A dozen taxis stood idle in the taxi-rank. Ed went to the head of the line.

The driver wound down the window. 'Sir?'

'I need a bolt-cutter,' Ed said.

'No unnerstann.'

The driver was sitting on the right side of his taxi, something Ed still found awkward. Ed went to the left door, opened it and sat down. He took the piece of paper out of his shirt pocket and signalled to the driver that he needed a pen. The driver gave him a ballpoint. Ed sketched a bolt. The driver nodded. Then a bolt-cutter.

'You wan'?' the driver asked, pointing at the cutter.

In the morning rush-hour, it took half an hour to reach an oil-blackened row of repair workshops and spare-part stores. The driver took the lead. He showed Ed's drawing to a mechanic in one of the workshops – an old friend it seemed. Five minutes later Ed had a bolt-cutter tough enough to cope with the chain on the twenty-ninth floor of the Kingdom Tower. The mechanic wrapped it awkwardly for him in brown paper.

Back at the Kingdom Tower, Ed gave the driver a 500 bill and told him to wait by the taxi-rank. He'd be back in a few minutes.

He pushed through the swing doors into the cool, splashy foyer – the fountains, the koi-fish, the waterfalls. The guard at the bottom of the escalator glanced at Ed's white card and then at the brown-paper package but didn't ask what it was. Past the altars, past the huge portrait of Queen Sirikit. This time Ed took the fast elevator.

The lobby of the twenty-ninth floor was exactly as Ed had left it. Taking his time, he unwrapped his package. He opened the jaws of the bolt-cutter and fitted them over a link in the chain. He pressed the handles of the cutter hard together, and the jaws bit through the link. Another bite on the other side of the link. The chain fell apart. If that was the best the Thai police could do… He put the bolt-cutter on the floor and began to tug at the rattling links of the chain, freeing the door-handles.

Something moved inside the office. The door of the Archive cracked open. Then he saw the silhouette of a woman against the light. A guard. In some kind of uniform. Skinny. Venomous. Unless there was another door, she was locked in. Who'd locked her in? Certainly not the police. Andronicus must have switched the police chain for one of their own. The guard saw Ed at the door and made straight for him, darting like a lizard through the cubicles. The chain clattered free. Ed shoved the door open and bent down to grab the bolt-cutter – it'd be handy if it came to a fight. He crouched in the doorway, looking up at the woman.

'*Falang?*' she said. She stopped a few paces in front of him, obviously puzzled.

Ed caught his breath – the woman was expecting someone, but obviously not him. 'They sent me instead,' Ed told her, standing up. For a second the initiative was his.

'Who send you?' The woman's eye took in the bolt-cutter and the unchained, unguarded door.

'Mr Bhatnagar,' Ed said.

The woman reached for her belt, perhaps for a telephone, perhaps for a gun. Ed raised the bolt-cutter. He saw the woman's hand pull a pager from its holster. With all his strength, he smashed the cutter down against her wrist. She screamed. The pager spun across the office and clattered into a distant cubicle. He pushed the screeching woman aside. Still gripping the cutter, he reached the door of the Archive.

Inside the room a woman sat tight-gagged and bound to a chair. Diana. It was over.

Day 375

Thursday 4th November 2010

They'd never been together before, all four of them in one place and at one time. It was Merr's revenge as he called it – making Ed his best man.

Ed and Diana had flown in the night before, and Merr had invited them for breakfast at the InterConti.

'So why Doha?' Diana asked him, starting on her second plate of fried eggs and beef-bacon.

'Rotation for one thing,' Merr told her, 'promotion for another. And there's work here for Irina. They like it here, what she does.'

Irina glanced ironically at Ed. 'Merr likes my stuff,' she said. 'How long it lasts after we are marry, I don't know.'

'Saturday's the big day, so we'll probably know by Sunday,' Ed said quietly. He was jet-lagged – it was a hell of a flight from LA to Qatar.

'How about *your* stuff?' Merr asked. 'Still doing reflections?'

'No. These days I agree with Dy – a severe case of *pseudo-philosophical bullshit.*'

'Ed…' Diana laughed at him fondly, putting down her fork and stretching out to touch his hand across the table.

'So just the Hollywood stuff then? For Warner Brothers, wasn't it?' Merr asked.

'Mostly,' Ed said. 'But it's been more interesting than I thought, doing those Leonardos. You see, I had this idea.

281

I can do all these styles, so why not mix them up in one painting. I did a *Holy Virgin Riding on a Unicorn* – a Duccio profile, Rafael drapery, and a Mondrian landscape? I mean, it brings the whole issue of style into question.' Ed was getting excited – his latest pictures were attracting comment, controversy even. Myron was seeing to that.

Irina was looking at him, her mouth gaping, incredulous.

'Do me a favour, Ed,' Merr asked him. 'Talk about something that doesn't impress the hell out of Irina.'

They laughed. It had been a good year.

After breakfast they went out to the beach. There had been November rain in the night, but the sand was dry again, and the sun was pleasantly warm. Simple boardwalks led across the sand to umbrellas, thatched roofs on poles. It was Thursday and the beach was already filling up.

Irina had to go shopping – some fabulous shops had opened in The Pearl, she said, and she needed a couple of things for the ceremony. Dy said she'd help Irina choose. Merr gave Irina the car keys, and the women clattered back along the boardwalk toward the hotel.

An Indian waiter approached the two men – if they were looking for a nice umbrella...

*****

'Why so many Indians?' Ed asked, sipping a Coke under their umbrella. 'Here? At the airport?'

'Pakistanis mostly,' Merr corrected him. 'They do the work. Along with the Filipinos.'

'That why you're here? Slave trade this time?'

'Doha's a kind of base,' Merr replied evasively. Then more frankly: 'Ed, after what happened in Bangkok, please... Please don't ask about work. Okay?'

They laughed. Even without Merr's new job, there was plenty of gossip to catch up on. But not quite yet. They had something to talk about first, something painful. Just before New Year the last activity in Terry's brain had flickered out. The hospital had said it was time to switch off the machines. They'd visited her most days, he and Dy, watching their little girl disappear, kept alive by the friendly, tireless machines. The end had been inevitable, but it hadn't been easy. This time though, they'd talked it through – found ways to accept the ugliness of it all. Merr listened reflectively, asking no questions. When Ed had finished, they sat in silence for a long time. Then Ed said: 'Somehow it brought us together. Losing Terry.'

'I can understand that,' Merr said.

'Then, afterward, we moved to LA.'

'Tell me about that,' Merr asked. 'Dy's new job.'

Ed began on the details. Diana was still an associate at Lambfields. They hadn't fired her – it would hardly have been decent after the brilliant report Matsuura had given her. But they'd switched her from DC to Los Angeles.

It amused Merr, the way that Dy had spun things at the UN. He'd seen the UN file. Matsuura had frozen Patel's project and then ransacked his office for traces of the original call – the whistle-blower's call about Andronicus. As it turned out, Chitanawa had taken the call and filed his notes in an old grey filing cabinet under *Miscellaneous: No Action Required*. Dozens of people might have accessed the *Miscellaneous* file – but there was no evidence that anyone had actually done so. And certainly nothing connected Diana with the call, nothing at all. As far as T-CAN was concerned, no one at the UN had blackmailed Andronicus. Somehow Matsuura had hung the whole mess on Patel's peg, and Patel had be recalled to India, to a bank somewhere in Uttar Pradesh. The glowing report on Diana had been Matsuura's last jeering stab at Patel's reputation.

And Merr had seen another file – the A-MISS file on Bhatnagar. Blood, organs, fake drugs – Andronicus had been persistent and busy, though mostly as a middleman.

Vadim? Merr knew about that too. Vadim's racket had been small and fledgling – importing BMWs in the diplomatic bag. Only a couple of cars a month, but the Thais had objected to the UN, and the Russian Government had removed Vadim. He was back in Russia now – something to do with the Volga-Don Canal.

But the Andronicus case was by no means closed. As far as Merr could tell, the investigation would roll on for years. Already it had lapped round the feet of a couple of politicians – one red, one yellow. That was good. As long as there was public mud-slinging, the blood business was dead and the organ business too, though the trade would certainly move on. Until they found out how to grow organs from stem-cells, there'd always be a market. Indonesia had been rumoured, and there were stories about Bosnia.

And Dy? Merr was curious. She'd changed, she didn't seem so spiky anymore.

Yes, Ed agreed, she'd changed – they both had. They hadn't tried to wind the clock back – you never could. But a lot of what they'd been to each other had survived – hidden, buried. And somehow they'd found it again.

Not that Dy had escaped scot-free. One shock sat very deep with her. Hirsch at the hospital, Merr, Irina, even Ed himself – they'd all thought she'd done something despicable, murderous even. Or, if she hadn't actually done it, that she was *capable* of doing it – she'd kept the blood racket secret and tried to squeeze money out of the racketeers. That had hurt her badly. What had she done to make everyone think such vile things about her? It was a question with no answer, an impasse she'd never completely escape. But now she was pregnant again…

'Pregnant! Irina thought she might be,' Merr said with a sudden explosion of pleasure. 'Just from how much she ate at breakfast: *I theenk eet eez pussible Dy eez ikspyecting.* You

know that accent of hers.' He laughed – proud of Irina's shrewdness, fond of everything about her.

'Dy never goes to weddings unless she's pregnant. You know that,' Ed said, his voice trailing off with a shiver. An expectant, black-haired waiter was hovering near their table. 'These Indian guys give me the creeps,' he said.

'Pakistani,' Merr corrected him again. 'Moslem.'

'How can you tell?'

'The Indians have money – they sit under the umbrellas. The Pakistanis put the umbrellas up, put them down, and fetch the drinks.'

'Arabs don't work?'

'Nothing backbreaking. Not in Qatar anyway.'

Ed waved the waiter away – *no thank you*.

'But – did you ever ask Dy? Why she went with Chaudhary that time? I mean…'

'Yes I asked her.'

'And…?'

'You still have doubts about her?' Ed asked suddenly defensive.

'No,' Merr answered. 'Not anymore.'

'Then let's just say, her answer was satisfactory.'

Merr fell silent, abashed. 'You're right,' he said. 'It was a crummy thing to ask. Please don't tell her I said it.'

'No, of course not,' Ed agreed. Then, to avoid hurting Merr's feelings: 'Chaudhary told her there really was a blood racket, told her he wanted to confess the whole thing. Confess to her because she was at the UN. So she went with him.'

The Pakistani waiter was still hovering, out of earshot, but somehow menacing.

'So you'll stay in Doha?' Ed asked, watching the waiter without catching his eye.

'It's a good place.'

'No problem with a work permit for Irina?'

'None at all.'

'But Merr…? What kind of career move is that? Marrying the KGB?'

'That's what they told me to do.'

'Washington?'

'Marry her or dump her.'

'Sounds like a Victorian father.'

'But you're right,' Merr agreed. 'Career-wise, any wife is one wife too many.'

'Such contempt for the institution of marriage!' Ed said piously.

'But in the end it makes no difference. This'll be my last posting. I can quit when I'm forty.'

'In 2013.'

'Exactly. Start my own security business. Somewhere safe. Here maybe. Qatar's fine. Irina likes it here.'

'Where did you catch up with her? After Thailand?'

'Well,' Merr replied causally. 'Definitely not…' Merr hesitated. 'In Vancouver.'

Get to Vancouver. Call me from there. Those were the last words Ed had spoken to Irina at the airport. So Merr knew all about it. And if he knew that, he must also know what had happened that last night at Schomberg's – it was on the surveillance tape after all.

The two men glanced at each other and began to laugh. One more barrier was gone.

'Why Vancouver, Ed? Of all places.'

'Vancouver? I went on holiday there one time. With my mom.'

Merr shrugged. 'Everything goes back to Mamma,' he said. 'Didn't Freud say that?'

'Maybe. But Shakespeare… No! I'm not going to tell you.'

'You really have given it up? Amazing!'

'Given up Shakespeare. But maybe I'll start on someone else. Any ideas?'

'Lee Kuan Yew?' Merr suggested. 'Grand Old Man of

Singapore – that's where I caught up with Irina, as she was getting off the plane from Phuket, matter of fact.'

'You didn't let the grass grow under your feet,' Ed laughed.

'For a girl like Irina…' Merr spread out his arms, embracing the world of things he'd have done to secure his lady-love.

'So one last question. Did you ever ask Irina where she was for those four missing years? Not that it's any of my business.'

'No harm in telling you. They recruited her in Moscow, fresh from art school. She did her basic training. Then she joined the prison service.'

'The prison service?'

'The Russians were decommissioning the Gulag. Setting up archives, that sort of thing. She met Andrey…'

'The weight-lifter.'

'Ex. Ex-husband. Ex-weight-lifter. She met him at a conference. A conference of police archivists – if you can believe it. In Lviv.'

'Where's that?'

'Ukraine.'

'And you guys didn't have it in her file?'

'No. When she quit the prison service, they gave her a new name.'

'And they didn't keep you posted?'

Merr shrugged.

'How unhelpful.'

'Yeah. So we ended up with two files on her. We just didn't know that Irina Porzova was the same person as… You needn't know her old name.'

'So,' Ed nodded. 'Dy and Irina, two lovely girls with spotless characters.'

'Spotless?' Merr repeated. 'I never understood what guys see in spotless women.'

'Me neither. Let's wait till we've got teenage daughters. Maybe it'll all come clear.'

'You got the jump on me there. The new one, the one on the way. Is it a girl? Do you know?'

'Yeah. A girl.'

'What you going to call her?'

'Dy was keen on something out of Shakespeare. Imogen. Miranda.'

'And?'

'Dy's mother was called June, so we settled for that.'

★★★★★

It was late afternoon before Dy and Irina finished shopping at The Pearl. The four of them had a drink on the beach, and then Ed went with Dy to their room so she could show him her new dress – a flowing caftany thing, peasant style at St-Honoré prices. Ed liked it – the embroidered front was perfect for one of his Leonardos. Dy posed near the window for him, letting the last sunlight play on the gold. He sat on the bed, admiring her. Loving her.

The doorbell rang discreetly, suburban, comfortable. Then the sound of a keycard unlatching the door. An Indian voice: 'Turndown service.' And the door opened.

Ed turned and saw the gun – saw it pointed at Diana. Ever since Hirsch's warning, ever since they'd left Bangkok, he'd been half-expecting it. His reaction was quicker than the Indian's aim. He flung himself at Diana, driving her to the floor, covering her with his body. He heard the shot. He felt the bullet shatter his thigh. Another shot. Another shot. Then the door slamming shut.

'The baby,' he moaned, the pain in his leg swelling up, overwhelming him. 'The baby.'

Silence. Nothing but the crying of his own voice.

Then: 'Ed?' It was Diana, so close and so far away. 'Ed? Don't go. Don't leave me. Ed, you promised.'